Mayhem

JAMIE SHAW

AVONIMPULSE

An Imprint of HarperCollinsPublishers

Excerpt from *Riot* copyright © 2015 by Jamie Shaw.

Excerpt from *Holding Holly* copyright © 2014 by Julie Revell Benjamin.

Excerpt from *It's a Wonderful Fireman* copyright © 2014 by Jennifer Bernard.

Excerpt from *Once Upon a Highland Christmas* copyright © 2014 by Lecia Cotton Cornwall.

Excerpt from *Running Hot* copyright © 2014 by HelenKay Dimon.

Excerpt from *Sinful Rewards 1* copyright © 2014 by Cynthia Sax.

Excerpt from *Return to Clan Sinclair* copyright © 2014 by Karen Ranney LLC.

Excerpt from *Return of the Bad Girl* copyright © 2014 by Codi Gary.

EPub Edition JANUARY 2015 ISBN: 9780062379610

Print Edition ISBN: 9780062379603

10 9 8 7 6 5 4 3 2

For every reader who falls in love with Adam.

Chapter One

"I CAN'T BELIEVE I let you talk me into this." I tug at the black hem of the stretchy nylon skirt my best friend squeezed me into, but unless I want to show the tops of my panties instead of the skin of my thighs, there's nothing I can do. After casting yet another uneasy glance at the long line of people stretched behind me on the sidewalk, I shift my eyes back to the sun-warmed fabric pinched between my fingers and grumble, "The least you could've done was let me wear some leggings."

Dee just laughs and bats my hands away from the material. "Stop your bitching, Ro. You'll thank me when we're old and gray and you look back on this night and realize that once, just *once*," she shoves her pointer finger in my face to emphasize the lonely number, "you actually flaunted that hot little body of yours before it got all old and saggy."

"I look ridiculous," I complain, pushing her finger

away and rolling my eyes for good measure. I look like Dee's closet drank too much and threw up on me. She somehow talked me into wearing this mini-skirt—which skintight doesn't even begin to describe—and a hot-pink top that shows more cleavage than should be legal. The front of it drapes all the way down to just above my navel, and the bottom exposes a pale sliver of skin between the hem of the shirt and the top of my skirt. The hot-pink fabric matches my killer hot-pink heels.

Literally, killer. Because I know I'm going to fall on my face and die.

I'm fiddling with the skirt again when one of the guys near us in line leans in close, a jackass smile on his lips. "I think you look hot."

Of course he thinks I look hot—I look like a freaking prostitute!

"I have a boyfriend," I counter, but Dee just scoffs at me.

"She means *thank you*," she shoots back, chastising me with her tone until the guy flashes us another arrogant smile—he's stuffed into an appallingly snug graphic-print tee that might as well say "douchebag" in its shiny metallic lettering, and even Dee can't help but make a face before we both turn away.

She and I are the first ones in line for the show tonight, standing by the doors to Mayhem under the red-orange glow of a setting summer sun. She's been looking forward to this night for weeks, but I was more excited about it before my boyfriend of three years had to back out.

"Brady is a jerk," she says, and all I can do is sigh because I wish those two could just get along. Deandra and

I have been best friends since preschool, but Brady and I have been dating since my sophomore year of high school and living together for the past two months. "He should be here to appreciate how gorgeous you look tonight, but nooo, it's always work first with him."

"He moved all the way here to be with me, Dee. Cut him some slack, alright?"

She grumbles her frustration until she catches me touching my eyelids for the zillionth time tonight. Yanking my fingers away, she orders, "Stop messing with it. You'll smear."

I stare down at my shadowy fingertips and rub them together. "Tell me the truth," I say, flicking the clumped powder away. "Do I look like a clown?"

"You look smoking hot!" she assures me with a smile. "If I was a lesbian, you'd be in trouble!"

I laugh until Douchebag leans in again, popping our personal bubble with his enormously hooked nose. "Don't let that stop you."

We both glare at him so sharply that he immediately stumbles a step back, his obnoxiously red sneakers suddenly becoming the most fascinating things he's ever seen. Dee and I turn back around, glancing at each other and trying not to laugh. She playfully elbows me in the arm, and I chuckle and nudge her right back. My smile settles back into place and I finally feel like I'm beginning to loosen up when a guy walks right past us like he's going to cut in line. In dark shades and a baggy black knit cap that droops in the back, he flicks a cigarette to the ground, and my eyes narrow on him.

Dee and I have been waiting for way too long to let some self-entitled jerk cut in front of us, so when he knocks on the door to the club, I force myself to speak up.

"They're not letting people in yet," I say, hoping he takes the hint. Even with my skyscraper heels, I feel dwarfed standing next to him. He has to be at least six-foot-two, maybe taller.

He turns his head toward me and lowers his shades, smirking like something's funny. His wrist is covered with string bracelets and rubber bracelets and a thick leather cuff, and three of his fingernails on each hand are painted black. But his eyes are what steal the words from my lips—a greenish shade of light gray. They're stunning.

When the door opens, he turns back to it and locks hands with the bouncer.

"You're late," the bouncer says, and the guy in the shades laughs and slips inside. Once he disappears, Dee pushes my shoulders.

"Oh my GOD! Do you know who you were just talking to?!"

I shake my head.

"That was *Adam* EVEREST! He's the lead freaking singer of the band we're here to see!"

Oh . . . God . . . No. "You're kidding . . ."

She shakes her head, stifling a laugh. "Did you see the way he looked at you?!"

"Like I'm an idiot!"

She pulls me in for a hug and finally lets loose the laughter she's been holding in.

"You couldn't have told me?!"

Dee squeezes me tight. "He was standing right there! What was I supposed to do?!" She laughs even harder. "Oh, babe, I'm sorry! That was—" Her body is still shaking with laughter when I feel her lift a hand behind my back to wipe a tear from her eye.

I groan and finish her sentence, "The most mortifying moment of my life."

"Come on, you've had worse. *Much* worse." She pulls away and grins at me. "Do you remember that time at David Miller's house when you—"

"Okay, Dee? Not making me feel better here!"

She chuckles to herself as she applies another coat of shiny pink lip gloss and then shoots her hand forward to do the same to me. "We'll call that the first of the many epic memories we're going to make tonight."

"Why in God's name would I want to remember that?" I ask after puckering my lips.

"Because you talked to Adam Everest!"

A tiny voice chimes from behind me. "Your friend is right," the girl says, nodding to herself. "And he looked right at you. He *smiled* at you."

"Isn't he gorgeous?!" Dee asks, never one to miss an opportunity to gush over boys. She and the girl behind us start gossiping about Adam while I lose myself in my thoughts. I just talked to a rock star, a freaking rock star. Granted, I had no idea who he was, but damn, did he look the part. If I could go back, what would I have said? Probably nothing, and then I never would have seen that smile, or those eyes.

"You're blushing," Dee says, breaking me from the memory.

"It's hot out here!" I lie.

"You're practically naked, and it is *not* that hot." Her lips pull into a knowing grin, which only makes my skin burn even pinker.

I'm saved when the door to Mayhem opens and I practically trip over myself to get inside. I have a boyfriend, and even though I'm sure I'll never speak to Adam again, I really shouldn't be replaying the moment in my mind wishing I would have done things differently.

In the dim haze of the club, a bouncer glances at our fake IDs and stamps our hands, and Dee pulls me straight to the bar. She holds up two fingers to signal the bartender and orders us two dirty girl scouts, but she hasn't even lowered her hand yet when a random guy sidles up next to her, threatening to choke us with his cologne.

"You look a little too . . ." his eyes scan over us, making me feel like I'm wearing even less than I already am, "*mature* to be Girl Scouts, but I'll believe anything a girl as pretty as you tells me." Corniest. Pick-up line. Ever. He grins like a cheeseball. "What can I get you ladies to drink?"

Dee turns to me and mouths "Just go with it," so I do. And, voilà, free shots. Cheeseball, who is apparently named Vinnie, pays for the first round, and some guy named . . . well, I have no idea what the hell his name is, buys the second round, and then Dee is dragging me onto the crowded dance floor. In advance of the show, the club is booming with house music, and it's fueling her hyper mood.

I laugh as she bounces in front of me with her wrists on

my shoulders. She looks incredible, as always, in a ruffled blue mini-skirt and a super low-cut white top. It's backless, flaunting the golden tan she's worked for all summer. Her long chocolate-brown curls are bouncing from side to side with the beat, and I finally give in and drop it low, rising back up ass-first like a freaking stripper. Dee laughs at me and twirls around with her hands in the air, and then we're lost to the alcohol pumping through our blood and the music vibrating beneath our feet.

By the third song, my thick blonde waves are glued to the back of my neck. I flip them away as Dee bends low and rolls her ass against my thighs. We're both laughing so hard that I'm surprised we haven't fallen over yet. My sides cramp like I'm out of practice.

When I feel stiff jeans press up behind me, my smile vanishes. I try to inch away, pressing tighter against Dee, but the jeans follow, and then grabby hands grip my sides. The floor is so crowded that I won't even be able to turn around without being pressed flush against whatever creeper is behind me, so I press my mouth into Dee's hair and tell her I'm heading to the bar. When I begin pushing through the crowd, her fingers curl around mine and she follows. Together, we find our way off the floor.

"What gives?" she shouts once we break free from the overheated crowd.

"Some asshole was getting way too touchy-feely."

"Damn. Was he hot?"

"I didn't get a look at him."

"Well next time, if he's cute, send him my way." She winks, and I laugh and brace my hands on the bar, still trying to catch my breath. Dee leans back against it, propping her elbows on top with her chest out in the most casually provocative pose she can muster. It works like a charm, because within seconds, two guys are in front of her.

"You girls looked amazing out there."

I'm still facing away from them, not interested. When they ask us to dance, Dee reaches over and grabs my hand.

I turn around and give the guys an apologetic smile. "I have a boyfriend."

"So?" Dee says. "Pleeease, Ro? Just one dance!"

"You go," I insist, nudging her toward the dance floor.

"You sure?"

"Yeah, go. I'm going to hang here for a while. I need a break."

Her perfectly shaped eyebrows pull together. "I'll stay if you want me to . . ."

I know she would, but I shoo her from the bar anyway. "GO!"

She laughs, her brown eyes sparkling with contagious excitement. "Okay, I'll be back soon!"

Both boys follow her like puppy dogs, and I smile to myself, knowing they're both in trouble.

After losing sight of her, I pull my phone out of my clutch purse and sigh when I realize there are no missed calls from Brady. It's almost ten o'clock, and I really wish he would've called to say goodnight. But he probably knew it would be loud in here, and he was probably exhausted from working all day. He's out of town for the weekend again, on yet another long-distance job for the advertising firm his uncle owns, and I've grown accustomed to sitting by the phone—he joined the company right after graduating, when I was still a sophomore, and traveling to meet with clients has always been a big part of the job. Still, the trips have been more and more frequent lately, and they always feel way longer than they really are.

My fingers type a quick text.

Miss you. Having a blast but wish you were here! Hope your day wasn't too rough. Can't wait to see you tomorrow! I love you.

I tuck my phone back into my purse and turn around, laughing when I spot Dee in the crowd, sandwiched between her two club gorillas and outshining them both. She looks amazing, and she knows it. In high school, she wasn't on the cheerleading squad but she dated most of the football team. Most of the other girls hated her, but she didn't care and neither did I. She had a well-earned bad reputation, but she never tried to be anyone she wasn't. She's *real*, and I love that about her.

When a stool opens up at the bar, I immediately dive onto it. My last drink is long gone, so I pull out my paper-thin wallet and flag the bartender.

I order another vodka cranberry and try to pull out cash to pay, but before I can manage, a thick hand covers mine. "A fox like you should never have to pay for her own drink." The guy uses his other hand to slip the bartender a credit card, and I sigh, looking up into plain brown eyes deeply set into a meathead face.

"I have a boyfriend," I say, trying not to sound rude but feeling pretty exasperated. With the number of times I'm having to repeat that tonight, it would've been easier to get the words tattooed on my forehead.

"Is he here?"

"No . . ."

"Then he's an idiot. Dance with me." The guy grabs my drink with one hand and tries to coax me off my stool with the other.

"No thanks."

"Aw, come on," he persists, refusing to stop tugging at my hand. "Don't make me beg."

"Sorry." I pull out of his grip and settle back on my seat.

"Why the hell would you come here dressed like that if you're just going to be a tease?" he snaps, but I ignore him completely, flagging the bartender again.

When the meathead calls me a slut and walks away—*with* my drink—I roll my eyes and order another, which I pay for myself before any other assholes have the chance to intercede. If I'm a slut, then Mother Teresa was too, because I might as well be her. Brady's father is a pastor, so Brady made the decision for both of us that we'd be waiting until marriage—whenever *that's* going to be. He agreed to live together, under the condition that we have separate bedrooms, but second base is getting harder and harder to stick to. I know I'm only eighteen, but we've been in a committed relationship for three years already, and now we're living together and, well, what the hell is he waiting for?

I gradually lose myself to people-watching while I sip on my drink and wait for Dee to tire herself out. The group beside me at the bar all look like college kids. They seem nice, and it makes me hopeful that I'll make at least a few new friends on Monday. Next to them is a girl dressed even sluttier than I am, surrounded by three guys who are all shamelessly hitting on her. I wonder if the guys are friends with each other, and I'm curious to see which will win the little competition they've got going on. The one with the blond faux-hawk is pretty damn cute; my money would be on him.

His eyes lift to catch me staring, and he smiles at me. I look away before he gets the wrong impression and decides to come over.

Next to him is a guy with his back to me, talking to a girl with bright purple eye shadow. She's gorgeous, with rich brown hair styled in a long bob. She laughs at something he says, and he places his hand on her forearm, caressing it tenderly with his thumb, giving her all the right signals. She's leaning slightly toward him, batting her lashes and brushing her fingers through her hair. I'm still staring when the guy turns toward the bar to order another drink.

And my heart shatters into a million jagged pieces.

Brady.

I blink, for a second believing that I can't trust my vision. I rub my eyes and stare harder, but it's definitely him. What the fuck is he doing here?

Maybe he came here to meet me. I scramble to check my phone.

No missed texts. No missed calls. I look from him to my phone and back again, remembering that Dee had mistakenly told me that we were going to a different club across town and that's what I told Brady. He didn't expect me to be here. With my eyes on my phone, I type another text.

Are you still working?

I watch as he pulls his phone from his shirt pocket, checks it, and then tucks it away. The girl he's with says something, and he leans in close to her ear, then kisses her cheek.

Maybe they're just friends. Please be just friends.

I watch as they laugh, as they talk, and then as Brady leans in and kisses her. And it isn't a friend kiss. He doesn't even come up for air, and I can't remember the last time he kissed me like that. I'm practically falling off of my stool before I know it, scrambling to find an exit door before I turn into a blubbering mess right there in front of everyone. I can barely see through the cloud of tears in my eyes as my hands push past people who stare at me or throw curses my way. Finally, I slam into a big metal door and fly outside just as a sob bubbles out of my throat.

I brace my hands on the cold stair railing and struggle to breathe. I suck in air, desperately trying to regain some semblance of composure. How could he? How could he?!

Three years. Three fucking years. He asked me to move in with him! We live together, for God's sake. I have never done *anything* to deserve this. I wouldn't even dance with those perfectly nice guys inside!

My knees feel like they're going to fail me, so I sit down on the top cement stair and curl my arms around my legs. It's gotten chilly, but that's the least of my problems. What am I going to do? I can't sleep under the same roof as him tomorrow night. I can't. I just can't.

It's pitch-dark except for a single light hanging above the door and some overhead lights across the parking lot. Bugs swarm in the spotlight above me, and normally I'd be paranoid about being so close to them since I'm allergic to pretty much all insect bites known to man, but right now, I don't care. They can eat me alive; hopefully they finish the job.

I reach my hand up to wipe the tears from my cheeks, realizing for the first time that I've been crying. God, what am I going to do? Should I go back in there? Should I tell Dee? She'll kill him.

I bury my face in my knees and let myself really cry then, sobs racking my body. I loved him. I loved him with every piece of me. I would've given him forever. My whole future . . .

When the door opens behind me, I sit up straight and hurriedly sniff in my tears as I wipe my shaking fingers across my slippery cheeks. I hear the flick of a lighter, and then someone sits down next to me on the stairs, puffing a cigarette. When I look over at him, I nearly choke.

He gazes back at me, starting at my hot-pink heels and then raking his way up, and then he chuckles. "Are they letting people in yet?"

Adam. He's ditched the shades and cap, and now his dark brown hair is framing his gorgeous face, stretching almost to his chin. I look away quickly, hoping he can't tell I've been crying.

"Sorry about that," I say. And I hear the hoarse sadness in my voice, but I couldn't keep it out.

When he reaches over and brushes my tangled hair away from my eyes, I tense.

"Is everything okay?" he asks, and I half laugh. No, everything is not okay.

"Everything's fine."

"Then why have you been crying?"

"No reason."

"You get all dolled up to sit outside of rock shows crying by yourself?"

I lift my gaze to stare into his eyes, and something in them makes me believe he really cares. Or maybe that's just what I want to see, but I suddenly need to tell someone. "My boyfriend's in there."

"And?"

"With another girl. I just caught him cheating."

Adam takes a deep puff of his cigarette, nodding as he sighs it back out. "Want me to fuck him up?"

I laugh, and he smiles at me. "Would you?"

"If you want me to."

"Why?"

He shrugs. "Because I offered."

"Why'd you offer?"

"Who knows why I do anything I do?" He stares at me while I wait for an answer. "I just do."

That's a good enough explanation for me, so I look back to my knees again, letting out a shaky breath. I can't believe I just laughed. At a time like this, Adam Everest made me laugh.

"Anyway, your boyfriend is a dumbass," he says out of nowhere.

"How do you know?"

His gray-green eyes wash over me. "Look at you."

I blush like hell, but I know he's just trying to make me feel better. "You thought I was an idiot when you first saw me."

Adam chuckles and shakes his head. "I thought you were cute as a peach." His lips hold the cigarette in his mouth as he stands up, holding a hand down to me. My heart stops; Adam Everest is offering me his hand. In faded denim jeans, all torn up at the knees, and a fit olive-green button-down rolled up to his elbows, he makes my heart race to a nonexistent finish line. "Come on, Peach."

I take his hand, and he lifts me to my feet, leading me away from the building. "Where are we going?"

"To get you a drink. I think you need one."

"I've had a few," I think out loud, slowing to a stop.

Adam gazes over his shoulder at me, his eyebrow cocked when he asks, "Are you saying you don't want another?"

I take a moment to consider his question.

Just a moment, and then I keep walking.

Chapter Two

WHILE WALKING ALONGSIDE Adam, I text Dee a quick message so she won't worry when she can't find me at the bar.

Getting some air--with a hot guy. Be back soon.

If I told her I was just getting some air, she'd be following me outside in a heartbeat. But if she thinks I'm showing interest in any guy who isn't Brady, I know she'll give me space.

I think the only person who hates him more than she does right now is *me*.

And anyway, it isn't a lie. Adam is hot as sin, but there's no way in hell I'm telling Dee that's who I'm out with. I cringe, imagining the high-pitched squeal that would tear from her lips. She'd be out here before I even finished typing the text, working some kind of voodoo telepathy and pushing me into his arms.

Adam crushes his cigarette under his shoe and then swings open the door to what I assume is his tour bus. It's a black double-decker, and inside, it smells like leather and men's cologne. Past the driver's seat is a row of leather bench seats, and sleeping on one of them with his arms crossed over his chest and his face half-buried in the gray leather is a guy almost as tall as Adam. One shredded-jean-clad leg is hanging over the edge.

Adam looks back at me and holds a finger against his lips; then he creeps up and crouches next to the seat. He leans in close, looking like he's going to kiss the guy's cheek, but then his tongue flattens against it in a big sloppy lick and the guy wakes up yelling.

"FUCK, Adam!"

Adam laughs loudly as the guy wipes his sleeved shoulder over his cheek.

"Fucking gross, man!"

"Show's gonna start in twenty minutes," Adam says, walking to the wet bar and pulling a bottle of liquor from the cabinet.

The guy sits up and rubs his hands roughly over his cropped black hair. "Shit." He finally spots me, and then his eyes travel over my face, my slinky top, my ten-sizes-too-small skirt, my hooker heels. He sighs. "Twenty minutes, Adam." Then he slides past me and out the door.

"Who was that?" I ask.

"That was Shawn. Our lead guitarist." Adam hands me a glass of whiskey and sits down where Shawn had just been sleeping, slouching in the seat. "So the way I see it, you have two options."

I sit down next to him, and it feels so weird sitting next to him, because he is so out of my league. "Only two, huh?"

He grins at me and downs his drink. "One, we can sit in here and get you so shit-faced that you can't remember what's-his-name's name."

I chuckle. "And two?"

"You can get even."

Okay, now I'm curious. "How?"

Adam sets his glass down and looks at me then—*really* looks at me. His eyes are locked with mine, and I swallow hard, every inch of me suddenly acutely aware of how close I am to him. His gaze drops to my lips, and when he starts leaning in, I panic. I know he's going to kiss me. Before I can regret my decision, I scoot away.

He eyes me carefully. "Are you sure?"

I play stupid, because I suddenly feel ten shades of embarrassed. Dee can never find out about this or I'll never hear the end of it. "Sure about what?" I swallow the rest of my drink, trying to calm my fire-cracking nerves.

Adam stays leaning forward for a moment before he carries both of our glasses back to the bar and I breathe a sigh of relief. "Shit-faced it is, Peach," he says as he pours me another glass.

"Where's the rest of your band?" I ask in an attempt to change the subject.

"Getting ready."

"Shouldn't *you* be getting ready?"

He turns around and swirls the amber liquid in his glass, a smile on his lips. "I am."

A knock at the door gets my attention, but my eyes stay glued on Adam as he goes to the front of the bus to answer it.

"Hi, Adam." It's a girl's voice, and it's shamelessly seductive.

"What do you want, Farrah?" Adam sounds bored, maybe a little irritated.

"Can I come in?"

Adam moves to the side enough so that Farrah can see me. And I can see her, all red-headed bombshell and legs, legs, legs. He sweeps an arm toward where I'm sitting. "I'm busy."

She smiles at me and sweetly asks, "Room enough for one more?"

"No," he says, and then he swings the door shut—right in her face.

My jaw is on the floor as he climbs back up the bus stairs and sits on the bench seat across from me, resting his elbows on his knees. "Sorry about that," he says.

Frowning, I apologize for ruining his night.

"If you were ruining my night," he replies, "I'd kick you off this bus without a second thought." He smiles at me, and I'm not sure how to feel about what he just said. Would he seriously kick me off? "Now tell me about this cheating boyfriend of yours."

"Can we not talk about him? I don't even want to think about him."

"Works for me. What do you want to do?"

I down my second drink of whiskey, my fifth drink of the night. It's starting to hit me, fast. "Give me a tour?" I stand up and instantly feel wobbly on my feet. Adam bolts to my side and presses a hand against my ribs, steadying me.

And I giggle. I giggle like crazy at myself for almost falling in front of Adam freaking Everest on his band's freaking tour bus, and he smiles at me like I'm the most adorable thing he's ever seen.

"Hold on." I crouch down and unbuckle my shoes, sliding them off and leaving them where they lay. "Okay, let's go." I'm suddenly much shorter than him, barely coming up to his chest. He takes a step deeper into the bus to begin the tour, but I reach up and grab his shoulder. "Wait." He looks back at me. "I need another drink."

He laughs and makes me another without any questions, handing it to me and then walking ahead of me through the tour bus. "This," he says, gesturing to the bench seats, "is where Shawn likes to pass out before shows and get licked on his not-so-tasty face."

I try not to giggle again, but I can't help it. He walks me deeper into the bus, pointing at a flat-screen TV in the corner that hovers over an entertainment center filled to the brim with video game consoles.

"This is where Mike's brain lives and dies."

I grin, and he leads me into a small kitchen full of stainless-steel appliances and a glass mini-fridge stocked with beer and energy drinks. He reaches in and pulls out a Red Bull, handing it to me. "How drunk are you?"

"Not drunk enough."

He gives me an appreciative smile. "Count backward from ten."

I do it with no problem, and then he steps into me and my back gets pressed against the counter. "In that case, this is where I bring girls to take a second shot at seducing them."

I brace my hands against his chest and stare up at him, trying not to faint from the way he's pressing against me and looking down at me and damn, he smells *so* good. A smile breaks across my face. "It happens so often that you have a designated place for it?"

His hands linger on my waist. "Actually, I think you're the first. But I think you deserve to have a spot named after you."

"Oooooh," I say, mocking his line. "That was sooo smooooooth, Adam Everest."

He laughs and pops open my Red Bull, taking a sip of it and handing it back to me. "Still haven't changed your mind, huh? Could be fun . . ."

"Oh, I'm sure it would be." My fingers smooth across his shirt, and I'm suddenly not so sure I want to turn him down. He could make me forget. I gaze up at him, realizing that boys like him leave girls broken. He's not the type of guy a girl has a fling with and gets over. He's the type of guy who ruins all the rest that come after him. "But no," I manage to say, knowing it's the right choice even though I want to slap myself.

"Damn," he says, backing off. "Break my heart, Peach." He winks at me and exits the kitchen, and I follow, feeling weak in the knees but not from the alcohol.

We make our way back to the front of the bus, where

we climb the stairs onto the second level. The first space is another sitting area with leather seats, but beyond that are closets and then twelve bunks, six on each side. All except three are neat and tidy.

"This is where the guys sleep," Adam says, gesturing to the bunks before leading me further into the bus and opening a door at the end of the hall. It's almost entirely occupied by a massive bed with black satin sheets.

"And this is where the magic happens?" I leap onto it and tuck my knees under myself, bouncing up and down from the impact.

"Dangerous, Peach," Adam says, leaning against the doorjamb and crossing his arms over his chest. "You're right where I want you."

I laugh until he takes a step forward, his knees pressing against the edge. I'm suddenly staring up at him. I swallow what's left of my Red Bull. "How long until the show?"

Adam pulls a phone out of his back pocket and checks the time. "Not long enough."

I chuckle and roll my eyes. "I don't want to sleep with you, Adam."

"Yes, you do," he says confidently. "But you won't, for whatever lame reason. Anyway, not *wanting* to is an entirely different thing."

Unable to argue, I repeat, "How long?"

"Seven minutes." I scoot further back onto the bed, and he sits down on the edge, studying me.

"Why are you being so nice to me?"

With a cavalier shrug, he says, "I told you, I do what I feel like. Don't try to figure it out. I don't."

"Why didn't you ditch me for that redhead? I'm sure she would've had you up here ten minutes ago."

He chuckles, and then he reasons, "I wanted to take a chance on you instead."

I frown and find myself telling him I'm sorry again, but he just smiles at me. It's a smile that could turn knees to jello and hearts to mush, so when he holds his hand down to me, I don't hesitate to take it.

"Don't be," he says, and then he lifts me to my feet and starts walking from the room. I'm in the doorway when I say, "Adam?"

He turns around.

"I'm not going to sleep with you, I'm not even going to come close, but . . . do you think you could make me forget what's-his-name for the next seven minutes?"

Adam studies me, and then he fishes his phone out again. "Six minutes," he corrects before tucking it back into his pocket. "Can you still count backward from ten?"

"Yes."

"Then start counting."

I count backward until I'm at five, and he steps in close. At four, his left hand is circling around my waist and pressing against the small of my back. At three, his right hand reaches up and cups my jaw, angling it up. At two, he leans in close, his lips a centimeter from mine. My breath hitches in my throat, and I suddenly can't speak. He's pressed flush against me, and I can feel *all* of him.

His mouth quirks into a smile. "What are you waiting for, Peach?"

"One."

Chapter Three

When Adam's phone beeps, he doesn't stop kissing me. His body is molded against every inch of me, pressing me deep into the black satin comforter. With one of his legs squeezed between mine, his jeans rub against my bare thighs, and it's like I can feel every single thread. One hand squeezes my skirted hip, and the other holds my neck in place as his lips explore mine. His kiss is agonizingly practiced—forget about what's-his-name, I can't even remember my *own* name.

His phone beeps again, and he groans.

I turn my head to the side, and his lips drop to my neck. Breathless as he licks his way down it, I say, "Shouldn't you get that?"

His lips travel lower, kissing a trail across my collarbone. I close my eyes and thread my fingers through his soft brown hair. "Adam," I say, but it's like he's refusing to hear me.

"Ignore it, Peach."

His phone beeps a third time, and I use my hands to coax his face back to mine. I'm trying to tell him he needs to check his phone because I think he might be late, but he covers my mouth with his before I can, doing this thing with his tongue that makes me forget whatever it was I was going to say.

His phone beeps again, and I wiggle down and reach into his back pocket. I check the time on his phone and see that he's five minutes late and has four missed texts from Shawn.

"You're late," I say between kisses.

"I'm always late."

The door to the room suddenly swings open and Shawn is standing there rolling his eyes. "For fuck's sake, Adam, you've just been *making out* for twenty-five damn minutes?"

I can't help laughing, too drunk by now to feel embarrassed. Adam smiles down at me. "She's a really good kisser."

Shawn walks over and grabs Adam by the back of his jeans, hauling him off of me. "Come on, man. You can see her after." Looking down at me, he adds, "Sorry."

I straighten my top and sit up, feeling all kinds of giggly inside. I just made out with Adam Everest, who was, hands down, the best kisser of my life.

"Shawn, this is Peach," Adam says, and as soon as I stand up, Shawn reluctantly reaches forward to shake my hand.

"Hi Shawn."

"Hi Peach."

Adam shakes the zipper of his jeans as he adjusts himself, and a fierce blush heats my cheeks. "See," he says, "we're all friends now. Stop getting your panties in a bunch, Shawn."

Shawn sighs. "Peach, you can hang backstage during the show if you want." He shoots a look at Adam. "But we *do* have a show we need to put on. Five minutes ago."

"I can't," I say as we're walking back through the hallway. "I'm here with a friend."

"So bring her back too," Adam says from behind me.

I don't reply because that is *such* a bad idea. Dee has been with a lot of guys, but none like Adam or Shawn. Bad combination. Bad.

I stay silent as I descend the stairs. Adam and Shawn patiently wait for me to put my shoes back on, and then we slip back into Mayhem, entering through a backstage door. Before I can leave to find Dee, Adam wraps his hand around my waist and tugs me into a corner.

"Come back to the bus after the show," he says.

I press my hands over his ears and pull him down to my lips, kissing him because I know it'll be the last time I ever get to. I make it count, savoring every last second of the way his silky-soft lips mesh with mine. When I release him, he looks like he's seriously contemplating mauling me right there on the backstage floor, and I grin up at him.

Then I walk away.

When I fish my phone out of my purse, I have three missed texts from Dee.

You're kidding.

You're not kidding!

OMG, what are you doing, getting pregnant?!

I chuckle and text her back, asking where she is, and she tells me she'll meet me at the bar. The whole time I'm walking, I'm paranoid I'll see Brady. My eyes dart to every guy with moussed blond hair I see. I kind of wish I had left my heels off, because I'm still tipsy as hell and using people's shoulders to keep me balanced as I weave through the crowd.

Dee suddenly bounds up to me from the direction of the bar and slaps her hands on my shoulders with a huge grin on her face. "You are DRUNK!"

I realize I'm squinting my right eye—my telltale give-away—at the same time I tip to the side from the impact of her hands. I grip her arms to steady myself. "A little," I admit with a sheepish grin.

"So what did he look like?!"

The squeal of a microphone interrupts our conversation, and we both look up to the stage as everyone starts screaming their heads off and surging to move closer to where Adam is standing, front and center. He grips the microphone and pulls it from its stand, swinging the cord around to move closer to the edge of the stage.

I turn back to Dee, needing to tell her about Brady before I lose my nerve. "Dee—"

Adam's voice interrupts me. "I see a lot of pretty girls in the crowd tonight." The girls scream even louder, making my attempts to speak to Dee futile. She screams right along with them, and I give up, surrendering all of my attention to Adam and feeling my skin heat at the sight of him. When Dee invited me to the show, she told me that the band is really popular around here and is only getting bigger; judging by the crowd's enthusiasm, they must be incredible.

Adam runs a hand through his hair, tugging it away from his eyes and dropping it to the side. "Shawn over here just pulled me away from the hottest one here less than two minutes ago!" Shawn laughs, and so does the crowd. Adam mumbles, "Thanks a lot, Shawn."

Shawn leans into his back-up microphone and says, "You're welcome, Adam." He points out at the audience. "Can I get a 'Thank you, Shawn'?"

Adam holds his microphone to the audience, and in unison, everyone shouts, "Thank you, Shawn!"

Adam shakes his head. "You all suck." He says it with a chuckle, and everyone laughs. "Peach!" he suddenly yells. And even though he has no idea where I am in the crowd, my skin flushes a fiery shade of pink. "I want you to know that your boyfriend is a goddamned idiot. I can't wait to help you forget about him some more as soon as we're done with this set!"

With that, the band starts playing, and Adam launches right into their first song. I suddenly feel the need to fan myself off, and when I glance at Dee, she looks like she could use some air just as much as I could. She turns to me and says, "He is so. fucking. hot!"

Before I have to lie to her, because I can *never* lie to Dee's face, I blurt, "Brady's here."

"What?!" she asks, pulling me farther from the stage so we can hear each other better.

"I said 'Brady's here!'"

"Where?!" Her eyes dart around the crowd, but there are so many people, it's useless.

"He's with another girl, Dee."

Her eyes snap back to me. "Another girl? Are you sure?"

"I saw him kiss her."

She frowns at me for a moment, and then she pulls me in for a hug so tight I can barely breathe. It's the exact kind of hug I need. The minute I'm in her arms, the tears break free again, dripping onto her bare shoulder. "Do you want to get out of here?" she asks.

I nod, and then she's pulling me out of the club. I cast one last look at Adam. He's shouting into the microphone over an ocean of raised hands. The front row is all girls, reaching like they're trying to touch him. And even though I *was* touching him just a few minutes ago, I know just how they feel.

Dee was right. This is a night I'll never forget.

Outside, we sit in her car as I cry into a stack of travel tissues. She shifts to face me, resting her knee on the center console. "You're *positive* it was him?" I blow my nose and let the tears fall, still not wanting to accept it. "Ro?" she says.

"I'm sure, Dee. I texted him and watched him pull his phone out of his pocket, look at my message, and put it away."

She's silent, and that scares me. When I look up at her, she's positively seething. "That fucking asshole," she growls, and I can see the wheels turning in her head as she contemplates all the horrible things she wants to do to him. "That motherfucking ASSHOLE. I can't believe this!"

She starts the car, and I sober up a little at the sound of the engine. "Are you good to drive?" I ask.

"I'm fine." She puts it in reverse and backs up, and I know that's the end of it. Never ask Dee twice if she's good enough to drive. She's not stupid, and if she says she's fine, she's fine.

"Where are we going?" I ask once we're on the road.

"We're getting your stuff." She glances over at me, reading the confusion on my face. "You're staying with me, babe. There's no way in hell you're going to be there when that asshole gets back tomorrow."

I never thought about where I would go, but she's right. I can't stay there. I can't see him. "I can't believe he did this to me right before I'm supposed to start school."

She casts a sympathetic glance in my direction, but she leaves the words unspoken. And just like that, because we've been best friends since forever, I know what she's thinking. He didn't *just* do this to me—he's been doing this to me for a long time. All those business trips, all lies.

I rest my forehead against the window as more silent tears fall. I'm thinking of Brady, of how I don't know what to do about him. I love him. Even after everything I saw tonight, I love him. But I'm not going to be *that* girl. I'm not going to be that girl who lets guys lie to her and walk all over her and cheat on her. I'm thinking of Adam, and how easy it was to be with him. How exciting. How he *did* make me forget, and how while I was with him, none of this shit with Brady mattered so much. How I walked away from him and now I'm all alone.

Dee reaches over and squeezes my arm, and I clasp my fingers with hers. "Thanks for always being there for me, Dee."

"Shut up," she says, and I let out a congested chuckle. She smiles over at me and gives my hand another squeeze.

By the time we're finished going through my and Brady's apartment, Dee's car is packed to the brim. I changed into a T-shirt and yoga pants and then packed every single last item of clothing I own. All my jewelry, cosmetics, personal effects. I took the damn panini maker, and I would've taken our big flat-screen TV too if only we had the room. I thought about leaving a note, but decided not to. What would it possibly say? *You broke my heart, I'm a blubbering mess, I love you, you asshole*? We got out of there as quickly as possible, and then we drove to campus.

On my third trip up the stairs to Dee's third-floor dorm room, I'm huffing. "Are you sure your roommate's okay with this?"

Dee drops one of my shoes down the stairs and curses under her breath. "Are you kidding? The girl has no friends. She's *thrilled*."

My arms are full, but using my thumb, I manage to snatch up the shoe Dee dropped. "Then why isn't she helping us lug all my crap upstairs?"

"Because she's socially retarded," Dee answers bluntly,

and I just shake my head. I have to lean against the wall for a minute because the stairwell starts tilting. When we arrived at my apartment, I was still way too drunk to drive, so we left my car there.

"We'll have to get my car on Monday," I say. "Brady never told me what time he's coming home tomorrow, and I don't want to run into him."

"I wish we *would* run into him," Dee snarls, and I don't have to ask why. I'm guessing he'd enter that encounter with two healthy testicles and leave with negative one.

Dee's roommate holds the door open for us as we carry my things in and collapse on Dee's bed.

"Macy," Dee says, "we're going to clean this mess up tomorrow, okay?"

Macy nods from where she's standing awkwardly in the center of the room, pinching the hem of her T-shirt. "Okay. It was nice to meet you, Rowan."

"Thanks for letting me stay here, Macy. You're the best."

Her smile is the facial equivalent of jumping for joy, and it makes me smile back. She finds her way back to her glowing desktop computer, and Dee and I lie on the bed trying not to immediately pass out.

"You need to get out of your stripper heels," I tell her.

Dee groans and throws her leg up over the bed, plopping her foot down right on my stomach. I *oomph* and then start laughing. I unbuckle her shoe and then she throws the other leg on top of me and I unbuckle that one too. She doesn't even bother changing clothes before we both crawl under the covers. She reaches over to turn off her bedside lamp, and then we're out like lights.

Chapter Four

THE PAIN IN my head this morning reminds me of last night first thing. I groan and shift in the bed, and then Dee groans and shifts too. And then we're both just lying there trying to out-groan each other until we giggle like goofballs and I smack a pillow over her face.

"You . . . bitch . . ." she groans without any conviction.

"What time is it?" I groan back. The room is filled with light, making me squeeze my eyes shut even tighter.

She fumbles around for her phone, knocking it off of her nightstand and then scooping it off the floor. "Noon. Why the hell are we up already?"

"Because we need aspirin and coffee and bacon."

After a long pause, she finally says, "Okay. Get up and get dressed."

"You first."

And then we both fall back asleep.

I wake up half an hour later, and even though I really

don't want to, I actually crawl out of bed this time. "Where's the shower?" I ask, pushing my finger into Dee's forehead.

She swats my hand away. "Down the hall and to the right. Take my tote with you. It's by the door."

After a quick shower, I come back to Dee's room positively starving. She snatches the tote from my hand and then takes her own shower as I try to find my brush and hair dryer and makeup in the pile of crap we tossed on the floor last night. I root through suitcases and overstuffed trash bags and other misfit luggage. By the time she gets back, I've only just found everything I was looking for. We end up competing for mirror space in front of her vanity as we get ready, and the bickering actually makes me feel a little better.

Dee had *pleaded* with me to room with her when we decided to go to school in Virginia, but was graciously understanding when I explained that I really wanted to live off campus with Brady.

Hah! Yeah, right.

She had guilt-tripped me for a month, ignored me for a week, and then tried to turn my own parents against me. She never liked Brady, and I never understood why. But maybe her intuition is just better than mine. I guess it's got to be, because I've been absolutely clueless.

"Hey." She bumps her shoulder against mine when she catches my reflection frowning, dangerously close to tearing up. "Don't. Not one more tear for him, Ro."

I take a deep, shaky breath. "Okay."

"Has he sent you any messages since last night?"

"Yeah." When I checked my phone while Dee was in the shower, I saw that I had one missed call and one missed text from him. He didn't leave a voicemail. I hand Dee my phone so she can read the text.

Sry I missed your txts, baby. It was a late night. Tried calling u this morning but I guess you're sleeping in. Be home in afew hours to kiss u awake. Love u more.

Dee makes gagging noises, but I can't even crack a smile. He sounds just like the Brady I knew, the Brady I fell in love with.

Did I ever really know him at all?

Dee snatches the hairbrush from my hand to prevent me from running it through my wavy blonde locks for the hundredth time. "Okay, let's get you the hell out of here."

We're halfway to her car when I ask, "Don't you have a cafeteria on campus?"

"Yes . . ."

"Then why are we walking to your car?"

Her shifty eyes aren't fooling me at all. "I thought maybe we could stop by your apartment . . ." she confesses. "Throw some of Brady's clothes on the lawn. Break some of his shit. I wasn't thinking clearly last night when we just got your stuff and left."

I shake my head. "No, Dee."

"Why not? Ro, he deserves so much worse than that. And maybe it'll make you feel better."

"It won't. When he comes home and has no idea why I left, *that* will make me feel better."

Dee gives me a skeptical look, but as if on cue, my phone starts vibrating. I lift it up, showing her that Brady is calling. "See? Better already."

"Don't you dare answer that."

"Wasn't planning on it." I decline the call and stuff the phone back into the side pouch of my purse. It's silent long enough for us to get to Dee's car, and then it starts vibrating again. I pull it out and turn it off completely.

"Did he leave you a voicemail?" Dee asks.

"Not yet. But he will."

She nods as we both hop inside of her plum-purple Civic. "I still say we should've broken some of his shit."

I shrug. "Then he'd be under the impression I care."

"But you *do* care . . ."

I find the strength to give her a half smile. "That'll be our little secret."

She rewards me with a grin of approval and starts the car. I waste no time buckling my seat belt and making sure it's pulled tight. Riding with Dee is . . . unpredictable. And with the nausea I'm still feeling from my hangover, this just isn't going to be good.

By the time we arrive at IHOP, I'm practically dry-heaving.

"Oh, stop being a baby," she says as she whips the car into a parking spot and hops out, stretching her arms behind her back. I brace my hands on the hood, trying to calm my contracting stomach.

"That should've been a twenty-minute ride," I say.

"I made it in ten!"

"I know!"

She laughs and starts walking toward the entrance, and I follow. Inside, we both order strawberry pancakes with coffee and sides of bacon. Dee fishes a hair tie from her purse and ties back her long dark chocolate curls. "So before *the incident* last night, did you have fun?"

I pour a heart-clogging amount of syrup over my pancakes, letting it soak in before adding another coat. "Yeah, I did." I look up at her. "Seriously. Thanks for making me go. And honestly, I'm glad I found out about Brady. Sooner rather than later, you know? If he would have proposed, like I wanted him to . . ." I don't even want to finish the sentence, but Dee knows. I would have said yes and given the rest of my life to him without ever looking back.

"So what about this hot guy you were with?" She's staring at her sugar packet as she tears it open and pours it into her coffee. Thank God, because that means she doesn't see the panic that flashes across my face. Adam comes back to me in a rush, making me feel . . . needy. That's the only word I can think of to describe it. Is it possible to miss someone you just met? And *miss* doesn't even feel like the right word . . . *yearn*? Is it possible to yearn for someone you just met?

I try to keep my voice even. "Um . . . what about him?"

"Did you get his number?"

I shake my head. I need to lie like I've never lied before to the only bloodhound who can smell my bullshit. "We were just talking. And then I saw Brady."

"You saw Brady while you were with him?"

"Yeah . . ." I'm trying to force my eyes to look trust-worthy as Dee stares at me suspiciously, but then she lets it go.

"Well, that's a shame."

I shrug. "It is what it is. Maybe next time." I pull my phone from my purse and turn it back on. Six missed calls, four missed voicemails, three missed texts. "You ready?" I ask, and she nods. We're in a corner booth and the restaurant is dead since we came between the lunch and dinner rushes, so I lay the phone in the middle of the table and play Brady's voicemail on speakerphone. His smooth voice breaks my heart all over again, but I need to hear what he has to say for himself.

"Rowan, I just got home and . . . all your stuff is gone. Baby, what's going on? I tried calling you three times now and I'm not getting any answer. You need to call me back as soon as you get this. I'm really worried . . . I love you. Please call me."

I look at Dee, and she rolls her eyes. I move on to the next one.

"Baby, seriously, I'm really getting worried here. Your car's still out there, but all your clothes are gone. *Every-thing* is gone. I have no idea what's going on. *Please* call me. I'm worried about you. I love you . . . I love you, so just . . . just call me back, okay?"

Now it's my turn to roll my eyes. I play the third one.

"Look, if this is some kind of joke, it's not funny, Rowan. Did I do something wrong? Please just talk to me. I have no idea where you are. I called Dee and I even called your Mom. Dee's phone went straight to voicemail and your mom hasn't heard anything either. You need to call me. I'm lost here, baby. I don't know what to do. Please come home. Or at least call me back . . . I love you."

"Shit!" I immediately snatch my phone off the table and call my mom.

"Rowan?!" She's panicked, and I feel so stupid for not predicting this would happen.

"Hey, Mom."

"Are you okay?!"

"Yeah, I'm fine. Nothing to worry about. There's just some stuff going on between Brady and me right now, so I moved my things out of the apartment and I'm staying with Dee for now."

"Oh, no, Ro . . ." She sounds so sad for me, and it's precisely what I don't need to hear right now because I do *not* want to cry again. "Are you alright, honey?"

"Yeah, I think so." And even if I'm not, I will be. I'm determined to make sure of that.

"Do you want to talk about it?"

"Maybe later, but not right now."

Dee yells loudly enough for my mom to hear, "I'm taking good care of her, Tracy!"

My mom breathes a sigh of relief. "Oh, good, Dee's with you? Tell her I say hi."

"My mom says hi, Dee." Dee smiles, and I tell my mom she says hi back.

"Rowan, honey, is there anything you need? Is there anything you need me to do?"

"Actually, yeah . . . Can you please not tell Brady that I

called you? If he tries to get ahold of you again, just don't answer the phone. Tell Dad to do the same."

"Honey . . . I don't know what's going on between you two, but he is *really* worried about you. Are you sure you don't want to—"

Cutting her off, I say, "Trust me, Mom. If you knew what he did . . ." I sigh. "Just trust me on this. Me making him worry is nothing compared to what he deserves." Dee nods emphatically and gives me a thumbs-up as she chews a massive mouthful of pancakes.

"Okay, sweetie. Whatever you want. I'll make sure Dad knows. And remember, if you need anything . . . money, whatever, you just call, okay?"

"Okay. I love you, Mom."

"Love you too, honey. And Dee too. I'll talk to you later."

I hang up the phone and slouch in my seat. "Jesus."

Dee chuckles. "I hope Brady gives himself a brain aneurysm or something."

"Dee!"

"What?!"

"We don't hope he *dies*!"

She smirks at me, clearly amused with herself. "Don't we?"

I ignore her and check my texts. More of the same. "I need to tell him *something* or I'm afraid he's going to call the police and file a Missing Persons or something."

Dee pulls her phone from her purse and scoffs at the missed calls and texts Brady left her. She starts typing, and I nervously ask what she's doing.

"Responding to his text. Like he asked me to. Because I'm *nice*."

I waste no time diving into her bench seat, looking to see what she's typing.

You know what you did. We know what you did. Fess up and maybe she'll consider talking to you again.

Okay, that's not so bad. I feel relieved, but then I watch as she hits RETURN a few times and quickly adds:

lol, that last part was a lie. EAT DICK, DOUCHEBAG.

She presses send before I can stop her, and I bang my forehead against the table. "I can't believe you just did that."

"Are you gonna eat your bacon?"

I groan and slide back into my seat, gnawing on a piece of bacon. If I don't eat it soon, she'll steal it from my plate and we both know it. "Did he say anything back yet?" I stuff another piece into my mouth.

She checks her phone. "Nothing."

But when I check mine, there's a brand new text.

Baby, come home. Let's talk about this.

I show Dee and then turn my phone all the way off again. "Well, at least we know he won't be calling the cops."

"What'd I tell ya?" she says, grinning as she points a fork full of pancakes at me. "I'm *nice*."

Chapter Five

On Monday, Dee and I wake up early to drive to my old apartment building. She turns into the lot out front, but then I'm immediately grabbing at the wheel, frantically yelling at her to turn around.

She crinkles her nose at Brady's silver Cobalt. "What the hell is his car still doing here?"

"Turn around!" My hands scramble over hers as the car swerves into a sharp U-turn, and then we're kicking up gravel as we skid back onto the road.

I melt into my seat, my nerves completely fried, while Dee looks at me like I've completely lost my mind. "He must have taken off work." I sigh. "He probably knows I'll come to pick up my car."

He left me more messages than I could count yesterday, and I read every single one of them. Not one mentioned that he was a cheating pig, so I didn't bother responding. I know he's trying to figure out exactly how much I know, which tells me he's not ready to come clean. And even if he is, he can kiss my ass.

Dee rolls her window down and props her elbow on it. "I say we go pick it up one night while he's sleeping. Then we can slash his tires and key his car as a parting gift."

"Fine," I say, still wondering how many secrets Brady has kept from me over the years. When Dee's surprised expression snaps in my direction, I rush to add, "To the picking it up at night, Dee! I told you, we're not slashing his *anything*."

She grumbles. "I can't be held responsible for my actions."

"Story of my life."

She giggles at me, and I lay my head back against the headrest.

"Are you nervous about your first class?" I ask after I get tired of watching the high-rises pass us by.

Dee shakes her head. "Nope, I'm excited! I bet it'll be filled with hot college guys." In Dee's world, I wonder if not-hot college guys even exist. "What about you? Nervous?"

"Extremely."

"You should've signed up for the same classes as me!"

My expression says, *really*? "Your first class is *biology*." I say the word like it's poison.

"Yours is *French*."

"French 201," I correct. "And anyway, I'll see you for speech *and* American history."

"We have speech at twelve thirty, right?" I laugh and tell her we do. "And history right after?"

"No, history is tomorrow. Jesus, Dee, what are you going to do without me?"

"Get lost somewhere on campus. Cry a little. Have some hot college guy try to comfort me. Then he'll agree to show me to my next class, but somehow we'll end up back at his fraternity house and—"

"You're going to miss our turn," I say flatly, cutting her off.

"Shit!" Dee squeals the car into the college entrance, and I grip the door handle and dashboard for dear life. When she parks the car, I sit there waiting for the past eighteen years to stop flashing before my eyes.

"We're here!" she chirps way too peppily, like she didn't almost just kill us both. "But we're super early."

I check my phone, growling when I have to ignore another three texts from Brady. "We're not that early. Only half an hour. We should head to our classes so we can get good seats."

Dee reluctantly agrees, and I can tell that she's a little nervous even though she'd never admit it. I smile when we part ways, knowing she'll be fine. She always is.

With my backpack hanging off one shoulder and a map in my hand, I find my way to Jackson Hall and navigate through a dense cluster of sorority girls to get to room 107. It's an auditorium way larger than I expected, and I have no idea how the professor is planning to successfully teach a language to a class this large. I automatically find a seat in the back corner farthest from the door, realizing too late that Dee isn't with me so I don't need to sit this far back. Since I think it would be awkward at this point to get up and switch seats, I stay put, pulling the fold-over desk over my lap and getting out my textbook and notepad. There weren't more than a few students scattered throughout the room when I entered, but now the seats are filling up.

Even though I'm a freshman, this isn't my first college class. I excelled so much in my high school AP classes that I was allowed to take a few courses at our local community college. One of them was French 101, which is why I'm already at the next level. I'm still not completely sure what I want to do with my future, but I've been thinking about pursuing a career as a translator, a job that would've been flexible enough to allow me to follow Brady wherever he needed to go for work. Now, I guess none of that really matters.

"Hey," one of my classmates says as he plunks down in the seat next to me.

I gaze over at him, taking in his faded Mr. Bubble T-shirt, his acid-washed jeans, and his hot-pink Chuck Taylors. "Hey." He's tall, nearly as tall as Adam but with a little more meat on his bones.

He reaches out a hand. "Leti."

"Rowan."

"I'm digging the polka-dot scarf, Rowan."

I blush, thinking of Adam as I fiddle with the petite scarf wrapped around my neck. When I looked in the mirror this morning, there was still the faintest little trace of a love mark. I barely managed to sneak it under Dee's radar yesterday, and today it was barely visible, but I knew she'd still lock on it like a heat-seeking missile. The scarf was a must-have, and I've paired it with black leggings, a loose white top, and bright red flats. My blonde hair is pulled up in a tight ponytail. If I looked any Frencher, I'd have to stop shaving my armpits. "Thanks."

"I hear this guy is tough," Leti says, referring to our professor, who hasn't made an appearance yet. "Did you have him last year?"

"No, this is actually my first class."

"You're a transfer?"

"A freshman." I give him a half smile.

"A freshman . . . ? Are you sure you're in the right place?"

I laugh when he looks at me like he feels sorry that I'm lost on my first day. "Yeah, I'm sure. I took French 101 while I was still in high school."

"Wow," he replies, his golden-brown eyes looking genuinely impressed. Oversized shades are sitting on top of his wavy ombré hair—deep bronze with sunrise-blond highlighting, it's buzzed short on the sides but left long on the top. "I'm glad I sat next to you then! I need all the help I can get."

I smile at him, realizing I've made my first new friend in record time. I pull my water bottle from my backpack and am taking a big sip when Leti suddenly grabs my forearm and points his chin toward the door. "Look who it is."

My eyes wash over the seats in front of me to land on—

Adam. Freaking. Everest.

I choke. Literally *choke*. Water forces itself into my sinuses as I try to not spit it all over the students sitting in front of me, and Leti claps me on the back, laughing. "Hey, are you okay?"

"Yeah," I cough. "I'm . . ." I'm too busy watching Adam to think straight. I can't even be bothered to finish my sentence. He's in another pair of torn-up jeans that are barely clinging to his hips, along with a gray T-shirt advertising some band I've never heard of. His braceleted wrist is reaching up to brush the hair away from his face. That face . . . I'd almost convinced myself that I remembered him being hotter than he really was.

Nope, didn't imagine it.

Most of the seats in the auditorium are taken, but a group of girls up front are calling his name, and Adam goes to sit with them. The girl who came in with him sits down on his lap and wraps her arms around his neck, giggling like she's oblivious to the stares of everyone else in the room. What the hell is he *doing* here?

With my eyes still on the back of Adam's head, I ask Leti, "Adam Everest goes to school here?"

"Hence the welcome party in the hall," Leti answers, and then his chin comes to rest on the heel of his palm. He stares dreamily at the boy who just had his hands all over me less than forty-eight hours ago and sighs. "I had French 101 with him last year."

"Why?" I ask. When he shoots me a confused glance, I clarify, "I mean, why is he taking classes?"

Leti shrugs. "I have no idea, but I'm definitely not complaining."

When our professor walks in, the chick on Adam's lap is forced to find a seat in the row behind him because the girls he sat with didn't save her a seat. Is she his girlfriend? Does he *have* a girlfriend?

"I'm Dr. Pullman," says our professor, a tall, bald man who I can't imagine smiling even if his life depended on it. "This class isn't going to be easy. You're going to have homework. A lot of it." A girl next to Adam giggles at something Adam said, and the professor shoots her a nasty look. She immediately bites her tongue, and he continues. "I have a strict attendance policy. I expect you to turn your cell phones off at the door. If you treat me with respect, I'll treat you with respect. Now, how many of you bothered to go online and print out our syllabus?"

Only a handful of people raise their hands. Adam isn't one of them, and neither am I. Even though I *did* go online and print it out, I don't want to draw attention to myself.

Dr. Pullman sighs. "Well, it's there if you want to take a look. Make sure to review it before you come to me whining with complaints about my class. If you don't want to be here, you have until next week to drop and still get a refund. As you can see," he waves his hand across the room, "I'll have a very full workload with or without you." He goes to the side of the room and opens up a laptop, starting the projector. "Let's get started, shall we?"

But there is no way in hell I'm going to be able to pay attention with the girl sitting next to Adam periodically lifting her fingers to comb them through the soft brown hair at the nape of his neck. I *know* how soft that hair is. My fingertips remember, and I'm having serious trouble not breaking my pencil in half and throwing the lethal pieces at her.

When class ends, Adam is the first one out of his seat and through the door. Leti nudges me with his elbow.

"Jealous much?"

"Huh?" I try and fail to act nonchalant as we pack our bags.

"If looks could kill, I swear there'd be three dead groupie tramps laying up there," he says with a teasing smile.

"I'm *not* jealous."

I'm *so* jealous. I'm jealous of the very thing I turned down less than two days ago, even though I know I made the right choice. I had just gotten out of a relationship, for God's sake. Like less than *five minutes* before I met Adam. And he's obviously a playboy—which may have been what I needed at that moment, but it's not what I need long term. Whatever this is that I'm feeling, I need to get over it.

Leti smirks at me. "If you say so, Ro-Yo."

As we make our way out of Jackson Hall, he's complaining about what a hard-ass Dr. Pullman is and what hell the class is going to be. I'm half paying attention to him and half flinging nervous glances down every hallway we pass to make sure I don't cross paths with Adam.

"Are you always this twitchy?"

I look up at him, frowning. "Am I seriously twitchy?"

"You're like a cute little chipmunk . . . on crack."

I laugh and adjust my scarf, making sure it's still covering the mark Adam left on me. "I guess I'm just still nervous about starting classes. Plus I had way too much caffeine this morning."

"No such thing!" Leti opens the door for me, his wide smile brightening my mood as he flicks his shades down over his eyes. At a fork in the sidewalk, we slow to a stop. "Hey, I'll see you on Wednesday?" he asks.

"Yep! See ya, Leti."

"Ciao, Ro-bot!"

The minute Leti is out of sight, my shoulders slump and I feel like a ton of bricks has just collapsed on top of me. I don't know where Adam disappeared to, but I hurry across the campus lawn like there's a sniper creeping on the rooftops trying to trap me in his sights. My eyes are everywhere, and my frantic heartbeat doesn't slow until I've dipped into Hoffman Hall, climbed the stairs, and am turning into Room 204.

"Ro!" Dee calls my name from the back, but I'm still in such a daze, I barely make eye contact before I slump into a chair beside her. This room is more traditional, with rows of small desks in front of a whiteboard. "How was your first class?!" Her excitement splashes me in the face, pulling me out of my own head.

"It was . . . interesting. I think I made a new friend. What about you?"

She starts rambling about the hot guy who sat next to her in biology. I nod and smile, smile and nod, add in an "oh" or a "wow" or a "that's awesome" every now and then. When our speech professor walks in and starts the lecture, I am beyond relieved. My brain is too full. Too full of Adam and . . . Adam. Oh, God.

Dr. V is much nicer than Dr. Pullman. She starts the class by asking us to tell the class our names, our majors, and something interesting about ourselves. When it's my turn, I've been too busy thinking about that girl's fingers in Adam's hair to come up with anything.

I stand up. "My name is Rowan Michaels. I haven't decided on a major yet, but I'm thinking of language studies. And, um . . . something interesting . . ." I'm completely tongue-tied as the pause stretches awkwardly on. "Um . . ."

Oh my God, I'm totally blank! Something interesting, about me? There's nothing! *I made out with Adam Everest on his tour bus last weekend* would be totally inappropriate, but I can't think of anything else!

"And she can fit eleven marshmallows in her mouth at once!" Dee shouts to fill the horrific silence. She's referring to the time we were sitting around a campfire with a group of friends, all trying to see who could stuff the most marshmallows in their mouth. I won by a landslide. When my loud laughter was muffled by all the marshmallows in my cheeks, everyone completely lost it. We all laughed hysterically until we were drowning in tears. Dee laughed like a hyena until she fell off her lawn chair, which made me laugh so hard I almost choked on a marshmallow.

The class laughs as Dr. V gives me an appreciative smile. "That's quite the talent, Rowan."

My cheeks are flush with embarrassment when I finally take my seat, fighting the urge to hide my face in my hands. Dee gives me a half smile and shrugs her shoulders, and I shake my head at myself, pressing the heel of my palm against my forehead. So much for first impressions.

When class ends, I'm done for the day, so I walk directly back to Dee's dorm and flop face-first onto her mattress. She has one class left and then we're going to meet back here to figure out dinner plans.

I want to tell her about Adam so freaking badly. But I just don't think she'd be the best person to give me any advice. She's still trying to convince me to light Brady's car on fire or replace all of his shampoo with . . . well, that conversation is just not one I want to commit to long-term memory.

When she bursts through the door an hour and half later, she hops onto the bed, making me bounce. "I love college!"

"Told you you would." I'm glad to see her so happy. She's been waiting for this day since before I can remember, and if I'm being honest, I had been a little worried it wouldn't meet her expectations. For once, I'm glad I was wrong.

Macy is sitting on her own bed in the opposite corner, a laptop on her lap. She looks up from it and asks, "Did you like your classes, Deandra?"

Dee freezes, eyes wide with shock that Macy is attempting to converse. In person. With a fellow human. "Yeah, I did, Mace. What about you?" Dee shoots an "oh my God" glance at me out of the corner of her eye, but I pretend not to notice and wait for Macy to reply.

"They were alright, I suppose."

"What are you taking?" I ask.

And that's how I lure Macy into a conversation that ends with me insisting she come to dinner with us. At a diner downtown—since Dee insists the food on campus tastes like feet—Dee rattles on like Macy isn't even there, so I guess she isn't put off by me inviting an extra wheel. Macy sits at the table silently nibbling on some fries. She's small and skinny, with straight black hair, a pale face, and eyes a little too large and dark for her face. But she has a friendly smile, and I find myself wanting to help her come out of her shell a little.

"So there's this guy in my class," I say. "His name's Leti."

"Oooh," Dee says. "Is he hot?"

"He's . . . he's definitely something." I chuckle, and Dee raises an eyebrow. "I'm pretty sure you two would love shoe-shopping together, if you know what I'm getting at."

"A gay friend?! You already made a gay friend?! No fair! I want one!"

I laugh and sip my Coke. "Maybe we should invite him to hang out sometime."

"We should *definitely* invite him to hang out sometime!"

"Next time we have class, I'll get his number and see if he wants to meet up with us some night."

When Macy speaks, it shocks us into silence again. "That's very kind of you."

I shrug it off. "It's no big deal. The more friends, the better. Right, Dee?"

"As long as this Leti doesn't try to steal my best girl, I'm golden." She sucks down a vanilla milkshake.

I grin at her and then at Macy. "Thanks again for letting me stay with you, Macy."

"Thank you for inviting me out tonight."

"Mace," Dee cuts in, shifting in her seat to face Macy, who is sitting beside her, pressed against the chipped yellow wall. "Let me ask you a question. You know Ro is staying with us because her scumbag piece-of-shit ex-boyfriend cheated on her, right?" Macy nods. "Well, don't you think she deserves to get some type of revenge? Flatten his tires or something? I mean, they were together for *three years*."

Macy gazes across the table at me. "I think Rowan is taking the higher road. It's an admirable quality."

"Higher road," Dee scoffs. "I'd like to catch him on a higher road," she mumbles, "and drive him right off it."

Macy and I both chuckle, and Dee finishes off the last of her milkshake. After she drives us back to her dorm, I pull a textbook onto my lap. The heavy weight is comforting, reminding me of simpler times, when the only thing I had to worry about was homework. Homework, I can do. Homework, I can bury myself in. I fall asleep with the textbook on my lap and Dee's knee jutting into my thigh. Much-needed sleep trumps the plan to go get my car, but it's not like I'll need it anytime soon anyway.

The next morning, I have to wake up earlier than Dee for my morning classes—she refused to take anything before 11 o'clock—so I try to keep quiet as I get ready for school. My first class is English 101. Then I have math, followed by an hour-and-a-half-long break during which I grab lunch in Lion's Den, and then I head to Benton Hall for history class with Dee.

If all three classes were about a certain brown-haired

rocker boy with ungodly skilled lips, I'd ace them with no problem. But as it stands, I'm pretty sure I'm going to fail.

My thoughts are back on Adam's tour bus, and they travel to that black satin bed. In history class, I chew on the end of my pencil, simultaneously regretting the moment and wishing I could go back and live it all over again. Making out with him had been so, *so* out of character for me. Before Adam, I'd only ever kissed two guys other than Brady. One was in fifth grade, so I'm not even sure if that counts, and the other was a guy I went on a few group dates with when I was a freshman, before Brady and I ever got together.

I have no idea why I've been thinking about Adam so much, probably even more than Brady. Maybe it's my brain's way of trying to protect itself from all the emotions I refuse to feel over the way Brady betrayed me. I loved him, I really did. But after seeing him with that girl . . . I almost feel like I never truly knew him. The Brady I knew never would have hurt me like that.

In a way, it feels like the boy I loved died, and part of me has accepted that . . . because when someone dies, there's nothing you can do to bring them back. The only thing you can do is let them go.

Dee and I walk from the building with some guy who she's apparently gotten friendly with from one of her other classes. My phone beeps again, and I peek at it while Dee talks the poor guy's ear off. Brady again. Of course. All it says is "I miss you," and it's the simplest text he's sent me so far—and the one that chokes me up the worst. His texts are like daily hauntings, apparitions reminding me of everything I lost.

"I'll see you guys later," I say, and then I'm practically speed-walking back to Dee's dorm before anyone can catch me.

The minute I get back to the room, I change into sweat pants and one of my dad's old work T-shirts. When Dee arrives later, I have a carton of Rocky Road in my lap and I'm staring off into space. She grabs a spoon and dips it in next to mine, but she doesn't ask any questions. Which is good, because I sure as hell don't have any answers.

Chapter Six

AT 3 A.M., I'm lying awake next to Dee. Eight hours until I see Adam again.

Eight. freaking. hours.

Eight turns into seven, and seven turns into six. By the time the alarm goes off, my eyes are red from sleep deprivation, but I hop out of bed like I've been lying on coals. After a quick shower, I stare down at the stacks of clothes that line almost an entire wall of Dee's dorm room. It sucks not having a dresser or any closet space for my stuff, but beggars can't be choosers. It's time to figure out what I'm going to wear today.

On one hand, I want to look decent in case Adam looks my way during French. The heavens would part, angels would sing, and he … . probably wouldn't even remember me. Ugh.

On the other hand, I don't want to draw any attention to myself. I made the right decision when I didn't go back to his tour bus that night after the show. It was the right call . . . It was, I know it was.

I sift through my neatly stacked piles until nearly every piece of clothing is lying in an unfolded mess on the floor, and then I sigh and find myself raiding Dee's closet. I opt for a short pair of jean shorts and a cute blue top that complements my deep blue eyes. In front of her vanity mirror, I yank my hair up into a ponytail and do my makeup before Dee gets back from her shower.

"Cute top," she says as her reflection enters the door behind me.

"Mind if I borrow it?"

"Hell no I don't mind! Keep borrowing my clothes and we'll have you a new boyfriend by the end of the week."

"How about this," I say with a snarky grin, stepping away from the mirror as Dee squeezes in front of it and leans in to rub moisturizer all over her face, "I'll get a boyfriend in no time."

She gives my reflection a serious look, and then she laughs. "Touché."

Dee has never had a serious boyfriend, and she's never wanted one. What she wants is to be admired by all, to be showered with flowers and candy from guys whose names she hasn't bothered to remember. She wants to hoard their affection but give none back, and even though she'd never admit it, I know that her aversion to relationships stems from how terribly things ended between her parents.

When she and I were in sixth grade, her dad discovered that her mom had been having a long-term affair, and Dee witnessed firsthand the devastation that love can leave in its wake. The first time she ever saw her dad cry—after her mom abandoned the family to move with the other man across the country—Dee snuck into my room and sobbed herself to sleep on my pillow while I assured her that her dad would be fine and she would be too. I told her she didn't need her stupid mom because she'd always have me instead, and then I smoothed her hair until she fell asleep.

That was the last time I saw her cry about her parents— after that, it was just anger, heated tears, and trashed bedrooms. Her dad has always been the most doting father I've ever known, but he couldn't fill the void her mom left behind, and even though Dee never said it out loud, I knew that she missed her mom as much as she hated her. Truthfully, since then, I don't think anything has terrified her more than commitment. I always suspected that maybe that was why she was so uncomfortable with me settling down with Brady so quickly—that and all the time he sucked away from her.

I wish I could give every minute of it back.

I rush Dee out the door, and we walk to campus as quickly as I can get her legs to move. I skirt through Adam's perfume-drenched welcome party and arrive at the auditorium for my French class extra early to make sure I get there before him. Then I scurry into the same seat I sat in two days earlier, making sure to save the one next to me for Leti.

" 'Sup, Ro-town?" he says as he slides in beside me. "Lovin' those blue piglets."

I gaze down at my blue toenails and then smile at him as he pushes his shades on top of his head. A girl could seriously get used to receiving compliments so often. Now, if only straight guys paid the same attention to detail. "Thanks. I love your T-shirt."

The pink ponies on his My Little Pony T-shirt match his hot-pink Chucks. "What can I say, I'm a total bronie."

I laugh and open my notebook to a blank page. "Hey, would you want to hang out with me and my roommate sometime? Like maybe this weekend?"

"Is she as cool as you are?"

"Way cooler."

He chuckles and tugs on my long ponytail. "Don't sell yourself short, Corn-Ro! I'd *love* to hang out with you and your roommate! What's her name?"

"Dee."

"She goes by a one-letter nickname? Wow, you're right, she *is* cooler than you."

My laughter is cut short when Dr. Pullman enters the room. Dressed in brown slacks and a pale yellow button-down, he reaches back to close the door behind him. But Adam hasn't shown up yet. Maybe he dropped the class. Or . . . did I freaking hallucinate him or something? Am I losing my damn mind?

The door is nearly shut when a hand slaps against it, preventing it from closing all the way. Adam appears in the open sliver and gives Dr. Pullman a charming smile that makes my heart sputter. He unapologetically slips into the room, two girls on his heels, and sits in his seat at the front.

I feel like a pathetic stalker as I steal glances at him throughout class. We only kissed—just like I'm sure he kissed every girl sitting with him in that front row. And I'm *nothing* compared to them. My chest isn't as big and my face isn't as pretty, my hair isn't as voluptuous and my ass isn't as va-va-voom. Whatever this is that I'm feeling, I need to quash it before it adds to the emotional cluster-fuck I'm already feeling over Brady. Adam was a nice re-bound. He did me a favor. Who knew we'd end up in the same damn class?

All rationality be damned, I leave class feeling almost as shattered as I felt that night at Mayhem. I shouldn't feel like Adam betrayed me like Brady did, but . . . ugh. I feel so . . . rejected. By both of them.

Leti flips his shades down when we step into the brightly lit courtyard. The sun beats down on us like a vampire's worst nightmare, and with the mood I'm in, I nearly hiss.

"You have class now, right?" Leti gazes down at me from behind black lenses.

"Yeah. Speech with Dee. Hey, give me your phone."

He hands it over and I give him mine. We punch our digits in and then trade back. "I'll text you about this weekend, 'kay?"

He tucks earbuds into his ears as he backs away. "You better!"

The next day, during my break between math class and my history class with Dee, I eat lunch alone in Lion's Den again, burying my face in my French textbook as I munch on a BLT and chips. We're spending the first week reviewing, and I read the word for *boyfriend* out loud. "*Petit ami.*" I glare at my textbook, thinking of Brady. "*Je déteste mon ex-petit ami!*" I'm tempted to end the sentiment by spitting on the floor next to my chair, but I'm guessing that might earn me more looks than I'm already getting. I'm officially that girl who eats alone and talks to herself.

In French.

Great.

I think of Brady until my brain starts following one association after another. Brady. That Girl. Mayhem. Adam. Adam's tour bus. That black satin bed. My skin starts to tingle, but then I remember French class, and all those girls. The giggling. The manicured fingernails combing through his hair.

I groan and close my textbook, letting my forehead fall against it. Adam. He's such a man-whore. I almost slept with a man-whore. A freaking man-whore.

And it was wonderful. And classes with him are going to be brutal. And my emotions are so all over the place that I seriously want to slap myself. I'm a mess. My whole freaking *life* is a mess.

By the time my lunch break is over, I've worked myself into one hell of a mood. I mope into my history class and slump into a seat next to Dee, who reaches over to play with the blonde pony tail cascading over my shoulder. "What's the matter?"

"Nothing," I lie. "Just . . . French homework I was working on during lunch. Totally has me drained."

"Well I have the perfect medicine!" Dee says, and already I'm suspicious. "Guess who got invited to a party this weekend!"

I shake my head. There's no way I'm going with her to a party. I think I'd rather get hit by a dump truck full of cow manure than try to brave a social event. A social event with lots of people—lots of smiling, happy people.

"Aw, come on, Ro! Pleeease? You need this! WE need this!"

Instead of telling her the truth, which is that I'm just not ready to put myself back out there after having my heart crushed under Brady's heel, I make up an excuse. "I already told Leti we'd hang out with him this weekend."

She narrows her eyes suspiciously, and I know she can tell I'm bullshitting, but she lets it go. "Leti had better be *amazing*," she warns.

"He is."

"I hate you."

"I love you."

She rolls her eyes playfully and straightens in her seat. I'm relieved she's not fighting me on this, but I guess she must realize that I'm just not ready to be thrown back into a social life. Soon, though, I know she'll start pestering me. She *is* Dee, after all.

After class, I spend my walk back to the dorm reading all the text messages from Brady that I've been ignoring. He left me another voicemail too, and I make the mistake of listening to it while out in public.

"Baby . . ." He sighs. "I messed up bad. I know I did. I . . . I don't even know what to say. I'm not going to try to defend myself. I just . . . Jesus, baby, I'm a broken man here. I feel like I lost my best friend. I don't deserve for you to call me back." He chokes up, and it brings tears to my eyes. "I never deserved you, but hell if I don't love you, Rowan. I love you so much, baby. I don't think I can go on without you." After a long pause, he says, "I hope you're liking school." Another long pause. "I love you, Ro."

By the time the message ends, silent tears are rolling trails of heat down my cheeks. I roughly wipe them away, angling my face toward the ground to avoid the stares of people walking past me on the sidewalk.

When Dee gets home, I'm a shell of her best friend, my face a tear-stained mess. My body feels utterly empty because I've cried every last shred of my energy out. Macy left the room to give me some privacy, and for the last half hour, I've just been sitting on Dee's bed staring at my phone. She immediately sits down in front of me, her knees practically on top of mine. She wraps her arms around me. "What'd he say?"

I give her the gist of the message, because I just can't bear to play it again. She sighs, and her eyes search mine. "You're not thinking of calling him, are you?"

I chew on the inside of my lip. Because I *am* thinking of calling him. I want to talk to him so badly. Each time I hear his voice, he puts another chink in the wall I've put up between us, and I can feel my anger fading.

"Oh, babe." Dee frowns. "Do you honestly think he'd never do it again?"

"I don't know, Dee." A sob escapes my throat, and I bury my face in my hands. She rubs my back.

"You know I'll stand by you no matter what you do, but . . . you know what I always say."

"Once a cheater, always a cheater."

She kisses the top of my head and then sits with me in silence until I gather the strength to show my face. "Sorry about bailing on the party." I haven't decided if I'm going to call Brady back or not, but I'm tired of talking about it. This is something I'll have to work out on my own.

"Don't be. I'm excited to meet this super-gay friend of yours!"

I love how easily she can make me laugh. "I don't think he's super-gay. I think he's just regular-gay."

"Well, he's gay, and you like him, so he must be super . . ." She stares at me expectantly.

"Super gay?"

"Super gay!" She stands up, yanking me off the bed. Her slender fingers straighten my too-depressed-to-be-bothered-with hair. "What do you wanna do for food today?"

Dee blasts girl-power music in the car all the way to the closest fast-food joint, and we pig out in the car, laughing and screaming karaoke—because what we do really can't be called singing. She serenades me with her soft drink microphone, and I play drums on her dashboard with my fries. By the time the song ends, I'm playing with only one fry because I ate the other halfway through my solo. I toss the last one into the air and catch it in my mouth, taking a bow when Dee busts up laughing.

"There she is!" she says with a contagious smile. "I missed you!"

"Sorry I've been so blah . . . I promise I'll lighten up and have fun this weekend."

"You're not going to have a choice!"

I text Leti later to ask if he can hang with us in Dee's dorm room on Saturday, and he texts me back a cheesy picture of him making a goofy-excited face and giving the camera a thumbs-up. I chuckle and show the picture to Dee as we drive home, and she laughs too.

On Saturday, he shows up wearing long khaki shorts, a tattered purple tank top, and rainbow flip-flops. His sunglasses hang from his V-necked tank as he spins around in Macy's office chair watching Dee and I paint our toenails.

"Leti," Dee complains as she paints her piggy nail glittery pink, "you really need to let us paint your toenails! You too, Mace!"

Leti and Macy share a look. She's sitting on her bed, curled up in the corner with a book.

"I'm a *dude*," Leti says.

I snicker as Dee pouts. "Yeah," she says, "But you're . . ."

The corner of his mouth quirks up. "I'm *what*?"

"You're . . . gay." She says the word quietly, like it's a secret, and I'm having serious trouble not cracking up.

"Really?" Leti asks. "That's news to me."

Uh, *what*?! I accidentally paint a streak of purple across the tip of my toe as my eyes dart up to his. "You're not?"

"I'd say I'm bi."

"You like girls too?"

"Well . . . just one . . . in fourth grade . . . but she was a total knockout!"

Dee laughs. "You're totally gay."

"Whatever," Leti says, spinning around again. "I'm still not letting you paint my toenails."

"Then at least let me paint your fingernails!" she says.

"Oh!" His spinning suddenly jerks to a stop. "You can paint three on each hand! Black, like Adam's!"

"Adam who?" Dee asks, and my throat instantly constricts, threatening to suffocate me—which would probably be for the best. How did I not see this coming?! *Of course* Leti would mention Adam! I still haven't told Dee about our make-out session or that he's in my class. Oh, God. Oh, no. No, no, no

"Adam Everest!" Leti says. "The lead singer of The Last Ones to Know!"

I'm frantically trying to brainstorm a way to stop this train wreck of a conversation from happening, but I can't think under pressure, damn it!

Dee finishes with her first foot and moves to the other, having no idea how panicked I feel sitting only inches away from her. "You're a fan? Ro and I just went to see him perform this past weekend! He is so *hot*!"

"Oh, we know, trust me!" Leti says. "He's the best part of French class!"

Boom, the bomb's been detonated. I cringe, waiting for the fallout.

Dee's eyebrows scrunch together in confusion. When she looks at me for answers, I sheepishly confess, "Shit, I forgot to mention that. He's. . . in our class."

She leaps from the bed like shock catapulted her off of it, completely ignoring the toenail polish she's probably smudging all over the place. "He's in your CLASS? Adam Everest is IN YOUR FRENCH CLASS?!" She and Leti are both staring at me like I'm a lunatic for not having mentioned it. "You FORGOT to tell me that? How can you FORGET to tell something like that!"

"Who is Adam Everest?" Macy peeps from the corner of the room.

Dee whirls on her. "Only a freaking rock god!" She spins back to me, and I have no idea how she isn't making herself light-headed with all the spinning and pacing she's doing. "I didn't even know he went to school with us! How did I not know this?!"

"Dee," I say cautiously, "your toenails are totally ruined."

Ignoring me, she braces her hands on my shoulders. "I *need* to be in your class! I need to make a switch!"

"You can't . . . It's a two-hundred-level class. You would've needed to take French 101 first."

She curses under her breath and slumps down on the bed. "God, I am so jealous of you."

"Don't be," I say. "It's impossible to concentrate."

Leti chuckles and props his feet on Macy's desk, but she doesn't seem to mind or notice. "It's true. I'm pretty sure Ro-bo Cop and I are going to fail."

"It'd be worth it!" Dee is all smiles as she dabs a cotton ball in polish remover and starts wiping all the glittery pink paint from her feet. "Have you talked to him?"

I nearly let out an irrational giggle that wouldn't make sense to anyone but me. Talked to him? Uh, yeah, that and then some. I bite my tongue.

"Nah," Leti says. "He comes in last and leaves first and he's always surrounded by bleached-blonde bimbos."

"Ugh." Dee rubs the last of the polish off and then begins to shake the pink bottle again, preparing to start over. "Ro, I swear I'm playing hooky one day just so I can walk you to class."

Not if I can help it! She takes my silence as agreement, but I'm already thinking of excuses to prevent that apocalyptic moment from happening. If Dee ever finds out I made out with Adam and didn't tell her about it . . . Yikes.

I get her mind off of it by telling Leti to slide his chair over to me so I can start painting some of his nails black like Adam's. As I run the brush over his pinky, his ring finger, and his thumb on one hand, and his ring finger, his pointer finger, and his thumb on the other hand—because I remember very clearly that those are the *exact* nails Adam had painted—I can't help wondering what it would be like to paint Adam's nails for him. It'd be intimate and tender and . . . ack, I really need to get that deliciously slutty boy out of my head. I had my chance with him, and I didn't take it.

End. Of. Story.

Chapter Seven

"I'm bored," Dee complains a little after eleven o'clock. She, Leti, and I are all crammed on her bed. I'm sitting with my back to the wall and Leti between my legs as I braid his hair into a million tiny braids like we've time-traveled to the nineties, and Dee is between his legs as he French-braids hers into pigtails.

"It's late," I counter.

When Dee suddenly gasps, I jerk, accidentally tugging on one of Leti's braids.

"Ow!"

"Sorry!"

Dee yanks her pigtail from his fingers and holds his spot while she spins around. "Your car!" she says to me.

Oh no.

"Your car?" Leti asks.

After sobering up from the three margaritas she made earlier tonight, Dee is officially getting her second wind.

Leti should have fled while he had the chance. "We still need to go get it!" she says.

And that's how I end up in the backseat of her car, leaning forward between my very best friend and Leti. "I don't even see the point in this, guys. I'm not even allowed to keep it parked on campus."

"The *point*," Dee replies, "is that it's your last loose end. And you can keep it parked in the Walmart parking lot on Fifth Street. It's not that far."

I groan and rest my head against Leti's seat. Dee got him all caught up to speed on Brady and insisted he come along. He said he had nothing better to do, so we both waited patiently while Dee changed into all-black clothing and tried to convince me to do the same. "We're not *stealing* my car," I told her, dangling my keys for her to see. She was one step away from donning a ski mask.

"What if he's still awake?" I ask as I nervously run my finger over the leather ridges of Dee's center console.

Leti shifts to face me. His hair is even wavier now that he's taken out the last of his braids. "What's the worst that could happen?"

When we park in the vacant lot next to the parking lot of my old apartment, the light in Brady's window answers Leti's question.

"Shit," I say under my breath. "I knew he'd be up." Normally, he'd be in bed by now. But with the way my luck has been going lately? Yeah, there was no chance he wouldn't be awake when we arrived for this impromptu black-ops mission.

Leti leans forward to stare through the windshield

up to the third-floor window. "Can't you just run over there real quick, start your car up, and get the hell out of there?"

I sigh. "Yeah, but if he comes out and I just speed away like a coward or something, that'd be *really* embarrassing. And awkward." I fish my keys from my purse and give Leti my sweetest smile. "Can you go over there and get it for me? Please?" I do my best to look pathetic and needy, which means I don't need to try very hard at all. I push my bottom lip out, curl my eyebrows in, and give him the biggest puppy dog eyes I can manage. "You can meet us at the gas station up the street and I'll ride back with you."

He purses his lips at me, but then takes the keys I hand him. "You *so* owe me."

Dee and I watch as he walks to the edge of the lot we're in, looks both ways, and then jogs across the street to my old parking lot. He glances back at us one last time before disappearing inside my car and driving off the lot. I breathe a sigh of relief when Brady doesn't burst from the building's front doors. Dee pats my knee, and I crawl into the front to sit next to her.

"Well, that was easy," she says as she turns her key in the ignition. Her ridiculous bundle of key chains jingles with the movement—a miniature platform shoe, a ceramic flower, a feather, a pink glass square that says 'sweetest bitch you'll ever meet'.

It sure doesn't *feel* like it was easy, since my neck still feels like it's been pumped full of steroids, but I guess it could've been worse. "I told you that you didn't need to go all ninja-mode."

"Well *someone* had to." Dee logic: it only makes sense if you're Dee. She karate chops my arm, but I'm too deep in thought to even crack a smile.

At the gas station, I climb out of her car and walk to where Leti is leaning against my trunk, dangling my keys from his finger. Before I take them from him, I wrap him in a warm hug. "Thank you."

He pats my back. "No problem, Roast Potato."

I chuckle and take my keys. When I climb into the driver's seat, I have to pull it way up so that I can reach the pedals. Leti climbs into the passenger seat and shifts his all the way back.

"That was fun," he says as I pull us onto the road. The look I give him says I would've rather had a root canal, but he just laughs. "Do you feel better now that you have your car back?"

"Kinda," I say, but I'm frowning.

"Then why don't you seem like it?"

I sigh and glance over at him, at his wavy highlighted hair and his concerned honey-shaded eyes. Even though we met less than a week ago, I feel like I can talk to him. Leti is a good guy. "It was the last thing tying me to him, you know? I have no other reason I'd need to see him now." Never seeing Brady again—it's hard for me to imagine. And painful.

"Are you thinking about giving him another chance?"

"I don't know . . ." Am I? "Dee would kill me."

"If she's a good friend, she'd understand." I know he's right, and I know she would.

"Leti . . . do you think people can change?" I'm thinking of Dee's motto: once a cheater, always a cheater. It can't be true . . . can it?

"Hm, that's a tough one." He runs his hand over his khaki-covered thigh. "There are some things about people that I think they can change, yes. Cheating? Yeah, I think people can learn their lesson. But I think it depends on the person."

"I guess the thing that's hanging me up is that I don't think it was just *cheating* . . . I think he was having an affair. I can't even remember how many 'business trips' he's had to go on since he started working for his uncle. I mean, how long was all of this going on before I found out about it?"

"I guess you'll never know unless you ask him."

Leti is keeping it real with me, which I appreciate more than he could possibly know. He listens and helps me sort through my own thoughts without pushing me one way or another. Talking to him is so much different than talking to Dee. He's so much more laid-back, and Dee is just . . . *Dee*.

"Alright," he says after we've been driving in silence for a few minutes while I consider everything he said, "enough about *that* drama. I want to know about some *other* drama."

Huh? When I glance at him, he looks positively devilish.

"Why didn't you tell Dee that Adam is in our class?"

I gulp and make sure to keep my eyes trained on the road, wishing I was a better liar. "I told you. I forgot."

Leti lifts his nose in the air and starts sniffing. "Do you smell that?"

I sniff the air too. What am I supposed to be smelling? Exhaust? City garbage? "No, what?"

"Bullshit," he says with a snarky grin, and I can't help laughing.

"Whatever."

"Come on! I really want to know!"

I chew on the side of my lip and spare a glance at him. "You can't tell anyone," I warn.

He crosses his heart. "I won't tell a soul!"

"*Especially* not Dee."

"Not even Dee!"

Oh my God, am I really going to do this? Before I can over-think it, I blurt, "I made out with Adam."

Leti stares at me, the tension-filled silence sucking all the oxygen out of the car . . . and then he busts up laughing. "Oh my God, you almost got me!"

"It's true!"

"Uh-huh." He grins at me. "Suuure it is."

"I'm not even kidding you right now!"

He laughs harder. "You are so full of it."

I shrug. "Fine, don't believe me."

Still laughing, he says, "Okay, Roly Poly, I'll bite. When did it happen?"

"Do you remember Dee told you that I saw Brady cheating on me while I was busy talking to another guy at Mayhem?" Leti nods. "That's not really true . . . I saw Brady at the bar with that girl. I ran out of the back of the building and started crying on a stoop. Adam came out to smoke a cigarette and saw me. We started talking, he invited me onto his tour bus, we started drinking, and . . . I don't know, one thing just kind of led to another . . ."

Leti is staring at me like I just sprouted an extra head. "You're not kidding . . ."

I stare nervously at him, still unable to believe that I actually just spilled my secret to someone.

"Oh . . . my . . . GOD." He flattens both hands against the dashboard, his fingers splayed like he needs to hold on to something to keep himself grounded. He stares out of the windshield until his head snaps in my direction. "You . . . made out . . . with Adam EVEREST."

I nod.

"I can't believe it!" he says. "That's why you always look at those skanks like you want to snap their twiggy little necks in half!"

"Do I seriously do that?" I worry my bottom lip again.

"Yes!" He laughs. "I mean, so does every other girl in the room, but . . . wow."

"You can NOT tell Dee about this!"

"I won't! I swear." He sucks in a deep breath. "That girl would straight-up *kill* you for not telling her. She'd go all Rambo in that hot black outfit of hers and flog you with her key chains until you confessed every juicy detail."

I might have laughed at that if it wasn't *way* too easy for me to picture. "I know!" I say.

I feel bad for not telling Dee about Adam but . . . I just can't. Maybe ten years from now, I'll tell her and we'll laugh. But right now, I just don't need the drama that would ensue. I've got enough as it is already.

I turn into the Walmart parking lot and give Leti a "you had better keep this secret or I'm a dead woman walking" look. He twists an imaginary key between his lips and tosses it over his shoulder.

Chapter Eight

TELLING LETI ABOUT Adam has been blissfully freeing.
I spend all Sunday feeling like a weight has been lifted
from my shoulders. But then Monday arrives and he sits
down next to me in class with a ridiculously goofy grin
on his stupid face. "What are you smiling about?" I ask,
already knowing the answer.

"Nothing," he chirps.

"Don't be stupid," I say, and he just laughs, his eyes
glued to the door. "Seriously," I warn. "Don't get weird
about this, okay?"

With humor in his tone, he says "okay," but his eyes
don't budge from the door, and I can already tell this class
is going to suck.

When Adam walks in, Leti's eyes dart from him to
me and back again, his smile growing wider and wider.
His lips stretch over his pearly whites, making me roll my
eyes. I smack him in the arm, and he laughs.

"I said to stop being weird!" I scold.

"I can't help it! This is too good!"

I groan. And I know I shouldn't gawk at Adam as his long legs carry him to his seat, but I really can't help it. He doesn't wear a backpack or even carry a notebook or a pen. The only thing he brings to class is a pack of cigarettes held loosely in his palm. How does he expect to take notes?

"Why don't you go talk to him?" Leti asks.

The corner of Adam's mouth quirks up in a devastatingly sexy smile when one of the girls up front bounces out of her seat, gives him a kiss on the cheek, and hands him a coffee. In well-worn jeans and a bright red T-shirt, he takes a sip and then smoothly slides into the seat next to her.

"What'd be the point?" I ask.

"Uh, do I have to spell it out for you?!" When I don't respond, Leti adds, "Because I *could* spell it out if you need me to. It wouldn't be that hard. Three little letters. S, E—"

Eyes wide, I yank on his shirtsleeve with one hand and shush him with the other. "Be quiet!" I look around to make sure no one else is eavesdropping on our hushed conversation, but all the students within earshot are busy either talking amongst themselves or texting on their phones during the final precious seconds before class starts.

Leti laughs. "I'm just saying!"

"I hear you!" I drop my voice even lower. "But there's no way in hell that would happen even if I *did* talk to him."

"Why not? He obviously thinks you're hot or he wouldn't have made out with you."

"Because I've never—" I stop myself. I can't believe I almost just confessed that I'm still a virgin.

"You've never . . ." When realization dawns in Leti's eyes, I can tell it's too late. "You've never—" He gives me a look, and I nod.

He shakes his head in astonishment, that amused smile still plastered on his lips. "This just keeps getting better and better."

Things just kept getting worse.

Later that week, Dr. Pullman gave a pop quiz to make sure everyone had been reviewing the basics like he had instructed us to do as homework, and I got a C. A freaking C! And of course, instead of blaming myself for being so easily distracted, I blamed a certain boy with disheveled brown hair, piercing gray eyes, and a *very* talented tongue.

The night before the quiz, I had dreamt about him. I'd woken up practically groping Dee. Talk about awkward . . . She hadn't woken up, but I felt embarrassed as hell. I'd never had a dream that *explicitly vivid* in my entire life. I woke up out of breath, all my muscles aching. For a few minutes, I lied there hating myself for turning Adam down. I wondered if the real thing would have been as amazing as that dream . . .

So when Dr. Pullman handed out the quiz the next day, my attempts to concentrate on the questions instead of the sex-god-of-my-dreams sitting up front was pretty much impossible. I'd been reviewing the basics all week, but my brain was filled with too much Adam to remember them.

I blamed that dream on pent-up sexual frustration caused by the good side of my two-faced pastor's son ex-boyfriend.

He texted me the day after we commandeered my car, left me messages begging me to just talk to him.

I caved and texted him back. I told him I would talk to him when I was ready.

Really, it was more courtesy than he deserved, but I felt a nagging need to end some of the pain he was feeling. Even after what he'd done to me, a part of me still loved him and hated seeing him so torn up. His constant texts and voicemails were numbing my anger to nonexistence, and I wasn't sure how I felt about that. If I let go of the anger, what did I have—besides a huge gaping hole?

By the second week of classes, Adam had started arriving at French class late. By the fourth week, I never knew if he was actually going to show or not. He usually arrived with a girl or two or three, and most of the time, they were girls I'd never seen before. He brought new faces with him to almost every class he showed up to, and I started realizing that the pretty girls who tagged along with him weren't even in our class at all—they just showed up with him, waited on him, and left with him. It was *highly* irritating.

A social life of my own probably would've helped, but every week, Dee got invited to parties and extended second-hand invitations to me, and every week, I found creative ways to turn her down.

Really, I don't know why she ever wanted to be seen in public with me. After the novelty of having Adam in my class wore off and it became clear he was never going to notice me, I switched to full-on college-bum mode. I walked to campus in two-day-old yoga pants and baggy T-shirts, with flip-flops on my socked feet and my unkempt hair twisted up into a messy bun. Half the time, I didn't even bother putting my contacts in and would show up wearing my rectangular black glasses instead. Dee would furrow her brow at me when I walked into history class, but I'd just grin at her. Once, I blew her a kiss, and she fiercely batted it away, which earned us strange looks from everyone who noticed.

I filled my nights with studying and my weekends with extra credit. After getting that first C in French, I really stepped it up. When Dr. Pullman offered extra credit to any students who were willing to help him set up the new language lab on a Saturday, I volunteered and dragged Leti along with me. We helped arrange the headphones and hardware and then installed software on the computers and tested it all out. Dr. Pullman bought us pizza and actually cracked a few jokes as we all worked together, and I realized he was actually pretty awesome. Tough as nails, but awesome.

The next weekend, he offered more extra credit to anyone willing to translate a short book from English to French. Apparently, I was the only person who took him up on the opportunity. I translated a children's book I wrote in eighth grade, and he gave me an exorbitant number of extra points, telling me that my story about the little unicorn without a horn was extremely touching in both languages. I nearly squealed with delight when I read the green-ink comments, rushing to shove the paper in Leti's face so he could see them too.

"You're such a nerd girl," he said with a laugh.

When fall break rolled around, I was almost sad to leave Leti's familiar face. He'd become a regular in our dorm room, and even Macy seemed to light up more when he was around. But I also missed my mom and dad, so I gave Leti a peck on the cheek and he saw Dee and me off from the Walmart parking lot. We drove home separately.

THAT SUNDAY, AFTER spending the week with my parents, I leave my car at their house and ride home with Dee. We stop at a gas station on the long trip back to school. As she fills up her tank, I go inside to use the restroom and stock up on gum. I'm walking back to the car when I notice Dee sitting inside it, talking on *my* phone. The windows are rolled down, so her voice swims out to me when she coldly finishes a sentence with, "because she *obviously* doesn't want to talk to you."

My feet fly across the last few steps of pavement in an instant, and I dive into the car like a bullet, snatching the phone roughly from Dee's hand. I pull it to my own ear to hear the tail end of Brady's reply.

"—don't like me, but this is between me and Rowan." A long moment of silence passes where I have no idea what to say. Should I just hang up? "Hello?" Brady says.

"It's me . . ." I shoot a glare at Dee and then step away from her car, swallowing my nerves. "Sorry about that," I say as I walk back to her trunk, leaning against it because I need the support.

"Rowan . . ." Brady says. He sounds hollow, like he never expected to hear my voice again. An awkward silence passes where we both have no idea what to say. Finally, he simply asks, "How are you?"

"I've been better . . ."

He could apologize, which would irritate me. He could say "me too," which would irritate me. He could plead his case, which would irritate me. Instead, he asks, "How is school?"

"It's alright, I guess." When another awkward silence begins, I offer, "I really like my English professor. And my French professor isn't too bad either." This is weird . . . This is so normal, it's weird.

"That's good . . . You've been staying with Dee?"

I spare a glance back to the car, where Dee is turned in her seat, listening to my every word with an agitated look on her face. If anyone should be irritated here, it's *me*. I push off the car and walk back to the gas station, circling around the side of the building for some privacy. "Yeah."

I hear Brady sigh, almost inaudibly, on the other line. "Rowan . . ." His voice sounds pained. "You can always come home. I—"

"I know, Brady." I take a deep breath. "I know."

"I miss you."

"I miss you too." I say it before thinking and immediately regret it. I *do* miss him, but I never intended for him to know that. I don't know why I told him . . . Why did I just tell him?! Before he can respond, I say, "Look, Brady, I have to go. Dee is waiting on me in the car."

He takes a minute, and then he says, "Can we talk again? Tonight?" When I don't answer, losing myself in the imperfections of the white paint on the side of the gas station wall, he adds, "Please?"

"Not tonight . . ." I sigh and rub my fingers over the center of my forehead. "But . . . soon, okay?"

He replies with "okay"—because we both know there's really nothing else he can say. The ball is in my court, and he knows it. And while that thought should probably make me feel empowered, it makes me feel weak. I want to wrap my arms around him. I want to forgive him. I want to forget what I saw that night and everything that has happened since.

"I love you, Rowan," he says.

"I'll see you later, Brady."

I end the call and rest my forehead against the cold brick of the building. Tears cloud my vision until I blink them away, letting them fall to the overgrown grass stretching around my bare ankles. I didn't think talking to him would affect me this much . . .

Wiping my tears away and sucking in a deep breath, I somehow manage to pull myself together. I walk back to Dee's car and climb inside, not looking her in the eye.

"I'm sorry," she says, her hand resting at the ignition but not turning the key. "I shouldn't have—"

"No," I interrupt, "you shouldn't have."

We drive most of the way back to school in silence, but

after an hour or so, she pulls an open bag of Cheetos from the center console and holds it out to me. I stare at it for a moment, recognizing it for the olive branch that it is, and then I reach my hand inside and take one.

"I told him I miss him," I finally say.

Dee says nothing, and I know it's taking all of her willpower to keep her mouth shut. I don't even know why I told her . . . Do I *want* her to say something? Do I want her to yell at me and tell me what an idiot I am?

Because I'm pretty sure I already know.

Chapter Nine

THAT NIGHT, I lie in bed thinking about Brady, trying to figure out why I'm so dead-set on avoiding seeing him. It's not because I'm still angry—I am, of course, but that's not the real reason.

The reason is that I don't know how strong I'll be if I have to look into his bright blue eyes again. I feel strong enough on the phone to hold my ground, to say goodbye. But if I need to say goodbye for good . . . can I do that with him standing in front of me, telling me he's sorry, telling me he loves me?

I miss being loved. Because I'm weak, and pathetic, and . . . God, I wish I didn't still miss him. I wish I was still as angry as the night I found him cheating on me. That night, he took my heart and tore it in two. Now, half of it still loves him, but the other half would rather struggle to beat on its own than mend together for the sake of a trust-abusing cheater.

If I talked to him now, I know I'd cave and tell him I forgive him, even if in my heart I never do. I'd hug him and kiss him and lose *myself* in him. And if I let myself do that once, I know I'll let myself do it again and again. And I don't want to be that person.

I'll talk to him. I will. Just . . . not yet.

The next day in French, Adam is a no-show. No surprise there. Some of the girls up front stand up and leave as soon as Dr. Pullman arrives, realizing that Adam won't be in class today. Leti laughs as I try to make them self-combust with my nonexistent superpowers. Dr. Pullman doesn't look happy either, his jaw working as he steps to the podium.

I don't see Adam until Wednesday, when he shows up twenty minutes late, a cigarette tucked behind his ear. Our night together is almost like a memory of a memory now. I still remember every detail, but it's like it was a movie I watched and rewatched a hundred times, not like it was something that actually happened to me. I admire Adam from afar just like all the girls who have never actually talked to him. And today, he is looking pretty damn admirable. He's dressed in midnight-black jeans—which, uncharacteristically, aren't torn up at the knees—and a long pale yellow band T-shirt with black lettering and designs. His hands always draw my attention, decorated with bulky rings and black nail polish, and framed by layers and layers of stringy leather bracelets. A long wallet chain hangs from his jeans, swinging as he walks to his seat at the front.

When class ends, Adam is the first one on his feet,

but Dr. Pullman immediately stops him from leaving. "Adam, hang around. I'd like to speak with you."

I watch Adam's back as he lets out a visible sigh and turns around. He leans against the wall by the door, watching everyone else leave, and I suddenly feel panicked. I'm actually going to cross paths with him now. There's no way I can avoid it!

I pack my things as slowly as humanly possible while Leti stands over me, grinning from ear to ear. I swear, it's like that boy can read my mind. "What's taking you so long?" he teases.

I shoot a glare at him from where I'm crouched on the floor, picking up a stack of papers I intentionally dropped to buy myself some time. I'm hoping Dr. Pullman will talk to Adam and get it over with before I make my way down the stairs.

By the time I stand up, I realize what a horrible plan that was—because Adam, Leti, and I are the last three students in the room.

Oh, God.

But maybe he won't even recognize me. I'm sure he's been with dozens of other girls since Mayhem. It's been over a month since then, and I look nothing like I did that night. My hair is pulled up in a lazy mess, I'm wearing my glasses, and I'm dressed in baggy winter-green yoga pants and an oversized royal blue college T-shirt. My nails are bright pink, my flip-flops are orange, and my face is pale, pale, pale.

Oh, God.

I take a deep breath and stand up, and Leti looks so

amused that I'm seriously going to smack the snot out of
him as soon as there aren't any witnesses. I make my way
to the stairs and then take one down, two down, three
down.

"Adam," Dr. Pullman says as he walks closer to where
Adam is standing. They meet halfway. "I've lost track of
how many times you've been tardy or absent in this class.
I might be willing to overlook it if you actually paid *any*
attention to the lessons or at least *attempted* to do well,
but it's become obvious you're here for . . . well, why *are*
you here?" Dr. Pullman shakes his head to himself and
continues before Adam can respond. "The last day to
drop this class is Friday. You won't get a refund, but you
won't get a failing grade. If you don't drop, I'm giving you
a zero. I'm tired of you coming in late and interrupting
my lectures."

"But I need this class to graduate . . ." Adam says, like
it never even occurred to him that he might not pass.

"Maybe you should have thought of that earlier," Dr.
Pullman informs him unapologetically.

And then, inexplicably, words start coming out of my
mouth before I even comprehend what I'm doing. "Dr.
Pullman, I'm so sorry," I say, coming to stand next to a
very curious-looking Adam. "Today was my fault . . ."
Uh, it was?! "I was . . . going over class notes with Adam
this morning, and . . . I lost track of time, and he hadn't
eaten anything at all, and so I told him he should really
stop at Lion's Den to get something, like maybe a BLT
or a chicken salad sandwich or even a bowl of soup or
something . . ." Okay, I'm full-on rambling now while ev-

eryone looks at me like I'm crazy. I smile sweetly. "You know, to help with his low blood sugar and all that jazz. But anyway, it was my fault and he really was trying to do better and he really was late because he was aspiring to improve in this class." Lies, lies, lies!

Dr. Pullman gazes at me suspiciously. "You were helping him polish his notes?"

"Yes." I nod vigorously. "We . . . we already arranged tutoring for this weekend and everything. He really wants to do better."

Dr. Pullman looks over at Adam then, who is staring at me with a still very-freaking-confused expression on his face. "You do?"

Adam's eyes slowly drift from my face to Dr. Pullman's. "Uh . . . yeah, I do. Tutoring . . . this weekend . . ."

Dr. Pullman inhales deeply as he considers this new information, glancing back and forth between me and Adam. "Okay. Rowan, if you're going to help him . . . and Adam, if you're serious about this . . . one more chance. Don't be late again."

I nod and exit the room, passing by Leti with Adam close behind. What in God's name did I just do, and better yet, why did I just do it?!

"Hey," Adam calls to me when I keep walking. Having no idea what to do about any of what just happened, I nervously turn around to face him. Over his shoulder, Leti is one gigantic smile. He winks at me and then slips away. "That was . . . uh . . ." Adam scratches the side of his chin adorably. "Why did you do that?"

By the way he looks at me, I can tell he has no idea

who I am. And I'm not sure if that makes me feel relieved or so disappointed that I need to skip speech class to wallow in Dee's room. "It just looked like you could use some help," I say, forcing my shoulders to shrug in an attempt at looking casual.

He studies me for a moment, and my assumption that he doesn't recognize me falters. He scrutinizes my features until his gaze locks with mine. "Do I know you?"

I shake my head a little too vigorously. "No, I don't think so."

"Are you sure?" His head tilts slightly to the side, and I nearly let out a swooning sigh. "You look really familiar."

"Positive," I lie.

"Are you sure you've never been to one of my shows?"

I contemplate acting like I have no idea who he is or that he's in a band, but decide that'd be overkill, and it would probably make him even more suspicious. "Nope. I just thought you could use a hand . . . Sorry, I acted impulsively."

"No," he blurts when I start to turn away from him. I turn back around. "No. No, you're fine . . . Thanks." He smiles, and it brings back an onslaught of memories. Him pressing me against the kitchenette counter. My pink heels lying in the walkway of the tour bus. Him leading me up the stairs. Me asking him to help me forget. Him smirking and asking me to count backward from ten. I feel my cheeks redden before he adds, "I actually think tutoring sounds like just what I need."

"Huh?"

"Tutoring. This weekend."

"Oh . . ."

"We kind of have to now anyway, don't we? I mean, if I don't do halfway decent on the test we have on Monday, we're both screwed. He'll know you were just covering for me."

Freaking hell. I hadn't thought of that.

"Just one problem," Adam says. "I have a few shows out of town this weekend . . ." He pulls a pack of cigarettes from his back pocket and packs them against his palm as he thinks about it, staring at the ground. Then his eyes lift back to mine. "You'll have to come along."

"I'll *what*?"

"I mean . . . can you? Do you have plans this weekend?"

"No, but I—"

"Good. We can leave tomorrow morning." He smiles at me, like there's no doubt I'll go with him.

"No, we definitely can *not* leave tomorrow morning!" I practically shout.

"Why not?"

"I have classes . . ."

Adam frowns. " 'Til when?"

"Two o'clock."

His eyes stare up then, his mouth moving as he does some math in his head. "Okay, that works. I'll pick you up out front after class. We won't get back until Sunday night, so make sure you pack some stuff."

"I don't even know you!" I protest.

Adam grins and then sticks out his hand. "Adam Everest." I stare at his hand, too shocked to take it, until he laughs and reaches forward, pulling mine from my side and shaking it. "Nice to meet you. Thanks for saving my ass."

Chapter Ten

DEE, LETI, MACY. Macy, Leti, Dee. My feet carry me down their row of faces and back again as I pace across Dee's room, pulling my hair through my fingers. "There is *no way* I can go!"

After my conversation with Adam, I skipped speech class to come back here and panic. By the time Dee and Leti showed up, I had worked myself into an anxiety attack.

Dee ignores me and pulls two nearly identical tops out of her closet—one pink, one aquamarine. When I first told her about Adam's offer, she squealed so loudly I literally cringed. She immediately launched into a high-pitched monologue about all the fun we'd have—since she proclaimed us a "package deal"—until I reminded her that her first shift at her new waitressing job was scheduled for this Saturday. She'd been putting in applications all month, had finally landed an interview last week, and must have sweet-talked the hell out of the owner, because he hired her for a job that she wasn't even remotely qualified for. Fast-forward to an hour later—after I've explained all the reasons why skipping her very first shift would be a really bad idea—and she's busy packing my suitcase, ignoring the hundred times that I've insisted I can't go.

Dee studies the pink and aqua tops she's holding up, and then she walks over to me, holding each against my body in turn. Satisfied, she hangs the aqua one back in her closet and tosses the pink one in the suitcase she's busy stuffing.

Leti watches us from his slouched position in Macy's computer chair, his ankles crossed on her desk. "Why can't you go?" he asks me. "You don't even have classes on Fridays, so it's not like you'd be missing anything."

"Because! It's insane!"

Macy, usually the voice of reason, asks, "Why is it insane?" Seriously?! Her too?

"Because I don't even know him!"

"*Everyone* knows him," Leti says, watching Dee as she lays three black skirts on the floor, looks them over, and then tosses the shortest one into the suitcase.

I slump on my bed, my elbows on my knees. "This is such a bad idea."

Dee holds up two pairs of hooker heels, and I pale at the sight of the hot-pink shoes I wore to Mayhem. "Leti," she says, "A," she holds up the pink pair, "or B?" She holds up a black pair.

"Hmm," Leti hums, smoothing a pretend-beard. "Both."

Dee grins at him appreciatively and then lays both pairs in the suitcase.

"Deandra!" I snap. "You're wasting your time!"

The next afternoon, I'm walking to campus with my suitcase rolling behind me. It's making a racket as it skips and tumbles over cracks in the sidewalk. How in God's name does Dee always succeed in talking me into things like this?

In the midst of our arguing, she got me to admit that I didn't believe Adam was a bad guy or that he'd take advantage of me, and she even got me to confess that I might have a little fun. Ultimately, though, I think it was her reminding me of the consequences of *not* going that finally sealed the deal. If I don't go, Adam will fail. And even though that would reflect poorly on me, I have to admit, the main reason I'm going is just that I sincerely want to help him. If he needs this class to graduate, he needs me to come along. And after what he did for me that night at Mayhem, I owe him that much.

When I finally arrive back at campus at two thirty, I look all around for him, but I don't see him anywhere. What I do see is a black Camaro convertible in the parking lot, surrounded by girls. A blonde is sitting on the back of the topless car, and two other girls are standing by its side, framing a pair of charcoal sneakers that are propped in the open window. It doesn't take a genius to figure out whose feet are in those sneakers, so I take a deep breath and walk over. As I get closer, the girls lift their heads to stare at me. At first, their expressions remind me of the look Leti gave me that first day in class when I told him I was a freshman and he thought I was lost. Then, hostility washes over them, like they can't believe I'm actually coming over to talk to—gasp—Adam Everest.

I ignore them and walk right up to his sneakers, looking down at him stretched out in the backseat. He has shades pulled over his eyes and both hands behind his head. The girl sitting on the back of his car has her pink-pedicured feet resting on his stomach, but he doesn't seem to mind. When he sees me, he slowly sits up, knocking the girl's feet off his body. She bristles and tries to paralyze me with the poisoned daggers she's staring, but Adam doesn't seem to notice. "I was starting to wonder if you were going to show or not," he says.

I use my hand to shield my eyes from the sun. "I had to run back to the dorms to get my stuff."

He hops over the side of the car, grabbing my suitcase and tossing it into his trunk. "Cool. I'm ready to get out of here." He looks to the girl still sitting on the back of his car, but she doesn't budge until he holds his hand out and helps her down.

"Adam," one of the other girls whines, "are you sure we can't come?"

"Sorry," he says as he hops behind the wheel. "I need to study."

The girl looks at me, her perfectly-shaped eyebrows furrowed as I toss my backpack in the back and slide in next to Adam. "I didn't think you were serious . . ." She takes in my bright blue leggings, my loose black T-shirt, my glasses. "But I guess you were."

I roll my eyes. I sure as hell didn't dress like this for

her amusement. I did it to make sure that Adam kept me locked me into his memory as the nerd-girl from class, not the cute Peach from Mayhem.

With me inside, Adam's Camaro purrs to life, and then we're on the road, the wind threatening to make my messy bun a whole new level of messy. "So," he says with one hand on the wheel, "you live on campus?"

"Yeah." I tuck some loose strands of hair back into my elastic band. "Er, no. I mean . . . kinda." Wow, smooth. This trip is already off to an epic start.

Adam pushes his shades up, which pulls his straight brown hair back too, and I'm once again left breathless over the color of his gray-green eyes. I force my gaze back to the road when he gazes over at me and asks, "How do you *kinda* live on campus?"

"My living situation fell through, so I'm staying with a friend of mine while I look for a place." That's mostly true, so I don't feel too guilty saying it. I haven't actually been looking for a place, but I know I need to. Dee's Resident Assistant knows I've been staying in her dorm room even though it's against the rules, and she's been getting on our case. If I don't leave soon, I know she'll report it, and the last thing I want is to get Dee or Macy in trouble.

When I ask Adam if he lives on campus too, he tells me he lives in an off-campus apartment with his band mate, Shawn. I remember the way Adam licked Shawn's face on the tour bus, and the memory makes me smile. I can only imagine what their apartment must be like. After a while, I pull out my phone and ask Adam exactly where we're going.

"All over," he says with an easy smile.

"Can you be more specific? I want to let some people know where I'll be." He raises his eyebrow at me, silent until I add, "You know, in case you decide to murder me. I want my friends to know where to look for the body."

Adam laughs, much to my relief, and a goofy smile finally forces its way onto my face. I listen as he gives me the full itinerary. Tonight, we'll be driving for roughly four hours before we get to the first concert venue. Tomorrow, we have a five-hour drive before we get to the second venue. Saturday, we've got a four-hour drive to the final venue, and Sunday, we have a six-hour drive back to school.

"Jeez," I say. "No wonder you're falling behind in class. That's nuts."

"It's not like this every weekend," he tells me, wrapping his black-nailed fingers around the gearshift to change gears as we merge onto the highway. "And most of the time, I'd be traveling on our tour bus, so I don't really have an excuse."

"You have your own tour bus?" I ask, remembering how nice it was and wondering how the band can afford it.

"It's not actually ours," he says, "but we have a friend that lets us use it."

"Why didn't you take the bus this time?"

He turns his head to smirk at me. "Because my French tutor had classes that didn't finish until two o'clock."

"Oh." God, now I'm blushing all over, and I'm not sure if it's because I'm happy he waited for me or if it's because I feel *bad* he waited for me. "Sorry . . ."

"What are you apologizing for?" He looks at me like one of us is seriously confused. "You covered for me when Pullman was about to kick my ass to the curb, and now you're taking a three-day road trip with me across two states to help me get caught up."

Okay, he makes a good point. "Well, in that case, you're welcome." He flashes a smile at me, and I joke, "I expect a backstage pass to all your shows."

"Whatever you want"—he stares over at me again—"just ask."

Okay, is he *flirting* with me? I might be imagining things, but the way he said that and the way he's looking at me . . . it makes a shiver dance through me from head to toe.

I swallow and concentrate on the telephone poles marking distance to my right. "Well, do you want to get started on French now?" Anything to get my mind off those lips and how soft they'd felt against the skin of my neck. I glance at my backpack in the backseat.

"Now?"

"Yeah."

"Honestly? I think I'd rather crash this car."

I laugh even though I know I probably shouldn't—from what I know about Adam, I don't doubt he's serious. "Alright. When then?"

"Later."

"Like, this-car-ride later?" I prop my elbow on the door and make waves in the wind with my hand. We're leaving the outskirts of the city now; I watch it get smaller behind us in the side-view mirror.

"Like, later-later."

"So, when we get to the venue?"

"More like . . . later-later-later." I laugh, and he grins at me.

"Tonight?" I pull my hand back in the car and rub the chill away.

After pulling a cigarette from its pack, Adam tucks it between his lips and pushes his car lighter into the dash. "Maybe?" He presses the lighter against the cigarette and puffs until the end burns hot. "I'm not really big on plans." He replaces the lighter, takes a long drag of the cigarette, and then holds it between two fingers with the hand he's using to steer. With his other elbow propped on the car door, he's hard not to ogle. Even when I turn my head away, I can't stop picturing him sitting inches away in his navy blue T-shirt and faded jeans. Maybe it's his black nails or his layered bracelets, his longish hair or the cigarette he keeps lifting to his lead-singer lips, but God, he's such a typical bad boy. He's the kind of boy girls love because there's no way they can ever bring him home to their parents.

After we're silent for a while, Adam plugs his phone into the sound system and hands it to me so I can pick some music. He has so much of it, it's ridiculous. There are tons of bands I've never heard of, so I take a chance and set it to a random shuffle. I'm glad when the first few songs are ones I've actually heard before. The music drowns out all the apprehension I'd been feeling about this trip, and I tilt my seat farther back, closing my eyes and letting the sun warm my barely tanned skin.

"So are you a fan?" Adam asks.

I'm guessing he's talking about his own band, not the one playing through the speakers. Without opening my eyes or turning my head, I say, "I haven't heard much of your stuff. But I liked what I did hear." I turn my face toward him and smile, using my hand to shield my eyes from the sun. "You're very talented."

He gives me a warm smile and then asks if I'm looking forward to the show tonight.

Actually, I feel super-nervous about not having Dee there. I've never gone to a concert or club without her, and flying solo would be intimidating even *without* adding Adam Everest to the mix. "It'll be kind of weird being there by myself."

Adam scoffs. "You're not going to be there by yourself. I'll be there. And I'll introduce you to all the guys. Don't worry. It'll be great."

I don't know what it is about him, but he's always so sure about everything he says that it makes me feel sure about it too. A warm sense of calm washes over me and I close my eyes again, turning my cheeks back toward the sun. "Okay."

We've been riding for almost half an hour when some terribly bad country song starts playing. "Oh my God," I say, my eyes popping open. "I can't believe you listen to country music!" I can't help laughing, but it only makes Adam smile. He shoots me a devilish grin and then starts singing along. Loudly. I laugh hysterically as he imitates the high-pitched country twang, singing about pick-up trucks, daisy dukes, and football games. "Make it stop!"

I joke, slapping my hands over my ears. But Adam just laughs and turns the music way up, singing even louder. At the top of his lungs, he exaggerates the yodel-pitch and Southern drawl. Still laughing my ass off, I snatch his phone from a cup holder to change the song, but as I'm looking for something better, a text message comes through from some girl named Jaylin.

Hope u have a fun wknd, but by the looks of that nerdy tutor girl, I can tell u won't! Call me when u want the fantasy. ;)

I immediately stop laughing. "Shit."

When Adam looks over and sees the expression on my face, he turns the music all the way down. I quickly push his phone into his hand. "Sorry, I didn't mean to read that. It just came through."

When he reads the text, he rolls his eyes and sighs. He hands the phone back to me. "Reply to that however you want. But don't tell her it's from you."

"Huh?"

"Let her have it. And whatever you say, I want her to think it's from me."

"Seriously?"

"Seriously."

I give Adam a skeptical look, but he just takes another drag of his cigarette and then puts it out in his ashtray, not looking worried in the slightest. I sit there thinking for a while, and then I type:

Herpes isn't really something I fantasize about. Sry!

I hand the phone back to Adam, hoping he'll get a kick out of the text before he deletes it. He laughs appreciatively and then hands the phone back to me. "Perfect. Send it."

I gape at him. "No way!"

He snatches the phone back and hits SEND before I can delete the message. I'm just sitting there with my mouth hanging open when he looks over at me and chuckles. "She deserved that."

"She's never going to talk to you again."

"Sure she will. Just watch. She's going to text me in three . . ." His eyes drift to his phone, which he's set back into his cup holder. "Two . . ." He points at the phone, like he can work magic. "One!" When nothing happens, he frowns and says, "Damn, how cool would that have been?"

I giggle at him and can't stand myself for it, but he's seriously cute as hell. His phone beeps a few seconds later, and he grins.

"Told you."

"She's probably telling you off."

He picks up his phone, reads it, and then shows me the screen with a triumphant smile on his face.

:(Did I do something wrong? Please don't be mad at me.

I shake my head. "That's just sad."

"Glad I'm not the only one who thinks so." His words surprise me, and I stare over at him, but his eyes are back on the road and his shades are back down. He turns his head to smile at me again, but it only lasts a second.

Before that smile, I'd never understood girls like Jaylin. Now? It's almost too easy.

Chapter Eleven

I'M STILL MUNCHING on a cheeseburger when Adam downshifts and turns into the venue's parking lot. Shawn is sitting on the steps of the open tour bus, scowling at his cell phone—which solves the mystery of who has been blowing up Adam's phone for the past twenty minutes. When he spots us, he immediately stands up, pockets his phone, and starts walking over. He does *not* look happy, and the bite I'm chewing is suddenly hard to get down. I really hope Adam isn't in trouble, but more than that, I really, really, *really* hope Shawn doesn't recognize me.

"You're late," he tells Adam. His eyes are narrowed at the fast-food bag in my lap, and I suddenly feel guilty for taking Adam up on his offer to grab me something to eat from a drive-thru on the way here. I would have turned him down if he had told me we were running late, but he acted as laid-back as ever, like we were in no big hurry.

"You're surprised," Adam replies, and if it weren't for

the look Shawn gives him, I would probably crack a smile. He walks over to my side of the car and leans against the black paint as I get out. "Shawn, this is the girl I told you about. The one who's helping me out with school."

"Rowan," I add for him, wondering if he even remembered my name.

Shawn extends his hand and introduces himself, but he still seems agitated and is giving me a weird look. "Do I know you?"

"Right?!" Adam interrupts as I shake my head no. "That's what I said!"

Not good, this is *so* not good.

The night I met Adam, Dee had done my eyes in smoky pink eye shadow with extra-thick mascara. She'd made my lips a pouty pink and had blushed my cheeks and curled my hair before tossing a micro-mini skirt at me, followed by bright pink heels and a scandalous pink top. I was practically music-video ready. When I looked in the mirror before leaving her dorm room, I hardly recognized myself, so I'm praying Shawn won't recognize me either.

I try to sound honest when I say, "Nope. I must just have one of those faces."

"Are you sure?" Shawn asks, still scrutinizing my every faded freckle. "I'm usually really good with faces. I swear I've seen you somewhere before . . ."

I shrug. "Not that I know of. But maybe, I guess." I walk to the back of the car, hoping some distance will keep Shawn's memory fuzzy, and ask Adam if he can pop the trunk.

As I get my stuff out, Adam walks over to me. "I have to go in now. We were supposed to start"—he looks at his phone—"fifteen minutes ago. But just give your stuff to Driver. He's . . . the bus driver." Adam chuckles at the look I give him. "Tell him you're with me, and then tell him to lock up and bring you backstage, okay?"

I nod. "Alright." I really feel like I should apologize for making Adam late again, but I know he'll tell me not to be sorry, so instead I thank him for the food.

He smiles warmly at me. "Sure thing. See you inside."

He doesn't bother putting the top of the convertible up before he disappears with Shawn. I close the trunk and walk to the bus. The door is still hanging open, so I step up to it and call out, "Hello?"

A young guy in jeans so worn they look older than I am jogs halfway down the stairs. His eyes go from me to the open door between us, and then he curses something about "Fucking Shawn" and complains, "I told him to close the damn door!" This guy looks Adam's age, with a mop-top of curly reddish-brown hair and a chin layered with days-old scruff. His long, baggy Ninja Turtles tank makes him look even taller and lankier than he already is.

"Uh . . . Hi, I'm Rowan." When it becomes clear that means nothing to him, I add, "Adam said to tell you I'm with him."

The guy looks me up and down. "So you're the tutor, huh?" I doubt I'm what he expected, but he smiles warmly at me and shakes my hand. "I'm Driver."

"Nice to meet you." I knock my toe against my suitcase. "Where should I put my stuff?"

"Oh, here, let me get that for you. Just hang tight." He takes my suitcase and backpack and disappears upstairs. After Dee finished packing for me, I emptied everything out and started over. She pouted the entire time, complaining about the non-attention-grabbing things I decided to bring along. Flats. Jeans. Leggings. T-shirts. Basically, the polar opposite of what Adam's "Peach" would wear.

After Driver hops back down to the lower level, I tell him what Adam said about locking up and taking me backstage. He closes up the bus and then walks me across the parking lot. There's still a long line out the door even though the show's already starting, but Driver cuts to the front and tells the bouncer I'm with him. Looking at all the girls in line, I suddenly feel way underdressed—which means I'm way *over*dressed—and way out of place in my black leggings, my blue T-shirt, and my black flip-flops. But it's not like I have anything better to change into. I frown, realizing I really should have listened to Dee for once, even though there's no way I'll admit that to her when she grills me about this the next time we talk on the phone.

When we get inside, my eyes take a moment to adjust to the darkness. And then I hear Adam's voice, and my eyes swing to the stage. Butterflies. So many butterflies. Why is it that the feeling I had sitting next to him gets multiplied by like . . . *a thousand times* when I see him standing onstage? The spotlight transforms his ordinary navy blue T-shirt and tattered jeans into . . . ugh, I don't even know. He is too damn sexy. The front of his shirt is tucked into a studded belt, and he's running a hand through his hair. I wonder if he knows the effect that has on the girls in the crowd.

By the confident smirk on his face, I'm guessing he does.

Adam talks to the crowd, laughing with Shawn and getting them worked up, while Driver and I skirt along the edges of the room to get backstage. When the first song starts, it makes the ground beneath my feet vibrate. And it's good. Seriously—*really* good. I find myself staring up at the band again. There are five of them, with Adam front and center and Shawn off to his right. To Adam's back-left is a guy much shorter and . . . well, *slighter* than he is. But maybe that's just because Adam is so . . . *Adam*, sucking up all the attention without even trying. The smaller guy has short, light blond hair and is looking down at his guitar as he plays. Closer to the front of the stage, there is another guitar player, this one sporting a spiked blond mohawk. He's just as tall as Adam, and his neon yellow T-shirt is hugging him so tightly I can tell he must work out. The drummer in back is a guy who is a little heavier, with cropped brown hair. He's banging on the drums so hard and fast that my eyes are getting a workout just from following his drumsticks. He's lost in the song, his entire body moving with the beat he's setting. I could probably watch him all night, but then the beat slows down and the instruments quiet, and all there is is Adam.

I suddenly feel a hand on my elbow, and I realize I've stopped walking. I'm just standing there practically undressing Adam with my eyes. I look up at Driver, who points with his chin toward a door a little farther back, and I follow him. He shows a pass to the security there, and then we both slip inside.

"Ever been backstage before?" he asks as he leads me down a hallway packed with rolling band equipment and people bustling back and forth.

I shake my head. "No."

He grins back at me. "Then this'll blow your mind!" He opens a door that leads to a set of stairs. The music is deafening in a way that makes my blood buzz with excitement. I'm mesmerized, watching the guys play from a vantage point that most people will never get to experience. Their backs are to me, but every time Adam turns in my direction to walk across the stage, it's like my heart stops beating. He looks as comfortable onstage as he did singing to me in the car, maybe even more so, as absurd as that is. When the song hits a chorus, he crouches down at the edge of the stage and holds his microphone out to the crowd. Everyone sings in unison as crowd surfers ride the waves. The front rows are surging forward to touch Adam's sneakers, the frayed edges of his jeans. He stands up and walks across the stage again, and when his eyes lock with mine, I'm sure I look as stunned as I feel. Adam smiles and winks at me—seriously *winks*—and I'm surprised I don't faint right then and there. But then he turns his back to me and continues the song, and I can breathe again.

Can I still call myself a virgin after that wink? Dear God . . .

The next song starts out quieter. Someone rushes past me, carrying a stool out for Adam to sit on. Adam puts the mic back in its stand and holds on to it as he sings in a voice as beautiful as it is haunting. He sings about breaking hearts and girls who should have known better, and there's no doubt he's the person who wrote this song. The lyrics convey a lack of emotion, but the way Adam sings it . . . it's like I can feel every word.

At some point, Driver disappears, but I'm not sure when he left or where he went, and really, I'm not all that concerned. I take every bit of the show in, knowing that I made the right choice when I decided to come along. Dee was right about it being a "once in a lifetime" opportunity. I'll have to make sure to play all of this down when I talk to her tomorrow so that she can't hold how right she was over my head for the rest of my life.

When the show ends, my stomach immediately twists itself into knots. I'm about to come face-to-face with Adam after witnessing the spectacle he just put on, and . . . ugh, I'm freaking *starstruck*! How am I supposed to talk to him after seeing that?! There are no words! Every girl in this building wants him, but I'm the one who will be sharing his tour bus tonight.

Will I be the *only* one sharing his tour bus tonight . . . ? I'd never even thought about it . . .

When Adam and the guys walk out of view of the crowd, the fans start chanting, "One more song!" But it's all part of the routine. Most of the guys stand to the side of the stage catching their breath, gulping down water, laughing and telling jokes. Adam swipes a water bottle off an instrument case and then practically skips down the stairs, spotting me standing sheepishly off to the side. He heads straight for me.

"So what did you think?" His eyes are wide with leftover excitement, and I let his energy wash over me, calming my nerves and making me smile.

"I thought you guys were awesome!"

Adam beams. "We have to do one more song, but then I'll introduce you to everyone."

After the last song, the entire band gathers around me—as if I didn't feel small enough already. "This is the girl from my class," Adam says by way of introduction, and then he points to the short blond guitarist. "That's Cody." Then to the mohawked guitarist. "That's Joel." Then to the drummer. "That's Mike. And you've already met Shawn."

I smile at Shawn and then give the rest of the guys a little wave. "Rowan. Hi." I vaguely wonder if Adam is ever going to bother introducing me by name, but it's really not my biggest concern right now. Looking around at all of the sweaty rock boys in front of me, I'm busy trying not to feel two inches tall. Forcing a smile, I say, "You guys were amazing out there." I nod at the drummer, Mike. "*You* were freaking incredible."

He looks absolutely stunned, glancing at the other guys and then over his shoulder, like he's not sure if I'm talking to him. "Me?"

"Yeah, you! I've never seen anything like that." By the look on his face, I'm guessing Mike doesn't usually get first dibs on after-show compliments—not with Adam and Shawn to compete with. He steps away from the rest of the guys to wrap his arm around my shoulder, and then he starts leading me away.

"Where are we going?" I ask, confused.

"To get married. Immediately. Sorry, Adam!" I look over my shoulder, but the guys are following behind us, laughing. Adam smiles so warmly at me that I can feel my heartbeat even in the tips of my ears. Mike leads us back the way I came, but once he opens the door to the venue, a wall of fans stops us from moving forward. The night turns into a chaotic mess of autographs and pictures. Mike's arm slips from my shoulder as he poses with fans, and then I'm just standing there, feeling out of place as hell and wishing I could melt into the floor or teleport to a less awkward layer of hell. I'm thinking about sneaking away—not that I'd actually have to sneak, since it seems no one remembers I'm still here—until another arm wraps around my shoulders. And this one gives me goose bumps, because when I look up, Adam is smiling down at me. The ends of his hair and the collar of his T-shirt are dark with sweat, and his body against mine is fire-hot from jumping around the stage all night.

He bends close to my ear so I can hear him over the crowd. "You ready to get out of here?" Even as he says it, I hear a chorus of girls calling his name.

I nod.

Adam takes my hand in his and leads me through the crowd, ignoring fans the whole way. We slip out of a guarded back door, and once we're out, he leans against it. "So you had fun tonight?" he asks as he pulls a cigarette out of its pack and lights it.

"*So* much fun," I say, and I mean it. "I've never experienced anything like that."

With one foot propped against the door, Adam smirks at me. "And Mike was the best part, huh?"

I shrug and tease, "You were alright too, I guess."

Adam chuckles and takes another drag. "I was feeling a little off tonight. I don't usually go on stone-cold sober."

"Oh yeah?" I remember the way he swirled the whiskey in his glass when I had been on his tour bus last time. I'd asked if he needed to get ready, and he'd told me he *was* getting ready. I guess pre-show drinks are a part of his normal routine.

"Yeah. It was . . . different."

"Good different or bad different?"

"Just different."

"Well, I thought you were great," I assure him.

He grins at me and scratches the side of his chin with the fingers he's not using to hold his cigarette. "So, better than just 'alright' then."

Letting my smile answer him, I tuck my legs into the stair railing and sit on the middle rail, resting my chin on my hands. I look up at Adam, watching him contentedly as I enjoy the cool night breeze that's blowing across my skin.

He takes one last long drag on the cigarette and then flicks it to the ground, smashing it with his toe. He points his chin toward where the bus is parked at the back of the lot. "Alright, come on."

When I unweave myself from the railing, he takes my hand again, and it startles me. Inside, he kind of needed to hold it just to get me out of there, but now? We're the only two people in the parking lot . . .

Adam walks me to the bus and unlocks it. I'm not sure where Driver is, but he hasn't gotten back yet. "Do you want a drink?" Adam asks.

"Nah, I think I'm going to go change." I'm feeling muggy from the long car ride, and I want to change into something a little less stale and bummy.

"Okay." He grins at me. "Your stuff is upstairs. In the room all the way at the end of the hall."

I climb the stairs and begin walking back through the bus. It's so weird being back here again. I remember the last time like it was yesterday and like it was a lifetime ago. I pass the bench seats, the rows of bunks—most of them looking thoroughly slept in—and then open the door to the bedroom. I walk inside and stare down at the black satin bed in front of my knees, remembering how it had felt to be stretched out on top of it with Adam pressed against me, kissing every bit of my skin that wasn't covered.

When I hear the door close behind me, it shocks me from the memory. I spin around to find Adam's chest right in front of my face. I gasp, inhaling his musky scent. He smells like clean sweat, day-old cologne, and cigarette smoke, which I wouldn't have considered a pleasant combination before I associated it with this moment. Before I know it, his hands are on the sides of my neck, his thumbs under my chin, tilting my head back. His gray-green eyes are focused on my mouth, and his lips are quick to follow.

For a second, I can't think straight and I instinctively

drink him in. His tongue slips between my lips, tracing and teasing and oh my God, I had forgotten what that tongue could do. Just before a moan slips from my mouth, I find the sense in myself to push him away. "What the hell are you doing?" I force myself to ask, trying to ignore how badly my heart is pounding in my chest.

Adam caresses my jaw with his thumb, staring down at me with bedroom eyes. "Kissing you." The desire in his voice causes a surge of heat to flood my entire body, thickening the haze in my head.

"*Why* are you kissing me?"

"Because . . . um . . ." He tilts his head to the side and looks at me curiously. "Okay, I think I'm confused . . ." His hands slide down my neck, over my shoulders, and then drop back to his sides. I immediately ache for them to be back on me, but that is *such* a bad idea. This isn't what I came on this trip for. "Don't you want me to?"

Dear God yes.

I mean—No!

My eyebrows furrow and I cross my arms over my chest as I stare up at him. "Why would you think I want you to?"

"Well . . . you saved me from getting kicked out of French class . . . and you made up this whole tutoring lie . . ." And that quickly, any desire I'd been feeling is blown to bits.

"Oh my GOD," I say, in utter disbelief. "You think I did that because I want to . . . to have *sex* with you?!" When he just stares at me like he's still confused as hell, any doubt I had vanishes. I'm angry, and beyond embarrassed, which makes me even angrier. "I can't BELIEVE this!" I shout. The room is suddenly way, way, way too freaking small for the both of us, so I slip around him and open the door, stepping into the hallway. "You thought—oh my God, I can't *believe* you thought that!" I whirl on him, and he's just standing in the doorway with wide eyes, like he doesn't know how to handle me. "And you were going to do it, too! Christ, Adam, you were going to sleep with me for French lessons? For tutoring?" When he doesn't deny it, I take a step toward him, pointing at his chest. "Please! Get some damn self-respect."

Loud laughter suddenly fills the lower level of the bus, and I realize that the rest of the guys have been on board for I-don't-know-how-long. I storm away from Adam and jog down the stairs, shooting them an irritated look, but they're all laughing so hard they barely notice me. Shawn is on his back on the gray bench seat, holding his hand over his stomach as he completely loses it. Mike is on his knees on the ground, his arms wrapped around himself as he keels over laughing. Cody is wiping his eyes with his palms as he laughs so hard he cries, and Joel is clapping him on the back, laughing so hard he sends himself into a coughing fit.

"Self-respect," Shawn chokes out in the middle of his laughter.

Ignoring them, I push open the door to the bus and step outside. I can't believe that this entire time—the car ride, the concert, the past thirty-six freaking hours—Adam thought I was just some groupie trying to weasel my way into his pants!

"Hey, uh . . ." His voice comes from behind me, but it only prompts me to start walking. I don't even know where I'm going, just as long as it's away from him. "Hold on!" he says as he jogs to keep up with me. "What the hell are you so mad about?"

I ignore him and keep walking.

"Where are you even going?"

"Away!"

Adam doesn't say anything else, but he falls into step beside me. And then we're just walking together through the dark parking lot. I have no idea where I'm going. Adam pulls shades from his back pocket and slips them on, messing up his hair and staring at the ground as we walk past a group of people who probably just left the show.

When we reach the sidewalk, I pause and stand beneath a street lamp as I wait for the crosswalk sign to tell me it's okay to keep running away from my embarrassment. No one is standing near us, so I turn to Adam and blurt, "I do NOT want to sleep with you!" I swat at a bug that flies in front of my face, making contact and knocking it straight into another hemisphere.

Adam gapes at me for a second, but then an irritating smirk curves his lips. "Really? I mean, are you *sure*?" Okay, now he's just intentionally being obnoxious.

I let out an exasperated sigh and turn away from him, crossing the street.

He starts laughing and chases after me. "I'm kidding!"

"I don't think you are!"

"Oh, come on. I really am!"

"Really?! Because it really seems like you think everything with a vagina wants to sleep with you!"

"Well, not *everything* with a vagina . . . I mean, lesbians, nuns . . . that'd just be weird."

I roll my eyes and keep walking. We've walked two blocks when Adam says, "Anyway, I don't know why you're so pissed I kissed you. You wanted me to."

I stop walking and spin to face him. "I did not!" Okay, so maybe I kind of did, but still, he had no way of knowing that. And I didn't *really* want him to. It's just . . . I mean . . . he's Adam freaking Everest!

"Then why did you kiss me back?"

"I didn't!"

"You definitely didn't stop me right away."

"I was in shock!"

Adam stares down at me, licking his bottom lip. Shit. He knows exactly what he's doing. "I wanted to kiss you. So I did." His gaze lifts from my lips to my eyes. "No need to throw a tantrum. Most girls would be . . . well, they wouldn't be storming around the city in the middle of the night."

"Well I'm not most girls!"

Adam chuckles. "No, you're definitely not."

Wow, what the hell is *that* supposed to mean?! I glare at him and start walking again, the cement beneath my feet receiving the brunt of my anger as my flip-flops tromp against it.

Adam jogs to catch up. "I meant that as a good thing!" I glare at him out of the corner of my eye, and he's nervously raking his hand through his hair. "Can you please just stop so I can talk to you?"

"We've *been* talking."

"No, we've been arguing . . . which is just . . . strange. I don't really do this that often . . . I'm no good at it."

I walk a few more steps before I growl and very angrily sit my ass down on a bench in front of a closed barber shop. "Fine. Talk."

He sits down next to me. "I . . . I didn't mean to assume that you wanted to . . . you know . . . hook up or anything. But it was an honest mistake."

"I'm not interested in being one of your one-night stands, Adam."

"Well . . . technically . . . you'd have me for three." The corner of his mouth quirks into a smile, and when he turns his head to look at me, his bangs tumble over his eyes, but he quickly swipes them away. Why is he so damn adorable? And irritating!

I glare at him. "Do I *seem* like that kind of girl?"

He pauses for a long time, and then he says, "Truthfully, you'd be surprised by some of the girls that want that type of thing. Not all of them fit the stereotype you have in your head."

Okay, fair enough. I sigh and ask, "Would you seriously sleep with someone for something as stupid as French tutoring?"

Adam grins at me and shakes his head. "Is that what you're mad about? It's not like that was the only reason."

I probably shouldn't ask what I ask next. "Then what are the other reasons?"

"I thought you wanted me to . . ."

"So you'd sleep with someone just because they want you to?"

He nervously rubs his palm over his thigh, staring at his knees until he makes eye contact with me again. "Do you really want me to answer that?"

I let out an irritated growl, still not exactly sure why I'm so worked up. "Look, I was mad because you just assumed I'd want you in my pants. But whatever. You said you're sorry, so . . . fine."

Adam frowns. "Do you want me to take you home?"

"You can't. You have a show tomorrow that's like ten hours away from school."

He shifts toward me. "If you want to go home, I'll take you. So just answer the question."

I study his unreadable expression, and then I say, "No. I don't want to go home."

He smiles softly and seems to let out a deep breath. Then he settles back into the bench and plays with the threads over his knee for a few seconds before looking at me again. "Okay, so don't get mad at me for this . . . but I just think we should be clear. If I tried to kiss you again, you'd get mad?"

I can't help laughing at his ridiculous question. But when I try to answer it, I realize it might not be so ridiculous. *Would* I get mad? I have absolutely no clue. Probably, but it would really just be because I'm mad at myself for letting him cloud my better judgment. Adam is bad news. He's a mountain of bad decisions wrapped in a beautiful package, and I hate the effect he has on me.

And I love it, which I hate. "Yes," I finally say. "So don't, okay? I just want to be friends."

"Friends . . ." he says, like he's testing out the concept.

"Friends."

He stands up and holds his hand down to me. "Okay. We'll be friends."

Chapter Twelve

ADAM WALKS ME back to the bus, opening the door for me so I can climb inside. The minute I step into view, Shawn pushes himself off the bench seat and walks over to me with a cheek-to-cheek grin on his face. "Can I . . . Can I just—" He abruptly pulls me in for a tight hug and starts laughing again. "Self-respect." His body shakes against me as his laughter gets louder, and then he sighs. "Oh my God, that was so great." He pulls away and smiles down at me. His jaw is dusted with day-old shadow, his forest-green eyes warm when he says, "I think I love you."

"Hey!" Mike shouts from where he's sitting on the floor playing video games with Cody. "I called her first!"

"Technically, I called her first," Adam says from behind me. When he walks past, he swoops in to plant an exaggerated smooch on my cheek. I blush and wipe it away, but I'm smiling when he looks back at me with a grin on his face. "Want something to drink now?"

I'm about to tell him "sure" when the bus door opens and Driver steps on, followed by a group of girls who look like models for Hoes-R-Us. Driver leads the five of them on board without introductions, but the girls don't seem to mind. They immediately flock to Adam, swarming him as he waits for my answer.

"Oh, yeah, sure," I finally say, feeling like an idiot for blatantly gawking at the new arrivals.

Adam mixes me some type of fruity cocktail, but his attention is already elsewhere. The blonde pressing against his side, the hottest one of the bunch, is giggling and tracing her fingernail over his neck, whispering something in his ear. There's a redhead and a brunette competing for his attention too. One of the other girls is sitting on the bench seat with Shawn, on his lap. Cody sets his game controller down and starts chatting up the fifth.

"Uh, I'm going to get ready for bed," I say to no one in particular. My voice seems to jar Adam back to the present, and he remembers to bring me my drink. When he hands it to me, he looks like he's about to say something, but before he can, Mike interrupts him.

"Rowan!" he shouts from the floor. "Come fill in for Cody!" I inch away from Adam, who is already the meat in a groupie-sandwich again, and stand behind Mike, staring at the war game on the screen. "Hop in here! I'm dying!"

"But I don't know how to play . . ."

Mike hands me the spare controller, playing one-handed with his eyes glued to the screen. "You can't be any worse than shorty over there." He nods his chin toward Cody, who doesn't notice or care as he flirts with the girl he's sitting with. I chuckle and sit down next to Mike, our knees squished together. I'm not a gamer, but I pick things up quickly.

"Holy shit!" Mike says after a few minutes, a second after I blow up an enemy compound. "Guys! You should see this girl!"

The guys are . . . otherwise occupied. Mike glances over his shoulder at them and scoffs. "Fricken groupies."

I can't help sneaking a peek at Adam, who is now sitting at the other end of the bus. He's leaning back in the bench seat near the front, sipping on a glass of whiskey while three of the girls chat him up. Their hands are all over him. My gaze lifts from their hands to his eyes and . . . is he *staring* at me? Yeah . . . he's definitely staring.

"Head in the game, Ro!" Mike says, and I quickly look away.

"Sorry."

Mike flashes a knowing glance in my direction. It isn't until I see that look on his face that I realize how irritated I feel that Adam is entertaining other girls—one under his arm with her hand on his chest, one with her leg draped over his knee, and one with her chin resting on her friend's shoulder, batting her eyelashes and playing with her hair.

"Hoes will be hoes," Mike offers with a shrug, and I can't help but crack a smile, because I'm not sure if he's referring to Adam or the entire band or the girls or all of the above.

After completely slaughtering the enemy for a few rounds, I stand up and stretch, watching as Joel follows a girl from where they were doing God-knows-what upstairs. His blond mohawk is still perfectly gelled into place, but her long chestnut waves look thoroughly tangled. He opens the door to the bus and starts to usher her off with his hand on her lower back. She turns around to give him a kiss, but it's so awkward—she's trying to make it passionate, he's trying to make it quick, and the resulting effect makes me cringe.

Should I feel sorry for her? Because I'm pretty sure I don't . . .

After practically steamrolling the girl off the bus, Joel walks over to stand next to me, admiring the scores that are still displayed on the screen. "Holy shit. Look at that kill count!" He nudges me with his elbow. "Mike really *is* going to marry you!"

"Hell yeah I am!" Mike says, turning his head to smile up at me. "You down for another round?"

"Nah, I think I'm going to go get some air."

I turn around, shock widenening my eyes when I see Adam now full-on making out with the blonde he's sitting with. She's on his lap practically eating his face. Her friend is kissing his neck, and the fourth wheel has moved to the other side of the bus to sit with Shawn and the girl he's with.

I'm going to have to walk right past all of them.

Fuck. My. Life.

I look anywhere but at Adam's gorgeous face as I move

down the aisle. I've barely passed him when he breaks his lips free and quite breathlessly says, "I'll come with you."

When I look back at him, the two girls he's with look just as confused as I feel. One of them squeaks, "But—"

"Hey, Joel," Adam interrupts, shifting the girl off his lap and peeling the other's hands from his neck so he can stand up. "Have you met . . . uh . . ." He's staring down at the blonde.

"Amber . . ." she finishes for him, and I bite back a snicker.

"Amber! And . . . her friend . . ." He's staring at the redhead now, and it's obvious he has no idea what her name is either. "This redheaded bombshell here."

Joel laughs and shakes his head. "Oh no you don't."

Adam stares down at the now pouting girls. His black-nailed thumb points back at me. "I'm going to take my friend here out for some air. But I'm sure one of the guys here would be happy to make you ladies some drinks."

"NOT IT!" Mike calls. Joel presses his pointer finger to his nose, and Shawn looks up, realizing he's the only one left since Cody has disappeared with one of the girls upstairs.

"Fuck," Shawn mutters, and Adam chuckles. He curls his hand around my shoulder, turning me around and leading me off the bus without another look back.

"You didn't have to come with me," I say once the door closes behind us.

He smiles at me, and any irritation I felt toward him instantly melts away. How the hell does he do that?!

"If we're going to be friends," he says, "there's something you should know about me."

"And what's that?"

"I never do *anything* I don't want to." He drapes his arm around my shoulders and leads me to where six or seven guys are sitting in a circle on coolers and lawn chairs under a bright parking-lot light. Many of them are roadies I recognize from when I was standing backstage. Driver is telling them some animated story about a party he was at last weekend—which apparently involved drugs, cops, and falling off a roof.

Adam plops down in the last empty chair, and I stand there awkwardly until he wraps his hands around my waist and suddenly pulls me into his lap. I gasp and immediately tense up. I'm a freaking statue.

"Relax," he whispers to me, "I'm not trying to get in your pants." His arms stay firmly wrapped around me as I shift a little to give him a doubtful look. He smiles up at me innocently and says, "I swear."

When Driver finishes his story, he looks around the circle and seems to notice us for the first time. "Hey! Rowan! How did you like the show?!"

"It was amazing," I say, trying to force my body to stop being so stiff. I can feel the rough denim of Adam's jeans through my leggings, the shape of his fingers clasped on my hip. I scoot myself deeper into him to get comfortable, turning so that my legs hang between his knees. Reluctantly, I wrap my arm around his shoulders for balance, and even though he's looking at Driver, a smirk sneaks onto his lips.

"Told you you'd love it!" Driver says from across the circle. Someone passes him a joint, and he puffs it a few times before passing it on. In that typical strained stoner voice that reminds me of one of Dee's old boyfriends, he asks, "Are you riding with us on the bus tomorrow?"

"She's riding with me," Adam answers for me.

One of the other guys says in an amused voice, "I heard she told you what's-what earlier tonight." Oh, God.

"She did!" Adam replies, not sounding at all upset about our earlier confrontation. But judging from how blazing hot my cheeks feel, I'm still embarrassed as hell.

"Self-respect." Another guy laughs.

Adam laughs too. "You should have seen it!" he says. "Broke my heart." My face is all-worry, but he just smiles up at me and squeezes me tighter.

I lean down and whisper in Adam's ear. "Sorry."

He lifts his chin like he wants to whisper something back, so I bend down further and place my ear near his mouth, surprised when he presses a soft kiss against my cheek. I pull away, and he chuckles at the stunned expression on my face. "Now we're even," he says quietly, and then his smile gets even bigger. "Want a beer?"

At this point, I'm pretty sure I need one. "Sure . . . thanks."

The other guys are already deep in a new conversation when he reaches into a cooler next to him and hands me one. "You *are* twenty-one, right?"

After a long pause, I smile sweetly and repeat, "Sure . . . thanks."

He laughs as I pop the tab and take a drink. We sit out

there for over an hour, listening to the guys tell stories and talk about plans for tomorrow. It's so weird being on Adam's lap, but eventually I get used to it and my body molds itself against him. It feels nice. Weird, and scary . . . and nice.

Each time the joint comes our way, I pass. I've never done drugs and don't plan to anytime soon. I'm happy when Adam passes too. He periodically sips my beer, which gives me butterflies even though I try to act as casual about it as he does.

When he tells stories of his own, I watch him intently, finding myself smiling at him and holding him a little tighter. When I feel his thumb rub absently over my side and that slight movement lights my entire body on fire, I realize exactly what's happening.

I am crushing on him. *Hard.*

"I'm heading to bed," I say, abruptly sitting up straight. Adam looks confused, and maybe a little disappointed, but he doesn't try to stop me.

"Aw, you sure?" Driver asks.

"Yeah. I'm not used to being up this late." I check my phone and see that it's half past three. "I'll see you guys tomorrow."

I crawl off of Adam's lap as the guys say goodbye to me, and then I walk to the bus without looking back. Adam doesn't follow me—or say anything to me at all—which is probably for the best. I pull open the door to the bus and climb the stairs to find Mike still on the floor playing games and Shawn and Joel sitting on a bench talking as they absently watch the TV. The girls must have left at some point. Good.

"I'm hitting the hay. I'll see you guys in the morning," I tell them.

They shout a round of "goodnights" to me, and then I climb to the second level. I walk through the upstairs sitting area and then past Cody, who is sound asleep on a bunk. When I get to the black satin bedroom, I'm surprised to find it completely untouched. I stare down at my stuff in the corner. Should I actually sleep in here? I don't want Adam to get any ideas . . . And he was expecting to sleep in here too, right? Is he *still* expecting to sleep in here?

I close the door behind me and change into my pajamas—a different baggy T-shirt and a pair of fuzzy pajama pants—and then I leave the room and crawl under the covers of an untouched bunk.

Chapter Thirteen

"HEY," A VOICE whispers.

I groan.

"Hey." A hand rubs my shoulder, and my eyes reluctantly peel open. Adam. "You don't have to sleep out here, you know . . ."

"I know," I say, my voice hoarse from sleep. "It's okay. I'm good."

"Okay . . ." He stares at me for a moment, his face close to mine and his hand still on my shoulder. "But if you change your mind, that bed is huge. You won't even know I'm there."

I giggle because I can't help it. Sleep next to Adam Everest and not know he's right there? Does he even realize how absurd that sounds?

His eyebrows turn in. "What?"

"Nothing." I giggle again and bury my face in the pillow. "Nothing. I'm really tired. I'll see you in the morning, Adam."

He stays crouched next to me for a moment, and then he says, "See you in the morning." After he goes into the bedroom and closes the door, I crawl out of bed to use the bathroom at the end of the hall. As I make my way back to my bunk, I notice that there are guys *everywhere*. There are twelve bunks, and the beds that aren't filled with band members are filled with what I assume are roadies. I quickly crawl back under the covers, suddenly wide awake.

I lie there. And lie there. And lie there.

Every time I'm about to fall asleep, I hear someone stir or groan or kick at their covers. And then the snoring starts. And it's not just one person. It's at least three. And one of those three is *loud*.

"Ohmygoddd," I groan when I'm on the verge of losing my mind. "Who *is* that?"

A voice I don't recognize chuckles and answers me. "That'd be Joel."

I fight the urge to strangle him in his sleep—or to perform an exorcism, since he obviously needs one—and force my eyes to close. I count backward, I count sheep, I count sheep jumping backward. I'm not sure what time I finally fall asleep, but when I wake up, the snoring is still going on and my eyes feel like the Sandman decided to be a douchebag and dump the Sahara on them.

Soft light is filtering through the white drapes, so I suck it up and crawl out of bed. I grab my bath stuff from my suitcase—which I've stashed in a nook near my bunk—and then I go to the bathroom downstairs to shower. It's pretty cramped, but I make do. I towel-dry my hair and dress in the bathroom, opting for a pair of jeans and a powder-blue tank top. I pull my hair up in a ponytail and put on my glasses, staring at myself in the mirror before I take my glasses back off and put on some mascara and lip gloss. Then I stare at myself again, sigh and take the glasses off again, and try to tone down the makeup. I want to look pretty, but I don't want my attempt to be obvious, and I *definitely* don't want Adam or Shawn to remember meeting me at Mayhem.

When I exit the bathroom, everyone is still upstairs. The bus is a mess, with clothes and dishes and trash everywhere, so I busy myself with picking up. I gather all the clothes into a pile, and then I put all the liquor away. I throw away all the trash and then take all the dirty dishes into the kitchen, grabbing a sponge and some dishwashing detergent and getting to work.

I'm scrubbing a whiskey glass smudged with prostitute-pink lipstick when I hear someone stretch and yawn at the front of the bus. I look up to see Shawn at the same time he sees me. He walks to the kitchen and leans against the counter next to me, scratching his fingers through his short-cropped black hair. "Keep this up and we might never let you leave."

I chuckle and shake my head. "I don't think I can live through another night like last night. How can you sleep through that?"

Shawn laughs. "I guess I'm just used to it." He grabs a dish towel and starts drying the glasses I'm washing. Gazing over at me, he says, "You know, I still swear I've met you somewhere before. What school did you go to?"

I answer him honestly, since the school I went to is over six hours away from the town we live in now and I know damn well that that's not how Shawn met me.

"Hm . . . what about at your job, then?" he asks. "Do you work?"

"Not right now. My parents are helping me out a lot. I'll probably work over the summers though."

"Oh well, I'm sure I'll remember eventually," he says, but not if I can help it!

When we finish with the dishes, he asks me if I want to go on a coffee run with him. We're already exiting the kitchen when I ask, "Won't the guys wonder where we are?"

"Nah," Shawn says, working a kink out of his neck. He's dressed in long, baggy cargo shorts and a worn-thin black band T-shirt. "They'll probably still be sleeping when we get back. The coffee shop is just around the corner."

The walk to the coffee shop is a little chilly, but Shawn was right—it's less than two blocks away, and we get there in no time. He pulls a chained wallet from his back pocket and approaches the counter, glancing at me over his shoulder. "What do you want?"

"Oh, you don't have to get me anything." I wish I would've brought my wallet though.

"Come on, just pick something," Shawn insists. "Everyone else is getting something. Call it your delivery fee."

"Okay," I agree, "Um . . ." I stare up at the menu posted on the wall behind the counter, and then I smile at the young barista waiting to take Shawn's order. "Can I please have a large iced mocha?"

As the girl makes my drink, Shawn stares through the window case that protects all of the pastries and cookies and muffins. "Do you like blueberry muffins?" he asks me.

"Yeah . . ."

"Can I get two blueberry muffins too, please?" he asks the barista. She hands him two, and he gives one to me. "Can I also get a chocolate-chip frap? Medium?" Shawn pulls a piece of paper from his back pocket. "And all of these drinks to go. In carriers, please."

It takes forever for the girl to ring him up. She holds the piece of paper in front of her as she does, and then she hands it to a second barista, who gets to work writing down names on cups and marking what the orders are. When our first two drinks are ready, Shawn grabs them for us and we sit down at a table, picking at our muffins.

It's a little awkward at first. I thank him for the coffee to fill the silence. "And the muffin," I add.

"No problem," he says. "So how are you liking hanging with the band so far?"

It's a damn good question. It went from fun to not-so-fun, back to fun again, and then weird, and now just kind of comfortable. "It's been interesting."

Shawn grins, amused. "Interesting how?"

"Well, I'm sure not many people get to see what goes on inside a tour bus."

"Is it how you imagined it?"

I remove the lid from my iced mocha to scoop out the whipped cream with my straw and eat that first. "I guess. I mean . . . I didn't really imagine it any particular way."

Shawn sips his coffee, staring at me thoughtfully.

"Adam told me what you did for him in class." He pauses for a while, and then he asks, "Why'd you do it?" When I raise my eyebrow, he adds, "I mean, obviously you aren't a groupie, and you're not interested in hooking up with him or anything. So why?"

After licking my straw clean, I shrug and put the cap back on. "He looked like he could use a hand, and . . . I don't know. I just felt like it, I guess."

Shawn chuckles. "Now you sound like Adam."

"Dear God, don't tell me that," I joke, and Shawn laughs.

"Adam's not so bad. I mean, he has his issues. But he's my best friend for a reason."

I smile. "I was just kidding. I actually think he's pretty great. I had a lot of fun with him yesterday."

"Before you demanded he get some self-respect," Shawn quips.

"Well, he should!"

He stands up to get our drinks, smiling brightly. "I'm not arguing!" He chuckles. "I was just shocked to hear you say it. What happened when you guys left the bus?"

I stand up to grab one of the drink carriers filled with coffees. "He chased me around town for a while, and then we agreed to be friends."

"Really?" Shawn gives me a weird look.

"Yeah . . . why?"

"No reason." He squeezes his drink into a carrier and then picks the other two up. I walk swiftly to the door to hold it open for him since his hands are full.

"No, what were you going to say?" I ask.

"Adam doesn't really have girl friends. So . . . just don't be surprised if he doesn't get what that means."

We walk down the sidewalk for a bit before Shawn asks, "How are you going to get him to study for that class you're in?"

"What do you mean?"

"I've been getting on his case about school since . . . well . . . middle school, I think." He chuckles. "If he doesn't want to go to class, he just doesn't. Same with studying."

"How the hell has he passed all his classes then?"

Shawn shrugs, and I guess it doesn't make any more sense to him than it does to me.

"Well I didn't come along just for the ride," I say. "What time are you guys planning on leaving today?"

"What time is it?"

I pull my phone from my back pocket, staring at a black screen. "No idea. My phone's dead."

"I think we're planning on heading out around eleven. But I'll have to talk to Driver to make sure."

"Then I'm waking Adam up as soon as we get back."

Shawn grins at me like I just handed him a winning lottery ticket. "Really?"

"Yes?"

"This is going to be good," he laughs. "Good luck!"

I tiptoe back along the bus hallway, between the bunks, trying not to wake the guys who are still sleeping. Most of them were awake by the time Shawn and I got back, but Adam wasn't among them. Neither was Mike, and I have to swallow a giggle when I walk past his bed and see that his short brown hair is disheveled into some unfortunate-looking bed-head. I walk past him and rest my hand on the doorknob to Adam's room, looking behind me to see Shawn peeking around the corner at the opposite end of the hall, looking *way* too giddy. I scowl and wave him away, and then I disappear into the room and close the door behind me.

Adam hears the door click closed and groans, "Shawn, I swear to God . . . if you don't leave me alone, I'm going to punch you in the dick."

I walk to the side of the bed and stare down at where Adam's face is buried in the pillow. He's shirtless, the definition in his back making my heart flip over. I try not to blush. "I brought you your coffee."

He shifts his face to the side and opens one eye. When he spots me, his lips slowly curl into an adorable smile, and then he starts laughing. "What time is it?" he finally asks, roughly rubbing his hand over his face. He props himself up on his elbow.

I'm too distracted with trying not to stare at him that I don't answer right away. When I realize I *really* need to say something, I clear my throat and say, "Eight thirty."

Adam rolls onto his back and scoots lower on the mattress, pulling the covers over his face. "Too early for coffee," he mumbles from under the covers.

I sit on the edge of the bed and pull the blankets down to just below his nose. "I think we should try to get some studying in before we need to hit the road again."

Adam sits up, the covers tumbling off his chest and to his waist. He stares at me for a long time, and now I *know* I'm blushing. "You're serious . . ." he says.

"Yeah. I mean, what did I come along for?"

"I have a better idea," he says, and I'm suddenly dying to know exactly what that idea is. "Lie down with me. Let's go back to sleep and we'll study in the car."

I bite my lip, *so* tempted. When he sees me do it, he gives me a sharp smile, and the dark look in his eyes reveals all the naughty ideas I just put into his head. I release my lip. "That's a terrible idea," I say.

Adam smirks at me. "Liar."

I stand up and move to leave the room, but he launches out of bed before I can open the door, jumping in front of me in just his boxers. He laughs and glues his hands to my shoulders. "I'm just joking!"

I give him a look.

"Okay . . . I wasn't . . . but I didn't mean it."

I give him another look.

"Okay, I did."

He smiles innocently at me, and I can't help laughing. "Don't you want to graduate?" I ask.

He groans and drops his hands. "Yeah."

"Then you have some serious work to do. This test on Monday isn't going to be easy, Adam. Cramming for it the night before isn't going to work, not with all the days you've missed."

He sighs and rubs his eyes before picking a T-shirt off the floor and pulling it on. "Can I shower first?"

"If you make it quick."

I'm back downstairs hanging with the guys when he emerges from the bathroom in a plain white T-shirt and faded torn-up jeans. "Shawn," he says while towel-drying his hair, "where's my muffin?"

Shawn laughs. "Your tutor ate it!"

"I did not!" I yell back.

Shawn points wickedly at me. "Did you or did you not eat a blueberry muffin this morning?"

I glare at him and grab a shirt that's lying on top of the pile I made this morning, hurling it at him. "Prove it!"

The guys all laugh, and Adam smiles wide, his pearly whites shining brightly. He shakes his head at us. "You're an asshole, Shawn."

"Hey!" Shawn protests. "She's the one who ate it."

Adam crooks his finger at me. "Alright, let's get this over with." I pass by him to go up the stairs, and he shouts back to the guys, "She told me to make it quick this morning, guys!"

They laugh, and I roll my eyes, not bothering to look back at the stupid grin that I'm sure is plastered on Adam's face. My backpack is still in the back room, so I grab it off of the floor and then bounce onto the bed, sitting cross-legged. "Alright, so . . . do you even remember how to conjugate verbs?"

"*Oui*?" Adam says. "*Je pense.*" I smile widely at his correct pronunciation of 'I think'.

"Alright, well let's start with some written stuff. We can work on verbal stuff in the car."

By the time I exit the bus with him at eleven o'clock, I'm feeling pretty hopeless. I can't fathom how Adam passed French 101, and he is *so* easily distracted, always getting off topic one way or another. At one point, I pressed my palms against his cheeks to quiet his yapping. When he stopped talking and just stared at me, I said, "You need to *con-cen-trate*."

Adam's gaze was fixed on me, and it was so intense that I loosened my hold. "If you don't let go of my face," he warned, "I'm *going* to kiss you." I immediately dropped my hands, blushing beet-red. He chuckled and flipped to the next page, getting back to work. But after that, *I* was the one who couldn't concentrate. When eleven o'clock finally rolled around, I was thankful for an excuse to get out of that room.

"Are we going to stop somewhere to eat?" I ask Adam as we walk to his topless black Camaro.

"I think so. If not, you and I can stop and just meet them there." I throw my backpack into the back and climb into the passenger seat. Adam frowns at the backpack and then at the textbook in my lap. "You're not going to make me study the whole way, are you?"

I shake my head. "No, I think I need a break."

He laughs and slides behind the wheel. "Is there any hope for me?"

I stare over at him, at his gorgeous eyes, his untamed rocker hair, and that heartbreaker smile that could make a smart girl stupid. "I guess we'll see."

Chapter Fourteen

"WHERE ARE WE?" I ask Adam as I stretch in his front seat, using my hand to block the blinding sun. I didn't mean to fall asleep, but I guess the sleep deprivation of last night finally caught up with me. I woke a minute ago to soft fingers rubbing gently over my arm, and I groggily opened my eyes.

"We're stopping for lunch," he says, nodding toward the tour bus parked at the back of the parking lot we're in. We're at a diner along the highway. A big red sign facing the road names it Rosy's.

I reach for my phone, which Adam connected to his car charger earlier in the trip, and turn it on to look at the time. We've been on the road for almost two hours, and I have tons of missed texts and calls—from my mom, Dee, Leti, and Brady. I ignore them and tuck the phone into my purse, and then I slide out of the car and stretch my legs, rolling my neck from side to side.

I walk into the diner with a literal *mob* of boys. In addition to the five guys from the band, there are five roadies, including Driver. I feel kind of awkward . . . and kind of really freaking awesome. Inside, there's no sign that tells people to wait to be seated, so everyone seats themselves. I slide into a booth seat, and Adam slides in next to me. Shawn and Joel sit across from us, and Mike, Cody, and Driver sit at a table next to us. The other four roadies sit in a booth farther down.

A middle-aged waitress comes by to take our orders, making pleasant conversation by asking about the band since she saw the tour bus out front. The weird look she gives me when she takes my order doesn't escape my notice, but I let it slide—I can only imagine what she's thinking, and I'd probably be wondering the same things if I were in her shoes. Still exhausted from my short nap in the car, I bury my face in my elbow while we wait for the food to arrive.

"Hey," Shawn says, lifting my blonde pony tail and letting it plop back down. I tilt my head back far enough to stare up at him. "How did studying go?"

I groan and bury my face again, and all three guys laugh.

"I thought I did awesome!" Adam says.

I sit up and rub my eyes. "You did *alright*. But we really need to get some studying done in the car."

Shawn is twisting his straw paper into knots when he asks, "Didn't you do that on the way here?"

"No, I fell asleep." I stare pointedly at Joel, who is busy sipping on his Coke. "Because *someone* kept me up all night."

Adam chuckles, and Joel looks from side to side with the straw still in his mouth, noticing we're all staring at him. "Who, me?"

"I think you need to see a doctor," I say. "Seriously. I swear you died at least thirty times last night."

Joel grins at me. "If you think *I'm* bad, you should hear my grandma."

I'm imagining what hell it would be to share a room with Joel and his grandma when our waitress brings our food. I immediately snatch up my burger, taking a very unladylike bite out of it. Most girls would probably order a salad or something when surrounded by the likes of Adam, Shawn, and Joel—who are, I have to admit, all sexy as sin—but I'm too hungry to care. And it's not like I'm trying to impress them.

Adam picks a steak fry off of my plate and replaces it with one of his onion rings. "I hate French," he grumbles.

Joel blows on a chicken wing, and it looks so perfectly crispy, I'm kind of wishing I had gotten those instead. "So why did you take it?" he asks.

"Needed a language to graduate."

I finish swallowing my bite of burger, watching Shawn as he trades one of his loaded potato skins for one of Joel's mozzarella sticks. "Why are you in school, anyway?" I ask Adam. "I doubt any degree you could get would help you out with the band."

Adam lays his pickle spear on my plate, which makes me smile since I absolutely love pickles, even though he doesn't know that. "I enrolled right out of high school," he says as I pick it up and take a bite, "back before we got as big as we are, and I just figured I might as well finish, I guess."

"What are you majoring in? Music?" I'm half paying attention to Adam, half watching Joel trade one of Adam's onion rings for a mozzarella stick. Watching the boys eat and pick off of each other's plates is making me smile. They're too freaking cute.

When Adam nods, I steal another one of his onion rings and give him three of my steak fries as a trade. He's smiling down at his plate when Cody turns toward us from the next table and says, "So, Rowan, how does it feel to be the only girl in history to ever turn Adam down?"

A better question would be *why the hell are we still talking about this*? Before I can respond, Mike says, "Aw, c'mon, Code. She's not the first girl to turn him down. There was that other one . . . What was her name . . ." His eyebrows scrunch together, and then he says, "Plum?"

"PEEEACH!" most of the guys near me suddenly shout out in unison.

Oh. My. God.

They break into loud laughter at Adam's expense, and I'm suddenly mid-anxiety attack. Shawn is laughing with the rest of them until he sees the expression on my face. And before I can hide it, he witnesses all of the panic I'm feeling. He studies me curiously, his eyes growing narrower and narrower. And then I see the precise moment when he realizes who I am, because his eyes get wide, wider, super-freaking-wide. I can see him imagining me with my hair down, my glasses off, my makeup done. He looks from me to Adam and back again. When it seems like he's about to say something, I shake my head almost imperceptibly at him, pleading with him to keep my secret.

Adam groans from the teasing and looks up at Shawn just in time to catch him staring at me with shock still written plainly across his face. He follows Shawn's eyes and gives me a weird look, and then Shawn coughs and lets out a forced chuckle. "Yeah, Peach. I'd almost forgotten about her."

My prayer for a distraction, any distraction—a fire in the kitchen, a five-car pileup on the highway, a nuclear freaking airstrike for all I care—is answered when the waitress pops back in to ask how everyone is doing. I stuff my face with more burger as I try to think of some way to change this disaster of a subject.

As soon as she leaves, Shawn says, "So." I look up to see a devilish smirk on his face. "Why didn't you get her number, Adam?"

"Because I'm an idiot," Adam says, and my heart pumps a flood of heat into my cheeks. "I didn't even get her real name."

"And you have no idea what it is?" Shawn asks, shooting me an amused grin that no one else catches.

"Not a damn clue."

"Do you even remember what she looked like?" Shawn chides. "You were drinking, weren't you?"

"I'll never forget," Adam argues, rising to the challenge while Shawn's smirk grows wider. "She was wearing these pink heels and this little black skirt. Her body, man . . ." This has got to be the universe's idea of a cruel joke. Adam shakes his head like the memory is too much, and then he glances in my direction like he's only now remembering that there's a female sitting right beside him. He clears his throat and quickly finishes, "Blonde hair. Long legs. Pink eyes."

"Pink eyes?" Joel asks.

"Her eye makeup," Adam explains. "It was shadowy and sort of sparkly. And she must've been wearing glitter lotion or something because there was glitter all in the bed afterward."

I swallow hard. Dee talked me into wearing shimmer body spray that night, and it had left glitter all in her bed too.

With a sharp glint in his eye, Shawn asks, "Her hair was kinda like Rowan's, wasn't it?"

I am going to MURDER him! My heart jackhammers in my chest when Adam glances in my direction, but he gives my hair only a cursory glance before dismissing the possibility that Peach's hair was similar to what I currently have twisted up in my ultra-messy bun. "Yeah kinda, I guess. But lighter and wavier."

My hair is always a little lighter in the summer, and Dee had worked her magic on my unruly waves.

"Maybe she'll be at the concert tonight," Shawn offers, his eyes sparking with trouble when I shoot him another warning look. It's taking all of my self-control to not kick him under the table, but if he keeps this up, he's going to learn what it feels like to have a kneecap lodged in his thigh.

Adam shrugs, and I interrupt the conversation by telling the guys I need to use the restroom. I tap Shawn's shin with my toe and then dart my eyes to the front of the restaurant, hoping he'll take the cue and follow. After Adam moves to let me scoot out of the booth, I walk around the corner to the front lobby and then stand there, waiting.

I can't believe Adam told all the guys about me. I can't believe he even *remembered* me.

When Shawn strolls around the corner, I practically steamroll him out the front doors so we can talk outside. He looks at me and starts laughing. "I *knew* I knew you!"

I sigh, worry settling on me like a blanket of ice. "Please don't tell anyone."

"Why? Why didn't you tell Adam?"

I tug on a loose strand of hair escaping from my bun. "I didn't want him to know." I frown at Shawn, who looks as confused as he does amused. I use my hands to indicate my plain tank top, my jeans, my sandals. "I'm not that girl, Shawn."

"But you *are* that girl . . ."

"But I'm *not*. I'm not interested in being one of Adam's groupies."

"He knows that, though."

"And that's *all* he needs to know."

Shawn stares at me like I'm a puzzle he can't put together. "Why did you *really* come along on this trip?"

I sigh again, rubbing the center of my forehead. "Our professor was threatening to fail him out of the class. I wanted to help, so I stepped in."

"But why? Why did you do it?"

"The night you and Adam met me . . . I had just broken up with my boyfriend," I confide. "I caught him cheating at that show, and Adam was really sweet to me. Honestly, that night would've been the worst night of my life if it weren't for him. I felt like I owed him."

Shawn stands there for a long time, thinking. Then he shakes his head. "I can't believe he doesn't recognize you."

"I looked a lot different that night, and he had been drinking . . ."

"Yeah, but he like *obsessed* about you for weeks."

"He *obsessed* about me?"

"Yeah. He talked about you a lot, and he always listed you on the backstage list, and he'd give you a shout-out every time we performed at Mayhem to see if you'd meet up with him afterward."

I don't even know how to process that, much less respond to it. I end up just standing there staring at Shawn, who still looks mildly stunned.

"So you're never going to tell him?" he asks.

I shake my head. "No, and I'd really appreciate it if you wouldn't either . . ."

Shawn studies my worried expression for a long moment, and then he sighs and scratches the back of his neck. "If you don't want me to, I won't. BUT, for the record, I really think you should."

"Nothing good would come of it, Shawn. He doesn't need to know."

He shrugs. "I still think you should."

When we walk back inside, I make a bee-line to the restroom to pull myself together. Adam *obsessed* over me? I find that hard to believe, since he definitely didn't recognize me when I saved him from Dr. Pullman, and he had sauntered *quite happily* into class with all of those sluts hanging all over him less than two days after we made out. But then again, it seems like most of the guys have heard about me—about Adam's "Peach"—so he must have told them about me . . .

None of this even matters. Even if that night *did* mean something to Adam, he's not relationship material. And even if he was, I'm not looking for a relationship.

I walk back to the table, intentionally avoiding meeting Shawn's eyes, and wait for Adam to stand up and let me squeeze back in.

"You okay?" he asks. I realize he's referring to my having been "in the bathroom" for so long.

"Yeah," I lie. "I think maybe I'm just feeling a little carsick."

"Oh . . . Do you want to ride on the bus?"

I glance at Shawn, who is attentively waiting for my answer to Adam's question. "No . . . No, that's alright," I say. "Just don't let me fall asleep again." I force a smile at Adam, whose concern for me is clear in the way his brows pull together over his gorgeous gray-green eyes. It reminds me of the way he looked at me at Mayhem when he saw that I was crying, and it makes me want to melt into his arms all over again. I quickly look back to my plate and finish off the last few bites of my now cold burger.

The guys insist on paying for my food, and then we're all walking back out into the bright afternoon sunshine. The diner's air-conditioning had been blasting the whole time, so the warm rays feel great against my goose-bumped skin. Adam and I split from the rest of the group, and then he flips down his shades and lights a cigarette before climbing back into the car.

On the road, I grab my textbook and start quizzing him on things we covered on the bus. I need the distraction, desperately. If Shawn tells Adam who I am . . . I don't even know what I'll do. What would Adam do? Would he be happy? Pissed? Would he even let me stay the rest of the weekend?

I dive into French tutoring, and to my surprise, Adam actually remembers most of what we covered earlier this morning and he seems much more focused. I guess there are fewer distractions while he's driving, and I intend to use that to our advantage and make the most of our car rides. We continue onto the next chapter, and I begin feeling a little more hopeful that we might be able to get him where he needs to be by the time we have our exam in a few days.

After about an hour of grilling him and making good progress, I slap the book closed and toss it into the backseat. "Time for a break."

I rummage through my purse for my phone and start checking the messages I've missed. The last one I got from Dee this morning makes me laugh.

Have you been thoroughly deflowered yet?!

Leti's text makes me laugh even harder.

I had a dream last night. You were there, and Adam was there . . . and I trampled you to get to him. Sorry! (Kind of.)

"My friends are ridiculous," I explain when Adam gives me a curious look.

"Oh yeah? What are they saying?"

"They're just gushing over how hot they think you are."

Adam grins and abruptly steers the car onto the shoulder, shutting it off.

"What are you doing?" I nervously ask.

He pulls one of his rings off and says, "Here, give me your hand." I do what he asks and he slides it onto my ring finger.

Butterflies. So many freaking butterflies.

"Take a picture of us and send it to them," he says. His smile is bright with trouble, and it makes me bust up laughing.

"You're a genius!"

I turn my back to Adam so I can get a picture of us together, but then his arm snakes around my waist and tugs me over the center console, pulling me flush against him. He presses his cheek against mine for the photo, and I know I'm blushing like an idiot. I fumble around for my camera app, and then I snap a picture of me holding my ring-clad hand up in an exaggeratedly giddy pose. I laugh and crawl back into my seat, texting the picture to Dee and Leti as Adam starts the car again and pulls back onto the highway.

Within seconds, my phone starts blowing up, and I laugh. Dee's messages are as loud as she is.

You are so full of shit! But OMG LOOK AT YOU!

He is so fucking hot!

MARRY HIM FOR REAL. OR GIVE HIM MY NUMBER!

Even as I'm reading her texts, my phone keeps beeping from the messages Leti is sending me.

I squealed like a schoolgirl!

Please tell me you've had a repeat of last month!

Bring him to my room! I promise I won't trample you (all the way) to death!

Look at how happy you two lovebirds look. AW!

"Did they buy it?" Adam asks.

"No," I laugh. "I think we just encouraged them."

He looks all too happy to hear it, smiling from ear to ear as I start responding to the texts. I tell Dee I'll call her later to tell her all about the trip, and I tell Leti I've been good. He sends me a picture of him pouting with his bottom lip pushed out, and I giggle and shake my head.

Turning the volume on my phone low so that Adam can't hear, I start listening to my voicemails. My mom just wanted to check in, so I text her to let her know that I'm alright and that I'll call her later in the week. Dee has left me multiple voicemails threatening "unforeseen consequences" if I haven't been "deflowered" by the time I come home. And finally, Brady.

His voice plays through my phone. "Hey, Ro . . . I'm just calling to see if you're free at all this weekend. I have both days off, and I just thought that maybe we could get together and talk . . . if you're up for it. Call me, please. Whenever you get a chance." A long pause. "I still love you, baby. I'm not giving up on us."

I manage to keep a blank poker face as I tuck my phone away, and then I look over at Adam, at his brace-leted wrist and black fingernails. He catches me staring and gazes over at me, and for a few seconds, our eyes stay locked, neither one of us smiling or speaking. What is he thinking?

I realize I'm still wearing his ring, which is too big for my finger anyway, so I take it off and hand it back to him. "Thanks for the picture," I quietly say. "That was awesome."

He slides the ring back onto his pinky finger. "Thanks for wearing my ring." He winks at me, and I giggle and roll my eyes.

"You should sing me another song." I recline my seat a little farther back and close my eyes.

"You want me to sing you to sleep?"

"No, I want you to keep me awake."

"What do you want to hear?"

"How about one of yours?"

Adam picks up his phone and sorts through his music, setting it to an instrumental, acoustic version of one of his band's calmer songs. He sings me the lyrics, about best friends and late nights and memories that will last forever. I watch him as he sings, thankful that he doesn't look down at me, because then I'd have to look away. His voice is quiet compared to when he's onstage, and here, like this, it sounds even more beautiful. It gives me chills.

When the song finishes, he finally looks down at me, and I'm smiling up at him. "You really are talented, you know."

He switches hands on the wheel and reaches over to cover my eyes. "Stop," he says bashfully. "You'll make me blush."

Adam? Shy? I laugh and pull his fingers away. "Yeah right."

He winks at me with a smirk on his face, and I have to look away from him, over at the trees to my right. I keep telling myself not to fall for him—because he is Adam freaking Everest and my heart's already been broken enough this year as it is.

I let the wind wash over my skin for a long while, listening to the music pouring out of Adam's speakers, before I pick up my phone and type a reply to Brady's voicemail.

**I'm busy this weekend, but we'll get to-
gether soon. I promise I'll call you in the
next few days and we'll set something up.**

Later, I'm on the tour bus alone while the rest of the band sets up inside. I curl my feet under myself on a bench seat and call Dee. The first thing she says when she answers the phone is "DETAILS!"

"What do you want to know?" I ask, and I'm sure she can hear the smile in my voice.

"How far have you gone with him?!"

Expecting that would be her first question, I answer, "We're just friends, Dee."

"Boys like that don't have girl *friends*, Ro. I mean, Jesus, how can you stand it?! I got a hot flash just from looking at that picture you sent me! Just ask Macy! I had to lie down!"

I laugh into the phone. "I'm not saying it's easy . . . But he's just a really sweet guy."

"So what's the problem?!"

"He's not really sweet to the girls he sleeps with . . ." I remember the way he shifted that girl off of his lap last night like she was nothing but a clingy housecat he was finished paying attention to.

"Oh . . . has he hooked up with girls since you've been with him?"

"No, but there were a bunch all over him last night."

"And? What happened?"

"He . . ." Okay, this is going to sound so much more

significant than it really was. "He kind of ditched them to hang out with me."

"WHAT!"

"Because we're friends! I felt totally out of place, and I think he could tell."

In a singsong voice, Dee says, "He liiikes you!"

I shake my head. "I mean, yeah, I guess I could probably hook up with him if I wanted to. He doesn't exactly have high standards . . . But he's not looking for a relationship, Dee. And neither am I, but I'm not looking for a one-night stand either. Especially not after . . ." I let the sentence hang, and she sighs, knowing exactly what I was going to say.

"Is he still calling you?" We're not talking about Adam anymore.

"Yeah . . . I told him we'd talk soon. Probably this week."

I can tell Dee is being deliberately careful about what she says next. Since stealing my phone and telling Brady off on our way back from fall break, she has definitely toned down her bossiness. "What are you going to say?"

"I don't know yet. I'll figure it out when I see him."

"You're not thinking of going back to him, are you?"

"I don't think so . . ."

"You don't *think* so?"

"We have a lot of history, Dee. I just . . . I'm just going to talk to him and figure things out. But I'm not stupid. You know that, so just trust me."

She sighs, and there's a long moment of silence before I ask, "So have I missed anything good since I left?"

"Carrie came by to officially kick you out of our room." She scoffs, and I roll my eyes at the mention of her RA. "You should have seen her face when you weren't here. She gave Macy and me an official written warning, but I'm not worried."

An official written warning? I frown. "What will happen if I keep staying there? What did the warning say?"

"Don't worry about it, Ro. She's just a bitch who has nothing better to do than harass people who actually have *friends*."

"I need to look into getting an apartment . . ."

"Can you afford that?"

I'm silent, because we both know the answer is no, and there's no way I'm asking my parents for more money.

"Maybe you can stay with Leti a few nights a week . . ."

"Yeah, maybe," I agree, but I don't mean it. I'm tired of being a burden on my friends, so I need to figure something else out. Soon. "Are you nervous about work tomorrow?"

"Nah," she says. "I'm ready to start raking in those tips! I'll even take you and lover boy out for drinks when you get back!" I'm chuckling when she says, "OH! And guess who I went out with last night!"

"Who?"

She tells me the guy's name, but I don't bother committing it to memory since in two weeks, she probably won't remember it either. By the time she's finished gushing, it's almost time for the concert to start. I brush the tangles from my hair and toss it up into a messy bun, and then I change into a pair of tighter jeans and freshen my lip gloss. When I step off the bus, locking the door behind me, I'm surprised to find Adam leaning against the siding with one leg propped against the black metal and a lit cigarette dangling from the hand hanging by his hip. He takes one last drag and smashes it when he sees me, walking over and draping his arm across my shoulders.

"What are you still doing here?" I ask, looking way up to meet his gray-green eyes. That night at Mayhem, I'd been wearing skyscraper heels. Without them, he towers over me. "I thought you were heading in to get ready."

"And be *on time*?" He scoffs and smiles down at me. "I'd rather walk you in."

Adam had a few drinks before he left the bus, and I can smell them on his breath, the smoky scent of the whiskey mixing with his cologne. When he walks me to the front of the line and we slip inside with his arm still around me, earning envious stares from every girl we pass, I find myself repeating a familiar mantra.

Don't fall for Adam. Don't fall for Adam. Don't fall for Adam freaking Everest.

He leads me backstage and I hang with the band until they take the stage. Then I stand with Driver and watch as they perform. Girls scream their heads off after every song, and by the third, I find myself joining them. Adam hears me and spins around, flashing me that smooth pearly-white grin that turns my insides into funfetti pudding. In spite of my blushing, I cup my hands over my mouth and scream even louder. I look over at Mike behind the drums, who laughs at me before he starts the beat to the next song. The guys are absolutely amazing, and when Adam and Shawn both sing at once, finishing each other's lines and singing over each other, it gives me goose bumps all over. Shawn's voice is lower than Adam's, but they work together perfectly. Shawn, Joel, and Cody all have quick fingers as they strum their guitars effortlessly, and Mike on the drums is as hectic and controlled as ever. I wonder if Adam would consider me a good enough friend to let me come backstage even after this trip . . . I'd love for Dee and Leti to be able to see this.

When the band ends its set, they're all drenched in sweat. Adam walks over to me and lifts his arm like he's going to rest his elbow on my shoulder, but I quickly step out of reach. When he gives me a look, I tell him, "You are *soaked*."

His eyes drop to his sweaty shirt, and then they lift back up filled with trouble and bad ideas. "Aw, c'mon, you're not afraid of a little hard-earned sweat are you?" He takes a threatening step toward me, and I take a matched step backward, throwing my hands up in self-defense.

"Don't you dare!"

His eyes dart to a spot over my shoulder, and I'm about to turn around to see what he's looking at, when long arms suddenly encircle me. Big green eyes meet mine from under short black hair—Shawn. Before I can wiggle out of his hold, Adam presses against my front, squeezing me into a sweaty Shawn-and-Adam sandwich.

"EW!" I squeal, cringing and trying to make myself paper-thin to escape their sweat-dampened T-shirts. But then another molten-hot body is pressing against my side.

Mike's arms wrap around Shawn's and Adam's shoulders. He smiles down at me and says, "I heard you have a thing for secondhand sweat."

"NO!"

Joel squeezes in on the other side. "Mike! I heard that too!" They're all laughing as I try to make myself as small as possible. I'm not trying to squirm out from between them because then I'd just end up getting even sweatier. They're all so tall, I doubt anyone looking at us from the outside would even be able to see me standing here helplessly in the middle. Eventually, I drop to the floor and crawl out from between someone's legs, sliding over to Driver and jumping up behind him. I grab onto his shoulders to use him as a shield.

The guys laugh as he tries to get away from me and I hold on tight, practically strangling him with the collar of his own T-shirt. When they finally go back to gulping down water and toweling themselves off, I release Driver and give him a sheepish smile before I take a seat next to Cody on the stairs. He's pouring water on a towel and rubbing it over his face and head. Cody and I haven't shared more than a few words, but I think that's because he's much quieter than the other guys. "You guys sounded really good tonight," I tell him, hoping to spark a conversation.

He smiles over at me. "Thanks."

"Is everyone planning on going back to the bus after this?"

"Hey Shawn!" Cody yells, interrupting the conversation that Shawn, Adam, and Driver are having. "Are we going out or staying in?" Like dominos, Shawn looks to Adam and Adam looks to me. Slowly, his lips curl into a smile, and then he's grinning at me like a Cheshire cat—one with *very* bad ideas.

Chapter Fifteen

"OUT" IS REALLY just a dive-bar across the street from the venue—which goes from being crowded to being *unbelievably* crowded when the band and their entourage walk through its doors, followed by masses of concertgoers.

Adam's hand stays glued to my lower back as he leads me to the only open bar stool, sitting me on top of it and standing behind me. He orders a round of shots for everyone in our group, and then he asks me if I've ever done a tequila shot before.

I shake my head. "Nope."

"You'll have to let me show you how then," he says near my ear.

If he thinks I'm letting him slurp tequila out of my belly button, he's got another thing coming. I turn around, prepared to tell him so, when I come face to face with the group of girls who have sidled up next to him.

"Hi," the clear leader of the harem says to him. She has long midnight-black hair that is curled to perfection, with thick fake eyelashes that she's batting for no reason, since Adam isn't even looking at her. When he finally notices she's talking to him, he turns to her and smiles.

"Hi."

"We just came from your show," she says with a seductive smile. "You were *so* amazing. I love the way you sing."

"Thanks," he says in that smooth voice of his. He doesn't look ruffled at all by all the heat she's throwing at him. I guess he must be used to it.

When our shots appear in front of me, I pick mine up and down it before Adam even has a chance to see they've arrived. He's still chatting with the black-haired hussy, and I need the liquor like I need air. I'm tempted to gulp his down too but decide that might be a little much. At some point in the conversation, Adam's eyes travel to our shot glasses, to my empty one, to me. He interrupts the girl mid-sentence to ask me, "You already drank yours?!"

I chuckle at his horrified expression. "Sorry."

"That's not how you do a tequila shot!"

"Oh!" the girl next to him says. "I *love* tequila." Her hazel eyes swing to me and she smiles. "You've never done a shot before?"

Before I can answer, she says, "Here, let me show you."

She takes a lime wedge in one hand and one of her friends' wrists in the other, sensually licking the pale skin there before covering the area with salt. She places the lime wedge between her friend's teeth—a short girl with a peroxide-blonde pixie haircut—and then her tongue glides provocatively over the salt on the girl's wrist. She swallows Adam's shot and then bites the wedge from her friend's mouth as sluttily as humanly possible.

I roll my eyes, but no one catches it. Adam is thoroughly engrossed with the spectacle in front of him, which makes my blood boil. "Lovely," I complain.

He peels his eyes away to give me a devilish smile. "Want to try?" I narrow my eyes at him, and he laughs. "Come on. It'd be fun."

I'm looking at the black-haired bimbo when I say, "Pass."

Adam leans in close, whispering in my ear. "Not with them."

"Rowan!" Shawn suddenly shouts from behind me, weaving his way through the crowd to stand next to Adam. "What are you drinking there?" He looks down at my empty shot glass and then smiles at me. "Schnapps? Peach?"

I ignore his stupid implication and hop off the stool, grabbing his elbow. "Play a game of pool with me." I need to get away from Adam before I lick him from head to toe, and away from his whores before I claw their eyes out.

Shawn leads me to the pool tables, where Cody and Joel are already mid-game. "Who's winning?" I ask, vaguely noticing that Adam has followed us—and so has his glitter-fueled convoy of girls. They blend in with the groupies already here watching Cody and Joel. Mike is standing off to the side with a beer, and even he has a girl trying—and failing—to get his attention. He's ignoring her like it's his job, standing with his arms crossed and his shoulder against a wooden pillar. When he hears me ask who's winning, he walks over to stand next to me.

"Cody," he says, "but they both suck ass."

I laugh, watching them both miss shot after shot until a waitress comes over to ask if we need any drinks. When Mike asks me what I want and tells me it's all going on the band's tab, I order a Long Island iced tea, desperately needing a liquid-induced buffer between me and all the pheromones in the air.

When a pool table opens up, I grab a stick and call to Shawn, "You ready?"

He shakes his head, chatting up a girl standing next to him. "I suck! Play Adam!"

Adam immediately steps away from the cluster of girls to grab a pool stick. Chalking it, he sheepishly says, "I'm really terrible at this game."

"You can't be as bad as Cody and Joel," I joke.

"What about you?" he asks, brushing his hair from his eyes. "You any good?"

"Not really," I lie.

"Then we should make this interesting."

I hold back a smile. It's already getting interesting. "What do you have in mind?"

"If I win, you have to do a body shot with me. Give or take, doesn't matter."

"And if I win?"

"What do you want?" He busies himself with racking the balls.

I think about it for a long time, and then a smile curls

my lips. "You have to get all the way through chapter seven tomorrow, even if that means studying after the show."

"That's four chapters!"

I smirk at him. "Take it or leave it."

He licks his lips as he thinks about it. "Can I at least break?"

"Sure," I say with an easy smile. Breaking or not, he's going down.

Adam leans over the table, aiming his shot. A confident grin lifts his eyes to mine. "You're on." He hits the cue ball hard and balls scatter all over the table, two immediately tumbling into pockets. His shot was so smooth, I can immediately tell he was lying about not being any good.

"Rowan!" Shawn laughs as Adam takes his next shot. "He's totally swindling you! Adam grew up with a pool table."

When Adam takes another shot and misses, I step to the cue ball and grin at Shawn. "So did I." I lean over the table and take my shot, sending my target sailing smoothly into a corner pocket. Everyone watches the red ball roll in, and then the guys immediately break into fits of laughter. Adam looks absolutely dumbstruck as I circle around the table, lining up my next shot and taking that one just as flawlessly.

"My dad got a pool table when I was eight," I say, sinking my third ball. "And I'm an only child, so we played together—a *lot*." I smirk up at Adam, who still looks like he thinks he might be dreaming. "Sorry, Adam, but you never stood a chance."

I'm sitting at the bar with Adam later when he whines from the stool beside me, "You're not seriously going to make me study after the show tomorrow, are you?"

I grin down at my drink, trying to ignore the girl standing behind him massaging his shoulders. She has long pink hair—pink, for God's sake—and she's wearing a toddler-sized halter top and a doll-sized skirt. I'm about to reply, when she circles around him and sits on his lap. "What are you studying for?"

"French," he groans.

"Oooh, I love French," she says, playing with his hair. I somehow resist the urge to bat her fingers away. "Say something to me in French."

Adam thinks about it for a moment, and then with a big smile, he looks up at her and says, "*Tu parles trop.*"

I bite back a snicker, raising my fingers to my mouth to keep from spitting my drink out as the girl squeals with delight and asks Adam what he said. He looks at me, the corners of his mouth twitching, and I can tell he's trying not to laugh. I can't very well tell her he said she talks too much, can I? Adam chuckles, and I realize he's not going to answer her, which makes this situation now incredibly uncomfortable.

"He said you're very pretty," I tell the girl, to fill his silence, and she blushes and plants a kiss on his cheek.

Adam grins at me. "*Tu es une . . .*" He leans in to whisper in my ear. "What's the word for 'big fat liar'?"

I laugh as he leans back, and the girl smiles at us, oblivious. "*Menteuse,*" I tell him.

"*Tu es une menteuse.*" He shakes his head and clucks his tongue against his teeth. "Tsk, tsk."

I playfully roll my eyes at him and spin back to the bar, ordering another drink. When Shawn comes by to ask me if I'm ready for that game of pool, I follow him to the pool tables at the other side of the room, leaving Adam with a girl on his lap, a cigarette in his hand, and a drink on the counter in front of him.

Shawn and I weave through the crowd, passing by Joel—whose blond mohawk makes him easy to spot standing by a pillar, making out with some brunette— and Driver, who is smoking something that smells especially suspicious. When we get to the open table, which Mike is standing by to hold for us, I pick up a stick and chalk it. "So what changed your mind?" I ask Shawn, wondering why he's finally decided to play with me.

"How many drinks have you had?"

I hold up three fingers, and then I raise my eyes to the wooden ceiling as I think about it, and I slowly lift my pinky finger too. He laughs.

"That's why. Maybe I'll actually stand a chance now."

Mike shouts back to us as he walks to the bar, "I wouldn't count on it!"

I laugh and nod my thanks to him as he disappears into the crowd. When Shawn finishes racking the balls, he stands back and says, "Alright, your break, Peach."

My eyes dart nervously to every face around us, but no one else seems to have heard or noticed. I glare at Shawn and walk over to him to line up my shot. "I'm going to kick your ass for that," I mutter as I lean over the table.

He laughs. "You were going to do that anyway."

After knocking a ball into a corner pocket on my break, I stand up and grin at him. "True story."

I walk to the side of the table closest to the wall to line up my second shot, which means I can see Adam across the room. There's a new girl already in my seat chatting him up, the old one is still on his lap, and another has her hand on his shoulder. I take my shot and completely botch it, cursing under my breath.

Shawn laughs. "Okay, or not."

As we play, I grow increasingly frustrated, because I am *seriously* sucking ass. I'm not sure if it's because of the drinks or because of the sluts, but I can't concentrate at all. Shawn walks over to stand next to me, staring at Adam, who is whispering in some girl's ear. "You know, I don't think he'd be paying any attention to them if you were still over there."

It irritates me that he's observant enough to know what's throwing me off my game. I scoff and say, "He doesn't need to babysit me."

Shawn gives me a weird look. "That's not what I meant . . ."

"Just take your shot, Shawn."

He stares at me for a moment longer before shrugging and leaning over the table, sinking a ball in a side pocket.

I win the game, but I swear it's because he let me. He probably feels sorry for me. Glancing at Adam, who is currently laughing with his own personal harem of giggling slutbags, I'm suddenly not really feeling this bar. I gaze up at Shawn and Mike, who are chatting in front of me. "I think I'm gonna get out of here."

"Aw, come on," Shawn says. "You weren't *that* bad. You wiped the floor with me!"

I force a smile. "It's not that. I'm just tired. I can't keep up with you guys."

Mike wraps his arm around my shoulders. "I'll walk you back."

Inside the bus, he immediately sits down in front of the TV and grabs a controller from the tangle of wires in the entertainment stand. He asks me if I want to play, but I pass and head upstairs to get ready for bed. I wash my face, brush my hair, and change into silky pajama pants and a clean tank top. When I walk back to my bunk, which someone has kindly made for me, I stare down at it with dread. I wasn't lying when I told Shawn I was tired. I feel like I haven't slept a wink in the past forty-eight hours, and the long drives in the warm sun and the alcohol-fueled nights with the band are catching up with me. Another night of Joel's snoring might very well kill me—and I *definitely* won't be able to pull a marathon tutoring session with Adam tomorrow.

My eyes drift to the closed door of the back room, and then, with a heavy sigh, I enter it. I move all of my things to a corner of the room and crawl under the black satin covers. The sheets are chilly, which feels amazing against my liquor-heated skin. I bury my face in a soft plush pillow, which smells deliciously like Adam, and fall asleep wondering if he's noticed I've left yet or not.

Chapter Sixteen

I'M SLEEPING WHEN I feel the bed shift. The covers lift, and then there's a weight behind me. It settles close, and I vaguely realize that it's Adam. It smells like cigarettes and a stronger version of the faded cologne still lingering my pillow. Sleep has almost pulled me back under when I feel something warm press against my shoulder. Something wet.

Adam kisses my shoulder and traces his tongue up the curve of my neck.

"Adam," I say quietly, still not quite awake. The four drinks I had are keeping me in a fog. "Don't."

"Why?" he replies just as quietly, kissing my neck again.

"We're friends."

His soft fingers trail lightly up my arm, giving me goose bumps all over as he plants soft kisses against my sensitive skin. "Really, really *good* friends."

I giggle and roll away, onto my stomach. With my cheek smushed against the pillow, I gaze over at his gorgeous moonlit face and let out a deep breath. "I like you."

He props himself on his elbow and reaches over to brush the heel of his thumb sensually over my lips, freezing me in place. "I like you too," he says, and then he drops his hand to the pillow before I find the strength to pull away from him.

I don't know what I would have done if he hadn't stopped touching me just now . . . What would I have done? Probably something stupid. Something really, really stupid. Frowning at him, I say, "Then let's not ruin things, okay? I don't want to mess around with you and have to hate you in the morning." And I mean it. Adam wouldn't think much of hooking up with me tonight, but I would. And then he'd get over it, and I wouldn't.

"I don't want that either . . ." He stares at me for a long moment. His grayish green eyes are impossible to look away from. "Okay," he says, leaning down to kiss my shoulder one last time, even more softly than before. And then he rolls away from me. I'm not sure if I just did the right thing, but I know *he* did.

"Thank you, Adam."

"Don't thank me yet. There's still a few hours 'til sunrise and I'm pretty sure I'm not going to fall asleep now."

I chuckle and flip away from him, onto my side. "Sweet dreams."

I feel the bed shift as he rolls back toward me. Knowing he's right behind me is bittersweet torture, but soon, his breathing gets heavy, and eventually, mine does too.

The next morning, something is tickling my face. I smack it away, almost back asleep when it feathers across my cheek again. I crack one eye open and see Adam's smiling face right in front of mine. His lips are stretched excitedly over his pearly teeth, his eyes sparkling with amusement. He's crouched next to my side of the bed, looking freshly shaved and showered, his hair still damp. He smells like expensive body wash and a morning cigarette, and I bury my face in the pillow to hide the smile threatening to reveal how girly he makes me feel.

"Good morning," he says.

When my cheeks are under control, I turn back to him. "Good morning."

"You ready?"

"Ready for what?" I ask, hoping the answer doesn't have anything to do with what he started last night.

Adam stands up to sit on the edge of the bed, practically on top of me. The covers pull tight against my body, and he rests his arm on the opposite side of me. "Studying!"

"Seriously?" I groan. "What time is it?"

"Time to get started!" When I give him a look, he laughs and says, "It's eight."

"Shouldn't you be sleeping in until . . . I don't know, noon or something?" Shawn made it sound like Adam was a late-riser, and after Adam threatened to punch me in my nonexistent dick for waking him up yesterday, I'm more than a little surprised to see him up so early.

"Yes, I really should." He shifts, his hand moving closer, squeezing my hips between his arm and the rest of him. "But there's no way you're going to get me to study after the show. No offense, but . . . it's just not going to happen. So you had better tutor the hell out of me while you have the chance."

At least he's being proactive. "Can I at least take a shower?"

"Make it quick," he says, echoing my sentiment to him yesterday morning. He winks at me. "We have four chapters to get through."

Adam and I are the only two people awake, so when I enter the hallway, I try to be as quiet as possible. I tiptoe between the bunks, but Adam makes an intentional racket, smacking at arms and legs that are hanging out of covers. He hops in bed with Shawn, snuggling his arm around him and saying "Oh SHAWN!" in a girl's voice. I giggle at them as I quicken my step to get to the shower before all hell breaks loose. Is it possible to beat someone to death with pillows and blankets? Because I'm pretty sure Adam is about to find out . . .

When I step into the shower, the bathroom is still hot with steam and the scent of Adam's body wash is still permeating the air. It smells like midnight—like loud music, hazy vision, and laser lights. Showering in here with him all around me feels kind of strange and . . . intimate. Brady's body wash never flooded the room like Adam's does.

I wash up quickly and dress in red leggings, a long black top, and my black sandals. Then I put on a little makeup—not too much—before sliding my glasses on. I'm pulling my wet hair up into a messy bun when I walk from the bathroom and spot Adam and Shawn sitting at one of the bench-seat tables. Shawn is sipping a coffee, scrolling through his phone, and Adam is scribbling in a pocket-sized notebook that I've seen him jotting in a few times throughout the trip. When he hears me, his eyes lift and he smiles. "That was *not* quick."

"That was *so* quick!" I argue.

"I don't know," Shawn teases. "Adam is kind of an authority on quick."

Adam doesn't miss a beat. "Did your mom tell you that?"

"Oooh!" I say, sitting down next to Adam and smiling widely at Shawn, who laughs and shakes his head at us as he goes back to scrolling through his phone.

I grab our French textbook from the table and slide it in front of me, asking Adam if he remembers what page we stopped on, but then his hand is commandeering the book and pulling it back his way. "Not here," he says.

"Huh?"

"We're going out."

O . . . kay. "Where to?"

Adam stands up, looking down at me. "Not sure yet." He starts walking toward the door to the bus, and I glance at Shawn, who is texting with one hand and sipping his coffee with the other. His short black hair is a mess, and it looks like he slept in the same clothes he wore last night and hasn't bothered changing into clean ones yet.

"You coming?" I ask him.

He looks from me to Adam and shakes his head. "Nope." When his eyes fall back to me, he gives me a wink that Adam doesn't see, and I know it was meant for Peach. With a quirky grin on his face, he tells me to have fun, and then he goes back to doing whatever it is he's doing.

I follow Adam off the bus and to his car. "So seriously, where are we going?"

He shrugs. "I seriously don't know."

I climb into the passenger seat a second before the engine roars to life. Adam's arm stretches behind my headrest as he backs out of the spot, and then we're pulling onto the main drag through town. "How are we supposed to get where we're going if you have no idea where you want to go?"

He chuckles and randomly turns right. "We'll manage. Stop worrying."

"Well, what are we trying to find?"

"Some place to have breakfast. Some place . . . Frenchy."

I have to laugh at that. "Frenchy?"

Adam grins at me, the strong breeze blowing strands of hair across his face. "Yeah. I need some inspiration if we're going to knock that many chapters out."

I spot a bistro up the street to our left and point it out. "What about that place?" It's a small brick building with a green-and-white striped awning and two tiny tables set up out front.

Adam's gaze travels the direction of my finger, and then he shakes his head. "That looks Italian." He turns left.

"French places probably aren't even open this early."

"Then we're going to be driving a long time." He turns up the radio just loud enough so we can hear it, not bothering to plug his phone in, and starts scanning through the stations.

Since it doesn't look or sound like he's joking, I open our textbook and start quizzing him as we drive. By the time he pulls into a parking lot and coasts into an open spot, we're nearly finished with the first chapter.

I look up and immediately start laughing. "IHOP?"

Adam leans back in the seat. "Do they or do they not have French toast?"

I laugh and shake my head. "They have the best French toast ever."

"Then it's settled." He shuts the car off, and we both get out.

Inside, he orders two different kinds of French toast and a crepe for good measure. I stick to my standard strawberry pancakes.

"Do you know where we could have gone instead?" I ask. When he waits for my answer, I tease, "McDonald's. We could've gotten French fries."

"Don't be ridiculous . . . Everyone knows McDonald's doesn't start serving fries 'til ten thirty." He smirks at me, and I laugh.

"You're kinda crazy," I tell him with a smile.

"Says the girl who came along on a three-day road trip with ten guys she'd never even met before."

It isn't exactly true, but the truth is even crazier. "Touché."

And thus begins our French lesson. I open the textbook and do a little review before saying, "Okay. We need to practice some of the written stuff . . . aaand we forgot to bring a notebook."

"No, we didn't." Adam wiggles the miniature notebook that I saw him writing in this morning out of his back pocket.

"*That* is your notebook?"

He nods and sips a coffee our server brought earlier. It's something French vanilla, and I highly suspect—no, I *know* that he ordered it just because it had "French" in the name.

"You use that for class?" I ask.

He nods again. I hold my palm out for the notebook, and he hands it over.

When I open it, I see that it's almost completely filled with scribbled lines. Lyrics. There are random phrases everywhere, written in varied sizes and slants—almost none of them actually following the lines of the paper. "There aren't any notes in here," I say as I flip through the pages.

"Sure there are." Adam takes the notebook back and flips through it before he finally finds what he's looking for. He slides it over to me. "See?"

The note—literally, just one—says to finish the homework on page 82 for Monday—which, if I remember correctly, means that it's more than two weeks old.

"Did you?" I ask Adam as I hand back his notebook.

"Did I what?" He flips to a blank page.

"Finish the homework?"

He hesitates before saying, "That's not the point."

I immediately start laughing again, and he grins at me. "I think we need to get you a new notebook."

"Or a cute note taker," he says with a smirk, and I scoff. "As if those girls would actually know how to take good notes." I'd be impressed if the girls he sits with in class even know how to read.

"What girls?" He looks thoroughly confused, his eyebrows scrunched together over eyes locked with mine.

"Those girls you always bring with you to class."

He laughs and scratches the back of his head. "I don't *bring* them. They just kind of follow me."

I want to comment on how unbothered he seems about that, but I bite my tongue, dropping the conversation and resuming the lesson. I assign Adam written exercises, and eventually, I slide into the booth seat beside him so I can show him exactly what he's doing wrong. When the server brings our food and sets it in front of us, I quickly move back to my side and pull my plate in front of me.

Adam is eyeing me curiously when I glance up at him. "What's your deal?" he asks me.

"What do you mean?"

He looks at our server, an elderly woman who is now helping a family of four sitting three tables down, and then back at me. "Why'd you dive back over there?"

I don't really know how to answer that. Because I'm getting way too cozy with you and I'm pretty sure your absence is going to feel like a giant gaping hole in my life when I have to get back to reality?

Adam sighs and sets his fork back down. "Look, if this is about last night—"

"It's not."

"I'm sorry. I'd had a lot to drink, and then you were in the room and I just thought—"

"Adam, it's not that. It's cool, alright?"

He frowns like he doesn't believe me. "Then what is it?"

"You don't think it would be weird if we sat on the same side?"

His head tilts slightly. "Why would it be weird?"

"It'd look like we were dating or something . . ."

"So?"

"So . . . I don't know."

"So what you're saying is you have no good reason?" A one-sided smile is sneaking onto his lips, making me feel a strange mix of emotions. Embarrassment and . . . something I don't want to think too hard about.

"I'm sure I have a good reason . . . I just can't think of it right now."

Adam laughs and picks his fork back up. "Then I think you should get back over here."

"Why?"

"Why not?"

I don't answer him. Because again, I have no idea what the hell to say to that. Instead, I busy myself with drenching my pancakes. I stir a mountain of sugar into my coffee as I let the syrup soak in, and then I pour another layer on. When Adam cuts off portions of both of his French toast piles and his crepe and slides them onto my plate, I cut off a big chunk of my pancakes and slide them onto his.

He smiles down at the pancakes as he carves into them. "The guys really like you."

The compliment makes me blush. I'm glad they don't hate me. "They're pretty awesome."

Adam takes a bite of my condiment-logged breakfast and chuckles with his mouth full. "Holy shit, this is syrupy."

I grin at him. "Only way to have it." While he's swallowing it down with a big gulp of coffee, I tell him, "My friend Dee and I eat at IHOP a lot. We always get the strawberry pancakes. And if we're hungover, we order them with sides of bacon, and she always tries to steal mine."

Adam starts cutting into a second bite. "Really? It happens enough that you have a routine set up?"

Okay . . . I *really* need to stop opening my big mouth. I attempt a casual shrug. "I guess. She's kind of a wild child. We've been friends since . . . well . . . forever." I hope that changing the focus from me to Dee will help steer this conversation away from drunken nights, one of which was notably spent with a very hot rocker boy who is currently sitting across from me paying nerve-racking attention to my every ill-conceived word.

"Shawn and I are kind of like that." Finally, a topic I'm comfortable with. The muscles in my shoulders immediately loosen, and I forgive Shawn for all of the stupid "Peach" comments he made yesterday.

"Yeah, I can tell you two have been friends for a long time. What about the other guys?"

"Shawn and I have been friends with Mike since middle school, and friends with Joel since high school when he moved to town. Cody is his stepdad's brother's cousin-in-law's son or some shit like that. He joined when we started getting big. Before that, it was just the four of us."

I nod and dig into Adam's blueberry French toast, which is pure amazingness. "He's kinda quiet."

"It's better that way. When he's not, he's usually saying something stupid."

I chuckle, remembering how Cody asked me how it felt to be the "only girl to turn Adam down." God, that had been awkward.

Adam adds, "He's cool for the most part though."

Really, they all are. Even the roadies seem great, especially Driver—even though his extracurricular activities leave something to be desired. Our server pops back in to ask if we need anything else, but so far, breakfast has been perfect. When she leaves, Adam slides from his booth seat to mine, pulling his plate over. I swallow hard and watch him. He's so freaking close. "Yes?"

He slides the textbook and notebook over without taking his eyes off mine. He looks far too amused. "We need to get back to work."

Oh, right. I flip to the page we were on and get back to it. By the time we're both finished with our meals, we've pounded through two whole chapters. We order more coffee and stay until we've gotten most of the way through the third, but I'm distracted. There is now a group of girls our age sitting two tables down, and they've been stealing glances at Adam for the past twenty minutes. Every time they look our way, I find myself glaring. If we weren't sitting on the same side of the table—looking utterly couple-ish—I don't doubt they would have come over to get his number, his home address, and his dick size for future convenience-store shopping purposes. I don't know if they keep staring because they recognize him or because of the whole sexy bad-boy vibe he gives off, but either way, it's getting under my skin.

When Adam shifts toward me in the seat, resting his knee between us, I'm distracted from my scowling. I give him my attention, and he brushes a loose strand of hair away from my face.

"What are you doing?" I ask, not stopping him.

He smiles warmly at me, but there's mischief in his eyes. "Don't you want to make them jealous?"

More than anything. "Why would I want to make them jealous?"

Adam snickers. "*All* girls want to make other girls jealous."

No arguing there. I let him play with my hair until he starts to lean in, and my eyes get wide. He doesn't go for my mouth though—he whispers in my ear. "Relax. I'm not going to kiss you. Just play along."

Adam kisses a spot next to my ear tenderly, and I don't know how he classifies this as not kissing—because I am definitely feeling *thoroughly* kissed. He marks a two-kiss trail along my jaw and then looks into my eyes as he comes in close. His lips are warm against my skin when he presses them against the outermost corner of my mouth in an agonizingly soft and teasing kiss.

My eyes close because I'm helpless to stop what happens to my body. My breathing stops, my heart stops.

Every ounce of energy I have is poured into *not* turning into the kiss. Because God, I *really* want to. I want to so bad it almost hurts. I should. I should just—

When Adam slowly pulls away, I open my eyes to find him smirking, and I feel self-conscious as hell. I try to control the breath I've been holding so that it doesn't come out in a humiliating sigh.

"Look," he says quietly, referring to the girls.

I peel my eyes away from Adam and look over to their table to find them frozen like statues, all four of them gawking at us. One literally has her mouth hanging open. They look away in a hurry, and I immediately start giggling. "Wow." I don't know if I'm referring to the effect we had on them or the kiss itself. My blood is still lava, struggling to pump oxygen to my brain.

Adam is serious when he says, "We could make them *more* jealous if you want . . ."

I chuckle nervously because yes, I *do* want to make them more jealous. I want to make them more jealous . . . in the privacy of a bedroom . . . where they aren't even present to witness how jealous we're making them.

I flip to the next page of the textbook and try to say in an even voice, "Time to move on to irregular verbs." I try to get my mind off of that non-kiss as Adam and I work our way through the third chapter, but I think it may have been the hottest kiss I've ever had in my entire life. Is that even possible?

I throw myself into teacher mode to try to calm myself down, and forty-five minutes later, the tingling memory of Adam's lips has finally faded from my nerves. When we're all the way through the third chapter, we decide to head back to his car.

"If you were this motivated in class," I chide after Adam insists on paying the check and we're walking out the door, "you'd pull straight A's."

"If classes were like this study session, maybe I'd be more motivated." He lights a cigarette as we walk, and then he slides his shades on and climbs behind the wheel. I rest my elbow on the door and let the wind wash over me as he speeds through the city streets. The sun is clinging to the last remnants of summer, heating my skin and beating into my eyes. I pull my glasses off since I'm fairly certain they're magnifying the sun's hellfire rays and scorching them right into my pupils.

Holding my hand over my forehead, I turn to Adam and ask, "Do you have an extra pair of shades?"

He stares over at me for a long moment, and then he takes his off and hands them to me. "Nope."

Crap, I didn't mean to put him on the spot or anything. Pushing them back toward his chest, I insist, "No, no. Don't worry about it."

"I'm *not* worried about it." He smiles and tosses them onto my lap. "They'll look better on you anyway."

Okay, I really need to get this blushing thing under control. "Thanks," I tell him, picking up his glasses and sliding them on. Parts of them are still warm from where they were snug against his skin, and I have to remind myself that friends do stuff like this all the time. Sharing his sunglasses is no big deal. No. Big. Thing.

I look at myself in the side-view mirror and chuckle. Turning to him, I ask, "How do I look?"

Adam gazes over at me, and the corner of his mouth pulls up in a grin. "*Tu sembles chaud.*"

I'm helpless to stop the giggle that escapes my mouth. *Adam Everest just said I look hot.* He smiles appreciatively at me.

"*Merci,*" I finally manage, and he winks at me, which nearly makes me giggle all over again. Who *is* this girl and why won't she get out of my body?!

"You ready to get started on that fourth chapter?" he asks after I've been staring out the open window long enough to get a grip on my ditzy alter ego.

I recline my seat and sink into it, whining, "Do we have to?" We've been studying in IHOP for almost three hours straight, and even though we're making good time and Adam is really like some sort of damn prodigy with all the progress he's making, I'm getting *really* tired of staring at that blasted textbook.

He shrugs. "I'm cool with not studying if you are, but I'm legally obligated to inform you that by refusing to tutor me, you will no longer reserve the right to hold me to the terms of our wager."

I groan. "Okay, we'll study. Give me . . . half an hour."

I lay my head against the headrest and inhale a deep breath of muggy afternoon air. It smells like asphalt and the decay of summer. Fall has been slow in getting here this year, but the October leaves are finally beginning to change color in spite of today's vengeful heat.

When Adam plugs his phone into the radio and hands it to me, I scroll through the song list to find instrumental versions of his band's music and pick a song that has a familiar title. When it plays through the speakers, I turn my head to him. "Sing for me again?"

He glances at me out of the corner of his eye, and then I watch as a bad idea curls the corner of his mouth. "Let's make a trade."

Uh-oh . . . "What kind of trade?"

"I'll sing you a song if you do a tequila shot with me tonight."

I shake my head. "No deal."

"Aw, come on! Why not?" He looks over at me, an indignant sparkle in his eyes.

I shrug. "Not a fair trade." Do a body shot with Adam Everest? Uh, yeah, it would be more than a fair trade. Girls would trample each other for the opportunity. Hell, maybe that's what Leti's dream had been about. Maybe it was a psychic vision.

I can't tell Adam that the real reason I won't do shots with him is because every time his lips are on me, I never want him to take them off. And if I put mine on him . . . I honestly can't even predict what would come of that. Probably Dee's dream come true. Unfortunately, my answer only encourages him.

"Alright, what do you want then?" he asks.

I chuckle and shake my head.

"Come on, just name it!"

"I don't want anything!"

"You have to want *something.*"

I pick up Adam's phone and change it to the noninstrumental version. His voice sings through the speakers, and I grin at him triumphantly.

But he's smiling right back. "Not what you really wanted though, is it?"

I huff and turn the radio down, and he laughs at me.

"I'll think about it," I say, pulling my phone from a cup holder so I can check my messages.

"Think about what you want, or think about doing a shot with me?"

"Both."

I'm not crazy—I'm so not going to think about it.

When I turn on my phone, I have texts from Dee and Leti, but none from Brady. I'm thankful this is one of the few days that he hasn't messaged me first thing in the morning—because today has been good so far and I really want to keep it that way.

Dee texted me a few times to "check the status" of my "imminent deflowering." I text her back to let her know that my daisies remain unplucked and healthy as ever, and to wish her good luck on her first day at the new job.

Leti texted me to let me know that he had another dream about Adam. In this one, I was apparently sitting on Adam's lap in French class telling him everything I wanted for Christmas, and Leti was pissed as hell because he had been in line to sit on Adam's lap first.

While reading his text, I bust up laughing so hard that tears pour from my eyes, and Adam turns a curious glance in my direction. Leti's next message asks me to send him another picture of Adam today to make up for my "bitch-slap-worthy line-cutting" last night. After I finish my hysterical laughing, I ask Adam if I can take another picture of him for a friend of mine.

"Only if you do a tequila shot with me tonight," he replies matter-of-factly.

I roll my eyes and tell him what I'm texting to Leti as I type it into my phone.

Sorry, but his highness Adam Everest is being a total freaking diva today.

Adam chuckles. "Tell your friend why I won't let you. Let's see whose side they're on then."

God, I can just imagine how that conversation would go. Dee would probably quit her new job just so she and Leti could drive all the way out to the next venue and hold me down while Adam licked salt off my stomach.

On second thought . . . telling them might not be such a bad idea.

"Time's up," Adam says, and I glance at the digital time on the radio. My half hour went way too fast. I sigh and grab the textbook from where I threw it into the backseat, and we immediately get back to work.

Chapter Seventeen

TWO HOURS LATER I slap the book closed, and Adam raises his eyebrow at me. "That's all she wrote," I say.

"We're done?"

I nod. "Yep. Except for practicing the written stuff."

"We'll have some time before the show."

"Sounds good." I smile over at him. "Congrats."

Adam reaches over and squeezes my shoulder. "Couldn't have done it without you, you know."

"Oh, believe me," I chuckle, "I know."

A smile stays on his lips as he asks, "Are you going to help me study for the rest of the semester?"

Are we seriously making plans for the future?! My feet twitch in anticipation of the nerdy dance I'd be doing if Adam wasn't sitting right next to me to see it. My lips are just as twitchy, threatening to beam a giddy full-faced smile at him. "Sure, if you want me to."

"I want you to." He flashes me that smooth white grin, his eyes happy and sincere.

"You *need* me to."

He laughs. "That too." In truth, Adam doesn't need me at all. He just needs to apply himself, but he doesn't seem capable of doing that without someone breathing down his neck.

When I finally toss our textbook into the back and sit up straight, the sun glints off a road sign saying we're ten miles outside of Fairview. I raise my eyebrow. "Where is this next concert, exactly?" We're less than twenty miles outside of my hometown, and Adam told me our locations in distance, not by name.

"Fairview. Why?"

I tell Adam about growing up near here and that my parents still live two towns over. He jokes about me taking him home to meet Mom and Dad, and I laugh. My dad would have a heart attack and my mom . . . well, she'd probably bake chocolate-chip cookies and smile as she gifted Adam with fingernail polish remover as a two-months-early Christmas gift.

When we pull up to the venue, we have an hour and a half until showtime. On the bus, I sit Adam down with the textbook and a notepad from my backpack and he dives into written exercises, determined to finish before the show so he doesn't have to do any studying afterward. I grab a Red Bull from the kitchen and sit nearby. The roadies are all inside the venue setting up, but most of the band is still on the bus, with the exception of Joel. After a while, I realize they've all been giving me super-weird looks.

I stare hard at Cody, who has been by far the least subtle. "What?"

He sniggers. "So much for all that stuff about self-respect, huh?"

"Uh, what?"

Mike snaps at Cody to shut the hell up, but Cody just chuckles some more. Mike casts me an apologetic glance, and from the way he looks at me and then quickly breaks eye contact, like he's embarrassed for me, it finally dawns on me.

They think I slept with Adam.

"WHOA, whoa, whoa!" I say, animating my words with my hands. "NOTHING happened last night! I slept in the back room because I didn't want to be held responsible for strangling Joel in his sleep. That's IT."

"Suuure ya did," Cody replies with a sarcastic sneer, and just like that, he cements himself as my least favorite member of the band.

Mike stares at me curiously from where he's gaming on the floor, and I whirl on Adam. "Tell them!"

Adam smirks at me. "I don't know . . . I'd had a lot to drink." He scratches his head, feigning a bad memory and looking downright wicked. "But if you promise to do body shots with me tonight, I'll tell them whatever you want me to."

I glare at him. "Tell them *the truth*. Right now! Or say goodbye to graduating in December!"

Adam laughs and shakes his head. He looks at Cody and Mike and shrugs. "I tried to put the moves on her, but she turned me down." His eyes drift back to me before he adds, "Again."

Shawn, who is descending the stairs in a fresh pair

of soft-worn jeans and a clean black band T-shirt, asks, "What are we talking about?"

Mike sets the controller down and pushes off the floor. "Rowan didn't hook up with Adam last night." He scratches his hand over his scalp and then stretches his arms behind his back. His brown hair is disheveled into messy chunks, and he's wearing dark denim jeans and a brown Guinness T-shirt.

Shawn raises an eyebrow at me. "Really?"

"Oh my God," I snap. "You too?!" When he doesn't deny it, I look around at everyone and bark, "Look, if I sleep with Adam, I'll make sure to make it so hot and heavy and LOUD that there's no damn confusion! Does that work for all of you?"

Four pairs of eyes bug and four jaws drop while I just stand there with my hands on my hips. I take turns scowling at all four boys—until I can't take it anymore and a wide smile blooms across my face. I can't believe I just said that. I start chuckling, and so does Shawn.

"Oh *wow*," he says, laughing. Mike smiles warmly at me, Cody looks thoroughly embarrassed, and Adam . . . Adam is just sitting there staring at me with his eyes wide and his lips still slightly parted. I can't imagine what he's thinking.

"I'm going upstairs to change," I say before any of them can form a coherent response to my outburst.

When I get upstairs, I throw myself onto my old bunk and pull the pillow over my head. I can't believe I just said that. Hot and heavy and *loud*? My disbelieving laughter is muffled by the pillow I'm holding over my cheeks. I'm officially losing my mind. Adam is driving me crazy!

When I feel someone push against the pillow and playfully shake it back and forth, I pull it away. Shawn is grinning down at me.

"On a scale of one to ten," I ask, "how crazy does everyone think I am?"

"Oh, definitely an eleven." He chuckles and sits on the edge of the bed. "So does he know yet?"

I shush him and sit up, casting a nervous glance to the stairs to make sure no one is listening. "No." I lean in closer and whisper, "I told you, I'm not going to tell him."

"You don't think he deserves to know?"

I frown. "He just doesn't *need* to know."

"Peach is still on the backstage list, you know. He never took her . . . you . . . off."

"He probably just forgot."

"Maybe," Shawn says, but he doesn't seem convinced. He stands back up and scratches the stubble under his jaw. "Just tell him, alright?"

I shake my head. "No."

Shawn groans and starts walking back toward the stairs. When I call to him and he turns around, I put my finger over my lips, silently asking him to keep my secret. He sighs and shakes his head in disapproval, but I know he'll keep this between us.

In the back room, I change into tight-ish jeans and a dark blue, lace-trimmed tank top, and then I brush my hair out and tie it back up. I'm really getting tired of having it up 24/7—and don't even get me started on wearing glasses instead of contacts—but I'm worried that wearing it down would jog Adam's memory. If we're going to be friends, I know he'll see me with it down eventually, but . . . just not yet. He hasn't even called me by my first name yet, so I'm not confident that I'm sealed into his memory as Rowan. I need to make sure there's no room for faded memories of Peach to sneak back in.

I jog downstairs to check Adam's exercises and correct the few he got wrong before handing the sheet back to him. "You pass."

He beams at me. "Body shots to celebrate?" I roll my eyes, and he laughs. "Whatever, fine. But we're definitely going out!"

After the show, which I'll never tire of watching, I walk with the guys directly into their usual onslaught of fans. Guys and girls . . . mostly girls . . . ask for pictures and autographs and the opportunity to take the guys out for after-show drinks. Michelle Hawthorne is the last person I ever expected to see.

"Hi, Adam," she says in her sultriest voice, batting her lashes as she gazes up at him.

"Hi." He smiles back, and I bristle because I hate when Adam smiles at girls like Michelle. She was the most popular girl in my high school—prom queen, cheerleading captain, most likely to marry an eighty-year-old billionaire and then divorce him two days later. She was in one grade higher than me, but my high school was so small, everybody knew everybody and most of us had been in the same district since kindergarten.

Michelle's sun-tanned skin makes mine look stark white by comparison, and whereas my hair is dirty blonde and wavy, hers is sunny and straight. Even her eyes are a brighter shade of blue than mine. She's like my prettier twin. *Much* prettier. Skinner and chestier and *gigglier*. For fuck's sake, what the hell is she giggling about? "Hi"? "Hi" is making her giggle?

"Do you remember me?" she asks Adam, paying no attention to me even though I'm standing less than a foot away.

"Um . . ."

She giggles again. "It's okay. We . . . met at a show you did here a few months ago." She stands on her tiptoes to whisper something in his ear, and Adam's lips curve into a smirk as he listens.

Gazing down at her, he says, "Sounds a little familiar."

Ugh, someone shoot me. I'm in the process of starting to walk to a less slut-infested part of the room when Adam's hand reaches out to grab mine.

"Hey," he says. "Hold up."

I let out a disgruntled sigh and turn around.

"*Rowan*?" Michelle asks, finally noticing me. "Rowan Michaels?"

I force a smile. "Hi Michelle."

"Oh my gosh!" She pulls me in for a hug, and my teeth clench. "How have you been?! I haven't seen you since graduation!"

"I've been alright," I say. I don't ask her how she's been because I really don't care.

"How do you know Adam?"

I glance over at Adam, who is watching us with amusement. I don't know what it is, but something about him is pissing me off. "We're friends."

"Seriously?" Michelle asks with more than a little astonishment. Why is that so damn hard to believe? My eyes turn to stone as I stare at her, but she peppily adds, "That's really neat! How is your friend . . . what was her name . . ."

"Dee."

"Dee! How is she?"

"She's fine too." I might be imagining things, but Michelle seems to be gravitating closer and closer to Adam as we talk, and I've now made a mental note of just how many inches are separating them.

"Is she here with you?"

"No. I came with Adam." Suspicions flash across Michelle's features like a funny movie I'll never get tired of watching, and pride flows through me like wine, making me feel like I could float two feet above her and laugh like an evil villain right down in her stupid sun-kissed face.

"Oh, that's cool," she says without her usual pep, but then she recovers. "We should all hang out! Catch up!"

Twenty minutes later, I'm trapped on the bus with too many groupies to count. We're taxiing a huge group of people to a little club across town, and I'm sitting as far away from them as I can get, brooding. I'm feeling strangely jealous and . . . territorial. I irrationally feel like these are *my* boys, *my* bus. My *friend*, who is currently surrounded by scantily clad bitches. When we first got on the bus, Adam tried to pull me down to sit next to him, but I honestly think I'd rather fork my own eyes and ears out than have any more of Michelle's giggling burned into my long-term memory.

I sit in the corner-most bench seat, keeping to myself and trying not to glare at Michelle or any of the other four girls flirting with Adam and making him laugh. I wish he and I had driven in his car instead of riding in this filthy slut-wagon. I know this Adam is the same Adam I've spent almost every waking minute with for the past two days, but . . . this one just feels different. Inaccessible. Agitating.

Heartbreaking.

I chew the inside of my lip raw as I stare out the dark window, watching the familiar businesses and shops pass by. Since my town is so small, Fairview is where everyone goes to do anything that's anything. Movies, shopping, restaurants—you've gotta go to Fairview. And I know exactly where we're headed, because Dee has dragged me there more times than I can count. Emily's is a tiny little club on the west side of town. It has a bar and a dance floor and a DJ booth, but aside from pink interior lighting, there's really nothing special about it.

When the bus is parked, I can't get off of it quickly enough. I nearly trip over Joel's ankle to get down the aisle, and Adam gives me a curious look as I pass by him. I kind of want to smack that look right off his stupid face. The girls pour out of the bus first, hanging off of band members and even roadies. Do they even know the freaking difference? By the way one slut is hanging off of Driver, I'm guessing that's a big no.

Mike comes to stand next to me, and we watch as everyone else files off the bus. "I think I'm going to go across the street to get something to eat first," I tell him. There's a little pizza joint literally right across the road that stays open super late. They do great business from all of the club-goers who need to sober up before driving home.

"Thank God," Mike says. "I'm coming with you."

"Hey Adam!" I shout. He looks up to find me standing a few people away. "I'll catch up with you later. Mike and I are going to get something to eat."

Adam weaves around people to get to me. Michelle is right on his heels. "Want me to come?"

"Nah," I say on impulse, not wanting him to feel like he has to babysit the poor nerdy tutor girl who doesn't quite fit in. And besides, the last thing I want right now is to have dinner with Michelle or any of the other girls who were practically drooling over him. "We'll probably be over in like twenty minutes."

Adam looks at Mike and then at me again. "You sure?"

"Yeah, it's cool. We'll see you later." Michelle is already gently pulling him toward the crowd of people now walking toward the club. She's dressed in a short skirt and super high high heels, and I kind of hope she trips and skins her knees so badly she has to have her legs amputated.

Okay, no . . . that's a lie.

I *really* hope that happens. Please fall, please fall, please fall.

"Alright," Adam says, interrupting all the bad karma I'm giving myself. "See you in twenty."

I force a smile and turn away from him, jaywalking across the street with Mike. "I can't stand her," I mumble once we cross the yellow line.

He chuckles. "The girl with Adam?"

"She went to my high school. Prom Queen and all that crap. She's so fake."

Mike shrugs. "That's kind of Adam's type."

I frown and clamp my jaw shut. This is so not a conversation I want to have.

Inside, Mike orders us an entire pizza. We get the plain cheese since there's one already made, and then we find a table and sit down. "God, I'm starving," I say, choosing a big piece with an airy bubble—my favorite.

Mike scoops three pieces onto a paper plate and sprinkles them with extra oregano and red pepper. "I *live* for pizza."

"If you were stranded on a deserted island and had to live on only three types of food for the rest of your life," I ask as I chew on a thick piece of cheesy goodness, "what would they be?"

Mike squints his eyes a little as he thinks and chews. "Pizza . . ." He pauses. "Pizza . . ." He pauses again. "And pizza."

I laugh. "Excellent choices."

He smiles around the piece he's biting into. "What about you?"

When I list pizza as my first choice, he smiles wide at me. "And strawberry pancakes," I add, "aaand . . . hm . . . what else . . . OH! Cookies, my mom's."

Mike chuckles. "I'd like to change my answer to that. Pizza, pancakes, and cookies . . ." He nods. "Yeah, ship me to this island."

Mike and I talk about everything from what kinds

of cookies my mom makes to why strawberry pancakes and bacon are the perfect cure for hangovers. He tells me that the parents of an ex-girlfriend of his actually owned a farm where they raised pigs *and* had a strawberry patch, and we make plans to grow strawberries in Dee's dorm and raise a pig on the bus—a pig named Breakfast.

"But we can't slaughter Breakfast!" I insist.

"How are we supposed to have bacon then?"

"We'll just have to go to IHOP . . . and bring Breakfast with us."

"And feed him bacon?!"

"Oh my God! You're a monster!"

Mike laughs harder than I've seen him laugh before, which makes me smile.

"So what ever happened to that girlfriend?" I ask.

He makes a noise. "She went off to college and expected me to follow. She didn't see a career with the band as being anything that was worth pursuing." He smirks. "I disagreed."

"That sucks."

With a shrug, he says, "Yeah, it kind of did, but what can you do."

"Why don't any of you guys have a girlfriend now?" I regret the question the second it slips from my mouth. It's really none of my business.

Mike chuckles. "Well, Adam, Shawn, and Joel don't really want one. Cody can't keep one. And I just haven't met the right girl yet."

I suspected as much—about all five of them—but hearing Mike say it out loud . . . eh, it kind of stings.

Adam doesn't want a girlfriend. I mean, not that I want a boyfriend, and even if I did, it wouldn't be a playboy like Adam, but . . .

I have no idea why that makes me feel all . . . blah.

"I'm sure you'll find her eventually," I assure Mike. "You probably need to look in better places though."

"Yeah, the girls we meet at these shows . . ." He shakes his head. "They're only interested in one thing."

"Sex?"

He chuckles and shakes his head some more. "No, sex I'd be okay with. They just want the fame. They want to be able to say that they bagged one of the guys in the band. I'm not interested in a chick that's going to bang me on a bus on the first night she met me, with my buddies hanging out two feet away, you know what I mean?"

If only Mike knew how close I had come to being one of those chicks. "Yeah" is all I can say.

After we finish the pizza, which I insist on paying for since I actually brought my wallet along this time, Mike walks me back to the club. Inside it looks—and smells— just like I remember it. It's dark and pinkly lit and smells so strongly of perfume that I might be tempted to wear a gas mask if I had one handy. I don't know if Emily's sprays the place down before they open, or if it's just the smell of all of the trashy girls crammed in here, but the effect is overwhelming.

Mike walks in front of me to part the sea of people as we make our way to the bar. I immediately know where Adam must be sitting because the crowd is much denser there.

"Adam's over there," Mike says with a nod in the direction I suspected. "I'm going to hit the bathroom. You cool on your own?"

"Yep. See ya later."

I weave and squeeze my way between people as I make my way to the end of the bar. I walk until I can't walk any farther—because I've reached a point where people are flat-out refusing to budge, giving me dirty looks for trying to force my way between them. I can see Adam, but there's no way he'll hear me from all the way over here. Michelle is still clinging to him, teetering on the edge of the stool next to him, practically tumbling face-first into his lap. There are people standing all around him, girls and guys alike. Frustrated, I stand there and huff.

"Need a little help?"

I look over my shoulder to see Joel. Thank freaking God. I turn around and smile up at him. "Hey." He has his arm around a brunette, and a girl who looks like her twin sister is clinging to his other side.

"Hey ADAM!" Joel yells over my shoulder, and Adam finally looks up to see us. The crowd follows his line of vision and makes room for us as we walk over. There's hardly anywhere to stand, but Adam pulls me in close, and I somehow find myself standing right between him and Michelle. My back is to her, and I know she must be seething.

Rowan: 1. Michelle: who the hell cares.

"Tequila shot?" Adam asks with a playful grin, and I look at the bar in front of him to see a few empty shot glasses already lined up.

"Looks like you've already had a few."

"But none with you!" he says. "We need to celebrate!" When he tugs me onto his lap, I squeal and grab his shoulders for balance.

"You haven't passed the test *yet*," I tease.

Adam's voice is subtly lower when he says, "What will I get when I do?"

Oh my.

I less-than-gracefully fumble off his lap. What was that about? And why is it so goddamn hot in here?

When the bartender takes our order, I ask for a White Russian and Adam orders two unsolicited shots. He either forgot about Michelle or he forgot about me, or maybe he didn't order one for himself . . . Either way, this is going to be interesting.

"Where is everyone?" I ask. Joel has disappeared, and I have no idea where any of the other guys are.

"Most of the guys are on the dance floor. Shawn went to see about getting us a table, I think. Or to check out the DJ booth. Or, actually, he might be in the bathroom too, maybe . . . I think . . ."

I can't help chuckling. "You have no idea, do you?"

When Adam shakes his head with a goofy grin on his face, I want to take his cheeks in my hands and kiss him. Or rub noses. Or . . . hell, I don't know. Something equally ridiculous.

"Adam," Michelle suddenly says from behind me, reminding me that she's alive, "come dance with me?"

Adam shakes his head, and I'm not sure if I should count this as 2 for Team Rowan, but I'm going to anyway. "I'm not *nearly* drunk enough for that yet."

When large hands land on my shoulders, making me jump, I look back to see Shawn's big green eyes staring at me from under his messy black hair. He smiles and leaves his hands on my shoulders as he tells Adam, "I got us a table."

Our drinks arrive with impeccable timing. I pick mine up and sip on it as we maneuver our way through the crowd to get to a back table where it's a little quieter. The table is a massive corner booth. The seat is soft pink leather, and there's a knee-high hot-pink circle table in the center. Mike, Joel, Joel's twins, and an extra girl I saw flirting with Shawn back on the bus are already there. Shawn slides in next to her, followed by Michelle and Adam. I stay standing off to the side, wanting a quick exit strategy in case Adam and Michelle decide to start sucking face, like God knows he's prone to doing. Adam tries to tug me in next to him, but I take his hand in mine and lower it back down. "I'm good," I say.

He frowns up at me, but I smile to reassure him. I don't want to ruin his last night on the road.

Ugh, the thought almost makes me teary-eyed. Is that why I've been feeling so crazy? Tonight is the last night I'll have with him and the guys. After tonight, it's back to my boring, depressing, Adamless life. Adamless and Shawnless and Mikeless. Joelless and Driverless. Hell, even Codyless.

Adam hands me one of the two shots he carried over, and I shake my head.

"Just take it," he says. "No hidden attachments."

"Can I have a lime and the salt?" I ask.

Adam hands it over, watching me curiously. Interested in seeing what a tequila shot tastes like when it's taken the way it's supposed to be, I lick the back of my hand, sprinkle some salt over top, lick it off, down the shot, and bite into the lime. I wipe my chin with the back of my clean hand and grin at the dazed look Adam is giving me.

"Thanks," I finally say.

His tongue flicks out to trace his bottom lip, and I have to look anywhere else. This place really needs air-conditioning, and a better ventilation system, and . . . air to ventilate.

"So Rowan," Michelle says, and I suck in a silent breath, welcoming the distraction. "How is Brady?"

Chapter Eighteen

THE TRUMPETS THAT should have accompanied the end of my world never sounded. I'm caught completely unprepared, staring at Michelle with shock stamped onto my face. I quickly mask my expression and hope no one else caught it, because my answer comes out sounding miraculously unfazed and flawless.

"I wouldn't know. We're not together anymore."

"Oh," she says. She's trying to seem sympathetic, but I can see right through her bullshit. "That's a shame. You two were so adorable together."

"Who's Brady?" Adam asks.

"No one," I answer, but Michelle can't keep her big mouth shut.

"You guys dated for like . . . how long? Like all of high school, right?"

"Yeah."

"What happened?"

"Are you seriously fucking asking me that?"

Whoa. I did *not* mean to snap like that.

Michelle's eyes get huge, and I'm stumbling to apologize. "Sorry . . . I mean . . . I just really don't want to talk about it."

"Well you could have just said so . . ."

I sigh and chew on my lip. I feel like everyone is staring at me—probably because they are. I sit down next to Adam mostly just to try to blend in so that I'm not so easy to gape at. I'm thankful when the conversation moves away from me and my horrendously failed love life, and even more thankful when a server pops by to take our drink orders. I order another shot and a Long Island iced tea.

"Going out with a bang?" Adam asks in my ear, reminding me again that this is our last night together.

With my cheek against his, I share a secret. "I'm going to miss you."

WHY DID I JUST SAY THAT?!

Adam pulls away to look at me, and I'm terrified of what he's going to say. I probably just freaked him the hell out. *I'm going to miss you?* He's known me for all of two days! He opens his mouth like he's going to say something, but then he closes it. Finally, he leans back in and says, "No, you won't."

When he pulls away to read my expression, I'm frowning. Like hell I won't miss him.

He leans in again. "You'll see me twice a week in class, and probably on weekends when I kidnap you for tutoring."

Okay, I seriously might cry. Instead, I laugh. "Promise?"

He shakes his head. "I don't make promises. But I'll show you."

It might be the drinks, or it might be Adam's non-promise, but I'm suddenly not feeling nearly so bitchy. When Joel asks me to dance, I even let him pull me onto the dance floor.

He spins me and dips me and grinds against me a little too provocatively, but I can tell that's just him and has nothing to do with me, so I let myself go with it, and we end up laughing hysterically on the dance floor at our ridiculous moves. By the time I'm following him back to the table, my hand fisted in the back of his button-down T-shirt as he leads me through the crowd, I've worked up a thin sheen of sweat. I nearly stop dead in my tracks when I see how cozy Michelle and Adam have gotten, but I somehow command my feet to keep moving forward.

Michelle has one hand cupped around Adam's jaw, turning his head into her. Their foreheads are touching, and he's grinning at her. She giggles and leans to the side to whisper something in his ear, and he licks his lips as he listens.

I roughly slide in next to him, accidentally throwing myself in a little too hard and slamming right into his back. When his head knocks against Michelle's and they both yelp, I start giggling uncontrollably.

"Oh my God," I say through giggles, "I'm sorry."

Adam chuckles and rubs his forehead. "Thanks for that."

"Any time." I giggle some more, my eyes drifting over everyone at the table until I catch Shawn smirking at me. His eyes are glassy, proof of the collection of empty glasses he's lined up over at his side of the table, not including any shots he had with Adam before we got here. "Feeling good, Shawn?" I tease.

He chuckles. "I'm feeling peachy!"

When my heart stops beating, he laughs a little harder. I really need to stop letting him catch me so off guard.

Michelle continues throwing herself at Adam as we all talk and drink, and just when I think I can't take anymore, she asks him if he's drunk enough to dance yet.

He chuckles and shakes his head. "Not even close."

"Then do you want to get out of here?" She says it quietly enough so that most of the table can't hear, but my ears were tuned in to their conversation as if national security depended on it. I immediately stand up to let Adam out of the seat, not wanting to hear the way his voice sounds when he eventually asks me to move. My sudden movement causes him to look up at me. His expression is completely blank, and I can't read it for shit, but his actions scream volumes. He starts scooting out of the seat, with Michelle practically joined to his hip.

I bite down so hard on the inside of my lip that I'm pretty sure I'm about to draw blood, but then I hear Shawn laughing. "Adam!" he shouts, and Adam stops scooting to look over at him. "Christ, man, you *still* don't know who she is, do you?!"

Adam turns back toward Michelle and scrunches his eyebrows. "Huh?"

"Not her!" Shawn yells. Oh God, Oh God, Oh God.

"Her!" He points his finger at me, and it freezes me to the bone.

Adam's eyes slowly swing back to mine. "What is he talking about?" he asks me, looking thoroughly confused.

"Nothing," I sputter. "He's drunk."

"Just tell him who you are!" Shawn shouts, and I shoot him a threatening glare. I'm going to kill him. I'm seriously going to kill him!

"Who is she?" Adam asks Shawn, and I practically lift him out of the seat by his elbow, curling my fingers around his arm and yanking him away from the table.

When Michelle hurries to follow, I stop dead in my tracks to glare back at her and spit, "NOT YOU!" She stumbles back a step as if my words literally slapped her in the face, but I'm too panicked to feel good about it and immediately start hauling Adam toward the door again.

"You better tell him!" Shawn calls after us, but I ignore him, getting Adam out of that club as fast as humanly possible. He's looking at me like I'm crazy, but he follows me without question.

Once we're outside, he stops walking, and my tug on his arm gets us nowhere. "What was that about?"

I turn around and stare at him, gnawing on the inside of my lip. It's going to be so sore tomorrow. "Can we just forget that happened?"

"No," he says, his tone so much more serious than I'm used to hearing him, "tell me what he was talking about."

I sigh and stare at the concrete beneath my feet; it takes me a moment, but I eventually summon the courage to look up at him. I take my glasses off and admit, "We've met before . . . Before this weekend."

Adam eyes me curiously. "Where?"

I don't want to say it, but Shawn is leaving me no choice. "Mayhem."

"When?"

I tug on my earlobe nervously. I don't want to have this conversation. This is the last thing I ever wanted. "A little over a month ago." When I realize I'm still not saying enough, I finally add, "You've only been turned down by *one* girl, Adam. Not two . . . just one."

Adam stares at me for a long moment, realization slowly washing over him. His eyes soften under the bright street lighting, the breeze gently blowing brown tendrils of hair across his forehead. "Just you," he agrees quietly, and then, with his eyes still on mine, he reaches behind me. His fingers wrap around my hair tie and pull it down, letting my blonde waves fall free. Then they comb over my temples, pulling my long hair forward and over my shoulders.

"I'm sorry I didn't tell you," I say, frowning as he plays with my hair, but then he reaches up and caresses my bottom lip with the heel of his thumb. And just like last night, I'm frozen. I watch as the memories of our first kisses play in his head. With him touching me like that and *looking* at me like that, I have no idea what to say or feel or do . . . or . . . or . . . am I even breathing? Holy shit, I need to breathe.

When his gaze falls to my lips and he starts leaning into me, I inhale a sharp breath and take a nervous step away from him. "Whoa."

He follows the step I take, his eyes smoldering. He slides one of his fingers through my belt loop to pull my hips forward as he forcefully closes the distance between us. My body is suddenly on fire, and I don't know how much longer I'll be able to fend off all the bad decisions it's begging me to make. At least he's not mad . . . I don't think . . .

"Adam," I somehow manage to say, my voice breathless and uneven, "we're still just friends."

He shakes his head, spinning our bodies around in one quick motion so that I'm pressed with my back against the brick wall. He steps in tight, with one hand still holding my belt loop and the other braced beside my ear. "Why didn't you tell me?" he asks. His voice is low, dangerous, and sexy as sin. It makes my head spin. Is he pissed? Shit . . . I can't even tell.

"I . . . I didn't want you to know."

"Well now I know." He's so close and so tall, I have to look up to meet his eyes. They're burning down into me, setting every cell in my body into a heat-induced frenzy.

I nod and swallow hard.

"You've been in my class for an entire *month*."

I nod again, biting down on my bottom lip. But that only draws his attention back to my mouth, so I release it.

"And now you've spent the past three days with me, and you told Shawn—"

Cutting him off, I say, "I did *not* tell Shawn."

"Then how does he know?"

"He recognized me. *You* didn't." I sound more irritated than I meant to.

"I knew I knew you." He leans in to press his mouth to my ear and whispers, "You lied to me, Peach." When he leans back again, his eyes are dark and his expression is unreadable.

"I . . . I'm sorry."

He slowly shakes his head. "Another lie."

I stare down at the ground. He's right, and he has me so damn flustered. Adam's finger lifts my chin so that I'll look up at him. "Why didn't you come backstage that night?"

"I was a mess."

"I wanted to see you again."

I want to tell him I'm sorry for the millionth time, but I manage to stay quiet.

Adam's hand cups the side of my neck, his thumb caressing the soft skin beneath my ear. "You come along on this trip with me . . . and you haven't even let me kiss you."

My breath catches in my throat. I . . . what am I supposed to say to that?

His body envelopes me, pressing my back tighter against the wall, shutting everything else out. I can feel how much he wants me. He leans down, agonizingly close to my lips. "Now that I know who you are, will you let me kiss you?"

I nervously shake my head from side to side.

He leans in a little closer, our noses brushing. "Why?" He's so close, I can feel his breath on my lips.

"I . . . I just . . ."

Before I can finish or even figure out what I want to

say, Adam's lips surge forward to claim mine. In one controlled movement, he closes the distance between us and sucks my bottom lip into his mouth. He presses his hips into me, and a breathless moan escapes my throat when I feel him, all of him. I want him to pick me up. I want him to wrap my legs around his waist and pin me to this wall so I can have him where I really want him. I don't think—I just kiss him back. I kiss him so desperately that there's no disguising how much I've wanted him.

Adam's hand slides up the back of my neck to tangle in my hair. He kisses me until my thoughts are nothing but haze, and then he drops his lips to my neck and grips my hip, pulling me even tighter against him. I'm putty in his hands. He's kissing me so passionately that I know there will probably be marks, but I don't care. It isn't until his cold fingers slip under the hem of my top, roughly clinging to my bare waist, that I'm shocked into opening my eyes.

We're in front of the club, out on the open sidewalk. I catch the disapproving stares of people walking by, and I inch myself away, panting. "Adam." I shake my head. "No."

He looks around, realizing the public display we're putting on. He seems equal parts agitated and amused as he roughly rubs his fingers over his eyes with a wide grin plastered on his face. "Bus," he says, and then he stops rubbing his eyes and reaches for my hand.

"No," I breathe, shaking my head. "We can't." My body screams in protest, but it really needs to learn to shut the hell up.

His face contorts with confusion. "Why?"

"Because . . . we're friends."

Adam growls and runs both hands through his hair, frustration rolling off him. "We are *not* friends."

His words cut right through me, and I'm afraid I might start crying right here in front of everyone. He must be able to see it, because he immediately backtracks. "No, no, that's not what I meant." He looks almost nervous, reaching his hands forward like he's afraid I'll shatter into a million pieces and he'll have to hold me together. I know he's telling the truth, which makes me feel better. But there's still the matter of the bus.

"Going back to the bus would be a *really* bad idea," I tell him.

"What would be so bad about it?"

Nothing. And everything.

"I'm not looking for a one-night stand . . ." I force a weak smile. "Not even with Adam Everest." *Especially* not with Adam Everest.

"How do you know it would be a one night stand?"

I give him a look that says it all. All Adam *does* is one-night stands. He can't even deny it.

"Why did you come along on this trip, Peach?"

"I wanted to help you . . ."

"Why?"

"I just did."

It's Adam's logic, so he can't argue with it. He sighs and takes a step back, running his hand through his hair. After a few seconds, he asks, "Can't we just see where this goes?"

I shake my head. "I still just want to be friends." We both *know* where it would go. It would go straight to bed and then leave me sitting by a phone that never rings, crying on Dee's shoulder.

"Honestly? After *that*?" Adam lets out a humorless chuckle. "I don't think this 'friends' thing is really going to work."

Frowning, I say, "This is exactly why I didn't want to tell you."

He steps forward again to rest his forehead against mine. "Peach," he says, gazing deeply into my eyes. "I don't think I've ever wanted anything as badly as I want to pick you up and carry you back to that bus right now."

I brace my hand on his chest and slowly push him away. He doesn't look happy, but he lets me move him.

"What am I supposed to do?" he asks me.

"Cool down," I say with a counterfeit smile.

"And then what?"

"Forget what happened at Mayhem." And just now. Because God knows *just now* has been scorched into my memory and will still be sizzling a year from now.

Adam shakes his head. "I can't do that."

"Then just pretend."

He shakes his head again, this time smiling. "Not gonna happen."

"Why?"

"Don't want to." He takes my hand and pulls me away from the wall so he can wrap his arm around my shoulders and walk me back toward the door.

"So you're cool with being friends?" I ask as we walk.

He laughs against me. "No."

"But . . . we're going to try, right?"

He grins down at me, not giving me an answer as he walks me back inside.

Chapter Nineteen

SEEING SHAWN SITTING at the kitchen table the next morning, with his shoulders slumped and his head in his hands like a fifty-pound bowling ball, brings the evil out of me. His messy hair and his dirty clothes from the night before scream killer hangover, and I owe him payback for forcing me to tell Adam my secret.

I make my way to the coffee maker and then rummage through the cabinets and drawers as loudly as humanly possible. I open cabinet after cabinet, slamming them closed as I search for the ground coffee. I find it and slap the can onto the counter. Then I find a drawer filled with miscellaneous spoons and spatulas and shove my hand into it, swirling it around like I can't find the tablespoon measurer even though it was lying right on top.

Shawn groans and buries his face in his arms. I smirk and pull out the tablespoon measurer.

"HEY SHAWN," I say in an obnoxiously loud voice as

I scoop coffee into a filter. "HOW ARE YOU FEELING THIS MORNING?" I pretend to "accidentally" kick the stove for good measure, the sound ringing through the kitchen.

"I'm sooorry," he groans into his arms.

"What was that? YOU'RE GOING TO HAVE TO SPEAK UP."

Shawn raises his bloodshot eyes from his elbow, looking downright pathetic. Then he lifts his head and holds his temples between his palms. "I'm sorry, okay? I was completely wasted."

I finish pouring water into the coffee maker and close the top, pushing the ON button before I turn around and lean back against the counter. "You're going to have to be more specific."

"I'm sorry for blowing up your spot. I shouldn't have said anything."

I nod, accepting his apology. I feel a little sorry too—I know he hated keeping that secret from his best friend, but he still should've kept his mouth shut. It wasn't his secret to tell.

"What do you need?" I ask. "Tylenol? Eggs? Pancakes?" It's my form of an apology, and it's the best he's going to get.

He gives me a bashful smile. "All of the above?"

I pour him some orange juice from the fridge, and then I find some Tylenol in a medicine cabinet in the bathroom. I set them both down in front of him as softly as possible, not making a sound. "Coming right up," I tell him, and then I shuffle him to the front of the bus so I can get to work.

Last night was definitely . . . interesting. Adam and I hadn't made it very far back into the club when the rest of the guys changed our direction, ushering us out. They took the party back to the bus, and I was grateful when I saw that Michelle wasn't part of it. I asked if we should give her a lift back to her car, but Joel assured me that a girl like her wouldn't have a hard time getting a ride.

When Adam told the band about me being the infamous Peach, my cheeks burned with embarrassment. It was a long story with a lot of questions and confusion and teasing. Ultimately, it culminated in a very drunk Shawn getting punched ruthlessly in the arm. Adam flexed his hand afterward, and I smirked with approval.

Once the upstairs was clear, I crawled into the black satin bed, hoping it wouldn't be weird. But I fell asleep before Adam ever came in, so I didn't have to find out. And this morning, I snuck out, tiptoeing between arms and legs and blankets that were hanging out of bunks.

By the time the other boys wake up, I've made bacon, scrambled eggs, buttermilk pancakes, and toast. There's not nearly enough for all of them, but they make do. The roadies eat quickly and then head out for a smoke break while the rest of the band stays on the bus. Adam isn't up yet, so I make him a plate and stash it in the microwave.

"Where's mine?" he asks groggily when he finally comes downstairs. He's wearing his shades, and I'm guessing it's because he's just as hungover as Shawn. He's also shirtless, with his faded, tattered jeans hanging low on his hips, revealing the waistband of his black CK boxers. Even though he sleeps without a shirt or pants on, I haven't indulged in a good look at him. Now, I can't help it.

A stilted laugh bursts from my mouth, and I hurry to cover it with my fist. When I'm confident I'm not going to burst out laughing again, I ask, "A unicorn?"

Adam looks down at the tiny unicorn stenciled on his lower abdomen and smiles wide. Then he looks back up and shrugs. "Shawn dared me. We were teenagers."

Adam's body is lean and toned. He doesn't have an eight-pack or anything, but the sight of his hard stomach still makes me blush all the way from the tops of my ears to the tips of my curling toes. He has slight indents marking the muscles beneath his skin, but I think it's the line traveling down the center that makes my cheeks heat the most. On his left pectoral is another tattoo—a Magic 8 Ball that says "Ask again later." It's so Adam, I'd smile if I wasn't busy trying to pretend I wasn't just shamelessly ogling him. I stand up and heat his breakfast in the microwave before carrying it over to where he's sitting at the kitchen table.

"You saved me some?" he asks as I set his plate down in front of him.

"You're welcome."

He chuckles and picks up a piece of bacon, eating that first.

Joel finishes his last bite of pancakes and leans back in his chair, patting his belly. "I think I'm going to miss you, Peach."

Shawn chuckles and says, "You're just saying that because of the pancakes."

"Am not. She's one hell of a dancer, too." He smirks over at me, and I blush, remembering how tipsy and dirty we got on the dance floor last night.

"Well," Mike interrupts, "I'm going to miss having *anyone* around here who's halfway decent at Call of Duty."

"Hey!" Cody protests, making us laugh. His legs are dangling from where he's sitting on the counter, distractedly texting on his phone.

"I'm going to miss you guys, too," I say, feeling all warm but sad inside.

Adam scoffs, pouring a layer of syrup on his pancakes. "I don't know why everyone is going all Hallmark on me. It's not like you're never going to see her again. You'll see her in two weeks."

"They will?" This is news to me.

Adam nods, letting the syrup soak in before he adds a second layer, just like I do. It makes me smile. "Yeah," he says, "you're coming to our show that Saturday."

"I am?"

Shawn laughs, and Adam smiles, sliding his shades up onto his head. "Yep. You've even got a backstage pass."

"Just one?" I'd really like to bring Dee with me, and maybe Leti.

"Or fifty. How many do you want?"

I chuckle and sip my coffee. If Adam wants me to go with him to Mayhem, I'll be there.

I exchange numbers and hugs with the rest of the

band before Adam drives me home, reserving my biggest hugs for Shawn and Mike. This trip would've been so awkward if it weren't for how awesome they both are. I'm glad Adam wants me to keep hanging around once in a while, because if he didn't, I'd definitely miss them.

We've been on the road for a while, the wind blowing through my hair—which I've left down for the first time in days—when Adam says, "So I managed to not pin you to the bed and have my way with you last night." My throat closes, and I stare over at him. His shades are back down, and one side of his mouth is curled up in a sexy smile. "Are you proud of me?"

I half chuckle, half choke. "Yes, Adam, I'm very proud of you."

"Because friends don't sleep with their friends, right?"

Okay, now I know he's just giving me a hard time. A really, really, really hard freaking time. "Right."

"I mean, not that much sleeping would've been going on, but—"

"Adam!"

"Right." He chuckles and pulls a cigarette from his pack, lighting it. "So do you think I'm going to pass this test tomorrow?"

"I think you'd better." After all the studying we've done? If he doesn't pass, I'm going to use our French textbook to beat him senseless.

"You don't think we need another late-night tutoring session?"

As appealing as that sounds, I've been psyching myself up for saying goodbye to Adam all morning, and I feel like I need to pull the Band-Aid off before I lose my nerve. He's said he'll keep in touch, but once we're back to real life and he's swamped by all of the pretty, familiar faces that follow him around every day, I wonder how long it will take mine to fade from his memory. Now that I'm no longer Peach from Mayhem—and I'm just Peach, the girl who won't sleep with him—he really has no reason to give me the time of day.

"Nah, I think you've got it covered," I say, forcing a smile at him. "I have faith in you."

"Careful, Peach," he warns, glancing over at me. "Famous last words."

I roll my eyes. "Faith or not, if you don't pass this test, those are going to be *your* last words."

Adam chuckles and rests his elbow on the door. "You're kind of a violent little thing, aren't you?"

"What can I say, you bring out the worst in me."

He gazes over at me again, the seductive look in his eyes making me blush again. "Do I now?"

I distract myself by fumbling my phone out of my purse and checking my messages. Dee texted me to tell me that she misses my annoying face and to remind me that my daisies will "wither and DIE" if I don't water them regularly. I snicker and move on to Leti's text next.

Dee said you might wanna stay with me this week?

Shit.
Shit, shit, shit.

Leti's text is a giant red flag. Dee wouldn't have messaged him unless this business with her RA has gotten serious. I chew on my thumbnail as my useless brain tries to devise some type of game plan. I can't go back to Dee's, but I don't want Leti to run into the same problems. And his roommate kind of gives me the creeps . . . Ugh. This is such bullshit. I wouldn't even *be* in this position if it wasn't for Brady. And now he has our two-bedroom apartment all to himself.

There's really only one choice.

When we get close to school, Adam asks me where to, and I tell him to take a right. "But this isn't the way to the dorms," he notes, his eyebrow lifting in question.

"I know."

"Where am I taking you?"

I sigh, running my clammy palm over the cold leather of his armrest. "Dee's RA gave her a notice that I can't stay there with her anymore. So I guess I'm going back to my apartment."

"To your ex . . ."

During the car ride, I'd told Adam the basics on Brady—that we dated for three years in high school, that we moved here together, that I never suspected him of cheating until that disastrous night at Mayhem. Adam had been uncharacteristically silent, listening without saying much.

"Yeah," I answer. Our apartment has two bedrooms, so I guess I'll just stay in my old room.

He stares ahead for a long time, and so do I. "Are you sure?" he finally asks me.

Hell no I'm not sure. But I don't really have any other options, now do I? "Yeah, I'm sure."

Chapter Twenty

I SIT IN Adam's passenger seat nervously wringing my hands in my lap until I bite the bullet and grab my backpack from the backseat. The trunk is popped, so I'm just going to grab my things and head in. I turn toward Adam, prepared to say my final goodbye, when he opens his door and gets out.

Okay . . . this is not how I planned this going. I had a clear vision in my head. I'd smile, nod, say I had fun, then tell him I'd see him in class on Monday. Thirteen words, tops. "Thanks." "I had a lot of fun this weekend." "I'll see you tomorrow." I recited them in my head a hundred times on the way here so that I wouldn't go blank or stutter when it came time to say them, but then that jerk had to go and get out of the damn car.

I scramble to meet him at the trunk, watching as he pulls my suitcase out and then stands there staring at me. It's so awkward, I don't know what to do. "Thanks for letting me come along this weekend," I stammer.

"You're sure this is what you want to do?" he asks, the concern in his eyes sneaking into his tone. Even though Adam is a total playboy, I know that deep down, he's a good guy. And I can tell that me going back to live with the man who broke my heart isn't sitting well with him. But it's not like I have any other choice.

I don't know what's making me feel sicker—that I'm about to talk to Brady face-to-face for the first time in almost two months, or that I'm about to leave Adam. That tomorrow, this weekend will officially be nothing but a memory.

"Yeah," I lie—as much to myself as to the deliciously unkempt rocker boy standing less than two feet in front of me. "I promised I'd talk to him. And I'll get Dee to bring my stuff over later."

Adam leans against his trunk staring at his shoes, black Vans with black laces and white soles. What's he thinking? Every second that he stands there, I feel weaker and weaker. I suck at goodbyes, and this one is already taking way too long. I hugged the other guys goodbye, but Adam? He's just standing there, looking perfect.

He suddenly reaches into his back pocket and plucks out his phone. "What's your number?"

I didn't give it to him on the bus because he didn't ask for it, and I'd grown pretty sure he never would. I didn't ask for his either because, well, there'd be no point. He's Adam freaking Everest—I'd never have the guts to actually call him, not even after spending so much time with him this weekend and realizing how amazing he is.

He stares down at his phone, his fingers waiting patiently against the touch screen. And then I say the first thing that comes to my mind, which also happens to be the dumbest. "Why?"

His eyes swing up, his cocked eyebrow showing how highly amused he is by my train wreck of a question. "Uh, because I'm going to call you?"

"*You're* going to call me?" I almost start laughing—I can't even imagine how many girls he's fed this line to.

But he just stares at me expectantly, the hint of a smile tugging at the corner of his mouth.

I hold out my hand, and he gives me his phone. I hand him mine as an exchange. "You first," I tell him, and he flashes me a smile before he starts typing his number into my phone.

"Alright, I'll call you," he says after I type in my number and hand him back his phone. He slides it into his pocket.

This time, I actually do let out a laugh. "Okay."

"I'm *going* to call you, Peach."

"I bet."

Adam's eyes narrow, but there's a goofy grin on his face. "You really don't believe me, do you?"

"My faith in you only goes so far, Adam Everest."

He reaches forward, gripping my fingers and pulling me to him as he pushes away from the trunk. His arms wrap tightly around me, his chin resting on my head. It's exactly what I wanted, and I smile against his soft-worn T-shirt, allowing myself to hug him just as tightly.

"You know," he says, "I think I'll call you tonight."

Even though my heart is doing back-flips from being

held by him like this, I can't help giving him a hard time. "If you say so."

We stand there like that for a long time. Way longer than friends would. I don't want to let go. What I really want is to slide my fingers under his T-shirt to see what the contours of his sun-warmed back feel like against my fingertips. Heat spikes through me, and I close my eyes. He's so tall, and he just feels so *right*. I sigh and pull away just enough to look up at him. "Hey, Adam?"

My eyes stare up, up, and his soft brown hair tumbles over his brow as he drops his chin to meet them. "Yeah, Peach?"

"I'm glad I met you."

He smiles sweetly down at me, the corners of his mouth crinkling. Part of me—the part that can't be trusted—wants to touch those crinkles. His lips. His cheeks. "So am I," he says sincerely. His eyelashes look so soft, I want to touch those too.

Finally, I summon enough strength to step away from his embrace. "I'll see you tomorrow?"

He nods once, looking like he doesn't want me to leave any more than I want to leave him.

"You had better be on time," I warn over my shoulder as I roll my suitcase toward the door to the apartment building.

That cocky smirk I love so much finally returns, brightening his eyes. "Promise to do a body shot with me and I'll even be early."

I chuckle and shake my head. "See ya, Adam."

When he says, "See ya, Peach," I don't look back. I

can't, because my knees are already shaking. I hear his driver's side door click open and closed just before I step up to the apartment building, and then I open the door and force my legs to carry me inside.

I immediately walk to the inside wall and press my back against it, squeezing my eyes shut and sucking in a deep breath. That was so much harder than I imagined it would be, and I'd already imagined it being pretty damn hard. Nothing is going to be the same when I see him tomorrow in class. Deep down in my clenching gut, I know I'll go right back to just being another girl to him. If I'm lucky, he'll say hi to me in passing. And then my heart will trip over itself to pump blood into my arm so I can wave at him before I take my usual seat beside Leti.

Eh, who am I kidding? There will be no words or waves because Adam and I will never actually pass each other. He gets to class after me and leaves before me. There won't even be any passing words or smiles, no friendly phone calls or breakfasts at IHOP. He said he wants me to come to Mayhem when his band performs in two weeks, and I'll go—hopefully Peach will still be on the backstage list. And if I actually get backstage, I know he'll let me stay, even if he's . . . preoccupied.

Which is my own damn fault.

For good reasons. Good reasons, good reasons. If I just keep reminding myself of that, maybe this will stop being so damn tough.

After collecting myself, I muster the courage to climb the stairs. Two flights, and then I'm standing in front of Brady's door. I probably should've called. Hell, I should probably call *now*. But this is my apartment too, and I'm not going to pretend it's not. I rummage around in my purse for my keys. If I'm going to be living here, I don't need to call or knock or *anything*, and I don't need to forgive him either. I don't owe him anything—if he wants my forgiveness, he's going to have to earn it, and no one said I had to make it easy.

I'm pretty sure that entering a conversation with him when I'm this irritated isn't the best way to start things, but it's too late for that because I'm already getting myself worked up, putting up a wall between us before I even step foot inside the apartment.

Good. It's probably for the best.

I could have called Dee and told her this is where I was coming, but I didn't want her to feel like she pushed me back into Brady's arms. Or worse, I didn't want her to jump in her car and speed over here to physically restrain me from making what I *know* she would think is a mistake of epic proportions. The real mistake would be allowing my best friend in the entire world to get kicked out of her dormitory her first semester of college. Dee's always been an amazing friend to me, and now I have to be one to her.

I'll call her after Brady and I talk—when it's too late for her to do anything drastic. I'll call her after resolutions have been reached and decisions have been made and all the uncertainty I'm feeling right now has been erased by a long, dramatic, exhausting conversation that I've been putting off for far too long.

I take a weighted breath and squeeze the key to the

apartment between my fingers. Then I twist it in the lock and push open the door—to see the last thing in the world I *ever* fucking expected. My sort-of-ex-boyfriend and that girl from the fucking club, half naked and writhing on the couch.

"You've got to be fucking KIDDING me!"

Brady looks up from where he's buried balls-deep in what I'm assuming is a herpes-infested vagina. A look of shock and then of absolute horror washes across his face, and he scrambles to pull on his pants. I'm already racing back down the hallway.

"Rowan! Wait! No!"

Suitcase in hand, I reach the end of the hall and throw myself into the stairwell, slamming the door behind me. I take the stairs faster than anyone with a sense of self-preservation would take them, thanking God that all I brought with me on the trip were flats.

Seconds after the door bangs closed, I hear Brady throw it open, and then his voice is echoing after me down the well. "Rowan! Baby, please!"

I'm practically tripping down the stairs, missing one here or there and stumbling to catch my footing. I'm not even looking where I'm going because my eyes are on my phone and Adam's number is on my screen.

"Baby! I can explain!"

Hah! Oh, if that isn't the line to end all lines. If he catches up with me, I am going to slap him across his goddamn face so hard he goes cross-eyed. We'll see if that bitch in my apartment likes him when he can't see straight.

Adam's phone is ringing for the second time without him picking up, but when I burst through the door, I see his car hasn't even finished pulling out of the parking lot. His brake lights are on, and then they flash white as he throws his Camaro in reverse. I run to him as he speeds back to me, and then I'm tossing my suitcase into the open backseat and literally *jumping* over the passenger-side door to get in. Brady bursts out of the apartment building like a cannonball, my name sounding all wrong as he shouts it across the lot.

"What happened?" Adam growls, throwing his arm around my seat, watching Brady run toward the car. "What did he do to you?" He jerks the car into park and reaches for the door handle, and I grab onto the sleeve of his T-shirt.

"Nothing! Just . . . he was with someone!" Brady is getting closer, and I'm full-on panicking. "Just get me out of here, okay?"

"Sorry," Adam says with a resolute shake of his head, and then he opens the door and gets out of the car.

Brady barely has the time to shout "Who the hell are y—" before Adam's fist punches him so hard that my ex flies backward and lands in a heap on the pavement. I gasp, and Adam shakes the sting from his hand.

"Peach, come here."

I do what I'm told because I'm really just too shocked to do anything else. When I step up to Adam's side, Brady is on the ground nursing his jaw, clearly too frightened to get up.

"Say what you want to say to this asshole," Adam

turns to me, his expression deadly serious, "because I'm taking you home with me, and I never want you seeing him again because you're too fucking good for a cheating piece of shit."

My eyes swim with tears, but I keep them directed at Adam so that Brady doesn't get the satisfaction of seeing how much he hurt me. Again. "There's nothing left to say."

Adam tucks me under his chin and plants a kiss against the top of my head. I feel him turn his chin toward Brady, and then he says, "You hear that? You fucking blew it, and if you ever try talking to her again, I'm not the only guy you'll have to fucking deal with."

Chapter Twenty-One

IN FRONT OF Adam's apartment building, I find myself in his arms again.

"It's okay," he says to calm me. "It's okay. Just . . . take a deep breath or something."

When we pulled up to his five-story apartment complex, I tried to pull my suitcase out of the backseat but ended up bursting into tears instead. Adam pressed up behind me, wrapping me tightly in his arms. Now, his chest is against my back, his cheek is against my temple, and his arms are laced around my stomach. He's holding me together like I might fall apart.

I just might.

"That guy is a fucking douchebag. I mean, that hair? Come on."

An airy laugh pushes its way out of my nose. Brady's blond hair is cropped short and always perfectly gelled, parted on his left side and swooped to the back. It's nothing like Adam's shaggy brown rocker hair.

"See? You're too good for an asshole like that," Adam says, planting a chaste kiss against my cheek. "Now, I'm going to take you upstairs, and we're going to get you a drink, and . . ."

And? What comes after "and"? Because the last time Brady made me feel like this, Adam took me to his bus, got me a drink, and then taught me all of the wonderful things he could do with his tongue.

"And?" I risk asking. If he doesn't finish that sentence soon, I'm pretty sure I'll need to sit down—right here in the middle of the parking lot while I wait for my head to stop swimming.

"And . . . we'll do whatever it is friends do when shit like this happens." Adam's gentle hands urge me to turn around. "I've never really done this before."

I imagine he hasn't. He's been on the other end though, I'm sure, making girls like me cry. They've probably called him every name under the sun. And maybe he deserved it . . . which is probably why he's stuck here with me now, losing what's left of his weekend. Karma's a bitch.

"Have you ever cheated on anyone?" I ask impulsively. I suddenly need to know, because . . . because I just need to.

"Cheated?"

I nod, afraid of the answer.

Adam leans against the car door, drumming his fingers against the shiny black metal. "Cheated . . . no. You have to be in a relationship to cheat on someone, right?" When I nod, he says, "I don't really do relationships. One crazy girl tried to accuse me of cheating, but she knew what she was getting into. They all know. It's not like it's a secret."

He's right, after all. Anyone who spends any time at all with Adam can see how he is. Flirty and reckless and noncommittal. But even though those qualities are what should warn girls to stay away, they're the exact things that draw girls to him. Girls like me. Adam is a bad boy, damaged goods. He's the boy that every girl in the world hopes she can fix.

Only I know better.

"Don't you ever want a girlfriend?" I ask, too numb to care about what I'm saying, even though I know I'll be kicking my own teeth out later.

Adam smirks down at me. "Why? Want to be my girlfriend?"

I force a chuckle, pretending to find the idea absurd. Hell, who needs to pretend? It *is* absurd. "I'm just wondering."

With a smile, he says, "Do I ever want a girlfriend . . . hm . . ." He fiddles absent-mindedly with a stringy black bracelet on his wrist, thinking. "Girlfriends are a lot of work."

"So that's a no?"

He chuckles and scoops my suitcase from the car, carrying it across the parking lot to the door of his apartment building. "It's an observation."

I take his cue and let the conversation drop as we walk through a lobby with polished granite floors and a five-story-high ceiling. We take an elevator to the fourth floor and then walk along a narrow hall to Adam's apartment. 4E.

The door opens into a large living room, and even if I didn't already know Adam and Shawn live here, I'd know that college-aged bachelors did. Hardwood floors stretch into the space, which features a plush gray couch and two mismatched recliners. They frame a wooden coffee table and face a massive entertainment setup with a large flat-screen TV and big, big speakers. In the corner of the room are more speakers and three guitar stands, two with guitars propped on them. The walls are muted gray and bare, except for a small patch where someone has written, in bright blue marker, DON'T COLOR ON THE WALLS! I recognize the handwriting from Adam's notebook and smile widely.

After setting my suitcase down, he walks into the kitchen to our left and sets two glasses on the counter. Then he opens a pair of cupboards filled to the brim with liquor bottles, his restless fingers drumming against the wooden doors. I hop onto a bar stool in front of the breakfast bar separating the kitchen from the living room and watch him. His back is to me, his black T-shirt hanging loosely over his shoulder blades, when he says, "Alright, I have an idea." He turns around with a mad-scientist glint his eye. "Let's make a new drink. We'll call it a forget that fucker cocktail or something. Just tell me what's in it."

I laugh. "Forget that fucker cocktail?"

"Hey, if you can come up with a better name, be my guest." He smiles warmly at me. "So what's in it, Peach? You name it, we've probably got it. And if not, there's a liquor store down the street."

I think about it for a while, staring up at bottles

stacked in front of bottles. A full fifth of gin catches my eye, reminding me of the only time I ever saw Brady get truly shit-faced. At a homecoming party my junior year, he drank way too much gin and was still throwing up a day and a half later. He hasn't touched the stuff since.

"Brady hates gin," I say, and the corner of Adam's lip curves up in approval.

"I love gin." He grabs the bottle from the cupboard and sets it on the counter. "What else?"

"He hates anything grape flavored." Grape lollipops, grape gum, grape soda—he'll scrunch up his nose and turn his head away like it's trying to escape from his neck. It's actually kind of adorable. But right now? I want to bathe in grape juice, wrap myself in grape-flavored taffy, and shove my grape-clad fist down his lying, cheating throat.

Adam roots through the cabinet, bottles clinking as he slides them around. "Aw, come on, I know we must have—Aha!" He pulls out a half-empty bottle of grape-flavored vodka, smiling triumphantly as the liquid sloshes around. "Anything else?"

I shrug. "I've discovered a love of tequila."

Adam leans in close, resting his elbows on the counter with his chin in his hands. "You have, have you?"

I chuckle and cover his goofy face with my hand. "I have."

With his black-nailed fingers, he pulls my hand to the side by my pinky so he can grin at me some more. "Good to know." He stands back up, turning around to root for the tequila. He mixes gratuitous amounts of all three liquors in both of the glasses, and then he slides one over to me.

I pick it up and study it. When I dip my nose over the rim and sniff, the scent is like a pool of acid behind my eyes. "This is going to be nasty," I cough.

"Good. More reason to make sure you never have to drink it again."

He has a damn good point. I raise my glass, and he clinks his to it. "On one?" I say.

He nods, and then I count down from three, trying not to think too hard about the last time I counted backward with Adam and all of the toe-curling things that happened afterward. On one, I gulp my drink down, and it blazes a river of fire all the way from my tongue to the pit of my belly. Eyes watering, I look back up to see Adam still holding his full glass, grinning at me.

"You have to drink yours too!" I complain, my throat and eyes stinging like unholy hellfire.

"Are you sure you don't want to be *extra* forgetful?" he asks, setting his glass in front of me.

"Adam!" I scold, sliding it back over. My hoarse voice alone is evidence of how strong the drink is.

Adam laughs and sighs, steeling himself. Then in one quick movement, he tilts his head back and empties the amber liquid down his throat. "Holy *Christ*," he chokes, setting the glass down and vigorously shaking his head back and forth like he might be able to shake the acid-hot taste away. "If that doesn't make you forget, I don't know what will!"

By the time Shawn comes home, Adam and I are totally tipsy. I tend to Adam's busted knuckles while he tells the story of punching Brady in the face, and then we both giggle like crazy. Even when I learn that Joel sleeps on their couch, so I'll have to sleep with Adam, I'm too drunk and exhausted to object. I crawl under his covers that night feeling the alcohol weighing me deep into his mattress. Adam is still in the living room with Shawn and Joel, which leaves me alone with way too much quiet.

Before I can stop them, memories of Brady flood my mind and escape in the form of salty tears dripping on Adam's pillow. I thought I was over him, but that didn't make the pain of seeing him with that *same* girl again hurt any less.

When Adam crawls in beside me a little later, I'm trying desperately to keep from sniffling, and instead I end up hiccupping.

"He's not worth it, Peach," he says, lying eye-level with me.

The pale moonlight illuminates the concerned expression on his face, and my voice breaks when I say, "I know."

Adam sighs, and I finally let myself sniffle. After a long moment of silence, he lifts his arm so that the covers are held up and there's nothing separating us but open space. "Come here."

"Why?" I nervously ask. I want to go to him. Badly. But my nerves are making me run my mouth instead of closing the distance between us.

"Because I'm going to hold you."

"You're going to hold me?"

Adam nods against his pillow.

"Why?"

He pauses for a moment, and then he says, "Peach?"

"Yeah?"

"Stop asking questions and just get over here."

While I battle my better judgment, Adam holds the covers in the air, waiting. I cautiously inch my way across the bed and press my front against him, and he wraps his arms around me. I don't know what to do with my hand, so I wrap my arm around him, placing my palm against his back. And then we're just holding each other.

Adam lets out a deep sigh, and I gaze up at him. "What?"

"Nothing," he answers without looking down at me. "Go to sleep."

I snuggle closer, trying to get comfortable, and Adam's hold on me tightens. My cheek molds to his hard chest, and I listen to him breathe. I want to thank him—for coming to my rescue tonight, for letting me stay with him, for holding me. For everything. But instead, I fall asleep to the perfect rhythm of his heart.

Chapter Twenty-Two

THE NEXT MORNING, I wake in Adam's arms—which is nice and does all sorts of butterfly things to my stomach until I realize that all of our studying is about to be for nothing because we are running *royally* freaking late.

"TEN FORTY?!" I launch myself out of bed so fast that my feet get tangled in the covers, and then I'm tripping and hopping and nearly eating floor. "No wonder you're always late!" When Adam just lies there staring at me, I throw the covers off of him—not caring that he's only in his boxers—and grab his hand, yanking him to his feet.

He smiles at me as I rant about how he needs to get dressed faster than he's ever gotten dressed before because I didn't bust my ass tutoring him all weekend just for fun. With one hand waving frantically in the air and the other clinging to the silky, oversized gym shorts I borrowed from him to wear to bed last night, I'm sure I look insane.

The shorts nearly drop from my waist as I usher Adam toward his closet and then rush out of the bedroom. I sprint to my suitcase in the living room, hastily unzip it, and grab a wrinkled pair of jeans. There's no sign of Joel or Shawn as I rush to the bathroom and dive into my pants. Adam's apartment is over ten minutes away from school. Between that and the time it will take to walk to class, we're barely going to make it. And if he's late one more time . . .

When I rush out of the bathroom, Adam is fully dressed in long black jeans and a charcoal-gray V-necked T-shirt. His wrists are decorated with bands and string bracelets that he never takes off, and he's pulling a mug from the kitchen cabinet. There's a full pot of coffee warming—I'm guessing Shawn made it—but we have time for coffee like we have time to fry up some eggs and bacon and toast and, hell, bake a freaking three-tiered cake while we're at it.

"No, no, no," I say, swiping the mug from Adam's hand and setting it on the counter.

He pouts, eyeing the mug like it contains the secret to immortal life. "Seriously?"

"I'll get you a coffee after the test!" I insist, circling behind him so I can push him toward the door.

He chuckles and lets me nudge him step by step. At the door, I throw my backpack over my shoulder, and then I grab his hand and drag him into the hall. When I let go, he slips his palm back into mine and grips it tight.

"Guess we better hurry," he says with a playful smile, and then he pulls me into a run. Hand in hand, we race past the elevator, down all four flights of stairs, and across the parking lot. Adam jumps behind the wheel of his Camaro and starts the engine, throwing his arm behind my headrest.

"You're going to need to run faster than that if you want to make it to class on time," I huff.

He flashes me a white smile and then whips the car out of the spot. But we don't get two full blocks before the worst happens. Orange cones. A burly woman in a yellow vest. A big orange sign that says DETOUR.

I lean forward in my seat, watching Adam's graduation go up in smoke. "No," I sigh.

Adam pulls up next to the woman. "Any way we can go around?"

"Is it an emergency?" she asks.

"Yes!" I shout, and her eyes dart to me.

"What kind of emergency?"

"My . . . dog . . . is in the hospital." When she eyes me doubtfully, her face full of deepened lines, I say, "He got hit . . . by a train."

Trying to look grave, Adam gazes up at her and says, "It was a very small train. The kind that wouldn't immediately flatten and kill a poor little Chihuahua like Tinker Bell."

Thirty seconds later, we're racing down the detour road, and I'm yelling, "A Chihuahua?!"

"A train?!" Adam laughs.

Dear God, we suck. We are the worst Bonnie and Clyde ever. I'm surprised that woman didn't bitch-slap us with her handheld stop sign.

My fingers claw into the seat as Adam guns the car through a yellow light. The next one flashes red seconds before we cross it, but he doesn't slow down. I sink lower in the seat, hoping we don't get a ticket . . . or, you know . . . die.

When we're on the last stretch of road that leads to the campus entrance, I'm chewing my nails into stubs. Three minutes left. We're never going to make it. It's a physical impossibility. Adam is going to fail and—

He jerks the wheel left, and his car dips into a ditch before roaring up onto the perfectly manicured campus lawn. We coast over the lush green grass until we pull directly up to Jackson Hall.

"You can't park here!" I protest as Adam pulls to a stop.

"I *have* to park here." He shuts the car off and pulls his keys from the ignition.

What the hell is he thinking? They'll tow his car! Or kick him out of school! "You . . . you . . . oh my God," I stutter, holding out my hand. "Give me your keys."

"No way," he says, shaking his head. "I don't want to make you late."

I'm panicking now because every second Adam argues with me means one second closer to us *both* being late. "Dr. Pullman loves me," I snap, gripping his shoulders, "but he HATES you, so just give me your damn keys, Adam!"

He hesitates, but then he hands them over. He stares at me for a moment longer and then leans in, planting a quick kiss against my cheek before jumping out of the car and running into the building. There are students *every-where* staring at me as I climb over the center console and tumble into the driver's seat, pulling it all the way up and adjusting the wheel. I turn the keys in the ignition and Adam's convertible roars to life. Thank God I know how to drive stick, or this would be a whole hell of a lot more interesting. I do a wide U-turn and pull back onto the road, bypassing the main entrance and sneaking into the back entrance of the parking garage just in case security has been called.

By the time I get to class—ten minutes late—the back of my neck is drenched with sweat from running all the way to Jackson Hall. My hair is unbrushed and ratty from the ride here, I have no makeup on, I'm wearing the same shirt I slept in—which I borrowed from Adam and is easily two sizes too big—and my jeans smell like they were worn three days ago and haven't been washed since . . . because they were, and because they haven't.

And Adam Everest is looking up from his exam to smile at me from the front row. A breathless sigh escapes me as I approach Dr. Pullman. "Sorry I'm late," I tell him.

"Are you feeling okay?" The concern on his face reaffirms just how terrible I look. "You can always take this exam later if you're not feeling up to it, Rowan."

"No, I'm okay. Thanks though." I force a smile as he hands me the exam, and then I drag myself up the stairs to sit next to Leti. He looks me up and down, and I can see all the questions he's dying to ask me spinning behind his golden-brown eyes.

"I'll tell you later," I whisper, and then I sit down and

get to work. The test is absolutely killer—which is why I nearly dive out of my seat when Adam stands up to be one of the first students to turn his in. I want to body surf over everyone in the rows in front of me so I can stop him from leaving. I want to scream at him to check and double-check and triple-check his answers. But then his exam is in Dr. Pullman's hands and he's walking out the door.

God, I hope he passed. He *better* have passed . . . or I'm going to kill him and then bring him back to life just so I can kill him again.

By the time I'm finished with the test, I feel drained—emotionally, physically, intellectually. I'm tempted to skip speech class and walk back to Dee's dorm for a nap, but I have a feeling she'd kill me for not showing up to give her all the details of last weekend. I'd wake up hanging upside down from the fire escape, with her standing in front of me with her arms crossed and a fire poker in her hand.

When I stand up to walk down the stairs of the auditorium, Leti stands up too, and I can tell he was waiting on me to leave. We hand Dr. Pullman our tests and then find an open bench in the hall. I sit with my legs sprawled out in front of me and my head resting against the cold white brick behind me. "That test was brutal."

Leti sits with his legs crossed, his entire body shifted toward me. "Sweetie, I have to ask . . ." I peek my eyes open to stare at him, and he picks at my sleeve. "Is this even your shirt you're wearing?"

I stare down at the oversized band T-shirt swallowing my torso. "It's Adam's."

"Mm," Leti muses, tapping his chin and then tapping my nose. "And why are you wearing Adam's T-shirt, pray tell?"

"This is going to sound really bad . . ."

He waits patiently, even though his arms are hanging awkwardly at his side like he wants to shake a confession out of me.

"I didn't have any clean clothes when I left his house this morning . . ." Since I'd only packed enough clean clothes for the weekend, Adam insisted I borrow his to wear to bed, and this morning, I barely had enough time to launch myself into a dirty pair of jeans, much less worry about changing my shirt.

Leti's mouth drops open, but no words come out.

I start giggling, and then I say, "I just spent the night. We didn't do anything. God, Leti, there's so much you've missed." I tell him all about the trip and then about walking in on Brady, glossing over the homicidal thoughts that now go hand in hand with the memory of my ex's face. By the time I'm done, I feel like I've just narrated a soap opera. An extremely unrealistic one.

"So let me get this straight," Leti says. "Adam wasn't even mad you lied to him, and then he *kissed you*, and you turned him down?"

"Not right away . . . but yeah."

Leti shakes his head. "I just don't even think we can be friends anymore. Some baby angel just lost its wings and *died* because of you."

I playfully roll my eyes and slap him on the knee. "Don't be a drama queen." But that nagging feeling is back, the one that tells me I blew a chance I should have taken. "You think I did the wrong thing?"

Leti pulls a pack of gum from his pocket and pops a piece into his mouth before offering me one. I take two. "I'm sure I haven't the slightest clue, baby-angel-killer. I guess what's right for me might not be what's right for you . . . Do you like him?"

I stare at my flip-flops and chew on my lip until I can't bear to hold it in anymore. "I like him a *lot*," I finally confess. "Like, seriously, Leti. He's like . . ." I sigh. He's Adam. He's *so* Adam.

"And I'm guessing that's why you didn't let things go further . . ."

I stare up at him, not understanding. "Huh?"

"Adam is a heartbreaker. And you've had your heart broken enough."

Leave it to Leti to hit the nail right on the head. I wrap my arms around his neck, squeezing him tight and breathing him in. He always smells faintly like mint chocolate chip, and he always seems to know exactly how I'm feeling. "Thanks, Leti."

"For what?"

I pull away and smile at him. "Always getting me."

One side of his mouth pulls into a smile, and then he asks, "Have you told Dee yet?"

I'm practically breaking into hives just thinking about it. "Not yet."

"Are you going to?"

If only it were that simple. I hate keeping secrets from Dee, but lately I feel like I have to. Which sucks. It sucks that I have to keep secrets from my very best friend—because if I don't, she'll whirlwind through my life and make things crazier than they already are. "Yeah . . . I'm just not sure how or when yet, so don't say anything, okay?"

After Leti vows his silence, he heads to his next class and I hopelessly try to comb my fingers through my hair in the girls' bathroom. I only succeed at making it even rattier until I give up and throw my backpack over my shoulder. Outside, I shield my eyes from the bright autumn sun, and then I hear my name.

Dee?

She's there, sitting on a bench and waving me over, and she's sitting with . . . Oh God.

Last night, I called her to tell her I'd be staying at Adam's for the foreseeable future, but I was so tipsy I don't even remember half of what I said. She must have waited outside our class like a freaking stalker, which I should have *known* she would do. I take a deep breath and walk over. "Hey."

Adam doesn't scoot over to make room for me. Instead, he pulls me to stand between his knees and wraps his arms around my legs. Dee grins at us like a fox—an evil fox with predatory ideas. "So I decided it was time for Adam and me to get acquainted. We're tight as spandex now."

I give Adam a questioning look, but he just smiles up at me.

"He told me you guys are headed to get coffee," Dee continues.

"We are?"

Adam nods up at me. "You said you'd get one with me after the test."

"And," Dee interrupts, "he asked if I wanted to come along."

"Do you?"

Invisible horns grow from her long chestnut locks, knocking the halo right off her head. "I do."

On the walk to the campus coffee shop, Adam wraps his arm around my shoulder and Dee grills me about what happened yesterday at Brady's. I still can't believe that slut was with him *again*. What happened to waiting until marriage? I mean, seriously. Fucking seriously.

Dee grabs us a spot in line to the register and turns around, pointing a finger at me. "I still can't BELIEVE you went back there! Honestly, Rowan, what were you thinking?" She steps up to the counter, orders a frappuccino, and then spins back around like she never stopped talking. "That man is the WORST kind of people. I am definitely going to go over there and fuck something of his up! I don't even care if you come with me anymore!"

"Be my guest," I say with a shrug, and Dee grins at me, surprised.

"FINALLY!" She clasps my face in her hands. "THANK YOU."

Adam chuckles at us as he orders his drink and asks me what I want. I order an iced mocha, and then we grab a table while we wait. He pulls a stool out for me and takes the one next to it.

"So I'm guessing you need to pick up some of your

stuff to take to Adam's?" Dee asks, staring back and forth at us like she's already planning our wedding colors and baby shower theme.

"She needs to get all of it," Adam corrects, which makes her grin even wider. "I'll get the guys to help."

I shoot her a warning look, but she ignores it and thoughtfully taps her finger on the table. "I really like your shirt," she tells me with a devilish glint in her eye. "Is it new?"

My eyes stab another warning look through her forehead, and then I answer, "It's Adam's."

"Hm," she hums, trying to control the impish dimple threatening to sink into her cheek.

"We're just friends, Dee." My tone is flat because I am *so* not amused.

"That's such a shame," she pouts. "His clothes look so good on you." She turns her attention to Adam and asks, "Don't you think so, Adam?"

Dead. She is so. freaking. dead.

I cast Adam an apologetic glance, but he returns it with a playful smile and then tells Dee, "I think she looks hot as hell."

He stands up to get our drinks, and as soon as he's out of earshot, Dee practically dives on top of the table and grabs my hands. "MARRY HIM. Oh my God, make beautiful babies!"

I shake my head, wishing my blushing cheeks would stop changing color like a manic-depressive mood ring. "You're crazy."

"YOU'RE crazy! How have you not hooked up with

him yet?! He's totally into you!" When I don't say anything, she says, "Wait, HAVE you hooked up with him?!"

I subtly shake my head no as Adam strolls back over to our table. He sets our drinks down and then looks back and forth between Dee and me as we try—and fail—to pretend we weren't just talking about him.

"Do I need to take another walk?" he asks with a suspecting glint in his eye.

Dee gives him her sweetest smile. "Would you?"

"Sure," he says, grabbing his drink from the table, "I could use a cigarette anyway."

First he teaches my ex a lesson for me, and now he's volunteering to give my best friend and me some privacy so we can gossip like giggly schoolgirls about him? God, he's perfect. If I thought he couldn't get *more* perfect, I was dead wrong.

Dee swoons as he walks away, resting her chin in her hands and letting her big brown eyes follow him out the door. "I think I'm in love."

"You and every other girl he's ever talked to."

Her eyes dart back to me, her finger pointing accusations. "Including YOU."

I shrug. "Anyway, no, we didn't hook up," I say, answering her earlier question.

"BUT?"

"He tried . . . He kissed me, but I turned him down."

Dee stares at me in shock for a minute, and then she lets out a deep breath. "Rowan . . ."

"Yes?"

"Why?"

"He'd break my heart, Dee. Just like Brady. Come on, you have to know that. I mean, this weekend, he almost hooked up with *Michelle Hawthorne.*"

"From high school?!"

"Yes!" I say, glad that she's just as disgusted as I am. "He had a concert in Fairview, and she was all over him! They apparently hooked up a few months ago."

"EW," Dee shouts, her face contorted with disgust. She stares down at her drink like she's watching a hi-def movie of something I don't want to imagine. "Ewww."

"Exactly." I remove the lid from my mocha to scoop the whipped cream out, eating that first.

"She's such a skanky whore-faced bitch. Do you know that she slept with BOTH of the Hazelton twins?!"

"So did you!" I laugh.

Dee's straw stops swirling around in her drink as she pauses and scrunches her nose. "I did?"

"Yes! You slept with Henry at Beth Miller's Halloween party in eleventh grade, and you slept with Hoyt at Laurel Lake that following summer."

She cocks her head to the side, clearly not remembering. "Are you sure?"

"Positive! You said it was weird that Hoyt was the quieter twin because he was so much louder in bed."

"Oh! That's right! Oh my God, he was so LOUD."

I laugh, remembering the way she had mocked the sounds he made. Her gorilla impression and her Hoyt impression were pretty much identical, minus some armpit scratching and imaginary-bug eating.

"Still though!" Dee says, looking positively disgusted.

"Michelle Hawthorne, ugh! Why would Adam be interested in a girl like *that*?"

"Because he's a total man-slut," I say casually, replacing the lid on my mocha. "You think Brady's bad? He and Adam aren't even in the same league."

"But Adam isn't in a three-year-long committed relationship with you . . . It's not the same."

"And he's not interested in a relationship, either."

"And if he was?"

"He isn't."

Dee grunts at me, and then she says, "So why not just have fun with him? Like friends with benefits?"

"Can you imagine me doing that?" I pause to sip my mocha as she considers. "I'd get attached, and then it would get weird and we'd have to stop hanging out. I'd rather just stay like we are now. We have a lot of fun together. He's cool."

Dee nods. "He does seem pretty cool . . ." She shrugs and stirs her frappuccino. "It's just a damn shame. Is he a good kisser?"

I giggle and blush a fierce rosy red. "What do you think?"

She groans. "I think I should've taken French in high school."

What transpires next can only be described as the Coffee Shop Inquisition. Dee shows no mercy; she's like an iron maiden, stabbing every last detail out of me—with one major secret I manage to keep hidden behind my teeth. I tell her about Adam crawling into bed with me on the bus and kissing my shoulder. I also tell her about making out with him outside of Emily's. But I still can't tell her about making out with him at Mayhem a month and a half ago. It's been too long; she'd kill me for not telling her sooner. This coffee shop is *filled* with potential weapons: plastic forks, scalding hot milk, sharp metal syrup taps. By the time Adam strolls back inside, I'm rubbing my right eye, trying to rid myself of the phantom pain that's taken root there in anticipation of the straw Dee would lodge in the socket if I dared breathe a word about my first time on Adam's tour bus.

"So are you two finished talking about what an amazing kisser I am?" he teases as he sits back down beside me.

I gape at him, resisting the urge to dive under the table to check for bugs because HOW THE HELL DOES HE KNOW THAT?!

Seeing my startled expression, he laughs. "Oh wow, you *were* talking about what a great kisser I am!" He glances at Dee, whose equally shocked expression hides nothing, and then his gaze swings back to me. "Scale of one to ten?"

"So *anyway*," I interject, ignoring him as I desperately try to get Dee on board with changing the subject, "I'm really just hanging out with him for the free backstage passes. I got you one for next Saturday."

She laughs and finishes off her frappuccino. "Yeah, that makes sense. Especially considering what a horrible kisser you said he was."

"Bullshit!" Adam protests.

I shrug. "You can't be good at everything."

He turns on his stool to face me, his knees pressing

against the side of my leg. One of his hands rests on the back of my chair and the other flattens on the table in front of me. "Let me try again," he insists, and my blood somehow manages to burn hot and flash cold at the exact same time.

Dee kicks me hard under the table. "Let him try again!"

"OW!" I yelp. "What the freaking hell, Dee!" I lift my leg so I can rub the throbbing pain away and scold, "You got me right on the bone!"

"Sorry! But did you hear what he said?"

"He's joking!"

She stares intensely at Adam, who is smiling innocently while his fingers drum on the table. "He didn't look like he was joking . . ."

"Well he was," I argue, even though she's right—he really didn't seem like it.

"Were you?" Dee asks him point-blank.

He smiles sweetly and shrugs, not saying a word. His eyes are locked on me, and I can feel the heat creeping up my neck.

I glance up at the clock on the wall, and it's like the heavens have parted to allow me this one tiny miracle. "Dee," I say, a grin spreading across my face, "don't you have class right about now?"

She follows my line of vision and curses, swiping her bag from the stool next to her and pointing a long pink fingernail at me. "I hate you! Call me later!" And with that, she's flying across the shop and spinning out the door like the erratic brown-haired cyclone that she is.

"She's nuts," I mutter to myself. I can't believe she

tried to get Adam to kiss me less than five freaking minutes after I told her what a bad idea that would be.

"She's perceptive," Adam replies.

I stare over at him, expecting to see that cocky "I'm just messing with you" smirk. But he's straight-faced and staring right back at me.

"You should let me try again," he says, all serious.

After swallowing the hard lump in my throat, I manage to murmur, "I thought we decided to be friends . . ."

"Yeah, we did. But can't I still kiss you?"

I shake my head.

"Not even once?" he says, his tongue tracing the seam of his lips. "Just to prove myself?"

"Trust me," I say, sliding off of my stool to throw my cup away because I desperately need the space, "you don't need to prove yourself." When I look back at him, he's watching me intently, waiting for me to explain. "I remember," I admit. "Vividly."

"And?"

"And I'll tell you your score if you promise not to bring it up again."

Adam shakes his head. "I don't do promises."

I shrug. "Then I don't do scores." I start walking toward the door, and he rushes to keep up.

Chapter Twenty-Three

THAT EVENING, as Adam, Shawn, and Joel yank a mountain of trash bags filled with my personal belongings out of the trunk of Adam's Camaro, I ask them the same question I've asked a million times since Adam told me I could stay with him. "Are you absolutely *sure* this is okay?"

"Are you kidding?" Joel asks, tossing one of the hefty black bags over his shoulder with another two hanging from his fist. By the time he slams the trunk shut, there's nothing left for me to carry. "This is like"—he laughs to himself as we walk across the parking lot—"the best thing ever. You realize how huge this is, right?"

Adam kicks the sole of Joel's sneaker as he takes a step. "Shut up, Joel."

Joel skips to land on his feet, snickering quietly. The evening sun is glinting off of the stiff blond spikes on top of his head, making them look downright deadly. "Sorry, man, but come on! This is—"

Adam kicks Joel's foot again, harder this time, and Joel trips forward, barely catching his balance.

"Asshole!" he shouts, still half laughing as he jogs ahead to get out of kicking distance. Adam smirks as he trails behind.

I really want to know what Joel meant, but it looks like he's finally taken the hint and decided to shut up. I cast a questioning glance over at Shawn, who is carrying four of my bags, and he catches my look.

"It's cool with us," he assures me. But that's not what I really wanted to know.

"Why is it 'the best thing ever'?"

Adam rolls his eyes. "Joel's just talking out of his ass. Isn't that right, Joel?"

Joel chuckles and swings open the door to the apartment building, holding it open for everyone. "Whatever you say, Adam."

Inside the apartment, I follow the boys down the hall into Adam's bedroom and they drop my stuff off on his black comforter, which is still hanging half on the floor after our mad rush to get out the door this morning. His walls are stark white with blue painter's tape crisscrossed in a random pattern, and filling the white shapes between the tape are lyrics—hundreds of lines written in bright blue marker. His curtains are black but sheer, and the only pieces of furniture in the room other than his bed are a small dresser and a corner desk. The dresser, the desk, and even the floor are covered with stacks and stacks of notebooks that I don't doubt are filled from front to back. The room is a mess, and it's beautiful, and every piece of it is Adam.

When Shawn and Joel leave for the living room, Adam stays behind, immediately pulling open half of his dresser drawers. He removes his clothes from the open drawers, stuffs them down into other drawers, and then carefully pushes the stuffed ones shut. When I realize what he's doing, I hurry to stop him.

"Oh, no. You don't have to do that," I insist, moving to stand next to him. I feel so intrusive, I want to physically grab his hands and make him stop going out of his way for me.

"I know," he says, but he's already walking to his closet and squishing the hangers together to make extra room. When he's not satisfied with how much space he's freed up, he unhooks a stack of shirt-filled hangers and tosses them on the floor inside the closet. He turns around, smiling at me.

"Seriously, Adam. At Dee's, I just had my stuff in piles on the floor. You saw."

"So? Here it'll be better."

I take a deep breath. "Look . . . I really appreciate what you're doing, but seriously, you don't have to do this. I really don't want you to think that you *have* to take me in or anything. I mean, we haven't known each other for that long and I don't want to be a burden and I know I don't have anywhere else to go but I don't want you to feel like—"

"Hey," Adam interrupts while I practically pull my hair out, "we're friends, right?"

"Yeah," I answer, staring apprehensively at the empty drawers still hanging open.

"And friends help each other out, right?"

Forcing myself to look him in the eye, I say, "Yeah, but—"

"Well, I want you to stay with me," he interrupts, giving me a warm smile. "So . . . you should help me out."

I chuckle and shake my head at him. "I should help *you* out?"

He nods, a goofy grin spread wide across his cheeks.

"You know I probably won't be back on my feet for the rest of the semester . . . right?"

"Yep."

"That's a long time . . ."

"It's not that long."

"You'll get tired of me."

"You'll get tired of me long before I get tired of you."

"You just met me."

"I've known you for almost two months now."

"You're crazy."

Adam flashes me his pearly white smile, and that alone is suddenly enough to convince me to stay with him for as long as he lets me. I thank him, he gives me a hug that makes my insides melt, and then he goes back out to the living room so I can finish unpacking.

As soon as he leaves, though, the warm feeling leaves with him and I'm suddenly freaking the hell out again. Am I seriously moving in with a boy I am *not* dating, who I've only actually known for less than a week, who also just so happens to be Adam freaking Everest?

I reluctantly fill his drawers with my clothes. Putting my bras and panties into his dresser feels beyond strange. Staring down at the white thong that tops the pile of panties in my new underwear drawer, I almost want to back out of my decision. I quickly snatch the silky garment up and bury it at the bottom, covering the bras and panties with a thick layer of boring socks.

God, this is crazy! My mom would so not approve. At least, I don't think she would . . . Would she even *like* Adam? My dad . . . oh God, my dad, my dad! Do I really feel like sending my parents to an early grave?

"Are you alright?" Shawn quietly asks as he enters the room.

I let out a deep breath, feeling light-headed and overheated. "This is weird, right? Please tell me I'm not the only one who thinks this is weird."

Shawn sits on Adam's black comforter, rubbing his hands over his knees. "It's definitely weird."

"Thank you!" I turn around and start pacing. "Adam acts like this is just *normal*. Like it's no big deal." I speak quietly and then slowly close the door, needing some private counseling from the sanest person available.

"Oh, it's a big deal," Shawn confirms. He's staring absently at the wall, and I can see his wheels turning.

"Does Adam do this all the time? Just randomly ask girls to live with him?" If he does, maybe it's not as weird as I think it is. And then I'll at least be able to ask Shawn what happens to those girls. Does Adam get tired of them? Does he kick them out?

If he *doesn't* do this all the time . . . then, well, I honestly don't even know what to make of this.

Shawn shakes his head. "Adam has never let a girl even spend *the night* here."

"I just spent the night here last night . . ."

"I mean before you," he corrects. "Adam has never let a girl spend the night here before *you*."

I stare at him for a long moment, letting that sink in. "Ever?"

"Ever." He raises a socked foot up onto the bed. "And now you're moving in . . ."

When the door suddenly clicks open, Adam looks back and forth between us like he might be interrupting something, and then he asks if he's doing just that.

"No," I say. "I just . . ." I just needed to pry some intel out of your closest confidante. I don't want to get Shawn in trouble, but . . . I need to ask. "Adam, you've *never* let a girl stay here before?"

He shoots a pointed look at Shawn, who raises his hands in surrender. "Sorry, man. She asked. She was kinda freaking out."

Adam's expression softens as he leans back against the door. "Why were you freaking out?"

Isn't it obvious? Because *that's what I do*! "I was *not* freaking out."

Shawn and Adam are both staring at me when Shawn nervously says, "Yeah . . . ya kinda were. I thought you were going to tread grooves in the floorboards."

Realizing I'm still shifting from foot to foot, I force myself to stop fidgeting. "Sorry . . . I don't mean to seem ungrateful or anything . . . but . . ." I sigh and sit down right where I was standing, right on the floor. "I can't help feeling like I'm taking advantage of you." That's only half of it. The other half of me is paranoid that I'm going to get kicked out on my ass the minute Adam finds something else to attract his attention. He's like a honey bee at a botanical garden, and I'm just a tiny daisy in a bed full of roses. I'm the only flower that won't put out.

Adam sits down in front of me on the floor. "Shawn, can you give us a minute?" When Shawn leaves, Adam rubs his hands roughly over my crisscrossed legs to loosen me up. "Peach . . . I've never let a girl stay here before because I've never been *friends* with a girl before. It's not a big deal. I let my friends stay here all the time."

"In your bed?" I ask, just to be smart.

He lets out a short laugh. "No, not in my bed . . . But, come on, was sleeping in my bed really so bad? It's big enough for the both of us. I bet you didn't even know I was there."

"Come on, Adam . . . This is weird."

He frowns, and his head does that adorable side-tilt thing that makes me want to sigh. "Why does it have to be weird?"

"Huh?"

"I guess I just don't get it." He stares at his knees and picks at the frays in his jeans before looking back up at me. "Why is it weird? If we're friends, why can't I do something nice for you? If you don't actually like me, Peach, just say so."

"Adam . . . I was just kidding around . . ."

He shakes his head and stands up to get some distance, eventually taking a seat on the edge of his bed. "No. I've been thinking about it, you know. About why you didn't come backstage that night. Why you never said hi to me in class. Why you lied about who you were and didn't want me to find out. I know you think I'm some kind of player or something, and I'm not denying it, but that really doesn't explain it. I mean, you said we can be friends, so why couldn't you have said that a month and a half ago? Why'd you have to disappear and then *hide*? And then *lie*?"

"I didn't think you cared," I say quietly. I feel like such a jerk.

"Well I did."

I sit down next to him and say, "I'm sorry."

"Why is it so easy for you to be around the other guys but not me? I mean, you can play video games all night with Mike. You can dance with Joel. You and Shawn have inside jokes like you've been friends for years. But I try to do something nice for you and you get all uptight about it."

"I've never shared a *bed* with Mike or Joel or Shawn," I answer.

"Would it freak you out as much?"

No . . . it wouldn't—because I just don't think of them the same way. Not like I think about Adam. "No, but not because I don't like you," I answer honestly.

"Then why?"

Because I like you way more than them, way more than I should. "I don't really want to answer that . . ."

Adam sighs and lets himself fall flat on the bed with his legs hanging over the edge.

"Adam?" I ask after a while.

He makes a noise that translates to, "Yeah?"

I twist my body to gaze down at him, at his shaggy

brown hair and those piercing eyes. His arms are relaxed above his head, pulling his shirt up so the barest sliver of skin is showing just above the waistband of his jeans.

"You're my favorite . . . That's why."

Staring up at me like he's not quite sure if I'm telling the truth, he asks, "I'm your favorite?"

Understatement of the century. I smile down at him. "By a hair."

Adam smiles, and then his expression grows more serious. He sits up, staring over at me. "How much do you like me?"

Oh, that question is so, so loaded. I bob and weave, weave and bob. "Enough to not make you sleep on the couch with Joel in exchange for tutoring."

He laughs, and then after a moment, he stands up. "I like you too, Peach . . . And I'm cool with just being your friend. So stop overthinking this, okay?"

I crawl under the covers and snuggle my cheek into Adam's pillow, feeling mixed emotions over how cool he is with being my friend. "Okay."

I roll toward the wall, expecting Adam to leave, but instead he takes off his jeans and crawls in next to me, wrapping his arms around me.

I don't really want to point out what I say next, but I'm too curious about what his reply will be to stop myself. "Friends don't do this, Adam."

"Well we're friends and we *are* doing this, so it looks like you're wrong for once."

I chuckle before snuggling even deeper into his arms.

Chapter Twenty-Four

EACH NIGHT FOR the next week and a half, I fall asleep with Adam's arms around me, and each morning, I fail the ultimate friend test. I usually wake up before the alarm, and with no reason to get out of bed, I don't. I lie with Adam until real life calls, and then I spend the rest of the day trying to convince myself that my reluctance to leave his bed each morning means nothing.

He drives me to school, and sits with me in French class, and we spend our evenings together, and . . . this is a mess. I'm a freaking mess.

I know it, and yet I still don't get out of bed on Friday morning. I lie in his arms until I fall back asleep. When I wake later, it's because he's crawled on top of the covers and laid his entire weight on me. He's dressed, and his freshly washed hair is dripping on my forehead.

"Guess what," he says, his eyes bright with excitement.

I try not to let a goofy smile consume my whole face. "What?"

"I got an A on that French test."

My eyes open wide. We studied for that exam harder than I've ever studied for anything in my entire life, but I never expected Adam to ace it! "You did?"

"Yep," he says, beaming down at me. "Ninety-two percent."

Without thinking, I lock his face between my hands, and his smile gets even wider. "Adam! Oh my God, that's awesome!"

"Grades got posted this morning," he says, laughing as I pull him into a strangling hug. "You should check yours. I bet I beat you."

He didn't beat me, of course, but I'm still super proud of him, and Adam decides to throw a party to celebrate. Later that night, I'm sitting across from him in a big circle on the living room floor. Low music is playing from the speakers nearby, mingling with the faint sounds coming from the video game that Mike and Macy are immersed in at the other side of the room. The rest of us are playing the drinking game Kings.

I'm glad Dee was able to drag Macy along, but we've barely worked Macy up to being relaxed enough to come to a party—getting shit-faced with a bunch of rock stars isn't exactly in her comfort zone. Mike seemed to pick up on her apprehension, asking if she'd like to play a video game with him instead. He said he was just happy to have the excuse to play, but I know it was more than that; he's sweeter than he likes to let on.

"Okay," Dee says, wiggling her fingers over the card pile since she enthusiastically volunteered to go first, "how do I play this game?"

She's sitting to my right, and Leti is to my left. Joel, Shawn, and Adam are playing too, along with two skanks from the ground floor that Joel took the liberty of inviting. Kayla and Zoey. Kayla is by far the more outspoken of the two, with long black hair, deep blue eyes, and fake boobs for days. Zoey is a tiny little thing with choppy bleached-blonde hair and, judging by the looks of her, an entire pharmacy's worth of diuretics.

Shawn hands Dee his phone, which displays a glossary of what each card means. "Pick a card and tell us what it is," he instructs, and Dee flashes him a shamelessly flirtatious smile as she plucks her first card.

"Okay, a five," she says, "so that means . . ."

The sound of six hands loudly slapping the hardwood floor surprises me into slapping mine down too, and all of the guys bust up laughing.

"What the hell?" Dee says, her nose scrunched with irritation.

"Last one to slap the ground has to drink!" Joel exclaims. He's dressed in dark denim jeans and a neon-yellow band T-shirt that highlights the blond spikes forming a runway down his head.

"That's no fair! I didn't know the rules!" Dee looks to me for backup, but I just shrug. After an aggravated huff, she picks up her cup. "Fine, but you guys are assholes."

All of the guys smile at her appreciatively, but with a body like Dee's, I'm pretty sure she could say she's a Satan-worshipper who eats babies for breakfast and they'd still smile at her the same way. Ever since she arrived wearing curve-hugging skinny jeans and a backless black top, Joel hasn't been able to take his eyes off her.

We each take turns picking cards and taking drinks, until Kayla—also known as the black-haired skanko-potomous sitting between Adam and Shawn—picks an "I never" card.

"Oh, yay!" she exclaims, sitting back on her knees and tugging on her black mini-skirt. She wouldn't have to fight with it so damn much if she had worn something sensible. To Dee's disdain, I'm still dressed in a navy-blue T-shirt and the light gray leggings Adam drew all over this morning when we were curled up on the couch. I was sitting by the arm and he was sitting next to me. He randomly tugged my legs into his lap, bit the cap off of his blue marker, and asked if he could draw on me. In that moment, with my legs stretched over his jeans and his hands on my thighs, I wanted him to do a hell of a lot more than write on me, but I managed a silent nod of my head.

"Hm," Kayla continues, tapping on her lips in an obvious move to draw attention to them, "I neverrr . . ."

There are so many ways she could finish that sentence. I never: read a book whole way through, passed a class with an A, closed my legs for more than five minutes, had an intelligent thought.

"I never had a threesome," she finally finishes with a sly smile in Zoey's direction.

I don't buy her 'confession' for a second. The sultry look she gives Adam screams that she *has* been in a threesome and already has another tentatively penciled in for tonight. Dee discreetly elbows me, breaking me from my glowering. My eyes are positively twitching in my poor attempt to keep them from narrowing into laser-shooting slits.

"Sure you haven't," Leti says, and if I thought I couldn't adore him more, I was wrong.

In a high-pitched voice that she apparently thinks is cute, Kayla adamantly insists that she really hasn't, while Adam, Shawn, Joel, and Zoey all take drinks.

I'm not surprised Adam has to drink on this one, but I am a little jealous—which doesn't make any damn sense at all. Why would I be jealous of Adam's threesome? I am in *no way* interested in having one. But the idea of him sleeping with not one, but two girls at the same time . . . it makes me want to snatch his hand from the card pile and drag him back to his room to make him forget all about past threesomes and future threesomes and every girl who isn't me.

Which is just insane. If Dee and Leti were really good friends, they'd have me committed.

Adam chooses his next card while I'm still having a heated internal debate with myself. "I'm the question master," he informs us, tossing the queen of diamonds onto the messy "discarded" pile. "That means I can ask any of you a question, and if you answer it, you have to drink." He immediately looks my way. "Need any clarification about that?" I shrug, refusing to fall into his trap, and he smiles approvingly at me before turning his attention to Kayla. "What about you? Any questions?"

His smooth voice elicits a satisfied grin from her, and she answers him without a second thought. "Nope."

Adam snickers as most of the circle laughs at Kayla's expense. She blushes beet red when she realizes her mistake, and then she swallows her penalty drink. When she sets her cup back down and her cheeks are still rosy, Adam rewards her with a big, genuine smile that makes me bristle.

Someone really needs to explain to him that harebrained idiocy is *not* freaking cute.

Neither is the way she keeps licking her lips or playing with her hair. When it's my turn again, I've spent the last few minutes daydreaming about holding her down and shaving her head. I reluctantly direct my attention back to the pile and take my turn, drawing another "I never" card.

"Here it comes," Dee says, fidgeting with anticipation. In high school, there was always one thing I could say that would ensure everyone else had to drink: "I never had sex." But frankly, that's the last thing I want Adam or any of the rest of these guys to know. I'd never hear the end of it—I'd be a walking, talking pariah. I can only imagine the way they'd look at me if they knew.

There are so many things I haven't done, my options for this turn are pathetically endless. I've never gotten a speeding ticket, I've never cheated on a test, I've never trespassed, I've never skinny-dipped. Finally, I settle on, "I never had a one-night stand." I'm not ashamed of this one, and I smirk, knowing I've still got everyone pegged.

Shawn nods appreciatively, and Adam raises his cup

in a mock toast. Everyone—even Leti—has to take a drink.

"You're missing out!" Zoey says to me, but it's obvious her comment is meant for Adam's benefit—letting him know just how down she is for a one-night stand. I don't even try to hide my eye-roll. Kayla catches it, but I don't care. She's been inching closer and closer to Adam since we started playing, and if she ends up on his lap, I swear to God I'm going to find an excuse to spill my beer on her.

When it's her turn again, she picks the "rule maker card," which means she gets to make a rule for the game. "Okay," she says, flicking her loosely curled midnight-black hair over her shoulder, "so how about . . . when a player picks a seven, they have to kiss someone in the circle." She smiles brazenly at Adam. "Their pick."

When Zoey giggles, the two sluts share a secret smile that seriously makes me want to bash their heads together. Even though Joel invited them here, we all know who they'd pick, and it definitely isn't Joel. Seven is a card that hasn't been drawn yet, so they're maximizing their chances. For hollow-skulled twits, they definitely know how to strategize.

Unfortunately for them, I pick the first seven. Dee's shrill squeal breaks me from my shock. She claps her hands together, and Leti stares at me with animated awe lighting his eyes like fireworks, like I'm about to unlock the secrets of the universe or do something equally epic.

"This should be good," Joel says, angling his body for a better view. Everyone's eyes are on me.

I look at Adam first, because I suck and have no impulse control. He's staring back at me, his expression utterly unreadable. I quickly force my eyes to the floor and curse myself for blatantly glancing at him the minute I saw my card. Knowing I have to cover up the slip, I look up at Joel, and then at Shawn. I force my eyes to travel all around the circle until my gaze lands on Dee. She widens her eyes in warning, and that's all she needs to do for me to know what she's thinking. I can practically hear her frantic inner monologue: *Don't you dare do what you're thinking of doing! Pick Adam! Pick him! Pick him or I'm going to glue your lips to his while you sleep!*

"Dee," I choose, ignoring her unspoken threats and shifting to face her. She's my only real option. If I pick Adam, he'll know I like him, and that will ruin everything. If I pick Joel or Shawn, they'll *think* I like them, and that will just be awkward. Dee is safe, and no one ever specified what kind of kiss. A peck and we'll be done.

"YES!" Joel abruptly shouts, slapping the ground. "THANK YOU GOD!"

"WAIT!" Mike hollers from where he's still gaming with Macy in the corner of the room. "Hold on a second!"

Shawn laughs. "Mike, better pause that game and get over here!"

"I can't pause it!" His fingers are moving like crazy over the controller, the glow of the TV illuminating his frantic face. "It doesn't . . . I can't . . . It doesn't pause!"

Dee leans in and whispers, low so that only I can hear, "What are you doing?! Just pick Adam!"

I shake my head and pull away. "Just a peck," I say loud enough for everyone to hear.

Dee sighs and impatiently puckers her lips, and I swear that Shawn, Adam, and Joel are all leaning in like they're trying to memorize the curves of our lips. Mike nearly trips over his own feet as he runs over for a courtside seat, and I have to shake my head. Men—they all suck.

"You ready?" I ask Dee.

"Lay it on me, lover."

Our lips touch and untouch in an instant, and I swear I can hear crickets chirping for a moment before Joel groans. "What the hell was that?" he complains. "That wasn't even a kiss!" I can't help smirking, but he frowns at us like we just stole his favorite childhood toy and smashed it with sledgehammers. "That could've been so fucking hot," he whines.

"We'll do it!" Kayla crawls toward Zoey, prompting Dee to say what I'm thinking.

"If you two do it, I swear to God I'm going to throw up."

"I second that," I add, and she smiles at me.

Kayla and Zoey ignore us and kiss anyway, directly in front of Adam's face. Dee makes gagging noises the whole time, but I can't even watch. I don't want to see Adam's reaction, so I stand up and walk back down the hallway.

"Where are you going?" Leti calls.

"Bathroom!"

I take a minute to collect myself, rolling my eyes at myself in the mirror. What the hell is my problem? It's not like he's my boyfriend or anything. We're just freaking friends! Friends who sleep together and cuddle and spend almost every waking moment together . . . but

still just freaking friends. Because that's what I wanted—
WANT—to be! I need to get a grip on whatever this is
I'm feeling. And then I need to toss it on the ground and
smash it, douse it in gasoline and light it on fire.

I open the door and begin walking back down the
hallway, shrieking when strong arms lock around me
from behind.

Adam laughs. "Not having fun?"

"Sure I am," I lie as he penguin-walks me down the
hallway.

"You didn't look like it."

I force a smile at him over my shoulder. "Maybe I'm
just not as fun as some of the other girls here." Sad, but
probably true.

Adam suddenly lifts me off the ground, making me
squeal. He carries me out to the kitchen and sets me down
on the counter. Shawn is leaning against the fridge ordering pizza, and Dee is sitting at the breakfast bar munching on some tortilla chips, watching us with amusement.

"What are you doing?" I ask Adam as he braces his
hands on either side of me.

"Do you remember that little game we played at IHOP?"

How could I forget? I recall exactly which game he's
talking about—the one where we pretended to be a couple
to make that table of girls jealous. That was before Adam
found out who I was, when he kissed the corner of my
mouth and nearly made me swoon to death. My heart
flutters at the memory. "Yeah . . ."

"Well, that was fun, wasn't it?" His smile is full of
trouble. I know where he's going with this.

"Yeah . . ."

Adam brushes my hair away from my ear, leaning in slowly and pressing his lips against it. His voice is quiet and smooth when he says, "So let's have some fun."

I can't help glancing back at Kayla and Zoey, who are both still sitting with Joel and Leti on the floor. They're pretending not to be watching Adam and me—and sucking at it, just like Joel is pretending not to be watching Dee—and sucking at it.

When Adam pulls away to gauge my reaction, I surprise myself—and him—by spreading my legs and pulling him between them. I tug on his neck until his ear is at my mouth. I know he's down with playing this little game, but I'm betting Kayla and Zoey have a hell of a lot more to offer. Worried, I ask, "Are you sure you don't want a threesome?"

Adam chuckles and leans back. "Are you offering?"

I playfully swat his chest, but he catches my hand, his eyes never leaving mine as he raises my wrist to his lips and presses a soft kiss against my pulse point. I wonder if he can feel my heart racing—because it's definitely threatening to pound out of my chest.

Dee's voice reminds me that she's literally sitting right by me. She's holding a chip near her gaping mouth, frozen in place. "This is better than porn."

An embarrassed giggle escapes me, and then Adam takes my hand and walks me to the couch, tugging me onto his lap while Kayla and Zoey openly stare at us.

For the next twenty minutes, he flirts with me, tracing his fingers down my arms, squeezing my knees, nuzzling my neck and whispering in my ear. When the pizza arrives, I'm all too grateful to launch myself off of his lap and practically teleport to the kitchen. The last thing he did was kiss my neck, and I seriously don't think I could take any more. I was experiencing the sweetest parts of hell.

After everyone stuffs themselves with pizza, we reclaim our spots on the floor and start the game back up. Joel picks the next rule maker card on his first turn and—because he's clearly still traumatized over my non-kiss with Dee—fervently demands that all future kisses include full tongue and last at least ten seconds. I'm surprised he didn't throw over-the-clothes groping in there, but I don't want to mention it—the last thing I want to do is give him ideas and then have him draw another rule maker card.

With each turn that Kayla or Zoey take, I'm paranoid they're going to pick a kiss card and make out with Adam right in front of my face. It would be the ultimate revenge for the faux PDA we put on before the pizza arrived. Even when Dee is actually the person who picks it, I have to hold my breath, worried that she'll pick Adam just to teach me a lesson.

She picks Leti, much to Shawn and Joel's disappointment, and they put on a show that leaves my jaw on the floor. The next person to pick a kiss card is Joel, and he picks Dee, who leaves him with *his* jaw on the floor.

With her finger under his chin, she gives him a kiss that plunges the rest of us into stunned silence. And then, in a daze, he crawls back to his seat, never taking his eyes off my best friend. Kayla and Zoey bristle, and when Dee catches it, her devilish smile widens and she releases a little chuckle. If I wasn't sure that Leti and Macy are going to walk her to her car tonight, I'm pretty sure I'd have to bribe Mike into being her bodyguard.

We continue going around the circle, the night getting darker and the stack of cards getting smaller and smaller until, finally, there's only one card left.

A smile spreads across Adam's lips when he flips the final kiss card over, and then he stretches his arms behind his back and rises to his feet.

He doesn't glance across the circle like I did when I picked that card, and I don't know if it's because Kayla and Zoey are so much hotter than I am, or if it's because of that stupid rule I made about us just being friends. Right now, I wish I had never said such a stupid thing. Last time he kissed me, I made him stop and insisted it could never happen again. Now, he's going to pick one of the girls who practically tackled him to sit beside him, and I'm going to be crushed.

My heart sinks when Adam walks behind Kayla and puts his hand on her head. He hasn't been with any girls in front of me since I moved in, but a part of me always knew it was bound to happen eventually. He's going to kiss her, and it's going to take every last shred of willpower I have to not break into tears. He's not mine. He's never going to be mine. But even if he leaves with her tonight, at least I know he won't be hers either. Not really.

Kayla grins and starts to stand up, but Adam presses his hand more firmly against her head, making her fall back on her ass. "Apple," he says, and Shawn snickers.

Adam walks behind Shawn and puts his hand on his head, but Shawn is too busy smiling at me to even look up. "Apple," Adam repeats, grinning down at Shawn. He walks behind Dee and puts his hand on her head, and I hold my breath. Dee is hot, probably even hotter than Kayla and Zoey. If Adam picks her, it will absolutely crush me. Dee would refuse to kiss him for my sake, but that wouldn't make his choice hurt me any less.

"Apple."

Adam walks behind me, and I wait to feel his hand on my head, but I never do. Everyone is staring at me, and I finally turn around to find him crouched behind me, his stunning eyes catching mine.

"Peach."

I swallow hard, and then—because I'm me—I say something really, really stupid. In a tiny voice, I ask, "What?"

Adam grins and leans in, pressing his lips against my ear. "You just got picked."

"If you don't want to do it," Kayla interrupts from across the circle, "you can just take a drink."

If I was having any doubts about doing it before, my mind is now completely made up. I turn and sit on my knees, and then I reach forward and curl my hands around the sides of Adam's neck. I don't have the courage to actually pull him to me though, so we're just sitting there, a satisfied smile curving his lips.

A second later, he slowly closes the distance between us, and his soft lips press gently against mine, parting them and frying every neuron in my brain. His kiss is silky smooth, and so is his tongue when it sneaks into my mouth. Without thinking, I suck on it lightly, and in the next instant, his arms are circled around my waist, tugging my body against his. Everyone else disappears. There is only the way he feels, the way he smells, the way he's touching me.

"That's ten," a distant female voice cuts in, but who the hell cares? Unless the building is on fire, she should probably shut the hell up, and even then . . . she should probably shut the hell up. "That's ten!" it repeats.

"Shut the hell up!" Dee scolds, and I finally stop kissing Adam long enough to open my eyes. He opens his eyes too, but then, eyes open, he pulls me in for another soft kiss. His lips caress mine once. Twice. He leans in next to my ear and whispers, low so that only I can hear, "We need to talk. In private."

Chapter Twenty-Five

I DON'T KNOW who stands up first, but then Adam and I are walking down the hallway, and . . . God, I have no idea why I'm following him to his room, but I ignore the jeers coming from the other direction and just let him lead me there. As soon as we're inside, he turns around to close the door behind me, trapping me with his body.

"You wanted that." His tone is accusing, but his eyes are questioning, and I'm too nervous to answer everything he's leaving unspoken.

What I want from Adam is so, so much more than kissing. I want a million things he won't ever give me. A million things he won't ever give anyone.

His smoldering eyes fix on the curve of my lips, heating them through his steady gaze alone. "Tell me you wanted that."

My nervous fingers slide up the downy-soft material of his T-shirt and curl around the back of his neck. I stare up at him and gently pull him down until I'm breathing the same air coming from his gorgeous, parted lips.

I can't say the words. I can't tell him what I want. So I continue what we started.

I kiss him.

Adam hesitates for only a second before kissing me back with even more urgency than he did in the living room. His hands grip beneath my thighs and lift me off the ground, and my legs wrap tight around his hips as he carries me to the bed.

He doesn't break his lips from mine until he sets me on the mattress and makes short work of stripping me of my shirt. As he takes his off too, my trembling fingers find the button of his jeans, unfastening it and pulling down his zipper. Adam has gone still, and I allow my gaze to travel up over his flat stomach, past his tattoos, and over his silky soft lips. His eyes hold me captive as he kicks off his jeans and crawls over top of me.

He kisses me like neither of us needs to breathe, and when his tongue is sliding between my lips like that, I'm pretty sure I don't. His body presses me into his soft black comforter, his fire-hot skin igniting the air around us and setting mine aflame. I'm lost in his scent, in his kisses, in his hands. He hitches my left knee up and rocks against my thin leggings, and the moan that escapes me prompts him to do it again. My head rolls back, and he does it yet again, his lips dropping to my neck as he sets an agonizing rhythm.

His fingers are flames licking over my skin, dancing higher and higher until they're cupping the silky material of my bra. The thin fabric feels brutally sensual against my pert nipple, and when he plucks with expert fingers, the inferno completely engulfs me. It steals all the oxygen from the room, but just when I'm sure I'm about to burst into flames, a knock on the door douses the moment.

"Adam, we're heading out!"

"Fuck off, Joel!" Adam barks at the door, and an irrational giggle bubbles from my throat.

I'm here . . . with Adam.

Me . . . and Adam.

His shaggy brown rocker hair frames his face when he smiles down at me. Then he settles at my side and slips his fingertip beneath the waistband of my leggings, snaking it in an agonizingly delicate line across my sensitive skin. Every cell in my body is tuned in to his touch, waiting impatiently for more.

"Why didn't you pick me tonight?" he asks, staring at me while I desperately try to think of something to say that won't ruin everything.

"Because we're friends," I quickly reason. It's not exactly a lie.

"Friends don't do what I'm about to do to you, Peach." Adam's hand slides lower inside my leggings, gliding over my moist panties. His fingers rub in a firm circle, and my breath hitches in my throat at the same time a moan tries to form. "Is this what you want?" he asks.

"Oh God."

Adam nibbles my earlobe, maintaining an agonizing pace with his fingers. "That's not an answer, Peach."

I turn my face to him and suck his bottom lip into

my mouth, which makes his rhythm falter a second before he slips his fingers into my panties and slicks them through my heat. They glide up to stroke my tight bundle of nerves, and I moan either his name or God's, which should probably be the same thing. My fingers thread into his hair and I kiss him like I've never kissed anyone.

"Adam," I breathe, and he deepens our kiss before sliding his finger into me. My back arches and I suck his tongue into my mouth, surprised and ridiculously turned on by the half growl, half moan that rumbles in his chest.

He pulls away only far enough to say against my mouth, "Tell me you want me."

"I want you," I moan. I've never wanted anything so badly in my entire life.

"Tell me why."

I'm breathless when I begin, "Because I—"

My eyes fly open when I realize I was about to tell Adam I love him.

His finger stops moving, and he cautiously leans back to search my eyes. "What were you just going to say?"

"I don't know," I stammer.

Oh my God, DO I love him? Is that even possible?! We've only known each other for two weeks—two freaking weeks—which might as well be five minutes! My head does a quick comparison of how I feel about Adam and how I felt about Brady, and I realize with a certain degree of horror that I think I love Adam *more*. Two weeks with Adam and the pain of losing him would hurt even *more* than losing the man I gave three years of my life to.

His hand slips out of my panties, and he stares at me

for a long moment while my heart thunders in my chest. I'm terrified he knows—terrified he's going to remind me how much he doesn't want a relationship right now, or ever—but then he leans back in and his lips find mine in a dizzying rush. His kiss is bruising and insistent, and my thoughts are foggy with lust when he breathes against my mouth, "Tell me."

When I shake my head, he drops his kisses to my neck and rolls his tongue in the hollow of my collarbone. "Tell me."

My toes curl and my eyes roll back. Adam's hand squeezes between the mattress and my leggings, gripping my ass as he roughly pulls me forward. His hardness grinds against my softness, and I trace my tongue over the shell of his ear.

"Please," I beg, needing him inside me. I've been so close to having him so many times, I'm afraid I'll fall apart if I have to give him up again.

Adam ignores my plea while kissing a soft line from my collarbone to the lacy trim of my bra, tugging the cup down over the swell of my breast and wrapping his wet lips around my primed nipple. When my back arches, it causes me to grind against him, and he moans against my nipple while I moan into nothing. The air grows thicker and the walls close in on us until there's only Adam's body and my body and the beads of sweat collecting on our skin.

"Please," I say again, and Adam swirls his warm tongue around my other nipple. Remnants of his kisses glisten on the one he just had his lips around, his teasing fingers rolling it between their slippery tips.

When he refuses to give me what I want, I squeeze my hand between us and slide the heel of my palm over his boxers, all the way down his length before wrapping my eager fingers around him and slowly drawing them back up. Our bodies are pressed so tightly together that I end up torturing myself just as much as him, my nerves fire-cracking under the firmness of my own touch.

With one of my hands between us and my other threaded in his hair, Adam plays with my nipples, and I savor every flick of his tongue, pinch of his fingers, and nibble of his teeth. I'm whimpering with pleasure and begging his name when he reaches into his desk drawer and pulls out a condom. He tears the wrapper and takes off his boxers while I rush to wiggle out of my leggings and panties. A second later, he's poised over top of me, his arms flexing at my sides while he positions himself between my legs.

He's seconds from taking my virginity, and he doesn't even know it.

A new tension takes root in me, and I'm about to suck my lip between my teeth when Adam sucks it between his instead. He eases forward, slowly stretching me to fit him, but I'm too tight and my nerves are only making me tighter.

"Adam," I pant, breaking my lips from his. This isn't fair to him. God, I want him, but I need to tell him. He's going to be my first, which means this will mean something to me even if he doesn't want it to.

His hips immediately pull back and leave me empty, his face full of concern. "What's wrong?"

"I . . ." I cover my eyes with my hand, my face burning red with embarrassment. I have to tell him I've never been with anyone. There's no way he's not going to know.

He gently covers my hand in his and pulls it away. "If you don't want to do this, we don't have to."

"It's not that," I say, squeezing my eyes closed because I can't bear to look at him. "I've just never done this before."

Utter silence. I don't even hear him breathe. When I open my eyes again, he's just staring at me like he's never seen me before. Like he doesn't even know me. "You're kidding . . ."

"No," I say, shaking my head in shame. I hate the way he's looking at me. I never wanted him to look at me like that, like we're strangers. Like I'm just another girl—a naïve one with no experience who doesn't belong in his bed.

"But you lived with your ex . . ."

I push up on the bed and frantically grab my shirt, pulling it back on while Adam stares at me. "We never did anything. I mean, we messed around . . . Not like we just messed around," I gesture toward his hard, naked body but try to avert my eyes, "but yeah . . . no . . ." Oh God. I just need to stop talking. Please God let me stop talking.

"You're a virgin," Adam says, like he can't quite wrap his head around it.

My bare feet hit the floor and I dive back into my leggings and panties, which are still bunched together. "Yeah, Adam, I'm a virgin."

"Where are you going?" he asks as I make for the door. He's on the bed, on his knees, the erect length between his legs begging for me to lie back down beneath him. But with the way he just stared at me, I doubt he'd want me anyway. I'm not his Peach. I'm just some lukewarm little girl who's way out of her league.

"I have to go to the bathroom," I say, and then I slip into the hallway and close Adam's door behind me.

Chapter Twenty-Six

IN THE BATHROOM, I brace my hands on the sink, cursing myself for wasting my teenage years on Brady instead of losing my virginity in the backseat of some random guy's car like Dee. I'm not the type of girl Adam likes no matter how much I wish I was or try to pretend I am. I've never had a one-night stand or a threesome, both of which would require not being a freaking virgin. He would have been better off bringing Kayla or Zoey back to his room—at least they would've known what the hell they were doing.

Since I'm too embarrassed to face him or anyone I might find in the living room—considering they now know what I sound like when I'm having the best almost-sex I've ever had in my life—I stay in the bathroom until I fall asleep on the floor, and I don't wake up until later when someone lifts me off the cold tile.

"What are you doing?" my groggy voice asks as I wrap

my arms around the someone's neck. I bury my face against their T-shirt, and Adam's scent envelopes me.

"Besides wondering why you're sleeping on the bathroom floor?" he asks, and I remember what happened between us in a rush.

I don't say another word. I don't say anything when he sets me on the bed, or when he tucks me under the covers, or when he crawls in next to me. We face each other under the dim glow of the city lights filtering in through his sheer black curtains, and I wish I could close my eyes and pretend to sleep, but I can't. He's impossible to look away from, gorgeous and staring at me like any girl in the world would want to be looked at by a boy like him, like I wished he would have looked at me before I fled to the bathroom.

He reaches forward and plays with a long lock of my wavy blonde hair, letting it spill between his fingers before his gaze finds mine again. "What were you going to say when I asked why you wanted me?"

My voice mirrors the nervous fluttering in my belly, tiny and uneven when I ask, "Why?"

"Because I want to know."

"I don't remember."

Adam studies me, and then he says, "Then ask me why I want you." His voice is quiet and smooth, in total opposition to mine. He stares at me like I'm something delicate and speaks to me like I might blow away. When I don't respond, he tucks my hair behind my ear and traces the curve of my jaw with his thumb. "Peach . . . ask me why."

His answer can't possibly be the same as mine, and I don't want to hear anything less. Not from him. So instead of asking, I lean forward until my lips are a breath from his, searching his eyes before I whisper, "*Do you want me?*" It's not the question he told me to ask, but it's the one I need an answer to.

I surprise myself by not waiting to for his reply. The pull of his lips is too strong to resist, and I close the distance between us just as he's opening his mouth to give me an answer. I navigate carefully to test his reaction, gasping when his arm circles around me and tugs me flush against him. With his hand splayed across my lower back, his lips explore mine—gentle, soft, and addicting.

He kisses me carefully, too carefully, so I roll onto my back and pull him with me, urging him to take control. Instead, he pulls away and stares down at me with those stormy eyes that melt me from the inside out. I can tell a thousand thoughts are swirling in his mind, each one probably screaming that I'm a virgin, so I sit up and slowly pull my shirt over my head, dropping it to the floor before unclasping my bra. I drop that to the floor as well, and then I lie back down, allowing Adam's hungry gaze to roam over every inch of my flushed skin. His fingertips graze my collarbone before he sweeps a feather-light curve to the swell of my breast and cups it in his palm.

Teasing my nipple between his fingers, he leans down and kisses me again, this time not so carefully. I moan against his mouth when he uses his knee to nudge mine apart and crawls between them, kissing all the way down to my naval and lower. With his lips at the waistband of my leggings, he bunches the material in both hands and slowly tugs them off. Then he settles on his stomach between my legs and splays his hand at the juncture of my inner thigh, watching his thumb as it rubs over the thin line of my pink cotton panties and soaks them all the way through. He continues torturing me even after his gaze lifts to meet mine. "I want to give you something."

His fingers hook into the lacy waistband of my panties and slowly pull them down, leaving my naked body on display in the suddenly too bright room. I close my eyes to ignore a rush of anxiety, but then Adam gently spreads my knees farther apart and the next thing I feel is his warm breath against the wetness between my legs.

I wait until I feel like I'm about to self-combust, and then I gaze down at him, wondering why he's not doing anything.

Which was exactly what he was waiting for.

His gray-green eyes watch my expression as his tongue swipes a slow stroke between my folds, flattening over my clit in a seductive tasting that causes the air to leave my lungs in a breathy moan. My muscles tighten and untighten until my knees start shaking, and Adam pulls away to plant soft, wet kisses against my thighs.

I groan and squeeze my eyes shut, drowning equally in the throes of ecstasy and agony. I need his lips back on me. I need his mouth and his hands and every single part of him all over and inside every single part of me.

"Peach," he says, demanding I open my eyes and look down at him again. "Do you know how long I've wanted to do this?" My bud blooms under his velvet kisses, each one bringing a rush of wetness between my legs that he uses to slide his finger deep inside of me. With his finger massaging just the right spot, he sucks me between his lips and savors me with the tip of his tongue. The sensation is so overwhelming that I instinctively reach toward his head to get him to stop, but instead of pushing him away, my fingers thread through his hair and hold him against me.

I'm moaning. I know I'm moaning, and if anyone is still awake in this house—which they definitely are now even if they weren't before—I know they can hear me. But God, I don't care. Nothing matters but Adam and what he's doing to me.

He withdraws his finger to swipe his tongue through me, sucking on my tiny nub like he's trying to dissolve it under his swirling tongue. My entire body feels like it's coiling too tightly, like it's going to unravel at any moment, and Adam must be able to sense it because his finger pumps back inside of me, curling against my insides as he devours me with his greedy mouth. He watches me watching him, and the sight of those eyes on me is enough to pull me apart. I burst all at once into a flood of white hot rapids, fighting the pull until it overtakes me. My hand flies out of Adam's hair to grip the pillow behind my head as I get swept away. My legs shake, my hips buck, and Adam pulls his finger out of me to grab my hips on both sides. He pins me to the bed and buries his face between my legs.

"Fuck, Adam!"

Moans rumble low in his throat as he drinks me up, and when I can't take anymore, I grip his hair between my fingers and pull him toward me. I sit up to meet him halfway and kiss him while my frantic heartbeat pulses between my legs. Adam's lips press against mine until I'm forced to lie back, and then he settles between my thighs, the hard-on in his boxers driving me wild with want.

"Get another condom," I beg against his mouth.

He shakes his head, our lips brushing in a soft caress.

"Why not?"

His gray-green eyes search mine, and then he pulls away to trace his thumb over the curve of my kiss-swollen lips. "I don't want you to regret it."

The questions I want to ask are drowned in the kisses he gives me, so soft and tender that the rapids in my belly calm into a bubbling pool. He kisses me until my muscles loosen and exhaustion sets in. Then he shifts to my side, leaving every inch of me chilled and wanting. His arm wraps around my waist and tugs me in until I'm spooned inside the length of his body, and then his nose buries in my hair and he deeply breathes me in.

My body wants to sleep, but my mind is filled with the echo of his words. *I don't want you to regret it.* Why does he think I'd regret it? Would he want to forget my name, just like all of the others?

The insecure part of me is shouting, *Of course he would! He's Adam freaking Everest! You're Rowan freaking Nobody! Even Brady didn't want you. What else did you expect?*

But the other part of me—the part of me that just accepted everything he was willing to give me, the part that almost confessed the three words that would have ruined everything—lies content in Adam's arms, wondering why he's holding me like he'll never let me go.

Chapter Twenty-Seven

Can you come pick me up?

The morning after my epically failed hookup with Adam, I'm desperate for an escape plan. I woke with his arms around me and his stubbly face smothered against the back of my neck, but I felt so nervous about how things would be between us that instead of falling back asleep in the only place my heart wanted to be, my stomach tossed and I felt like I was going to throw up.

Dee's response is immediate. She knows me well enough to know that I wouldn't ask unless I needed her, and right now, I need her more than ever.

On my way.

With Adam and Shawn still asleep, and Joel nowhere to be found, I sit on Adam's couch gnawing my cuticles to bits since my fingernails have long since met their maker. I'm saying silent prayers that Adam won't wake up and find me out here and want to talk about why I snuck out of bed, or why I'm using my best friend as a getaway driver, or why I practically begged for him to take my virginity last night after almost telling him I loved him.

He did me a favor. He still wants to be friends.

Friends . . . Unless in the light of a new morning, he realizes we are *so* far beyond that and one of us—the one who has never had and never *wants* a friend like that—will never be able to go back.

My thumb is bleeding and my foot is bouncing up and down when a key turns in the lock and Joel strolls in ahead of my thoroughly tousled best friend. Her chestnut locks are pulled up into a haphazard ponytail, and Joel's normally meticulously styled blond hair is all over the place in the most sexed-up bed-head I've ever seen. I raise my eyebrow at Dee, but she tugs me to my feet before I can even ask.

"Let's go get breakfast."

She and I are almost out the door when Joel catches her hand and pulls her into a not-meant-for-still-virgin-eyes kiss that makes my toes curl in my already-tight flats. Dee's hands flutter to his chest, and his wrap around her arms. Mine hold onto the doorknob because if they take this show to the couch, I don't plan on hanging around to watch. I'll have to steal Dee's keys because there's no way in hell I'm staying in Adam's general vicinity, but that shouldn't be too difficult if Joel keeps her distracted.

Fortunately for me, their lips break apart, and Dee is left just as speechless as I am.

"I'll call you," Joel says, his voice like melting sugar.

Dee takes only a second to recover, and smirking at him, says, "I never gave you my number." She consoles him with a light pat against his chest, and then she leads me out the door.

As soon as we're in the elevator, her hands clamp onto my shoulders, her eyes full of concern. "What happened last night?"

"You first," I say, trying to buy myself some time. I definitely do *not* want to hear the details of what she did last night, but I'd rather talk about that than the disaster that happened in Adam's bedroom.

Dee tries and fails to prevent a smile. She lets her hands drop and shrugs a shoulder, but then her fingers drift to her lips and I can tell last night wasn't as ordinary as she's trying to pretend it was. "Joel came back to my room with me."

Yeah, no kidding. When all I can do is frown, she says, "What?"

"Joel's not like the other guys you've been with, Dee . . ."

The other guys she's been with worship the ground she walks on. She's a siren; once they've had her, they always want more. She thrives on their undivided attention, and if they don't give it to her, she does what it takes to get it. Then, as soon as she has it, she doesn't want it anymore.

The problem is, Joel isn't going to be that guy. She's met her match in him—I just doubt she knows it yet— and I have no idea how she's going to handle it when she's not the center of his world.

"And I'm not like the other girls *he's* been with," she

replies with a confident smirk, her high heels clicking onto the lobby floor as soon as the elevator dings open.

We cross the quiet parking lot together and I pause at her passenger-side door, staring at her over the plum-purple hood of her Civic. "You realize he's kind of a rock star . . ." A rock star, a sex fiend, a groupie hoarder. A name forgetter, a phone number discarder, and hopefully not the guy who detonates my drama-bomb best friend.

"Oh, he's a rock star alright."

"Oh my God." I slide into her front seat before she starts spilling the details of her sexcapades with my couch-dwelling roommate, hoping that Macy was able to stay with Leti last night or the poor girl is going to be traumatized for life. Memories of a senior year camping trip when I had to sleep in a tent next to Dee and Matt Anderson still haunt me to this day.

Dee laughs and slides in next to me, and on the ride to IHOP, I attempt to distract myself from my own train wreck of a love life by stressing about hers instead. I know she's right about Joel never having been with a girl like her before—because there is *no one* like Dee—but I can't help the sinking feeling I get when I think about them together.

"If you and Joel go south," I warn after she finishes scolding me for not telling her about a nipple ring I'd have no way of knowing about, "I don't want to get dragged into it, okay?" Thanks to me, things are already messed up between me and Adam; I don't need them getting messed up between me and Joel too. If he and Dee end up going atomic, I know I'll get caught in the blast.

She scoffs at me. "How could things possibly go south?"

I don't bother answering because there'd be no point. Dee does what she wants, and right now, she wants a bad boy with a mohawk, a nipple ring, and more fame than he knows what to do with. Trying to stop her would be useless, and it's not like I don't have bigger things to worry about.

We're seated in IHOP and have placed our orders when she clasps her fingers on the table and says, "Okay. Time to spill it."

I sigh and rub my eyes, and then I lean forward and concentrate on a scuff mark on the plastic table. "Adam gave me my first—" I hold my fingers in the shape of an O, and Dee gasps, drawing my eyes back to hers.

"You had your first—OH MY GOD. Are you still a—"

"YES," I interrupt, slouching in the seat and rubbing my temple. "I mean . . . I offered. I wanted to . . . But he turned me down."

"Wait, so did he," she turns her hand palm-up and wiggles her middle finger, and my face nearly melts right off, "or did he go," her index finger points down and slowly lowers beneath the lip of the table.

"Both," I answer, and her eyes widen with disbelief.

"And then he *turned you down*?"

Like it wasn't mortifying enough that it happened, now I have to talk about it. With words. And eye contact. I sigh and let my head fall to the cushion behind me, preferring to stare at the weathered ceiling instead of the utter confusion in Dee's eyes—like no guy would ever turn a girl down after doing that to her. Unless of course that guy is Adam and that girl is me.

"Yeah," I say. Turned me down, broke my heart—whatever you want to call it.

Dee takes my hands and pulls me forward so that I have to look at her again. "Tell me everything."

I stop chewing on the inside of my lip long enough to share in limited detail what happened between Adam and me last night, because I'm hoping she'll have all the answers I don't.

But she doesn't.

"Were you really going to give it to him?" she asks about my virginity after our pancakes arrive, adding yet another question to a list that's already impossibly long. But at least this one, I can answer.

"Yes." I was going to give him everything, but he didn't want it.

He told me I'd regret it.

My heart throbs painfully against the cage of my chest because I *already* regret it. I should have known Adam didn't want me like I wanted him. I guess I should be happy he cared about me enough to be honest *before* we crossed that line instead of after.

Dee carves into her pancakes while I let mine grow cold, her brow furrowed while she tries to dissect everything I just said. "Okay, not one damn word of that makes any sense. Why would he turn you down after messing around with you like that?"

I have the answer, but that doesn't make it any easier

to say. Dee lifts her eyes to gaze across the table at me, and I suck in a quiet breath.

"Because I basically told him I loved him," I admit. I almost said the words, and then my actions screamed it, and both of those told Adam the one thing he didn't want to hear. He's always treated me differently than he treats other girls, but then I had to go and act just like them. I had to fall for him just like they *all* do.

"Sweetie," Dee says, the concern in her eyes forcing me to look away again, "you *do* love him."

My forehead falls to the table, and I groan. I don't know when it happened or how it happened, but the way my heart is aching makes it impossible to deny. The only thing holding me together right now is the hope that maybe I can fix this somehow before it's too late.

My text ringtone dings loudly next to my ear, and I lift my head to see Adam's face appear on my phone. His perfect smile pulls at the frayed strings of my heart, and I stare at the screen until Dee orders me to read it.

Why did you sneak out?

I rub my stinging eyes, hating that he knows that's what I did. He doesn't ask where I am, because I'm sure Joel told him, but he knows I'm avoiding him. Because we're not going to be friends anymore and it's all my fucking fault.

"Ro," Dee says, her voice soft but insistent, "tell him how you feel. I've seen the way he is with you, babe. That's not the way a guy treats a one-night stand. He doesn't pick her when he has skanks throwing themselves at his feet, and he doesn't hold her until she falls asleep every night. Adam *likes* you."

I ignore her and type back, *Sorry about last night. I know you don't want a girlfriend. I didn't mean to be one of those girls.*

Dee and I fall into a nervous silence, staring at my phone until Adam's next text rings through.

One of those girls?

I don't wait for her to coach me this time. Instead, I answer honestly. *The ones that want more from you.*

When seconds without a response turn into minutes, I know I must have said the wrong thing, and I scramble to take it back. *Friends?*

But Adam never responds to that text either, and by the time we leave IHOP, I feel like the world ending would be less terrifying than going back to his apartment. I feel like I'm walking face-first into bad news when all I want to do is run from it.

"Well you're going to get an answer one way or another later tonight," Dee reminds me.

We're supposed to go to Mayhem—Adam invited me back when the guys were touring—but after last night? I think I'd rather walk on the sun.

"I'm not feeling so well . . ."

She glares at me before I slip into her passenger seat,

and she's still glaring when she slides into the driver's seat beside me. "If you hide from him forever, things between you two really *will* be over. Is that what you want?"

I shake my head no, and she gives me a wicked smile. "Good, because I know just what you're going to wear."

Chapter Twenty-Eight

THAT EVENING, AFTER waging World War III in front of Dee's closet, she and I reached a compromise. I'm dressed in a stretchy black skirt and a slinky silver top, courtesy of Dee, but I've paired them with long black leggings, sparkly silver flats, and a chic black jacket.

"Stop being so nervous," she orders as my foot bounces up and down. I'm sitting on her bed with my legs crossed, chewing on my thumbnail with my jacket tossed to the side because I'm roasting in my own skin.

"I'm not."

I so am. What's Adam going to think when he sees me? Is he going to think I'm pretty? Desperate? Classy? Boring? Will he wait until after the show to kick me out or will he do it right away?

"You look fucking *hot*," Leti says, pulling me to my feet. So does he—dressed in dark denim jeans and a tailored lavender button-down. "Let's see a little spin."

I reluctantly do a carefully footed twirl, and then I plop back down on the bed and laugh when Leti takes Dee's hand and she does a much more dramatic version. She's decked out in a blood-red peek-a-boo dress with eyelets in all the right places, and gorgeous black ankle boots that even *I* wouldn't mind borrowing.

Dee always dresses to the nines, but she's never spent so much money on a pair of shoes before. We spent the entire day shopping, and she dropped an entire week's salary on them. I can tell the outfit is for Joel's benefit, despite how many times I've warned her over the past few hours about what a player he is. I did my best to recount some of the raunchier things that happened on the bus, but I think it only made her want him even more.

"You know Joel is going to be with other girls tonight, right?" I ask, trying to prepare her.

She flicks her hair over her shoulder and ushers us from the room before flicking off her light switch and smirking at me. "We'll see."

It isn't until I see his jaw drop when we approach him at the bar in Mayhem that I realize how talented she is at playing this game. He has two girls clinging to his sides, but as soon as his blue eyes land on Dee, his arms drop from their shoulders. He gravitates toward her like he can't resist her pull, and then his arms wrap possessively around her.

"Let me show you the bus," he purrs, and she giggles up at him.

"Maybe later. Where is everyone?"

Joel finally notices me then, and his eyes bug out of his head. "Whoa, Peach!"

God, I don't look *that* different. So I have some freaking eye shadow on and Dee worked her magic on my hair . . . and I'm sparkly—super freaking sparkly . . . Not a big deal!

Joel laughs and takes a step back to rake his eyes over me. "Damn."

I'm cherry-red from the roots of my hair to the tips of my toes when Dee says, "Where *is* Adam?"

"Yeah," Leti adds. "Weren't you guys supposed to be onstage already?"

The tussle Dee and I had by her closet, and then the fuss she made over my hair, made us ridiculously late. I was hoping Adam would be onstage so I wouldn't have to have the inevitable awkward conversation with him without at least getting a few drinks in me first, but of course, God hates me.

"He wouldn't go on until Peach got here," Joel says, pulling out his phone to text someone.

Dee winks at me while he's occupied, but I feel the sudden need to be near a trash can in case I need to throw up. He wouldn't go on until I got here? That can't be good . . .

Joel hasn't even finished typing the text when Shawn materializes at the other end of the bar, stopping dead in his tracks when he sees me. His eyes get just as wide as Joel's did, but he recovers much more quickly. "I was worried you weren't going to show."

"Why were you worried?" I ask, feeling more worried than anyone.

Shawn just smiles at me, and then he smacks the back of his hand against Joel's shoulder. "Time for the show."

Joel smiles widely at me. "You need to go to the bathroom or anything?"

I raise my eyebrow. "No . . ."

"Good."

He and Shawn lead me to the bar and sit me on a stool, somehow convincing the people on either side of me to get up and leave so that Dee and Leti can take their spots.

"Stay right here, okay?" Joel asks, already backing away from me.

"O . . . kay?"

"Best seats in the house!" Shawn calls as he walks away, and then he and Joel disappear in the crowd.

"What was *that* about?" Leti asks, still staring at the spot where Shawn and Joel were swallowed up.

I have no idea. All I know is that I need a freaking drink. I spin around on my stool and order an extra strong vodka cranberry, forgoing the straw and taking a big swallow when it arrives. I sip on my drink and talk about anything *but* Adam until the crowd starts screaming and I know he's just taken the stage. Dee and Leti immediately spin around for the show, but I'm too busy ignoring the chills racing up my spine.

"Hello MAYHEM!" Adam shouts, and the crowd rewards him with a chorus of deafening screams. "How is everyone tonight?!"

His voice coats my insides like spiced honey, and I

finally turn around to face him. My heart hiccups and trips over itself when I take in his shaggy brown hair, his ripped-up jeans, his mountain of bracelets and wristbands. He tugs the disheveled hair from his eyes, his black fingernails combing it back until it falls thick on one side. In a fitted black button-down rolled to his elbows, he looks utterly irresistible, and I squirm in my seat remembering everything he did to me last night.

Adam waits until the guys have finished strapping their guitars around their necks and the crowd has quieted down before he smiles and says, "I'm going to start the show a little differently tonight . . . See, I met this girl."

All of the blood drains from my face, and I swear I can hear Dee gasp even over the girls screaming their heads off in the front row.

"Her name's Rowan, but I call her Peach, and this morning she broke my heart."

Dee's grip bites into my arm, but I'm pretty sure my body would require blood flow to actually feel it—which would require my heart to beat which it is definitely *not* doing. I broke his heart? He's got to be joking . . .

Adam smiles that smile that kicks my useless heart into overdrive. "I fell asleep with her in my bed last night, but this morning, she was gone."

I'm pretty sure the girls in the front row are yelling at him to forget me, but Adam ignores them and continues. "Ever since I met this girl, I haven't been able to stop thinking about her."

Joel puts his hand to his forehead and swoons down to his knees, cooing into his microphone, and Adam laughs.

"Last night, I wanted to tell her all sorts of things I've never wanted to tell anyone, but I was an idiot. I thought she just wanted to be friends."

"What'd ya want to tell her?" Shawn prompts, leaning into his microphone with his head turned toward Adam.

Adam stammers, "Uh . . . stuff." He chuckles and continues, "Right now, I want to ask her something."

Joel strums a random chord on his guitar. "What are you waiting for, man?"

Adam takes a deep, shuddering breath and says, "Peach . . . you know I never make promises, but I'm going to make you one right now. I promise I would never, *ever* hurt you like your asshole ex-boyfriend did."

Shawn's smile is bigger than anyone's. "That's not a question, man."

"I'm getting to it," Adam scoffs, nervously raking his hand through his hair again. "God, this feels so middle school . . ."

The crowd laughs, and Shawn chides, "That's not a question either."

"I'm nervous!" Adam shouts, earning high-pitched declarations of love from at least five girls in front of the stage.

Dee whirls on me with her mouth gaping wide. Her hands are in her hair, and I'm pretty sure I'd be freaking out just as much as her if I wasn't in total, utter, mind-numbing shock.

"Peach, I want to be with you."

My breath hitches in my throat.

"We were never friends, and I'm tired of trying to be."

My heart pounds in my chest.

"I want you to be my girlfriend . . . So I guess my question is, can I be your boyfriend?"

A blanket of shock wraps itself around me, and Joel motions like he's cracking a whip. Shawn teases, "I think you should say 'please,' man."

Adam flicks him off, but then he scratches his hand adorably through his hair and says, "Please?" I swoon along with every other girl in the building. "Think about it," he adds, "and tell me after the show."

"Ya ready?" Shawn asks, and Adam nods. They cue the lights-guy and the lights cut a second before spotlights cast the band in a blue glow. When the band starts performing its first song, Dee grabs my arm and hauls me toward the bathrooms, where we can talk without needing to shout.

She apparently didn't get the memo, because without warning, she turns and screams, "OH MY FUCKING GOD! ROWAN!" She latches onto my shoulders. "ROWAN! OH MY GOD!"

"Did Adam seriously just ask me out?" I ask, still too shocked to comprehend what just happened.

"IN FRONT OF EVERYONE!"

My knees are suddenly Jell-O, so I kneel down right where we're standing. "Oh my God."

With me out of grabbing range, Dee latches onto Leti, and they jump around squealing like lunatics.

"Oh my God," I say again, and then my eyes start to sting and I don't know what to do with myself.

When Dee and Leti drop down to my level, waves of

confusion wash over their faces. "Why are you crying?" Dee asks me, brushing her thumb across my cheek and then staring at her wet skin like it's a foreign substance instead of real tears.

"Adam just asked me out."

"I know! Aren't you happy?"

I lift my gaze from the floor and tell her, "I'm in love with him, Dee."

"Uh, DUH!" She starts laughing and pulls me in for a big hug. "I told you, babe! A blind person could see the way you are together. You two are perfect for each other."

"What if he changes his mind?"

"Didn't you hear a word he said?" Leti asks me, rubbing a hand over my shoulder. "That boy just told the whole world that he is *your* man."

A smile breaks through my cloud of tears when I realize he's right. Adam isn't Brady. He made me a promise, and he made it in front of everyone, and he wouldn't have done either of those things if he didn't really mean it. Adam Everest never does anything he doesn't want to—he told me that himself.

"I'm going to be Adam's girlfriend," I say, laughing to myself.

Dee squeals and lifts me to my feet, pulling me into a group hug that makes the night feel even more perfect.

I don't go backstage until after the band does their final "last song." The guys all shoot smiles at me as they exit the stage, but the person I'm waiting for is last in line. Everyone else gives us our privacy, and Adam walks up to me looking a thousand times more nervous than he did in front of throngs of screaming fans.

"I broke your heart?" I ask, and he gives me a sad smile.

"I thought I pushed you too far. I was worried you wouldn't come back."

A chuckle escapes me, and at the look he gives me, I rush to explain, "I thought you wouldn't *want* me to come back."

"Why wouldn't I want you to come back?"

"Because I wanted to be your girlfriend," I murmur, the confession making my heart race even though Adam just told me in front of hundreds of people that he wants that too.

He smiles and curls his hands around either side of my waist. "Do you still want that?"

I stare up into the gray-green eyes that stole my breath before I even knew his name. Before he was a real person who comforted a stranger on a stoop, invited a classmate on a road trip, held a friend in his arms, and asked a girl he cares about to be his girlfriend. "Are you sure this is what you want?"

"I'm more sure of what I *don't* want," he says, the sincerity in his eyes pulling at my heart. "And that's to ever lose you."

My hands slide over his sleeves until my arms are wrapped around his neck, and then I rise onto my tiptoes, aching to kiss the beautiful mouth that just told me everything I wanted to hear. Adam drops his lips to mine, and the world falls away. That empty spot in my heart where I've wanted to keep him fills until it bursts, and then my fingers are threading into the back of his hair and Adam is lifting me off of my feet. I want him to carry me somewhere, anywhere private where I can kiss him for as long as I want to, but then a chorus of high-pitched whistles and cheers sounds behind us, and I laugh against his mouth.

He sets me back on my toes and gives me a smile that warms me from the inside out. "So is that a yes?"

"Oh," I say, giggling when I realize I never answered him. My fingers twirl in the soft hair at the nape of his neck, and I smile at him with all the love I've kept hidden deep in my heart. "Yeah, Adam. *Of course* it's a yes."

Chapter Twenty-Nine

WHEN WE EMERGE back onto the main floor of Mayhem, I'm swallowed by the chaos. Everyone wants to know if I'm the infamous Peach and if I'm Adam's new girlfriend. Each time I confirm that I am, Adam lights up the room with his smile and squeezes me tighter against his side. He poses for pictures with fans but refuses to take his eyes off me while I play the role of photographer; he always smiles at me instead of the camera and makes my butterflies wild.

At the bar, I sit on a stool surrounded by all of my favorite people. Dee is busy arguing with Mike over his lack of fashion sense, Joel is egging them on, Leti is laughing at the three of them, Shawn is nursing a drink while he watches the show they're all putting on, and Adam is pressed behind me with his fingertips brushing discreetly under my top and over my bare sides. I grip my glass with both hands, knowing that he knows *exactly* what he's doing to me.

His whisper in my ear sends shivers down my spine. "It's killing me not to kiss you right now."

"Why don't you?" I whisper back, already feeling the phantom of his lips on mine.

"Because I wouldn't stop at kissing."

His fingers slide higher until his thumbs are tracing the underwire of my bra and my toes are curling in my sparkly flats. I desperately need to get his hands out of my shirt or I'm seriously going to lose my virginity on the bar or on the floor or right here on this freaking stool.

I gently push his hands down, and he groans against my ear, but I don't leave him hanging. Feeling reckless, I turn my head toward him and say, "Shots?"

His eyes spark with anticipation. "What kind of shots?"

I flag the bartender and order a round of tequila shots for everyone. When they arrive, I lift a lime wedge off the tray that accompanies them and spin around to face Adam. He spent the entire road trip trying to convince me to do a body shot with him, and now, I'm finally going to. "Open."

I resist the urge to bite my lip between my teeth when his gorgeous lips part at my command, his eyes filled with a storm that promises to consume us both. I can feel other eyes on me too, but I ignore them and place the lime wedge between his teeth.

Adam closes his lips around my fingertips, the warm wetness on my fingers creating warm wetness between my thighs. I flick my tongue over the hollow of his neck before I lose my nerve, sprinkling salt onto his skin and dipping my tongue slowly, slowly into it. His fingers tighten around my sides when I suck the last of the salt off of his neck, and I quickly swallow the tequila shot. The fiery liquid blazes down my throat and into my belly as I lean forward to bite the lime wedge from his teeth.

Adam lets it fall from his mouth before I can. His lips crush against mine and his fingers scrape against the back of my scalp to lock me in place. My hands fist in his shirt, and he steps tight between my knees, tugging me forward on the stool until he's fitted against my heat. I whimper against his mouth, and he breaks his lips from mine to press his lips against my ear.

"Here or the bus?" he purrs.

Last time he kissed me like that and asked me to go to the bus, I told him I just wanted to be friends. This time, I say, "Bus."

Adam is lifting me off the stool a second later. He takes my hand and whispers something in Shawn's ear on our way out, giving clipped responses to every fan who tries to spark up a conversation along the way.

"What did you say to Shawn?" I ask when we emerge outside, on the same stoop Adam comforted me on the night we first met.

He wraps his arm around my shoulder to ward off the cold while we practically sprint toward the bus. "I told him the bus is off limits to anyone without a death wish."

"You did not!" I gasp, and Adam laughs at me. He unlocks the door to the bus and opens it for me, and then he steps on behind me and immediately tugs me back against him, his hands splayed along the front of my hips. "Do you know what I wanted to do inside?" he asks.

"Hm?"

His fingertips glide under my top again, snaking up my stomach and over my bra. He clutches me possessively, his hands squeezing and kneading until my head falls back against his chest. His lips feast on the curve of my neck a moment later, and I wrap my arms behind his neck, drunk with desire for the man who put my heart back together and finally has his hands on me.

"Fuck," Adam breathes when I grind my ass against him. He reaches down to hold me still, and I know he's holding back. He said he was afraid of pushing me too far, so I take the lead, threading my fingers with his and tugging him away from the door. I don't stop until we're in the black-satin bedroom.

"Peach," Adam says from the doorway, his voice cracking with restraint.

I turn around and flatten my hands against his chest, staring up into the same eyes I fell in love with in a line outside of Mayhem. "Ten."

His brow dips with confusion, and I continue staring up at him. The first time he brought me to this room, he asked me to count backward from ten to prove I was still sober enough to not be taken advantage of. I need him to know that I know exactly what I'm doing and I'm doing exactly what I want. "Nine."

Recognition begins to dawn across his features, and I continue counting. "Eight."

The sexiest smile tugs at his lips, and he takes a step forward. I take a step back.

"Seven," I say with my knees pressed against the edge of the bed, and he begins crawling over top of me. The restraint in his expression is gone, replaced by a predatory smile that makes my heart patter against the wall of my chest while I inch farther onto the bed.

"Six," I say, and Adam's hands push my top up until he's sliding it over my head and tossing it over his shoulder. He drops his lips to my neck, and my breaths quicken.

"Five," I breathe, reaching behind my back and unclasping my bra.

Adam's fingertips graze softly over my shoulders as he pushes the straps down. He drops the bra to the floor, and I say, "Four."

He kisses an invisible line between my breasts and down my stomach, and then he slips off my shoes, planting a soft kiss against my ankle before grasping the waistbands of my skirt, leggings, and panties. He pulls them down in one slow motion and sits on his knees to rake his eyes over every inch of me. His tongue traces the seam of his lips, and I moisten between my legs.

"Three," I say, bringing him back to the moment.

He takes off his shirt, and I quickly say, "Two."

Adam crawls back over top of me, his hair tickling my cheeks until his lips are a breath away. I trace a fingertip over the Magic 8 Ball tattoo inked on his pectoral before sliding my fingers over his sides, relishing in the freedom to finally touch him wherever and however I want.

"What are you waiting for, Peach?" Adam asks, and I

never get to one. I kiss him fiercely, and he moans against my mouth. His hips rock against me, and I moan right back. His fingers thread into my hair, his elbows weigh into the pillow under my head, and he kisses me until I can't think straight. I'm writhing beneath him, needing so much more of him than he's giving me.

I reach between us to unbutton his jeans and then I push them as low as I can manage. My thumbs hook into his boxers, but then Adam pulls out of my reach. He rests his forehead against my chest, breathing heavily. "Peach, we don't have to go all the way right now. I swear to God I just wanted to kiss you."

I comb my fingers through his hair, knowing he doesn't want to push me. But this feels right, *so* right, and I need him to understand how ready I am.

"I wouldn't have regretted it," I say, and his beautiful eyes gaze up at me from beneath thick, dark lashes. "Last night . . . you told me I'd regret it, but I wouldn't have . . ." I swallow the lump in my throat, distracting myself by brushing his soft hair away from his forehead with my fingertips. My gaze finds his again, and I muster the courage to say, "I want it to be you, Adam . . . I'm yours if you want me."

When he kisses me this time, it's different. It's slow and soft, but it makes me just as dizzy. He finishes taking his jeans and boxers off, and then he pulls a condom from his wallet and rolls it on. When his tip presses firmly against me, I suck his tongue into my mouth to draw him in. A moan rumbles low in his chest, but then he wrestles control away from me, nipping at my tongue and lips until I'm soaking wet with want for him.

"Peach," he says, and I open my lust-filled eyes to stare up at him. "Ask me why I want you."

He wanted me to ask him this last night, but I was too scared. I'm still scared—I'm freaking terrified—but I trust him. He said he wouldn't hurt me, and I know he won't. "Why do you want me, Adam?"

With one hand holding himself up and the other tenderly brushing his thumb beneath my ear, he stares down at me and answers, "Because I love you."

His lips follow his words, kissing me hungrily as his hips press forward. A sharp sting breaks between my legs, and I gasp against his mouth and dig my fingers into his shoulders. Adam pauses, pulls back, and then kisses me so insistently that all I can feel is his lips bruising mine. The pain between my legs ebbs, replaced by the overwhelming crush of his lips, and he rocks back into me, a little farther this time while my fingers scratch between his shoulders. He continues easing in and out of me until he's buried all the way inside and I'm able to loosen my hold on him.

"Are you okay?" he pants, but I'm still lost in the three words he said before he broke the last barrier between us.

"You love me?" I ask, happy tears welling in my eyes.

The concern on Adam's face is replaced with a warm smile. "More than anything."

He kisses me until the entire room is swirling with heat, and then he resumes rocking, the sting inside me gradually overwhelmed by sensations that leave me whimpering sounds of pleasure into the shell of Adam's ear. His soft lips explore every inch of my body—my mouth, my chin, my neck, my breasts—until the flood inside me starts welling again, threatening to burst all around him.

I hold him so tightly that I'm surprised he can even move, but his hips are relentless. Our hearts pound against each other and sweat beads across our skin, and Adam thrusts into me over and over again, nibbling at my ear as I plummet over the edge. I call out his name as I fall, and the sexiest sound of surrender rumbles in his chest as he follows me over. His body grows heavier against me with each thrust, and I hold him tight against me, my pulsing matching his throbbing while I struggle to catch my breath.

When Adam lifts onto his elbows to stare down at me, I'm barely holding back tears. I thought I had loved Brady, but that was the love of a girl who barely knew herself. She didn't know what she wanted out of life, and she didn't know what she was capable of. My love for Brady was born of sacrifice—sacrificing my own goals for his, my own needs for his, my own self for him. With Adam, we're both willing to give each other everything.

"Ask me why I want you, Adam," I say, and he stares down at me with so much love in his eyes that I almost tell him right then.

"Why do you want me?" he asks, and a thousand reasons come to mind. I want him because of his eyes and his smile and his laugh and his heart. I want him because of his dreams and his goals and his sense of humor and his light. I want him because he made me promises even though he never makes promises, because of the way he looks at me like he looks at no one else. I want him because of the way I feel when I'm with him and the way I feel when I'm not. But all of those are really just one reason waiting to be said, and I'm not afraid to say it anymore, because I know he wants to hear it.

With Adam in my arms and in my heart, I finally say the words I'm no longer afraid to admit to him or myself or anyone.

"Because I love you."

Epilogue: Adam

___

WHEN MY ALARM goes off that morning, two months after making things official with Peach, I ignore it, wrapping my arms tight around her so that she's snug inside the curve of my body. I bury my face in her long blonde hair and breathe in her strawberry shampoo, hoping that if I just ignore the alarm, she will too.

"Adam," she groans, her voice heavy with sleep.

I hug her tighter and squeeze my face into the space between her neck and pillow. The alarm keeps screaming.

"Adammm."

When I continue ignoring her, a smirk already sneaking onto my face because I know what's coming next, Peach grunts and starts rolling over. She rolls me onto my back as she reaches across me for the alarm. She can't reach it—she never can, because I'm a brilliant strategist encouraged by positive reinforcement—so she crawls over top of me to hit the OFF button, and then she collapses on my chest, her face smothered in my pillow.

Seeing my opportunity, I brush her hair away from her neck and kiss her there—softly, knowing it drives her crazy. I'm rewarded with an involuntary squirm that makes me harden between us, and my fingers dip beneath her soft cotton top. I trace feather-light lines up her back until her skin goose bumps under my fingertips, loving how her body responds to me.

When her lips find mine, *I'm* the one who moans, which might embarrass the hell out of me if I wasn't so busy concentrating on trying to keep my hands from literally tearing her thin top and adorable bunny shorts off her tiny little body. I don't know how she does this to me, but she always does—makes me fucking crazy to be as close to her as possible. No one—*no one*—has ever made me feel so desperate. I'd probably hate it if I didn't love her so damn much.

Three and a half seconds later, I've had more than I can take. I flip her over, and she lets me. I drop my lips to her neck, finding the spot that makes her moan even louder than I did, restoring some of my dignity. My fingers graze under her top, and her back arches when I trace my tongue across her collarbone, making her skin flush my favorite shade of pink. Her hands curl between my bare shoulder blades, scratching at my skin and threatening to steal what's left of my self-control. If I don't get inside her soon, I'm pretty sure those bunny shorts are done for.

"Adam," she moans, and it completely does me in. My name on her lips, sounding like *that* . . . Yeah, I'm not a damn saint, and she knows that as well as anyone.

Her bunny shorts are tossed on the floor a second later, and then I show her why that obnoxious alarm is the best fucking device mankind ever invented.

Afterward, she's breathing deeply, sound asleep in my arms, and I'm remembering the first time I ever held her like this. That first time I held her in my arms as she drifted to sleep—the night I nearly broke my fist on her asshole ex-boyfriend's face—I was fucking terrified. I held her to make her feel better, but once I had her in my arms, I couldn't let go. All night, I had the opportunity to roll away from her—and I knew I should—but I couldn't bring myself to do it. Instead, I squeezed her tighter, scared shitless about the feelings I was having, and about fucking it up and losing her. I'm not sure if that's the night I fell in love with her, but it's the night I started realizing I'd do anything to keep her.

"SHIT!" Peach suddenly yells, jerking out of my arms and launching herself out of bed. "THE ALARM, ADAM!"

"Yeah?" I say, shifting until I'm sunken deep in the warm center of the mattress.

"I promised Dee I'd meet her at IHOP! Why didn't you—"

When I start chuckling, she glares at me. It's not my damn fault she's so irresistible, and she should know better than to trust me to share her with anyone else— even her best friend—when I'd rather keep her for myself.

She growls at me, reading my thoughts, and then she stomps over and whacks me with a pillow. When I grab her wrist and yank her back onto the bed, she squeals and frantically scrambles to get away. I wrestle her beneath me, giving her a smirk she can never resist. My hair is hanging down over her face, and she's pretending not to want me. Even though she just had me less than half an hour ago, she's not doing a very good job.

When I wink at her, she giggles, and I plant a quick kiss on her nose before letting her back up. Peach wouldn't mind if I kept her here another few hours, but Dee . . . that girl is another story, and I know better than to get on her bad side. A few days after Peach and I became official, I accidentally brought up the night she and I met at Mayhem. I didn't know I wasn't supposed to mention it in front of Dee because I had no idea Peach had been keeping what happened between us that night a secret from her. The girl had a meltdown that I'm surprised didn't take out the entire East Coast. Peach spent days texting her and calling her. She even tried prying intel out of Joel, who was the only one of us Dee would still bother talking to, and considered forcing him to deliver flowers and chocolate until I warned her he'd probably take all the credit. Eventually, she had enough of Dee's drama and asked me to drop her off at her dorms. Twenty-four hours later, it was like nothing had ever happened between them, and I knew better than to try to make sense of it.

When Peach bends over to grab a pair of jeans from a bottom drawer of our dresser, I enjoy the view, disappointed when she slips from the room for a shower. If I hadn't already worn myself the hell out, I'd be tempted to try and join her. With other girls, sex was sex, but with Peach, each time is like . . . God, I don't even know. It's exhausting in a way that leaves a satisfied smile on my face and heavy weight in my bones. With her, I'm in it. I'm in every second of it, giving as much as I take because sex isn't just sex with her. It's so much more than that, and if I tried to describe it, I'm pretty sure the guys would have my balls in a jar.

The first time we almost went all the way . . . well, that entire night was just confusing as fuck. First, when I asked her why she wanted me and she clamped her mouth shut in the middle of a sentence that started with "Because I . . ." I thought she was going to tell me she loved me. My heart thundered in my chest, with as much fear as hope. I wanted to hear it, but looking back, I don't know if I was ready—because when she refused to tell me, I started doubting. We both pretended like nothing happened, until I was wrapped in a rubber and pushing into her, and she told me she was a virgin and blew my fucking mind.

I still have no idea how or why that shithead ex of hers dated her for three fucking years and then lived with her and never once crossed that line, but I'm glad he didn't.

When I found her sleeping on the bathroom floor, I felt like the biggest asshole in the entire world. I picked her up and brought her to my room, and it dawned on me with blinding clarity why I wanted to kick my own ass for embarrassing her and why taking her virginity— something I had *always* avoided doing with other girls— was suddenly the only thing I could think about.

I loved her, and I wanted to tell her, but I was terrified of losing her if she didn't feel the same way. So instead of just saying it, I told her to ask me why I wanted her. If she wanted to know, I'd tell her, but if she didn't, I wouldn't push it on her and mess things up. When she refused, I should have been hurt, but then she kissed me and fried every circuit in my brain. I went down on her because I just wanted to give her something, anything, and when she melted in my mouth, I savored every last bit of her.

She told me to get a condom, and my heart galloped like a prize-winning Clydesdale in my suddenly tight chest, but one look in her eyes told me she was still high off her orgasm and that I'd be taking advantage of her if I pushed her any further. I loved her too much to do that to her, even though I was pretty sure I'd be dead from blue balls by morning, so I rolled to her side and spooned her tight against me, holding her in my arms until she drifted off to sleep.

The next morning, when I woke up and she was gone, I panicked. I rushed from my bedroom to find Joel on the couch, and he told me Peach had left with Dee. I raked my fingers through my hair, asking over and over again if she said anything or if he knew anything. The guys wanted to know why I was freaking the fuck out, but what could I tell them? I pushed her too far and now she couldn't even look at me? I sat on the floor in my room staring at my phone until I got the guts to text her. I asked why she snuck out, and a second later, the most confusing text I've ever read flashed onto my screen.

Sorry about last night. I know you don't want a girlfriend. I didn't mean to be one of those girls.

She was *apologizing*? To *me*? My brain couldn't wrap around any of it, so I texted back, *One of those girls?*

The ones that want more from you.

I stared cross-eyed at the phone for a few seconds before yelling for Shawn and Joel. Then I told them what happened with Peach—skimming over the good parts and the part about her being a virgin, since that was a secret she shared with me and I'd take it to my grave— and asked them if the text meant what I thought it did. Did it mean she wanted to be my girlfriend?

They told me I was a fucking idiot for needing a text message to tell me that, and I slowly realized what a tool I'd been. She thought I didn't want a girlfriend, and in a way, I really didn't. Other girls wanted to date me for a lot of fucked-up reasons, but those girls weren't Peach. I didn't want a girlfriend—I just wanted her, in every way possible.

Another text rang through, this one asking if we were still friends, but hell no we weren't friends. I was so tired of pretending not to want the world from her. Waking up without her next to me and worrying that I'd never get to fall asleep with her again knocked some sense into me, and I knew I had to grow a pair and do what it took to be with her.

When she asked me a few weeks after Mayhem why I asked her to be my girlfriend onstage, I told her it was because I wanted the whole world to know how I felt about her, but that was only part of the truth. I also had that word *friends* ringing in my head and was terrified of being rejected for what would have felt like the hundredth time in my life, all one hundred times by the only girl with the power to break my heart. I finished the set and walked offstage, my heart leaping into my throat when I saw her waiting with her answer.

I thought that hearing her say yes made me the happiest man alive, but it didn't even compare to the moment she told me she loved me. Before Peach, love was just a word that girls threw at me from the crowd, but now I know what it really means.

It's mayhem. It's forever.

It's her.

Don't miss Joel and Dee's story . . .

Riot

Coming February 10th from
Avon Impulse!
Read on for a sneak peek!

"KISS ME," I order the luckiest guy in Mayhem tonight. When he sat next to me at the bar earlier with his Leave It to Beaver haircut, I made sure to avoid eye contact and cross my legs in the opposite direction. I didn't think I'd end up making out with him, but now I have no choice.

A dumb expression washes over his face. He might be cute if he didn't look so. freaking. dumb. "Huh?"

"Oh for God's sake."

I curl my fingers behind his neck and yank him to my mouth, tilting my head to the side and hoping he's a quick learner. My lips part, my tongue comes out to play, and after a moment, he finally catches on. His greedy fingers thread into my chocolate brown curls—which I spent *hours* on this morning.

UGH.

Peeking out of the corner of my eye, I spot Joel Gibbon stroll past me, a bleached-blonde groupie tucked under his arm. He's too busy whispering in her ear to notice me, and my fingers itch to punch him in the back of his stupid mohawked head to get his attention.

I'm preparing to push Leave-It-To-Beaver off me when Joel's gaze finally lifts to meet mine. I bite Beaver's bottom lip between my teeth and give it a little tug, and the corner of Joel's mouth lifts up into an infuriating smirk that is *so* not the reaction I wanted. He continues walking, and when he's finally out of sight, I break my lips from Beaver's and nudge him back toward his own stool, immediately spinning in the opposite direction to scowl at my giggling best friend.

"I can't BELIEVE him!" I shout at a far too amused-looking Rowan. How does she not recognize the gravity of this situation?!

I'm about to shake some sense into her when Beaver taps me on the shoulder. "Um—"

"You're welcome," I say with a flick of my wrist, not wanting to waste another minute on a guy who can't appreciate how long it took me to get my hair to curl like this—or at least make messing it up worth my while.

Rowan gives him an apologetic half smile, and I let out a deep sigh.

I don't feel bad about Beaver. I feel bad about the dickhead bass guitarist for The Last Ones to Know.

"That boy is making me insane," I growl.

Rowan turns a bright smile on me, her blue eyes sparkling with humor. "You were already insane."

"He's making me homicidal," I clarify, and she laughs.

"Why don't you just tell him you like him?" She twirls two tiny straws in her cocktail, her eyes periodically flitting up to the stage. She's waiting for Adam, and I'd probably be jealous of her if those two weren't so disgustingly perfect for each other.

Last semester, I nearly got kicked out of my dorm when I let Rowan move in with me and my roommate.

But Rowan's asshole live-in boyfriend had cheated on her, and she had nowhere to go, and she's been my *best* friend since kindergarten. I ignored the written warnings from my RA, and Rowan ultimately ended up moving in with Adam before I got kicked out. Fast-forward to one too many "overnight visitors" later, I still ended up getting reported, and Rowan and I got a two-bedroom in an apartment complex near campus. Her name is on the lease right next to mine, but really, the apartment is just a decoy she uses to avoid telling her parents that she's actually living with three ungodly hot rock stars. She sleeps in Adam's bed, his bandmate Shawn is in the second bedroom, and Joel sleeps on their couch most nights because he's a hot, stupid, infuriating freaking nomad.

"Because I *don't* like him," I answer. When I realize my drink is gone, I steal Rowan's, down the last of it, and flag the bartender.

"Then why is he making you insane?"

"Because *he* doesn't like *me*."

Rowan lifts a sandy blonde eyebrow at me, but I don't expect her to understand. Hell, *I* don't understand. I've never wanted a boy to like me so badly in my entire life. I don't even want Joel to just *like* me—I want him to worship the ground I walk on and throw himself at my feet. I want him to beg me to be with him and then cry his eyes out when I tell him I'm not a relationship kind of girl.

When the bartender arrives to take our orders, I order shots for both of us. At eighteen, Rowan and I are far from being old enough to drink, but our fake IDs and the stamps on our hands say otherwise.

"Make hers a double," Rowan says, pointing a thumb in my direction.

I finally stop scowling long enough to smile. "See? This is why I love you."

We've just gulped down our shots and slapped our glasses on the bar top when something heavy lands on my shoulder. Leti rests his left elbow on me and his right elbow on Rowan. He's been dancing his butt off on the dance floor with some tattooed beefcake, but he smells like he just stepped out of the shower, fresh and sexy-clean.

"What are we celebrating?"

I groan, and Rowan shakes her head in warning.

"Oh," Leti says. "Joel?"

"He's such an ass," I complain.

"Didn't you just spend the night with him this past weekend?"

"Yes!" I shout. "God, what is his problem?!"

Leti laughs and massages my shoulders. "If you like him, just tell him."

Okay, number one, in what freaking universe do they think that would ever work? Joel is a serial player. He lures girls in with his bad-boy hair and his panty-dropping smile, and then he chews them up and spits them out. 'Liking' him would be like 'liking' ice cream. Sure, it's great when you're stuffing your face with it, but then it's gone and you're just left with this all-consuming empti-ness. Yeah, you can go to the store and get more, but what if they don't have the flavor you want? What then?!

And number two, have these two ever met me? Boys chase after ME, not the other way around.

"I don't like him!" I protest.

Rowan and Leti share a look and speak at the same time. "She likes him."

"I hate you bitches."

I hop off of my stool and head toward the crowd. Mayhem is the biggest club in town, and tonight, The Last Ones to Know are opening for a band even bigger than they are, so *mayhem* is an understatement for the vibe on the floor. Before the bands take the stage, the club pulses with house music that makes the floors throb and the walls shiver. I have every intention of dancing my ass off until my brain overheats and shuts down from mind-numbing exhaustion.

"Aw, come on, Dee!" Rowan pleads before I get too far.

"Don't be mad!" Leti adds.

I turn around and prop my hands on my hips. "Are you two coming or what?"

After four songs of me being the meat in a Rowan-and-Leti sandwich, the house music fades out and the roadies begin the sound check. The crowd splits in half—half surging toward the stage to get good spots, and half retreating to the bar to catch their breath and drown themselves in liquor. Rowan, Leti, and I join the latter half, grabbing the best seats at the bar and spinning around to face the stage.

Every time Adam is about to perform, Rowan gets antsy, her feet dancing and her fingers curling. She picks at the pretty pink polish I painted her nails in this morning, and I tell her to stop, but I'm pretty sure she'd self-combust if she ever actually listened to me.

Adam is the first to walk onstage, and the crowd goes insane. He's followed by Shawn, the lead guitarist and backup vocalist. Then Cody, the annoying rhythm guitarist who had the nerve to ask me for my number; Mike, the adorable drummer who has grown on me these past couple months; and Joel, the bane of my existence.

His eyes rove over the front row, and I know what he's looking at: eager faces and barely covered boobs. Those girls are just eye shadow and tits on legs, which is just how Joel likes them. And now, with Adam making it widely known that he's off the market, Joel and Shawn have their pick of the litter. Cody gets the leftovers, and Mike avoids them like the plague—which each of those girls probably has, along with a million other communicable diseases that health teachers lecture horny freshman about in high school.

"Let's go backstage," I tell Rowan, already hopping off my stool. I have one thing those girls don't—a best friend with a permanent backstage pass I intend to use to my advantage.

"I thought you wanted to stay out here?" Rowan asks. Adam wanted to drag her backstage before he left to perform—since Rowan's dirty blonde hair, big blue eyes, and tight little figure aren't exactly dick-repellant, in *any* sense of the word—but I insisted I wanted to stay at the bar so we could drink.

"I did want to. Now I don't."

She and Leti follow me to the backstage door, where Rowan doesn't even need to tell security her nickname to get them to let us in. Most of the guys know her as Peach, which Adam took to calling her back before he bothered learning girls' names or remembering their faces. Now, she has him wrapped around her little finger.

"What?" she asks when she catches me studying her. Sure, she's gorgeous, but so are lots of other girls who throw themselves at Adam. Something about her won him over . . . Maybe her innocence. Maybe I should give it a try. Stop being so forward, wear flats more often, keep my mouth shut once in a while.

I laugh when I realize I can't even imagine that. "Nothing."

I lead Rowan and Leti past the side of the stage where Shawn stands, circling around the back to get to the side where Joel stands. My heels click against the stage stairs, and once we're at the top, I pull my long chocolate hair over my shoulders, hike my skintight dress up a little higher, and freshen my lip gloss.

It's hard not to scream like a groupie while I watch the guys command the stage, especially from this vantage point. The way Joel's blond spikes shine deadly under the foggy blue glow of the spotlights above him. The way he doesn't even need to look down at his guitar while he plucks the strings. The way his blue eyes periodically find mine and his mouth tips up at the corners. His presence on the stage is magnetic. It turns my blood to lava and makes it impossible to think. Part of me wants to play hard to get, but the other part of me knows all too well the rewards of letting him have me.

When Joel's dark eyes capture mine and hold them long enough to make me melt under their heat, my skin flushes and I know I need to do something to put myself back in control. With a devilish smile, I say, "Ro, you might want to close your eyes for this."

Without lifting my dress up, I wiggle out of my lacy black thong and dangle it from a manicured pointer finger. Joel's hands are busy playing his guitar, but his eyes remain fixed on me, and when I toss my panties at him, he snatches them out of the air. He finishes the song with them dangling from his wrist, and then he stuffs them in his back pocket, giving me a wink that would make any other girl weak in her knees.

"I can't believe you just did that!" Leti shouts over the music.

"I can!" Rowan shouts back, making me laugh.

"I'm heading back to the bar," I tell them, and Rowan questions me with a look.

"Why?"

The truth is, I want to see if he'll come after me. And if he doesn't, I need to have enough distance to pretend that I don't care.

At the bottom of the stairs, I turn around to stop Rowan from following me. "I want another drink. You stay here. Wait for Adam."

She frowns at me, but I give her a smile and walk backward toward the door. "I'll see you after."

At the bar, I sit next to the hottest guy I can find and flash a smile in his direction. Two minutes later, I have a drink and a distraction.

"So do you like the band?" he asks, nodding toward the stage.

I shrug. "They're alright." They're also the last thing I want to talk about right now, since I desperately need to stop agonizing over what's going to happen when their set ends, but God apparently hates me.

"I went to high school with most of them," the guy brags, like he can claim some kind of residual rock-star status for having shared a zip code. I almost burst out laughing, barely managing to hide it behind the drink I'm sipping.

"Were you friends?" I ask, not caring but knowing it's my turn to say something.

He goes on and on about the classes they shared and the time he got to see them in the talent show and how he went to one of Adam's parties his senior year. I'm mentally plotting my escape when the guy's eyes flit over my shoulder and open wide, sending untamed eyebrows jumping up into his forehead. His hand latches onto my forearm like a lifeline, and I turn my head just in time for my lips to brush Joel's cheek. "Is this guy bothering you?" he questions in my ear, his blue eyes turning to read mine before narrowing on the guy's hand, which recoils from my arm even though the rest of the guy looks totally dazed. With his wide eyes and unhinged jaw, he's so starstruck that I can't help but cast a quick glance at his lap to check for a man-for-man hard-on.

"You know Joel Gibbon?" he gasps, startling me from my detective work.

"Who, him?" I ask, pointing a lazy finger at the boy standing behind me. Inside, I'm giddy as hell that Joel came to find me. Outside, I'm mildly bored and totally unfazed.

"Oh my God," the guy says. "I'm such a huge fan!"

"You apparently went to school together," I add without turning to face Joel, who loosens up behind me even as his both of his heavy arms come to wrap around my shoulders. Since no one else has popped up at my sides, I'm guessing the rest of our group stayed backstage to watch the closing band perform.

Joel's chuckle rumbles against my back. "Oh yeah? What year were you?"

The guys talk and I tune them out until the hot fanboy eventually gets a picture with Joel and leaves. And then Joel's suggestive voice is in my ear again.

"Are you ready to get out of here?"

"Are you ready to stop being a man-whore?"

He has the nerve to laugh. "Why, are you jealous?"

Insanely. "Why would I be jealous?" I peel his arms away and turn on my stool to face him. "I'm the one you always go home with."

"Isn't that interesting," he muses with an agitating glimmer in his arctic-blue eyes.

Joel usually begins the night with someone else—or a *few* someone elses—and on nights I'm not around, he goes home with them. But on nights I *am* around, I always end up winning his attention—through exhaustive effort that I'm really getting tired of exerting.

"If I say no, what will you do? Go home with one of them instead?"

"You won't say no."

I scoff at him. "Shows what you know."

When I spin away from him, he squeezes up behind

me again and presses his lips against my ear. "You won't say no because you know all the things I want to do to you."

He starts telling me exactly what those things are, and my toes curl in my peep-toe pumps. Goosebumps spread from my ankles to my ears, and I abruptly hop off my stool.

"Where are you going?" Joel calls after me.

"To see if you're a man of your word!"

Acknowledgments

MAYHEM IS MY debut novel, which means that the people named on this page took a chance on me and on this story, and for that I'm saying *thank you* from the bottom of my heart.

To my three best friends—Kelleigh McHenry, Rocky Allinger, and Kim Mong—for being the most phenomenal critique partners and cheerleaders I could have asked for. Kelleigh, thank you for making T-shirts with my characters' names on them long before this book was published. Rocky, thank you for loaning me the first romance novel I ever read, which forever changed my life. And Kim, thank you for encouraging me to try my hand at creative writing back before it was something I ever thought I'd be good at. Without you three (and our emergency Panera dates!), this book might still be just a dream.

To my mom, Claudia, for *always* believing in me.

Your lifelong encouragement of my dreams—even when they were crazy—is why I'm accomplishing them today. Thank you for your unconditional love and unwavering support—and for reading my drafts even when the dirty scenes made it weird.

To my husband, Mike, for putting up with the mood swings that went along with me living inside Rowan's head. You've supported me throughout this entire process, and I love you more than words can say.

To my agent, Stacey Donaghy, for always knowing when I need a laugh, a phone call, or a glass of wine. Thank you for being Type A right along with me, and for being the best advocate for this story I could have asked for.

To my editor, Nicole Fischer, for helping make my dreamiest dream a reality. Thank you for giving this story a home, for loving Rowan and Adam as much as I do, and for making sure I didn't skimp on the naughty parts.

To Liis McKinstry for looking out for Adam's rep. To Amanda Bergeron for seeing the potential in this story. To everyone at HarperCollins for working their magic. And to everyone else who has supported me—because there are a *lot* of you and you know who you are—

Thank you for being rock stars.

About the Author

Born and raised in South Central Pennsylvania, JAMIE SHAW earned her M.S. in Professional Writing from Towson University before realizing that the creative side of writing was her calling. An incurable night owl, she spends late hours crafting novels with relatable heroines and swoon-worthy leading men. She's a loyal drinker of white mochas, a fierce defender of emo music, and a passionate enthusiast of all things romance. She loves interacting with readers and always aims to add new names to their book-boyfriend lists.

www.authorjamieshaw.blogspot.com
www.facebook.com/jamieshawauthor

Discover great authors, exclusive offers, and more at hc.com.

Give in to your impulses . . .
Read on for a sneak peek at seven brand-new
e-book original tales of romance
from Avon Impulse.
Available now wherever e-books are sold.

HOLDING HOLLY
A LOVE AND FOOTBALL NOVELLA
By Julie Brannagh

IT'S A WONDERFUL FIREMAN
A BACHELOR FIREMEN NOVELLA
By Jennifer Bernard

ONCE UPON A HIGHLAND CHRISTMAS
By Lecia Cornwall

RUNNING HOT
A BAD BOYS UNDERCOVER NOVELLA
By HelenKay Dimon

SINFUL REWARDS 1
A BILLIONAIRES AND BIKERS NOVELLA
By Cynthia Sax

RETURN TO CLAN SINCLAIR
A CLAN SINCLAIR NOVELLA
By Karen Ranney

RETURN OF THE BAD GIRL
By Codi Gary

An Excerpt from

HOLDING HOLLY
A Love and Football Novella
by Julie Brannagh

Holly Reynolds has a secret. Make that two.
The first involves upholding her grandmother's
hobby of answering Dear Santa letters from
dozens of local schoolchildren. The second . . .
well, he just came strolling in the door.

Derrick has never met a woman he wanted to
bring home to meet his family, mostly because
he keeps picking the wrong ones—until he
runs into sweet, shy Holly Reynolds. Different
from anyone he's ever known, Derrick realizes
she might just be everything he needs.

"**D**o you need anything else right now?"

"I'm good," he said. "Then again, there's something I forgot."

"What do you need? Maybe I can help."

He moved closer to her, and she tipped her head back to look up at him. He reached out to cup one of her cheeks in his big hand. "I had a great time tonight. Thanks for having pizza with me."

"I had a nice time too. Th-thank you for inviting me," she stammered. There was so much more she'd like to say, but she was tongue-tied again. He was moving closer to her, and he reached out to put his drinking glass down on the counter.

"Maybe we could try this again when we're not in the middle of a snowstorm," he said. "I'd like a second date."

She started nodding like one of those bobbleheads, and forced herself to stop before he thought she was even more of a dork.

"Yes. I . . . Yes, I would too. I . . . that would be fun."

He took another half-step toward her. She did her best to pull in a breath.

"Normally, I would have kissed you good night at your front door, but getting us inside before we froze to death seemed like the best thing to do right then," he said.

"Oh, yes. Absolutely. I—"

He reached out, slid his arms around her waist, and pulled her close. "I don't want to disrespect your grandma's wishes," he softly said. "She said I needed to treat you like a lady."

Holly almost let out a groan. She loved Grandma, but they needed to have a little chat later. "Sorry," she whispered.

He grinned at her. "I promise I'll behave myself, unless you don't want me to." She couldn't help it; she laughed. "Plus," he continued, "she said you have to be up very early in the morning to go to work, so we'll have to say good night."

Maybe she didn't need sleep. One thing's for sure, she had no interest in stepping away from him right now. He surrounded her, and she wanted to stay in his arms. Her heart was beating double-time, the blood was effervescent in her veins, and she summoned the nerve to move a little closer to him as she let out a happy sigh.

He kissed her cheek, and laid his scratchier one against hers. A few seconds later, she slid her arms around his neck too. "Good night, sweet Holly. Thanks for saving me from the snowstorm."

She had to laugh a little. "I think you saved *me*."

"We'll figure out who saved who later," he said. She felt his deep voice vibrating through her. She wished he'd kiss her again. Maybe she should kiss *him*.

He must have read her mind. He took her face in both of his hands. "Don't tell your grandma," he whispered. His breath was warm on her cheek.

"Tell her what?"

"I'm going to kiss you."

Her head was bobbing around as she frantically nodded yes. She probably looked ridiculous, but he didn't seem to care. Her eyelids fluttered closed as his mouth touched hers, sweet and soft. It wasn't a long kiss, but she knew she'd never forget it. She felt the zing at his tender touch from the top of her head to her toes.

"A little more?" he asked.

"Oh, yes."

His arms wrapped around her again, and he slowly traced her lips with his tongue. It slid into her mouth. He tasted like the peppermints Noel Pizza kept in a jar on the front counter. They explored each other for a while as quietly as possible, but maybe not quietly enough.

"Holly, honey," her grandma called out from the family room. Holly was *absolutely* going to have a conversation with Grandma when Derrick was out of earshot, and she stifled a groan. All they were doing was a little kissing. He rested one big hand on her butt, which she enjoyed. "Would you please bring me some salad?"

Derrick let out a snort. "I'll get it for you, Miss Ruth," he said loudly enough for her grandma to hear.

"She's onto us," Holly said softly.

"Damn right." He grinned at her. "I'll see you tomorrow morning." His voice dropped. "We're *definitely* kissing on the second date."

"I'll look forward to that." She tried to pull in a breath. Her head was spinning. She couldn't have stopped smiling if her life depended on it. "Are you sure you don't want to stay in my room instead? You need a good night's sleep. Don't you have to go to practice?"

"I'm sure your room is very comfortable, but I'll be fine out here. Sweet dreams," he said.

She felt him kiss the top of her head as he held her. She took a deep breath of his scent: clean skin, a whiff of expensive cologne, and freshly pressed clothes. "You, too," she whispered. She reached up to kiss his cheek. "Good night."

An Excerpt from

IT'S A WONDERFUL FIREMAN
A Bachelor Firemen Novella
by Jennifer Bernard

Hard-edged fireman Dean Mulligan has never
been a big fan of Christmas. Twinkly lights and
sparkly tinsel can't brighten the memories of too
many years spent in ramshackle foster homes.
When he's trapped in the burning wreckage of
a holiday store, a Christmas angel arrives to
open his eyes. But is it too late? This Christmas,
it'll take an angel, a determined woman in love,
and the entire Bachelor Firemen crew to make
him believe . . . it is indeed a wonderful life.

He'd fallen. Memory returned like water seeping into a basement. He'd been on the roof, and then he'd fallen through, and now he was . . . here. His PASS device was sounding in a high-decibel shriek, and its strobe light flashed, giving him quick, garish glimpses of his surroundings.

Mulligan looked around cautiously. The collapse must have put out much of the fire, because he saw only a few remnants of flames flickering listlessly on the far end of the space. Every surface was blackened and charred except for one corner, in which he spotted blurry flashes of gold and red and green.

He squinted and blinked his stinging eyes, trying to get them to focus. Finally the glimpse of gold formed itself into a display of dangling ball-shaped ornaments. He gawked at them. What were those things made from? How had they managed to survive the fire? He sought out the red and squinted at it through his face mask. A Santa suit, that's what it was, with great, blackened holes in the sleeves. It was propped on a rocking chair, which looked quite scorched. Mulligan wondered if a mannequin or something had been wearing the suit. If so, it was long gone. Next to the chair stood half of a plastic Christmas tree. One side had melted into black goo, while the other side looked pretty good.

Where am I? He formed the words with his mouth, though no sound came out. And it came back to him. Under the Mistletoe. He'd been about to die inside a Christmas store. But he hadn't. So far.

He tried to sit up, but something was pinning him down. Taking careful inventory, he realized that he lay on his left side, his tank pressing uncomfortably against his back, his left arm immobilized beneath him. What was on top of him? He craned his neck, feeling his face mask press against his chest. A tree. A freaking Christmas tree. Fully decorated and only slightly charred. It was enormous, at least ten feet high, its trunk a good foot in diameter. At its tip, an angel in a gold pleated skirt dangled precariously, as if she wanted to leap to the floor but couldn't summon the nerve. Steel brackets hung from the tree's trunk; it must have been mounted somewhere, maybe on a balcony or something. A few twisted ironwork bars confirmed that theory.

How the hell had a Christmas tree survived the inferno in here? It was wood! Granted, it was still a live tree, and its trunk and needles held plenty of sap. And fires were always unpredictable. The one thing you could be sure of was that they'd surprise you. Maybe the balcony had been protected somehow.

He moved his body, trying to shift the tree, but it was extremely heavy and he was pinned so flat he had no leverage. He spotted his radio a few feet away. It must have been knocked out of his pouch. Underneath the horrible, insistent whine of his PASS device, he heard the murmuring chatter of communication on the radio. If he could get a finger on it, he could hit his emergency trigger and switch to Channel 6, the May Day channel. His left arm was useless, but he could try with his right. But when he moved it, pain ripped through his shoulder.

Hell. Well, he could at least shut off the freaking PASS device. If a rapid intervention team made it in here, he'd yell for them. But no way could he stand listening to that sound for the next whatever-amount-of-time it took. Gritting his teeth against the agony, he reached for the device at the front of his turnout, then hit the button. The strobe light stopped and sudden silence descended, though his ears still rang. While he was at it, he checked the gauge that indicated how much air he had left in his tank. Ten minutes. He must have been in here for some time, sucking up air, since it was a thirty-minute tank.

A croak issued from his throat. "I'm in hell. No surprise."

Water. He needed water.

"I can't give you any water," a bright female voice said. For some reason, he had the impression that the angel on the tip of the Christmas tree had spoken. So he answered her back.

"Of course you can't. Because I'm in hell. They don't exactly hand out water bottles in hell."

"Who said you're in hell?"

Even though he watched the angel's lips closely, he didn't see them move. So it must not be her speaking. Besides, the voice seemed to be coming from behind him. "I figured it out all by myself."

Amazingly, he had no more trouble with his throat. Maybe he wasn't really speaking aloud. Maybe he was having this bizarre conversation with his own imagination. That theory was confirmed when a girl's shapely calves stepped into his field of vision. She wore red silk stockings the exact color of holly berries. She wore nothing else on her feet, which had a very familiar shape.

Lizzie.

His gaze traveled upward, along the swell of her calves. The stockings stopped just above her knees, where they were fastened by a red velvet bow. "Christmas stockings," he murmured.

"I told you."

"All right. I was wrong. Maybe it's heaven after all. Come here." He wanted to hold her close. His heart wanted to burst with joy that she was here with him, that he wasn't alone. That he wasn't going to die without seeing Lizzie again.

"I can't. There's a tree on top of you," she said in a teasing voice. "Either that, or you're very happy to see me."

"Oh, you noticed that? You can move it, can't you? Either you're an angel and have magical powers, or you're real and you can push it off me."

She laughed. A real Lizzie laugh, starting as a giggle and swooping up the register until it became a whoop. "Do you really think an angel would dress like this?"

"Hmm, good point. What are you wearing besides those stockings? I can't even see. At least step closer so I can see."

"Fine." A blur of holly red, and then she perched on the pile of beams and concrete that blocked the east end of his world. In addition to the red stockings, she wore a red velvet teddy and a green peaked hat, which sat at an angle on her flowing dark hair. Talk about a "hot elf" look.

"Whoa. How'd you do that?"

"You did it."

"I did it?" How could he do it? He was incapacitated. Couldn't even move a finger. Well, maybe he could move a finger. He gave it a shot, wiggling the fingers on both hands. At least he wasn't paralyzed.

But he did seem to be mentally unstable. "I'm hallucinating, aren't I?"

"Bingo."

An Excerpt from

ONCE UPON A HIGHLAND CHRISTMAS

by Lecia Cornwall

Lady Alanna McNabb is bound by duty
to her family, who insist she must marry a
gentleman of wealth and title. When she meets
the man of her dreams, she knows it's much
too late, but her heart is no longer hers.

Laird Iain MacGillivray is on his way to propose
to another woman when he discovers Alanna
half-frozen in the snow and barely alive. She isn't
his to love, yet she's everything he's ever wanted.

As Christmas comes closer, the snow
thickens, and the magic grows stronger.
Alanna and Iain must choose between
desire and duty, love and obligation.

Alanna McNabb woke with a terrible headache. In fact, every inch of her body ached. She could smell peat smoke, and dampness, and hear wind. She remembered the storm and opened her eyes. She was in a small dark room, a hut, she realized, a shieling, perhaps, or was it one of the crofter's cottages at Glenlorne? Was she home, among the people who knew her, loved her? She looked around, trying to decide where exactly she was, whose home she was in. The roof beams above her head were blackened with age and soot, and a thick stoneware jug dangled from a nail hammered into the beam as a hook. But that offered no clues at all—it was the same in every Highland cott. She turned her head a little, knowing there would be a hearth, and—

A few feet from her, a man crouched by the fire.

A very big, very naked man.

She stared at his back, which was broad and smooth. She took note of well-muscled arms as he poked the fire. She followed the bumps of his spine down to a pair of dimples just above his round white buttocks.

Her throat dried. She tried to sit up, but pain shot through her body, and the room wavered before her eyes. Her leg was on fire, pure agony. She let out a soft cry.

He half turned at the sound and glanced over his shoulder, and she had a quick impression of a high cheekbone lit by the firelight, and a gleaming eye that instantly widened with surprise. He dropped the poker and fell on his backside with a grunt.

"You're awake!" he cried. She stared at him sprawled on the hearthstones, and he gasped again and cupped his hands over his— She shut her eyes tight, as he grabbed the nearest thing at hand to cover himself—a corner of the plaid— but she yanked it back, holding tight. He instantly let go and reached for the closest garment dangling from the line above him, which turned out to be her red cloak. He wrapped it awkwardly around his waist, trying to rise to his feet at the same time. He stood above her in his makeshift kilt, holding it in place with a white knuckled grip, his face almost as red as the wool. She kept her eyes on his face and pulled her own blanket tight around her throat.

"I see you're awake," he said, staring at her, his voice an octave lower now. "How do you feel?"

How *did* she feel? She assessed her injuries, tried to remember the details of how she came to be here, wherever here might be. She recalled being lost in a storm, and falling. There'd been blood on her glove. She frowned. After that she didn't remember anything at all.

She shifted carefully, and the room dissolved. She saw stars, and black spots, and excruciating pain streaked through her body, radiating from her knee. She gasped, panted, stiffened against it.

"Don't move," he said, holding out a hand, fingers splayed, though he didn't touch her. He grinned, a sudden flash of white teeth, the firelight bright in his eyes. "I found you out in the snow. I feared . . . well, it doesn't matter now. Your knee is injured, cut, and probably sprained, but it isn't broken," he said in a rush. He grinned again, as if that was all very good news, and dropped to one knee beside her. "You've got some color back."

He reached out and touched her cheek with the back of his hand, a gentle enough caress, but she flinched away and gasped at the pain that caused. He dropped his hand at once, looked apologetic. "I mean no harm, lass—I was just checking that you're warm, but not too warm. Or too cold . . ." He was babbling, and he broke off, gave her a wan smile, and stood up again, holding onto her cloak, taking a step back away from her. Was he blushing, or was it the light of the fire on his skin? She tried not to stare at the breadth of his naked chest, or the naked legs that showed beneath the trailing edge of the cloak.

She gingerly reached down under the covers and found her knee was bound up in a bandage of some sort. He turned away, flushing again, and she realized the plaid had slipped down. She was as naked as he was. She gasped, drew the blanket tight to her chin, and stared at him. She looked up and saw that her clothes were hanging on a line above the fireplace—all of them, even her shift.

"Where—?" she swallowed. Her voice was hoarse, her throat as raw as her knee. "Who are you?" she tried again. She felt hot blood fill her cheeks, and panic formed a tight knot in her chest, and she tried again to remember what had happened, but her mind was blank. If he was—unclothed, and she was equally unclothed—

"What—" she began again, then swallowed the question

she couldn't frame. She hardly knew what to ask first, Where, Who, or What? Her mind was moving slowly, her thoughts as thick and rusty as her tongue.

"You're safe, lass," he said, and she wondered if she was. She stared at him. She'd seen men working in the summer sun, their shirts off, their bodies tanned, their muscles straining, but she'd never thought anything of it. This—he—was different. And she was as naked as he was.

An Excerpt from

RUNNING HOT
A Bad Boys Undercover Novella
by HelenKay Dimon

Ward Bennett and Tasha Gregory aren't on the same team. But while hunting a dictator on the run, these two must decide whether they can trust one another—and their ability to stay professional. Working together might just make everyone safer, but getting cozy . . . might just get them killed.

"Take your clothes off."

He looked at her as if she'd lost her mind. "Excuse me?"

"You're attracted to me." Good Lord, now Tasha was waving her hands in the air. Once she realized it, she stopped. Curled her hands into balls at her sides. "I find you . . . fine."

Ward covered his mouth and produced a fake cough. She assumed it hid a smile. That was almost enough to make her rescind the offer.

"Really? That's all you can muster?" This time he did smile. "You think I'm fine?"

He was hot and tall and had a face that played in her head long after she closed her eyes each night. And that body. Long and lean, with the stalk of a predator. Ward was a man who protected and fought. She got the impression he wrestled demons that had to do with reconciling chivalry and decency with the work they performed.

The combination of all that made her wild with need. "Your clothes are still on."

"Are you saying you want to—"

Since he was saying the sentence so slowly—emphasizing, and halting after, each word—she finished it fast. "Shag."

Both eyebrows rose now. "Please tell me that's British for 'have sex.'"

"Yes."

He blew out a long, staggered breath. "Thank God, because right now my body is in a race to see what will explode first, my brain or my dick."

Uh? "Is that a compliment?"

"Believe it or not, yes." Two steps, and he was in front of her, his fingers playing with the small white button at the top of her slim tee. "So, are you talking about now or sometime in the future to celebrate ending Tigana?"

Both. "I need to work off this extra energy and get back in control." She was half-ready to rip off her clothes and throw him on the mattress.

Maybe he knew because he just stood there and stared at her, his gaze not leaving her face.

She stared back.

Just as he started to lower his head, a ripple moved through her. She shoved a hand against his shoulder. "Don't think that I always break protocol like this."

"I don't care if you do." He ripped his shirt out of his pants and whipped it over his head, revealing miles of tanned muscles and skin.

"You're taking off your clothes." Not the smartest thing she'd ever said, but it was out there and she couldn't snatch it back.

"You're the boss, remember?"

A shot of regret nearly knocked her over. Not at making the pass but at wanting him this much in the first place. Here and now, when her mind should be on the assignment, not on his chest.

She'd buried this part of herself for so long under a pile of work and professionalism that bringing it out now made her twitchy. "This isn't—"

His hands went to her arms, and he brushed those palms up and down, soothing her. "Do you want me?"

She couldn't lie. He had to feel it in the tremor shaking through her. "Yes."

"Then stop justifying not working this very second and enjoy. It won't make you less of a professional."

That was exactly what she needed to hear. "Okay."

His hands stopped at her elbows, and he dragged her in closer, until the heat of his body radiated against her. "You're a stunning woman, and we've been circling each other for days. Honestly, your ability to handle weapons only makes you hotter in my eyes."

The words spun through her. They felt so good. So right. "Not the way I would say it, but okay."

"You want me. I sure as hell want you. We need to lie low until it gets dark and we can hide our movements better." The corner of his mouth kicked up in a smile filled with promise. "And, for the record, there is nothing sexier than a woman who goes after what she wants."

He meant it. She knew it with every cell inside her.

Screw being safe.

An Excerpt from

SINFUL REWARDS 1
A Billionaires and Bikers Novella
by Cynthia Sax

Belinda "Bee" Carter is a good girl; at least, that's
what she tells herself. And a good girl deserves
a nice guy—just like the gorgeous and moody
billionaire Nicolas Rainer. Or so she thinks,
until she takes a look through her telescope
and sees a naked, tattooed man on the balcony
across the courtyard. He has been watching
her, and that makes him all the more enticing.
But when a mysterious and anonymous text
message dares her to do something bad, she
must decide if she is really the good girl she has
always claimed to be, or if she's willing to risk
everything for her secret fantasy of being watched.

An Avon Red Novella

I'd told Cyndi I'd never use it, that it was an instrument purchased by perverts to spy on their neighbors. She'd laughed and called me a prude, not knowing that I was one of those perverts, that I secretly yearned to watch and be watched, to care and be cared for.

If I'm cautious, and I'm always cautious, she'll never realize I used her telescope this morning. I swing the tube toward the bench and adjust the knob, bringing the mysterious object into focus.

It's a phone. Nicolas's phone. I bounce on the balls of my feet. This is a sign, another declaration from fate that we belong together. I'll return Nicolas's much-needed device to him. As a thank you, he'll invite me to dinner. We'll talk. He'll realize how perfect I am for him, fall in love with me, marry me.

Cyndi will find a fiancé also—everyone loves her—and we'll have a double wedding, as sisters of the heart often do. It'll be the first wedding my family has had in generations.

Everyone will watch us as we walk down the aisle. I'll wear a strapless white Vera Wang mermaid gown with organza and lace details, crystal and pearl embroidery accents, the bodice fitted, and the skirt hemmed for my shorter height. My hair will be swept up. My shoes—

Voices murmur outside the condo's door, the sound piercing my delightful daydream. I swing the telescope upward, not wanting to be caught using it. The snippets of conversation drift away.

I don't relax. If the telescope isn't positioned in the same way as it was last night, Cyndi will realize I've been using it. She'll tease me about being a fellow pervert, sharing the story, embellished for dramatic effect, with her stern, serious dad—or, worse, with Angel, that snobby friend of hers.

I'll die. It'll be worse than being the butt of jokes in high school because that ridicule was about my clothes and this will center on the part of my soul I've always kept hidden. It'll also be the truth, and I won't be able to deny it. I am a pervert.

I have to return the telescope to its original position. This is the only acceptable solution. I tap the metal tube.

Last night, my man-crazy roommate was giggling over the new guy in three-eleven north. The previous occupant was a gray-haired, bowtie-wearing tax auditor, his luxurious accommodations supplied by Nicolas. The most exciting thing he ever did was drink his tea on the balcony.

According to Cyndi, the new occupant is a delicious piece of man candy—tattooed, buff, and head-to-toe lickable. He was completing armcurls outside, and she enthusiastically counted his reps, oohing and aahing over his bulging biceps, calling to me to take a look.

I resisted that temptation, focusing on making macaroni and cheese for the two of us, the recipe snagged from the diner my mom works in. After we scarfed down dinner, Cyndi licking her plate clean, she left for the club and hasn't returned.

Three-eleven north is the mirror condo to ours. I

straighten the telescope. That position looks about right, but then, the imitation UGGs I bought in my second year of college looked about right also. The first time I wore the boots in the rain, the sheepskin fell apart, leaving me barefoot in Economics 201.

Unwilling to risk Cyndi's friendship on "about right," I gaze through the eyepiece. The view consists of rippling golden planes, almost like . . .

Tanned skin pulled over defined abs.

I blink. It can't be. I take another look. A perfect pearl of perspiration clings to a puckered scar. The drop elongates more and more, stretching, snapping. It trickles downward, navigating the swells and valleys of a man's honed torso.

No. I straighten. This is wrong. I shouldn't watch our sexy neighbor as he stands on his balcony. If anyone catches me . . .

Parts 1 – 6 available now!

An Excerpt from

RETURN TO CLAN SINCLAIR
A Clan Sinclair Novella
by Karen Ranney

When Ceana Sinclair Mead married the youngest
son of an Irish duke, she never dreamed that
seven years later her beloved Peter would die.
Her three brothers-in-law think she should
be grateful to remain a proper widow. After
three years of this, she's ready to scream. She
escapes to Scotland, only to discover she's so
much more than just the Widow Mead.

In Scotland, Ceana crosses paths with Bruce
Preston, an American tasked with a dangerous
mission by her brother, Macrath. Bruce is too
attractive for her peace of mind, but she still
finds him fascinating. Their one night together
is more wonderful than Ceana could have
imagined, and she has never felt more alive.

The darkness was nearly absolute, leaving her no choice but to stretch her hands out on either side of her, fingertips brushing against the stone walls. The incline was steep, further necessitating she take her time. Yet at the back of her mind was the last image she had of Carlton, his bright impish grin turning to horror as he glanced down.

The passage abruptly ended in a mushroom-shaped cavern. This was the grotto she'd heard so much about, with its flue in the middle and its broad, wide window looking out over the beach and the sea. She raced to the window, hopped up on the sill nature had created over thousands of years and leaned out.

A naked man reached up, grabbed Carlton as he fell. After he lowered the boy to the sand, he turned and smiled at her.

Carlton was racing across the beach, glancing back once or twice to see if he was indeed free. The rope made of sheets was hanging limply from his window.

The naked man was standing there with hands on his hips, staring at her in full frontal glory.

She hadn't seen many naked men, the last being her husband. The image in front of her now was so startling she couldn't help but stare. A smile was dawning on the stranger's full lips, one matched by his intent brown eyes. No, not quite brown, were they? They were like the finest Scottish whiskey touched with sunlight.

Her gaze danced down his strong and corded neck to broad shoulders etched with muscle. His chest was broad and muscled as well, tapering down to a slim waist and hips.

Even semiflaccid, his manhood was quite impressive.

The longer she watched, the more impressive it became.

What on earth was a naked man doing on Macrath's beach?

To her utter chagrin, the stranger turned and presented his backside to her, glancing over his shoulder to see if she approved of the sight.

She withdrew from the window, cheeks flaming. What on earth had she been doing? Who was she to gawk at a naked man as if she'd never before seen one?

Now that she knew Carlton was going to survive his escape, she should retreat immediately to the library.

"You'd better tell Alistair his brother's gotten loose again. Are you the new governess?"

She turned to find him standing in the doorway, still naked.

She pressed her fingers against the base of her throat and counseled herself to appear unaffected.

"I warn you, the imp escapes at any chance. You'll have your hands full there."

The look of fright on Carlton's face hadn't been fear of the distance to the beach, but the fact that he'd been caught.

She couldn't quite place the man's accent, but it wasn't Scottish. American, perhaps. What did she care where he came from? The problem was what he was doing here.

"I'm not a governess," she said. "I'm Macrath's sister, Ceana."

He bent and retrieved his shirt from a pile of clothes beside the door, taking his time with it. Shouldn't he have begun with his trousers instead?

"Who are you?" she asked, looking away as he began to don the rest of his clothing.

She'd had two children. She was well versed in matters of nature. She knew quite well what a man's body looked like. The fact that his struck her as singularly attractive was no doubt due to the fact she'd been a widow for three years.

"Well, Ceana Sinclair, is it all that important you know who I am?"

"It isn't Sinclair," she said. "It's Mead."

He tilted his head and studied her.

"Is Mr. Mead visiting along with you?"

She stared down at her dress of unremitting black. "I'm a widow," she said.

A shadow flitted over his face "Are you? Did Macrath know you were coming?"

"No," she said. "Does it matter? He's my brother. He's family. And why would you be wanting to know?"

He shrugged, finished buttoning his pants and began to don his shoes.

"Who are you?" she asked again.

"I'm a detective," he said. "My company was hired by your brother."

"Why?"

"Now that's something I'm most assuredly not going to tell you," he said. "It was nice meeting you, Mrs. Mead. I hope to see more of you before I leave."

And she hoped to see much, much less of him.

An Excerpt from

RETURN OF THE BAD GIRL

by Codi Gary

When Caroline Willis learns that her perfect
apartment has been double-booked—to a
dangerously hot bad boy—her bad-girl reputation
comes out in full force. But as close quarters
begin to ignite the sizzling chemistry between
them, she's left wondering: Bad boy plus bad
girl equals nothing but trouble . . . right?

"I feel like you keep looking for something more to me, but what you know about me is it. There's no 'deep down,' no mistaking my true character. I am bad news." He waited, listening for the tap of her retreating feet or the slam of the door, but only silence met his ears, then the soft sound of shoes on the cement floor—getting closer to him instead of farther away.

Fingers trailed feather-light touches over his lower back. "This scar on your back—is that from the accident?"

Her caress made his skin tingle as he shook his head. "I was knocked down by one of my mother's boyfriends and landed on a glass table."

"What about here?" Her hand had moved onto his right shoulder.

"It was a tattoo I had removed. In prison, you're safer if you belong, so—"

"I understand," she said, cutting him off. Had she heard the pain in his voice, or did she really understand?

He turned around before she could point out any more scars. "What are you doing?"

She looked him in the eye and touched the side of his neck, where his tattoo began, spreading all the way down past his shoulder and over his chest. "You say you're damaged. That you're bad news and won't ever change."

"Yeah?"

To his surprise, she dropped her hand to his and brought it up to her collarbone, where his finger felt a rough, puckered line.

"This is a knife wound—just a scratch, really—that I got from a man who used to come see me dance at the strip club. He was constantly asking me out, and I always let him down easy. But one night, after I'd had a shitty day, I told him I would never go out with an old, ugly fuck like him. He was waiting by my car when I got off work."

His rage blazed at this phantom from her past. "What happened?"

"I pulled a move I'd learned from one of the bouncers. Even though he still cut me, I was able to pick up a handful of gravel and throw it in his face. I made it to the front door of the club, and he took off. They arrested him on assault charges, and it turned out he had an outstanding warrant. I never saw him again."

Caroline pulled him closer, lifting her arm for him to see a jagged scar along her forearm. "This is from a broken beer bottle I got sliced with when a woman came into my bar in San Antonio, looking for her husband. She didn't take it well when she found out he had a girlfriend on the side, and when I stepped in to stop her from attacking him, she sliced me."

He couldn't stop his hand from sliding up over her soft skin until it rested on the back of her neck, his fingers pressing into her flesh until she tilted her chin up to meet his gaze.

"What's your point with all the show-and-tell, Caroline?"

She reached out and smoothed his chest with her hand. "I don't care how damaged you are, because I am just as broken, maybe more so."

Her words tore at him, twisting him up inside as his other hand cupped the back of her head. "You don't want to go here with me, princess. I'm only going to break your heart."

The laugh that passed those beautiful lips was bitter and sad. "Trust me, my heart was shattered long before I ever met you."

Gabe wanted her, wanted to believe that he could find comfort in her body without the complications that would inevitably come, but he'd seen her heart firsthand. She had one. It might be wrapped up in a mile-thick layer of cowhide, but a part of Caroline Willis was still open to new emotions. New love.

And he wasn't.

But he wanted to kiss her anyway.

He dropped his head until his lips hovered above hers, and he watched as they parted when he came closer. Her hot breath teased his mouth, and he couldn't stop while she was warm and willing. He might not get another chance to taste her, and while a better man would have walked away, he wasn't that guy.